THE GATEKEEPERS

THE GATEKEEPERS

DANIEL GRAHAM, JR.

THE GATEKEEPERS

Copyright © 1995 by Daniel Graham, Jr.

A Baen Books Original

Baen Publishing Enterprises
P.O. Box 1403
Riverdale, NY 10471

ISBN: 0-671-87684-8

Cover art by Doug Chaffee

First printing, September 1995

Distributed by Simon & Schuster
1230 Avenue of the Americas
New York, NY 10020

Library of Congress Cataloging-in-Publication Data

Graham, Daniel, 1952–
    The gatekeepers / Daniel Graham, Jr.
      p. cm.
    ISBN 0-671-87684-8
    I. Title
PS3557.R192G37 1995
813'.54—dc20   95-15305
                                                          CIP

For my father and his visionary comrades . . .

Soldiers also asked him, "And what is it that we should do?" He told them, "Do not practice extortion, do not falsely accuse anyone, and be satisfied with your wages."　　Luke 3:14

Other than that, seize and hold the strategic high ground.

Preface

Although *The Gatekeepers* is fiction, the technologies described herein are real. *The Gatekeepers'* plot relies on three technologies that I have watched develop over my career. Brilliant Pebbles is the ballistic missile interceptor system developed under the Strategic Defense Initiative. The Single-Stage-to-Orbit spacecraft, one promising design for totally re-usable spacecraft, has been successfully test-flown. You may have seen photographs of the McDonnell Douglas DCX hovering over the desert. The Solar Power Satellite, capable of providing clean, inexhaustible electric power, remains in the laboratory.

Any nation, or any individual like the hero Rolf Bernard, who controls these technologies, controls access to low earth orbit. Therefore, they control access to the unlimited wealth in Space. They become the gatekeepers to national security, technological and indeed, economical progress— our future. In a dramatic way, Dan Graham makes the case for deploying each of these technologies. The tiny but vigilant Brilliant Pebbles parked in various low earth orbits can protect the United States and our allies—even our erstwhile foes—from attack by ballistic missiles. Today, as you read this book, more than twenty countries have ballistic missile capability or will have such capability by the turn of the century. Some such as Libya, Iran—and now Korea—threaten us and our allies with weapons of mass destruction.

To effectively deploy Brilliant Pebbles and secure space for free men, we need inexpensive and reliable transportation to space. Re-usable spacecraft can provide routine airline-style operations to and from low earth orbit, lowering the costs dramatically. With these technologies, ordinary citizens can afford to fly into space, a thrill heretofore reserved for pioneers like me.

By dropping the cost of putting material into space, we make commercial projects possible. The Solar Power Satellite demonstrates the technological boon of exploiting space as a resource. If we want to continue our cultural and technological progress, we must look beyond fossil fuels for cheap, safe sources of energy. What better place than our sun? In space, the sun never sets. By putting solar collectors in orbit, we can tap that virtually unlimited energy and send it back safely to Earth in the form of weak microwaves, gathered by antenna "farms" then distributed to consumers.

Make no mistake. These technologies exist. They will be built. They will be used. The only question is: *By whom?* Who will become the gatekeeper of space? Let us hope the United States exercises that responsibility for our nation's benefit, and the world's.

Dr. Buzz Aldrin

An aerospace industrialist
attempts to seize and control
space.

Chapter 1

Paul Bernard stood at the thick plate glass with a pair of binoculars hanging from his neck. He cleaned his wire-rim glasses on his necktie, then slipped them back onto his equine face. He fiddled with the red and white striped security badge clipped to his shirt, glancing at a two-year-old photo in the center of the badge. He had not looked straight at the camera; a curly shock of brown hair hung over his forehead. Above the photo, in bold letters, EVERGREEN AVIATION, INC.

Paul didn't work for Evergreen Aviation, Inc. He leased a hangar and a slab of concrete runway at their secure airfield, the Marana Regional Airpark, secluded in rough country north of Tucson, Arizona. And he followed the landlord's strict rules. He and his staff watched, but did not discuss, the comings and goings of the matte black helicopters. As curious as they were about exotic gadgetry, they never asked questions about the special modifications made to civilian and military aircraft. They avoided the men wearing black berets and camouflage fatigues devoid of insignia. And they did not listen to the conversations in Spanish and stranger Arabic dialects.

Paul hitched up his pants. Round-shouldered and gangly, Paul had spent his youth hunched over books and keyboards, away from playing fields. As an adult, he

1

preferred the solitude of desert, ocean, and sky, so he took comfort surveying the panorama of rock, cactus, and buffalo grass—the sun-baked desert at the northeast corner of Marana Regional Airpark.

Paul shifted his gaze to the steel-gray Felix-P spaceship standing stoically on a cement apron at the end of the runway in the pitiless heat. The sound man handed Paul a wireless headset—earphones and mike—plus a paper cup filled with ice water. "Dr. Bernard, you tell me who you want to talk with and I switch the channel. You got Max Yeager in the blockhouse, the ground-safety crew in the hangar, and Mr. Winston with the camera crews."

"Thank you." Paul forced a smile and put the headset on. "Switch off for the time being." Paul needed to collect his thoughts as well as his nerve. *Everybody's being too nice. Could it be something's wrong? Or, maybe they're patronizing me? No, that's ridiculous. I'm just nervous, justifiably so. Twenty-seven years old, just got my Ph.D. from MIT, I got more than $150 million of R&D sitting out there, and I wouldn't be here except Dad owns BAP— the biggest aerospace company in the world—and Mom put up the capital for this gig. If Felix blows up on the pad, everyone else just goes back to work. I gotta explain the mess for the rest of my natural life. Oh, what the hell, Dad'll probably kill me, which ought to put an end to my explanations. . . .*

Paul loosened his tie and unfastened his collar. He signaled to the sound booth to switch to Channel One, the blockhouse. "Okay, everybody, look lively. Here comes the herd. T minus ten and holding. Stand by."

Paul listened to the blockhouse chatter with one ear while watching his father, Rolf Bernard, usher the dignitaries, policy wonks, and press into the viewing room. The guests, each tagged with a hot pink Marana guest badge, shuffled into the viewing room.

Rolf took the microphone from the podium and stepped toward the small crowd. In his dark gray suit and lemon-yellow tie, Rolf looked taller than his God-given five feet ten inches. His neat hair, turned silver at the temples, gave him an Old-World touch of dignity and polish: by any standards, he was handsome. "My esteemed colleagues, welcome, to BAP's Tucson Propulsion Lab. In a few minutes, you'll witness history. You'll see the world's first single-stage-to-orbit craft, our Felix prototype, lift off and climb to a modest altitude of three hundred feet, then hover at a positive thrust of exactly 1.0 for two minutes and thirty seconds. Our remote pilot, Captain Charles Rogers, whom you may remember from his Space Shuttle Columbia days, sits in the small blockhouse to the left of the craft. From there, he'll maneuver Felix up, hold her in a hover, then move the twenty-ton ship in a broad circle, and finally land the ship on the same spot from which it launched.

"At present, the Felix-P uses eight small aerospike rocket motors configured to burn kerosene. The Tucson Propulsion Lab, headed by Dr. Bernard, my son, is working on a version of the aerospike that can burn kerosene in the atmosphere, then hydrogen in space, but to be blunt, we've only gotten to the point where we can burn one or the other. So today the Felix-P burns kerosene."

A question came from the back. "Mr. Bernard, what are those lines or cables attached to the Felix-P?"

"Lines?" Rolf turned to look out the window.

Paul pulled his headset off and stepped out of the booth to answer the question for his father. "I'm Dr. Bernard, the project manager for today's test. The FAA requires either restraining bolts or safety tethers for static tests. Although we don't think today's test is static—more of a bunny hop really—we don't want to waste time battling semantics with the FAA, so we put on the tethers. Besides, our host, Evergreen Aviation, wants the tethers so we don't bunny hop too close to their hangars. And of course, the tethers ensure that we don't prang our ship."

The press stood still, dictating machines running. Paul

spoke again to fill the void. "The tethers are made of one-inch steel cables attached to a heavy nylon collar slipped over the nose. Sort of like having . . ." Paul groped for the right analogy. "Well, they're like training wheels." Paul turned to his father and whispered, "Beats the hell out of installing a self-destruct device."

The voice from the back prodded, "So you're just going to go up three hundred feet and come down—a bunny hop, you called it? With training wheels?"

Paul chafed. Rolf whispered, "Son, you worry about operations. Leave the colorful analogies to me." Paul returned to his booth and put on his headset.

Then Rolf raised the microphone and smiled at the press. "Although we try to make these tests look simple and easy, please don't underestimate the engineering involved. We're using eight fully throttleable aerospike rocket motors—radically new technology. We can lift off, pulling a fraction of g. Felix's Cray computers keep her position over the earth within a square meter. Think about what happens as she hovers. She's got the constant force of gravity, complicated by air disturbances. As she burns fuel, her weight changes, which changes the thrust needed to hover. If you think holding a flying machine steady in midair isn't the toughest flying maneuver, you need to have a talk with a helicopter pilot."

"I hear you!" a voice from the side piped up.

"As for going up only three hundred feet: Can you name another twenty-ton rocket that can go up three hundred feet; then come down in one piece? With our ability to bunny hop, as Dr. Bernard so colorfully called it, we can run inexpensive, low-risk tests, and thereby develop Felix at a fraction of the investment put into other launch systems. We'll learn more today from our little bunny hop than the Redstone project learned from their first twenty attempts."

The intercom interrupted Rolf: "We're ready to ignite the rockets."

Rolf looked up at the control booth and gave a thumbs-up. "Proceed. And good luck."

Paul signaled the sound man to patch the blockhouse chatter through the lab's sound system. The small crowd in the viewing room pressed against the thick glass. They squinted at the bright desert sun. A thousand meters to the east, they saw Felix-P standing alone on a thick slab of concrete. A simple cone-shaped, wingless craft, without launch tower, Felix sat companionless, like some diminutive monument built in the Sonora desert. Whatever life graced the area, hid in the shade under rocks, in the blockhouse, or in the Evergreen Aviation hangars. The scruffy foreground showed no other signs of man except chain-link, razor-wire fences and warnings to trespassers. To the south sat the Evergreen boneyard: mothballed Phantoms, Globemasters, 707s, and other fuselages wrapped in ghostly shrouds like warriors denied a proper burial.

Suddenly the desert roared to life. Felix fired her engines. Quail leapt into the air in panicked flight from the crushing noise, the piercing light, and the smothering dust. The close-up monitors showed the restraining bolts blow and the stubby legs lift off the cement apron. Within moments, Felix rose two hundred fifty feet and strained against her nylon collar and five steel cables.

The long plume of fire reached the ground, sending out wave after wave of dust and debris. The blockhouse reported: "She's as stable as rock. You could shoot pool in that bird. We're giving the cables some slack."

Monitors showed the inch-thick cable reeling out. From a thousand meters away, looking through a wall of dust, Felix did not appear to move. Nevertheless, voices from the blockhouse said she moved. The voices told how she had carved a perfect circle in the air, then stepped back to the center of her circle. And there Felix stood atop her bright fire and waited for a minute.

Captain Rogers' voice betrayed enforced calm. "Two

minutes into test. Altitude 2,847 mean sea level, three
hundred from ground surface. We're reeling in cable and
bringing Felix down. All systems nominal."

Felix drifted slowly down to her perch and rested. Paul
tore his headset off, giving a loud whoop. "Did you see
that! Have you ever seen such a beautiful spaceship? Like
Scarlett O'Hara coming down the staircase in her hoop
skirt. All that power and just as gentle as . . ." Paul rejoiced
inside. " 'Scuse me, I gotta go to the blockhouse."

Paul drove past the blockhouse, straight to the Felix-P
where he met members of the ground-safety crew, as
well as Max Yeager and Captain Rogers. Max, recently
retired from BAP and recalled to consult for young Paul,
held out his meaty hand. "We did good today, boy."

Paul clasped Max's hand. "We did, didn't we?"

"I don't need to look at the readouts to know a perfect
test when I see one."

"We got one helluva spaceship, eh?"

Then Max raised a cautionary finger. "Let's not get giddy,
Paul. She's not a spaceship yet. You know she can't fly to
low earth orbit on kerosene. Either we solve the dual-
fuel problem, or we go with hydrogen."

"But we're so close."

Yeager nodded. "You and Rogers had better get to the
luncheon. I'll get the briefing slides ready for the post-
test report. We'll wrestle with fuel tomorrow."

Paul and Rogers drove back to the lab for the catered
luncheon. A saguaro cactus stood sentry at the lab entrance.

Half the tables sat empty. Paul found Ted Winston,
BAP's public relations expert, and asked "Where's the
press? We had reporters, camera crews. Where are they?"

"They left, most of them."

"Why?" Paul couldn't believe they'd gone.

"Frankly, Paul, they think they've been suckered, and
they hate being suckered."

"What do you mean?"

"First, they thought they were here to see a launch,

not a hover. They didn't buy Mr. Bernard's story: launches are easy; hovers are hard. Second, they figured we were scamming them with the tethers. They really liked your training wheel analogy. You're going to get to read and hear your prosaic analogy till you're sick of it. You've got to be more careful, Paul. Third, they wanted to see the blockhouse and look around the airfield, but Evergreen Aviation forbade it; instead, they got herded around like diseased cattle. Fourth, they insisted they get close to Felix, whereupon we tell them our insurance won't let us put civilians within a thousand meters of a fueled spaceship. So again, they smell a scam. Fifth, they couldn't get decent pictures of the launch—excuse me, hover—because of all the dust. Sixth, they asked a lot of operational questions that the Air Force won't let us answer due to security reasons. In short, we wasted their time with our rinky-dink dust storm, and they're pissed. Underwhelmed. One wag showed me a couple of lines from the story she's putting on the wire. To quote: 'The poor little rocket looked like a weather-beaten traffic cone forgotten at the end of a desert runway, in weather so hot that I swear it just burst into flames, although BAP swears it was a launch.' Don't look for any great clippings in tomorrow's papers. There won't be any."

"Then they don't know what they're talking about." Paul wiped the nervous sweat from his brow. "Ted, get back with them. Do your spin doctor stuff . . . geez man, you sound like you agree with them."

Ted stood like a bear: low-centered, thick, strong, dark, and aggressive. "Listen, Paul. We could've have put on a really sexy show, but we blew it. The press had nothing to touch and very little to see. Your 'training wheels' cables seemed rather chicken, and blaming it on Evergreen only made it worse. Bunny hop? You guys must put in overtime thinking of ways to cut your own throats. Never, never, never ad lib in front of the press—you're not good at it. Now, if you'll excuse me . . ." Ted turned and walked away.

Paul stood red-faced. Captain Rogers remarked, "Where did your father find that little ray of sunshine? No wonder sales are down."

"Dad hired Ted as a favor to then White House Chief of Staff Sununu. Supposedly Ted knows his craft, but you can kinda see why Sununu wanted Winston off the White House payroll—definitely not your kinder, gentler public relations man, is he?"

"Hardly."

"Find Max and help him set up the briefing. I guess we might as well preach to the choir. We've no potential converts today. I'm going to find my dad." Paul knew where to look. He found his father working the phones, just finishing a call.

"What did you think of Felix?"

Rolf finished scribbling a note in his day-planner book, "Just finishing a thought . . . there." He tucked the book into his breast pocket. "I thought the test went perfectly. I couldn't be happier with the test. The press effort stank. I'll jack Winston up a few notches and see if we can sell Felix. Too bad your mother wasn't here to see your big triumph. I sent her a personal invitation."

"She's a busy woman."

"She ought to find time to show her only son some moral support."

"Her investment bank put up more than a hundred million dollars for Felix research and development. I call that moral support."

"Whatever you say, boy, but you underestimate your chances. She doesn't invest a hundred million dollars unless she expects two hundred million back. She knows what I know: Felix is going to be our biggest sell since your grandfather built the BP-3."

Paul tried to shift the burden of the conversation. "Maybe Mom doesn't feel like she needs to come out here and check up on me."

"You think I'm checking up on you? Well, I'm not. Felix

is a joint venture: BAP set up the lab and kicked in fifty million, your mother put up the rest of the money. And, don't forget, hotshot, your mom can't produce and sell spaceships; you can't produce and sell spaceships; BAP can. No offense."

Paul folded his arms. "None taken."

Rolf put a hand on Paul's shoulder. "If we don't build and sell a fleet of Felix ships, then all you've got here, son, is a 150 million-dollar science-fair project. You keep that in mind. Your mother, as much as she'd hate to admit it, would agree with me about this."

"Really?"

"Something else—you ought to ask her to your next big test. She might come if *you* ask her. You need to keep your investors informed, especially when they're family. You might need another shot of capital, and looking at our projected losses for the next three quarters, I'd say BAP won't be able to help. That's your finance lesson for today. Now, come with me and watch the master schmooze this pathetic little crowd Ted arranged for you."

"Lead on." Paul opened the door.

Rolf stopped in his tracks and grinned through his perfect, white false teeth. "I've just had a brainstorm! I know how to get you press coverage beyond your wildest dreams."

Chapter 2

Bobby Tyler checked his rearview mirror, then turned his Bronco four-by-four off the George Washington Parkway into a scenic overlook on the Virginia side, downriver from Great Falls. The Potomac ran low, exposing rocks and sandbars. The hot, dry July breeze withered the large poplars and maples. Tyler parked in a patch of shade, where he paused to enjoy a last blast of air conditioning and collect his thoughts.

Tyler plucked his aviator sunglasses from his face and wiped them clean with a clean tissue. As he checked his watch, Tyler heard tires crushing gravel and he looked up to see a black Lincoln Town Car pull in beside him. He noticed the blue Military District of Washington decal with the two silver stars. General Marshall was punctual—perhaps to a fault. Marshall got out, took off his gray jacket, peeled off his silk tie, and tossed both onto the car seat. He brought a brown paper bag—an ordinary lunch sack. Reaching for the pack of cigarettes in his shirt pocket, he walked to a short stone wall, and standing in the shade, looked over the precipice.

Tyler sat in the Bronco and watched from behind the dark tinted glass. Marshall looked, as always, like an overdressed high school wrestling coach—short-cropped hair peppered with gray, stocky in build, and bristling with nervous energy.

Tyler got out and took his place beside the older man. "Hello."

"Bobby. I didn't recognize your car."

"Brand-new, sir."

"Well, you can afford it." Marshall gazed down at the rapids below Minnie Island. "You still playing racquetball? Looks like you put on a couple pounds."

Tyler thought his clothes hung a bit loose from his six-foot frame. He loosened his tie. "I can still beat you, sir, if that's what you mean. Say, why don't we get back into the air-conditioning. It's like a damn oven out here."

"You could use the sun. You're pale." General Marshall sat down on the short wall, with his back to the parkway. With his toe, he nudged an empty beer can that rattled down the steep hill. "Years ago, I used to sit on a short stone wall a lot like this one up at West Point. And I'd just look out over the Hudson River."

"Really. I'll bet it never got this hot up there." Tyler took his coat off and draped it over the wall.

"Hot enough. I'd look down at the spot where the new Americans put a great chain across the Hudson, like an iron gate to block British shipping to Manhattan. Pretty darn big gate. The British captured the huge iron chain and hauled it to Gibraltar where they used it to build their own gate across their harbor entrance."

Tyler felt a bead of sweat trickle down his back. He said nothing. Marshall would get to the point soon enough after the folksy dumb-like-a-fox preliminaries.

General Marshall opened the brown paper bag and pulled out a handful of roasted peanuts. "I used to sit up on that stone wall, look over the Hudson River, and eat roasted peanuts my mom sent me from our home in Surry County. Ever been to Surry?"

"Yes, sir." Tyler instinctively reached over to accept a handful of peanuts.

Marshall shucked a peanut and asked, "How are things going with Rolf Bernard?" He put a cigarette in his mouth and flicked open a chrome Zippo—his Ranger Tab lighter—and cranked the flint wheel with his thumb.

"Not so good." Tyler saw from Marshall's quizzical face that he wanted details. "No surprise, really. We plug the Defense Department's five-year budget into our revenue model and presto—we've got to cut our workforce from 140,000 employees to 80,000."

"I figured it might be that bad."

"You figured right, General. In addition, this recession in the aerospace industry has hurt BAP more than most. Airbus undercut us for some big orders. Foreign military sales can't pull up the slack. We make decent money doing airframe maintenance, and our space division makes money, but what BAP needs right now is nice little war."

"We don't start 'em, Bobby. And at the rate we're shrinking, we won't be able to finish 'em either." Marshall threw a handful of peanut shells on the ground. "Rolf's going to have some bigger headaches coming up. So are we for that matter."

"Like what?"

"Three hundred and twenty Brilliant Pebbles."

Tyler looked around and whispered, "Sir, we shouldn't talk about that here. That's black work and you know it."

"So don't talk. Just listen." Marshall took a long drag from his cigarette, then crushed it against the stone wall. "Problem is, the Pebbles are so black that we can't find the funding for them."

"Is that supposed to be funny?"

Marshall shook his head. "Am I laughing? Listen up, Bobby, we're all out on the same limb; Rolf knew what he was getting into."

"You sure?"

"He had to know. Anyway, that's academic, now. We didn't exactly advertise our project as Brilliant Pebbles— Congress killed it twice under that title, you know. So we committed enough black money to buy bits and pieces of high technology. We got the Air Force to ante up for the kinetic kill device under the cover of antisatellite research—just built a lot of test devices—say perhaps three hundred and twenty. That's all. CIA developed the command and control mechanisms for a generic geodesic dome, purpose not specified. I influenced the National Reconnaissance Office to invest research dollars on small spaceborne IR sensors parts. That's all, just lots of parts."

"Parts? Who's going to believe that?"

"Nobody. The bigger question is, who's going to find out? We know it's no sheer coincidence that we all used the same contractor, and that our bits of technology add up to three hundred and twenty Pebbles. Technically speaking, we didn't break any laws."

"But somebody's got to find out someday."

"You're right. We figured Bush would understand— he was CIA; he knew the missile threat. Bush didn't like the politics of SDI, but we figured he'd pay off the contract and . . . it doesn't matter anymore. Bush ain't here, the money for black projects dried up, and we're screwed. We don't have anything to pay Rolf with. How do you think he'll react?"

Tyler tensed. "Sir, BAP's in big trouble. Rolf can barely hold it together. You guys still owe a billion dollars for the Pebbles; if you stiff us, we might go under. If you're asking me to break the news to Rolf, forget it—I can't. You'll have to deliver this bit of news in person."

"Not just yet. It's not over yet. We can contain this situation as long as we keep it under wraps. Everybody's cutting the Stealth program to ribbons, and some of that money might fall our way. So basically, we can ride this out if Rolf lies low."

"Rolf will drag you guys into court faster than you—"

Marshall interrupted. "He won't get a dime for at least ten years, and he knows it. In the meantime, he'd be just as broke. Listen Bobby, here's what we want you to do. Keep an eye on Rolf, for his sake. Keep a lid on things. We have no choice but to stall payments on the Pebbles. We need you to keep us informed about Bernard's reaction—none of us can afford to let this get out. We'll think of something—I don't know what yet. At least, this present administration can't last forever."

"Neither can Rolf. . . ."

"We'll make it up to him." Marshall crushed a handful of peanut shells.

"Like how? Our little surveillance effort in Paris? That's a low yield, high-risk bit of nonsense that I ought to shut down tomorrow."

"That might be our ace in the hole—no pun intended."

"Real cute, sir."

"We just try to use human weakness to our advantage. Don't get squeamish on me, boy. I'll call you at home from time to time. Don't call us. Also, you'll see a slight bump up in your consulting fee. And give my best to your lovely wife, Mariam."

Both men rose. Marshall emptied the leftover peanuts onto the ground for the squirrels, then folded the little bag into his pocket. Tyler walked Marshall to the big Lincoln. As Marshall opened his door he mused, "Too bad Rolf can't just deploy the Pebbles himself; then he could sell them, I'd bet you. His old man started BAP that way. Old Vincent Bernard hocked his house, sold his car, borrowed all he could get, then built three BP-3's without orders. Talk about going out on a limb. The Army Air Corps loved his little plane and bought 46,000 of them—biggest run BAP ever had. Yeah . . ."

"That was a long time ago."

"Just a thought. If Rolf put the Pebbles up, somebody would have to buy them."

"Cigars?" Rolf Bernard passed an ebony humidor around the table. "George? You'll have one, won't you? Cuban Coronas, hand rolled, leaf, no fill."

"Don't mind if I do." George Harchord took the cigar and a small device—a gold-plated, handheld guillotine—to snip the end. He struck a match and singed the flat end, saying, "Can't smoke these at home—not since my triple bypass. So boys, if this magnificent cigar kills me, I trust you to lie to my wife and the flight surgeon, then bury me with the stub."

"Got our word on it, General." Don Benson raised his cigar.

Congressman Rob Doherty fingered the cards and grinned. "Benson, you yellow dog, you've never kept a secret in your journalistic life."

"Why sir, you cut me to the quick!" Benson flourished his cigar in mock protestation. "I have never—maybe once or twice—been accused of spilling the beans." He blew a ring of smoke into the blades of a slow ceiling fan.

Rolf cleared his throat to interrupt, "Rob, you know Don would never violate the sanctity of our poker table. That's *the* prime directive." Rolf passed out small stacks of red, white and blue chips and collected twenty dollars from each man, including the taciturn fifth, his son, Paul.

Paul looked around the table. While the other men sorted their chips, Benson addressed Paul. "Are you any good at poker?"

"I play a little in Vegas on my time off."

"He counts cards." Rolf warned the group.

Doherty chuckled, "That won't help you here. Ever play Seven-Card-High-Low-Wild? Mrs. Mulligatawny's Stew? Deal Seven Pass the Trash? Dead Dog's Bone? Rolf's Wild Ride? Pick Your Friends? We've been making these games up for over fifteen years."

Paul just stared at Benson.

"Apparently, your old man didn't brief you about our harmless little game. We just come here to gab."

"I come for the food and to take your money," General Harchord interjected.

Benson ignored Harchord. "We come here to gab, and

no offense to the general, but he's the biggest bag of wind at the table."

Rolf and Rob Doherty guffawed. Harchord raised an eyebrow.

"The rules for our low-stakes poker game are simple enough: no women, no rank, no snitching. We rotate the game. Last month we played at Harchord's house. You should try to be in town for one of his games; Quarters 2, Fort Myers—sitting on the grand verandah, overlooking the monuments, sippin' whiskey served by orderlies. That's the life for me."

"But we can't smoke these heavenly cigars." Harchord tapped a thick ash into the thick crystal ashtray at his side.

"Mrs. Harchord won't let us smoke in the presence of the general. Scary thought: the Air Force Chief of Staff is whipped." Benson nodded in Harchord's direction and added, "Don't worry, Rob. I won't print that."

Paul prompted Benson. "You were telling me about the game."

"Oh, yes. There are seven of us regulars that play. We have one thing in common: we flew aircraft in combat. General Harchord, long before he earned his stars, was a mere mortal B-52 bomber pilot. The Honorable Congressman Doherty flew F-4C Phantoms in Vietnam. His specialty: knocking out SAM sites."

Doherty couldn't resist a dig. "That's right. We had to clear out the SAMs so the B-52 wimps could just cruise on by unmolested and drop their payloads."

"You missed a few SAM sites, I can tell you."

"Touché, General." Benson shuffled the cards. "I flew the old F-86E Sabre in Korea, back when men were men, and women were proud to get groped by a pilot. Of course, you know about your dad. He flew the RF-4C Phantom reconnaissance jet. What do you fly?"

"I fly a Gates Learjet 54. Strictly commercial. I never got into the armed services. Bad eyes." Paul tapped his glasses, knowing that had his astigmatic eyes not kept him out of service, his mother surely would have. "I know it's not the same as flying in combat."

"Tsk, tsk, my lad" —Benson flourished his cigar— "you've got as much right to join this council of warriors as any old B-52 pilot, bunch of softies."

Harchord rose in his defense. "Soft, my ass. I don't want you giving young Paul here, any wrong ideas about buff pilots."

"Buff?"

Benson answered, "Acronym for Big Ugly F---ers. Right, General?"

"Big, ugly, and then some. You guys don't know deprivation until you've done your time in a B-52."

Benson set his cigar down. "Uh-oh. I asked for it. Here comes the eye patch story."

Harchord scowled. "Paul's never heard it."

Benson stood up. "Gentlemen, I think I'll take advantage of this lull in the action to visit the men's room."

Doherty defended the general, "I love the eye patch story. I used it on the House floor back in 1988 when we debated funding B-1 production."

"Thank you, Rob." Harchord paused to wet his lips with a spare taste of whiskey. "In the mid-seventies we changed tactics for our strategic bombers. We planned to fly under their air defense—nap-of-the-earth stuff—then rise above our targets and drop nuclear bombs with drag fins on them, so we'd get far enough away before the bomb detonated. There was a problem with that. We'd still be too close to the detonations, so close that the light would instantly blind anyone who saw a detonation. So our genius engineers built thick blast curtains that the pilot would pull around to seal off the cockpit . . ."

"But you couldn't see," Paul interjected.

"Right. We'd fly on instruments only. Only problem was, the first bomb that went off would put out enough electromagnetic pulse to cook our avionics. Honest, I'm telling you what was in the procedures manual. If EMP knocked out the avionics, the pilot would put on an eye patch—they issued one eye patch per bomber—over his best eye, then open a peephole in the blast curtain, then fly the giant supersonic bomber with his hand on the yoke and his weak eye up to a little hole. If a nuclear blast blinded his good eye, he'd hand the eye patch to the copilot, and they'd trade places."

"You've got to be kidding," Paul smirked.

"Nope. I trained with an eye patch, flying out of Griffith Air Force Base."

"What happened if the copilot lost an eye?"

"The procedures manual sort of stops there, but the second-eye option remained a source of speculation among pilots and copilots. B-52 flight crews have a heightened appreciation for the old expression, 'the one-eyed man is king.'"

Doherty added a postscript. "Old warriors like your dad and General Harchord tell Congress, 'If you really want us to defend this great country, you need to provide us antimissile defense, a new bomber, better submarine detection' . . . so Congress gives them an eye patch."

A tall man in waiter's jacket took drink orders and disappeared. Benson returned and dealt a round of straight poker, in deference to newcomer Paul. Paul won, beating his dad with a pair of red queens.

"An unpropitious start, Paul." General Harchord fingered his blue suspenders. "It's bad luck to take the first pot."

And so it was. The deck of cards circumnavigated the table twice, stopping at each port of call where each dealer announced another ridiculously contrived game—except Paul: he stuck to draw poker.

Even then, the older men prevailed. They played straight poker as well as their whimsical games, and Paul bought another twenty dollars of chips.

Rolf interrupted play, raised his voice. "Margaret?"

"Yes, Mr. Bernard." A middle-aged woman wearing an ivory cocktail dress walked into the room and smiled through the cigar smoke. She wore long strands of pearls, and pearl earrings. She looked pale, even fragile. She wore her natural blond hair in a tight bun, bound to the top of her head. Margaret was, from her head to her shoes, an off-white. Not a bright white. Perhaps a white yellowed with age—except for her violet eyes, and her crimson lipstick and fingernail polish.

"You all remember Margaret Bergen, my social secretary and house manager. . . ."

Margaret Bergen spoke with a Boston Brahmin accent. "It's a pleasure to see you gentlemen again. You too, Paul. The buffet is ready."

"Thank you, Margaret." Rolf spoke for the table. "We're hungry."

Rolf led the small party into a glass porch overlooking an illuminated Japanese garden. Silver platters caught flashes from scores of candles. Cut crystal wineglasses sparkled, standing in a row before a pair of squat green bottles called *Bocksbeutels* in which they put Franken wine. Rolf opened the first. "This wine is a Spätlese— that means they use a late-picked grape with more sugar content for a sweeter wine. It's from Sulzfeld, 1988. It won a gold medallion." Rolf set the Spätlese down and picked up the second *Bocksbeutel*. "And here we have a dry wine, a Müller-Thurgau grape from Iphöfer Kronsberg, a Qualitätswein mit Prädikat, only a silver medal, but forgive me, I prefer the drier wine." Rolf poured himself a glass, adding, "Please, gentlemen, help yourselves."

The men turned their attention to a lace-covered marble table laden with *Schnitten*—cold cuts. Margaret had procured a half-dozen different wurst: *Jagdwurst*, *Pilswurst*, *Kalbslebewurst*, *Blutwurst*, *Zungenwurst*, and *Bierwurst*. A smoked eel, complete with head and brittle teeth, lay in rigor mortis on an oblong silver tray at the top of the table. Various cheeses sat upon a monkeypod board: *Jarlsberg, Münster, Handkäse, Jetöst,* and *Brie.* Small china bowls held Bavarian sweet mustard, one Prussian hot-as-hell mustard, and a concoction of *Schlagsahne mit Meerettich*—whipped cream and horseradish. A basket of *Brötchen* and rye bread sat next to the meats. Good old American lettuce and tomatoes lined the trays. Once Margaret saw that the men had found everything, she disappeared into the house.

"This is delicious!" Benson effused. He pointed at a pile of plum-colored slices mottled with bits of meat and white squares. "What is this stuff?"

Rolf replied, "*Zungenwurst*—it's tongue."

"Too bad my wife isn't here. She loves tongue."

A moment of stunned silence erupted as Harchord burst into laughter. "I dare you to print that!"

The others roared. "Hear! Hear!"

The mirth subsided, and Harchord took a seat in a large wicker chair beside Paul Bernard. "What do you do for your dad?"

"I run the BAP skunk works at Marana."

"Oh, *you* run it?"

Paul blushed. "Yes, as a matter of fact. BAP's like a big family business."

"Don't ever feel defensive about being in charge. Never apologize for working in a family business. At least your dad put you where the opportunities are." Harchord smiled. "It's like the old patriarch of the Rothschild family, Meyer Amschel Rothschild. He built the biggest financial empire Europe has ever seen. He started with a small money-changing business, five sons, and six opportunities. He sent his ablest son, Nathan, to the fast-growing, cutthroat financial markets in London. He sent his most astute son, James, to Paris to sift through the intrigue. He sent his refined and patient son, Salomon, to Vienna to provide banking services to the Hapsburg court. He kept his namesake, the meticulous Amschel, Jr., back in Frankfurt to run the back office and manage the intrafamily communications and intelligence operations. The fifth son, Kalmann, was incompetent. Although Papa Rothschild needed a family agent in Amsterdam and Hamburg, he refused to invest an opportunity on his mediocre son. Instead, he spent a fortune to buy his dear, but flaky offspring the kingdom of Naples, and poured money down that hole to keep Kalmann out of trouble. So, your dad must have you figured for a Nathan, not a Kalmann."

"I hope so."

"What are you doing at Marana, or can you say?"

"We're building the Felix prototype."

"Your dad never told me you ran the single-stage-to-orbit project—son of a gun. Then I guess I'll get to see your ship pretty soon. I hear you're going to test fly Felix near D.C., aren't you?"

"In September, yes. It's my dad's idea. We're going to launch from our site at Rixeyville, more publicity stunt than research. We're going to put a crew aboard, then send her up as far as she'll go. We can't get her into orbit burning kerosene, but we can put her out of sight."

"Why don't you use liquid hydrogen like the shuttle?"

"We're trying to develop a dual-fuel rocket—actually it's my pet project. The Russians researched the dual-fuel technology for years. We'll burn denser kerosene for greater thrust through the atmosphere, then when we leave the atmosphere, we switch to hydrogen, which is less dense but burns at greater velocity. I guess I'm fixated. I wrote my dissertation on dual-fuel rocket motors. You'd think I could build the damn thing."

"Why mess with it?"

"If we crack the dual-fuel problem, we can use smaller fuel tanks and gain cargo-hold area. We instantly increase the Felix payload to twenty thousand pounds, which means we can compete for most Shuttle payloads. Then, maybe NASA will listen to us."

"I wouldn't go to all that trouble for NASA's business." Harchord shook his head and sipped from his glass of

Müller-Thurgau. He puckered. "Maybe you oughta burn this stuff instead of kerosene—damn, but it's dry as hydrogen."

"Don't let Dad hear you criticize his favorite wine."

"Right." Harchord set his glass down. "So how do you solve your dual-fuel problem?"

"I hired a pair of Russians from NOP Energiya to help me: the two happiest engineers in North America. They got to trade in their sledgehammers for micrometers. And they love the women in Arizona. You'd think they'd died and gone to heaven."

"So you're going back to Tucson?"

"Not directly. I go to England; BAP has a small lab outside Mindenhall, where we do some joint R and D with the Brits."

"Then, you'll pop over to Paris to see your mom, I suppose."

Paul glanced sideways. "No, I've barely enough time to visit the Mindenhall lab."

Harchord sensed Paul's discomfort. He withdrew to the conversation at the other end of the porch. General Harchord steered Rolf aside. "I don't want to leave before we have a chance to talk privately."

"What's on your mind, George?"

"I'm on my way out, Rolf."

"This isn't the first time you've predicted your demise. What makes you think you're in trouble now?"

"One of my little spies at National Security Council keeps me up to date. I've been a little too disagreeable with the new Commander in Chief and his lapdog Defense Secretary."

"You should tell your wife to scrape the Perot bumper sticker off your car. . . ."

Harchord shook his head, "You never know. I might find myself working for Perot someday."

"Not bloody likely." Rolf checked himself. "What I mean is, I don't think Perot will be in position. . . ."

"I know what you mean," Harchord chuckled. "No, Rolf, the politicians figure the Cold War has ended; we won, now it's time to cashier the Cold War warriors. I'd go a lot happier if I thought they were right. Anyway, I just wanted to tell you I don't think I can be much help pushing our projects anymore. You can't count on me anymore, I don't have the clout."

Rolf hesitated, then spoke. "George, ever since you made major general, you figured your days were numbered, and the politicians were going to toss you out on your ass. You'll outlast them. They'll keep you in the Pentagon just so they can keep tabs on you. They'd rather have you inside the tent pissing out."

"I'll take that as a compliment."

"And if you ever do hang up your uniform, it'll be my turn to help you."

"You can help us both now. I want you to promise me one thing."

"Ask."

"The Administration floated a proposal by the Chiefs whereby we'd give—or at least share—our SDI technology to the world in an effort to combat state-sponsored nuclear terror—or some such nonsense. That means sharing our technology with the Russians. In an effort to ease the new policy through, the Administration wants BAP to give the Russians the grand tour of your Pueblo facilities. Don't do it, Rolf. Not even our side knows what we've got squirreled away at Pueblo. We sure can't afford to let the Russians see our stash. The Russians are still a bunch of wolves; worse, they're wolves in sheeps' clothing. Even worse, they're starving. You can't let them see Pueblo. I don't care how you do it: lose the Pebbles, hide the Pebbles, burn the warehouse. It doesn't matter. You don't let anybody—especially some twenty-two-year-old congressman's aide and an entourage of Russian scientists—into Pueblo to see how you make Pebbles. Are we clear on that, Rolf?"

"There are limits. . . ."

"Don't tell me that. That's not what I envision on our tombstones: There Were Limits! We're too set in our ways to think like a bunch of lawyers. Promise me, Rolf. You'll keep Pueblo black."

"I'll do what I can."

"Not good enough. You know damned well, whoever controls low earth orbit controls the military, political, and economic destiny of mankind for the next century. Shall we take control of low earth orbit or give it to the United Nations, or Russia perhaps?" Harchord's doctoral dissertation had expounded his theory of spatial strategic dominance. Stripped of academic embellishment, Harchord's argument went: for two thousand years, Athenians, Romans, and Vikings dominated their worlds by controlling intercoastal waterways; for two hundred years, the British dominated the world by controlling the oceans; after World War II, until the threat of ballistic missiles, Americans dominated the world by controlling the air. History repeats, therefore, whoever takes control of low earth orbit will dominate the world into the foreseeable future.

"All right, George, I promise."

"That's better. Thank you."

Rolf wiped his forehead with a linen napkin, then sought the easy banter of Benson, the newspaper man. Soon, they set their plates and glasses down, and retired to the den for more cigars, cards, and large snifters of Asbach Uralt, a modest brandy made from the Reisling grape.

They cashed in their chips just before midnight, and Rolf walked his guests to their cars in the driveway. Harchord clasped Rolf's hand with a firm shake. "Thanks again, Rolf. I know I can count on your promise."

Before the taillights disappeared down the asphalt drive, Paul and Rolf climbed the granite steps back into the house. Paul wandered through the house to the guest bedroom, and Rolf returned to his study. In the background, Rolf overheard Margaret bid the housekeeper "Buenas noches."

A few lights burned randomly throughout the Bernard mansion. There were no sounds except for old clocks ticking, the central air hushing, and the stop-and-go tapping on a small computer keyboard. An amber light from the screen lit Rolf Bernard's tired face as he carefully composed a letter to Cynthia, his estranged wife.

Rolf printed the one-page letter on his laser printer, signed it simply, "Rolf," and stuffed it in a plain white envelope addressed to Mrs. Rolf Bernard, 182H, Rue Dauphin, Paris. He threw the envelope onto a wooden tray with other outgoing mail.

Rolf sighed. He lifted a heavy crystal glass filled with whiskey, rattled the ice, and wiped away the water ring with his sleeve. He took a big swallow and spat a solitary splinter of ice back into the glass. He wondered, *What on earth has gotten into George Harchord?*

He picked up his empty glass and considered refilling it, but he'd had enough alcohol to meet his needs. Rolf closed his eyes and contemplated the fresh, heart-shaped face of the Nicaraguan woman, Miss Escondido, the new house servant. In his mind, the young woman looked knowingly back at him with moist brown eyes, for why else does a rich older man hire a young illegal alien and pay her twice the going wage? But Rolf would not touch her: would merely contemplate her, and congratulate his virtue for choosing the simplicity of alcohol. Rolf glanced at the plain white envelope lying in the wooden tray.

Chapter 3

Two men sat behind a window, shrouded by shadows. Below lay rue Saint-Jacques, and beyond a nest of buildings stood the treetops of the Hôtel Cluny. Nightlife in the Latin Quarter had fizzled out, and stragglers, students mostly, wandered up the street, arm-in-arm, huddled against the slight nip in the autumn air. Dry beech leaves danced down the street like sprites beneath the full moon.

The faceless man in charge turned to his partner who steadied the long camera lens on the tripod, and said sarcastically, "Ah, this night was made for love." Gaining no response, he said, "You've got no appreciation of why we're here."

"I get paid to take pictures." The cameraman peeked through the lens. "I'd rather work for *National Geographic*."

"You underestimate the value of your work. She's a very important woman, very rich, very well connected in France and Germany. Her husband, Rolf Bernard, has even more clout; he's an aerospace industrialist with strong ties to United States security. Unfortunately, she's developed an appetite for younger men, an appetite soon discovered by our adversaries. The GRU set her up with a fake baron from Montenegro with designs to blackmail the industrialist husband. We found out, removed Baron

What's-his-name, then substituted our man Chip. If she's going to be compromised, why not be compromised with us? Besides, people do the most useful things when blackmailed. Now maybe you'll appreciate your work."

"Shh." He clicked the camera shutter.

Through the lens he saw a slender woman quickly and methodically undress: shoes, slip, hose, blouse. Next, she deftly shed each shoulder strap of her brassiere, spun the clasp from back to front beneath her pale breasts, and tossed the gangly apparatus onto a chair.

The camera clicked. The little motor advanced the film. The man with the notebook asked, "Clothes off or on?"

The shutter clicked, the little motor whined, the shutter clicked again. "Would I waste film?"

The woman walked to her side of the bed and sat down with her back to the camera. She modestly slipped out of her panties, turned out the lamp, then slid under the covers where Chip waited.

"What's Chip doing?"

"What do you think?" The man with the camera leaned back in a shadow and lit a cigarette, giving the camera a rest. He turned to the agent and stifled the man's next question by saying, "They're under the sheets. You want pictures of sheets?"

"No, no. This is very disappointing." The agent looked at his watch. "I could get us something to eat. You think we got maybe fifteen, twenty minutes?"

The cameraman looked through the infrared scope. Most definitely, there was heat coming from under the sheets. "At least fifteen minutes, maybe twenty." The cameraman drank cold coffee from a white styrofoam cup. "Get me some hot coffee, will you?"

The agent left. The cameraman glanced at an old copy of *Paris Match*. In spite of the gloom, his eye caught an ad for group tours to what was left of Yugoslavia—a picture of smiling Croats wearing hard hats, inviting tourists back to Dubrovnic. The picture was poorly composed, he

thought. Contrived. The fake smiles and spotless hard
hats only enhanced the sense of dread and false hope.
The cameraman sighed. He should freelance pictures for
Paris Match, *The Economist*, and *Time*, but the Company
paid a steady wage.

He peeked through the camera lens. The blue satin
sheets tossed, rose and fell like a calm Mediterranean
Sea catching flashes of moonlight. The camera could not
feel the heat beneath those satin waves.

The cameraman shut the magazine and pitched it onto
the floor. The whole job was a botch. As their supervisor
had explained, their mission was to "get pictures of a
smoking crotch." In six months the cameraman had taken
hundreds of pictures to prove that Mrs. Bernard had slept
with another man, but in these cynical times, mere
infidelity couldn't break a man like Rolf Bernard—so the
Company thought. They wanted photographs so obscene,
so painful, so humiliating that *Hustler* magazine would
blush as they printed them. Chip's job was to set up those
photos, but what did the camera see? It saw one shapeless
form under sheets, like two middle-aged parents enjoying
themselves quietly so as not to scandalize the children.
From time to time, the agent in charge of the project
complained, "It's disgusting. It's so unprofessional."

They had botched the job from the beginning. On one
sweaty summer afternoon, a more enthusiastic Chip had
Mrs. Bernard bent over a chest of drawers. The agent
pressed his binoculars to the window. The light, the subject,
everything favored success. The camera clicked and
whined through two rolls of film. But when the cameraman
developed the film, they saw what the camera had seen.
"It's so unprofessional! You rank amateurs!"

The camera had seen Chip, all six foot two inches of
him, his broad shoulders, massive chiseled back, large
arms, thick muscular waist and buttocks, a contorted
athlete bent over a chest of drawers. One could barely
make out a second pair of slender feet on tiptoes—but

aside from that, it looked as if Chip had caught his doodad in the sock drawer. The agent fumed, "Disgusting! Amateurish!"

The agent critiqued Chip's first effort in paternal tones, encouraging the young man, suggesting that he move the chest of drawers to another wall to facilitate a profile shot. Then he asked for physical, sensory details about Mrs. Bernard; and Chip, a young, has-been tennis pro, a man without scruples, a perfect Company man, replied, "You vulgar pervert." He turned and left the meeting while the agent barked, "Get back here! I'm not through with you!" And Chip retaliated by shutting the window blinds the next night, and for a couple of nights after that.

The agent complained to his bosses that Chip didn't take his job seriously, but the man in charge of the Bernard case, an agent known only by the name Iago, decided it would be a bit too awkward—even for the Company— to replace Chip just now. Iago told the supervisor; the supervisor told the field agent, who argued with the supervisor. The supervisor explained the pecking order to the field agent, ending the discussion by saying, "You've never seen Iago, but he's seen you. Just do what you're told and no one will get hurt."

That raised a few eyebrows.

The cameraman suspected (and he was right) that Chip liked Cynthia (and why not?) a lot more than his Company handler. Even in the beginning, Chip saw nothing but profit in dragging his assignment out.

In a naturally physical way, Chip grew fond of Cynthia. She was his first monogamous relationship. The higher authorities in the Company emphatically insisted that Chip not pass a disease to the "subject," as that might compromise the "project." Cynthia, similarly emphatic, convinced Chip that the retribution for such indiscretion would be the ultimate price—she'd have him altered. So as time passed, threats directed below motivated better than threats from above. Chip mostly feared that she might discover his link to the Company, call off their mutually beneficial affair, and summon the veterinarian.

Whenever Cynthia's blood rose in one of her energetic moods, Chip made sure Cynthia closed the window blinds. He'd whisper, "I'd be so embarrassed if anyone saw."

"Sweetheart, this is Paris," she'd chide, shaking her head. Then she'd lower the venetian blinds.

The agent came back with coffee. He walked over and peered into the camera's eyepiece. Just two people sleeping—soundly.

Chapter 4

Bobby Tyler rubbed the sleep from his eyes—three o'clock in the morning. He sat in a wicker rocking chair, nursing a large cup of coffee, watching moonlit patches of fog settle into the draws. From his perch on the Carter farmhouse porch at the top of a hill, Tyler faced southeast where the little town Rixeyville sat. Generators hummed. Large trucks revved their engines. Occasionally a public address system squawked. A whiff of diesel exhaust wafted up the hill. The night, the chill, the sounds, and smells reminded Tyler of night maneuvers at the Hohenfels Training Area in rural West Germany—a memory made fond by a gulf of passed time. Even so, the rocking chair made a more comfortable resting place than the back seat of a jeep with its top down.

On the next hill, the night crew moved a section of chain-link fence, brought in the crane, adjusted the xenon lights, tested the communications gear, and waited to receive the Felix-P.

Behind him, the screen door slammed, and Tyler turned to see Max Yeager stepping onto the porch, speaking through a yawn. "Getting up at three in the morning makes for a long day, doesn't it?"

"Not much choice—someone's got to superintend this road march. On a Heavy Equipment Transport, Felix takes

33

up the whole highway. You know what happens if you clog up the roads during rush hour around Washington: a mob of angry commuters hangs you from the nearest telephone pole. We've got to move her at night. Anyway, Max, you can go back to bed—you're retired."

"I didn't retire. I became a free agent." Yeager yawned again.

Tyler's handheld cellular phone chirruped. He unfolded the wallet-size phone and pulled out the stubby antenna. "Tyler speaking."

"This is Paul. We just passed Warrenton, and we're about to turn south onto Route 229. ETA to Rixeyville about three-fifty."

"We're ready. And we're cooking breakfast."

Max reached over and took the phone, "Paul, this is Max."

"Yes?"

"You make that HET driver go slow on the turns."

"I'm sitting next to him. He heard you, Max. He's nodding his head."

"You tell him to nod his head slowly."

"Okay." Paul rubbed the sleep from his eyes. "We'll see you in forty-five minutes."

The caravan wound its way down Route 229 flashing yellow, blue, and red lights. Felix lay on the HET, covered with a metallic silver blanket. One might have thought the caravan hauled a seventy-foot yacht. They turned into BAP's Carter Farm Facility. Dust from the gravel road screened the HET, which drove up the hill to the launch platform. A ground guide moved the HET in beside a large gold circle painted on the cement.

Tyler walked around the vehicle, peeking under the shroud. He'd never seen Felix before—only pictures and models. He bumped into a shabby cameraman whose gaffer turned a blinding light on a woman who wore too much makeup, a yellow scarf, navy blue suit, and a tiny microphone clipped to her lapel.

"Just what the hell are you doing here?" Bobby stepped forward and put his hand in front of the camera.

"Cut!" the woman barked. The gaffer turned the lights off. Tyler and the threesome stood blinking. The woman softened her tone and spoke. "A Mr. Theodore Winston, Vice President of Government Sales, BAP, Inc., hired us to shoot a documentary of your test flight. He wrote us a script. Want to see?"

"Well, Winston didn't clear this through me. And he's not here to vouch for you. Not that it matters, but I'm supposed to handle security. So wait here a second, will ya." Tyler turned and yelled, "Hey, Dr. Bernard!"

"Yes, Bobby?" Paul stepped out of a shadow.

"Did these movie people come down with you?"

Paul walked closer to get away from the loud machinery. "Yeah, part of the big promo. I'm in charge of them until Ted gets here. They're okay. Hi, Gloria." Paul waved at the woman with the sculpted blond hair.

"They need badges. Everyone here has a blue BAP company badge. Where's yours, by the way?"

"I left it in my other pants."

"For crying out loud, we might as well host an open house and let Lockheed, Boeing, and Ariane just walk in and help themselves to our secrets."

"This *is* an open house of sorts." Paul sloughed off Tyler's criticism.

"Irregular. Damned irregular." Tyler turned to the woman. "I'll send a man down with badges for you three. Humor me and wear them. Meanwhile, continue to do your job, but until I get this sorted out with Mr. Winston, you'll have to leave your gear inside this facility. It should be safer here . . ." Tyler scowled at Paul. "Theoretically safer."

She nodded. "Fair enough." The gaffer switched the lights on, and the cameraman hefted his camera onto his shoulder.

Tyler wandered off shaking his head.

Max Yeager handed Paul a light-blue hard hat, and together they watched the ground crew—sixteen men and four women in lime green jumpsuits—unfasten the straps. The crane dangled cables and a harness over Felix, and in short order they raised her (without fuel, Felix-P weighed less than fifteen thousand pounds), and set her down with her five stubby legs squarely upon the steel pads. They secured Felix to the ground with exploding bolts. Yeager looked at his watch and called above the din, "Timekeeper!"

"Yo!"

"Mark six fifty-seven. Felix secure."

The actress stepped out of the bright light and asked, "What's all that about?"

Paul answered, "We're timing ground operations. We can set Felix for a launch in less than forty-eight hours, with fewer than a hundred technicians. That's the real beauty of the system. A Shuttle launch takes sixteen weeks to set up, and fourteen thousand high-paid technicians. When you do the math, you see that Felix requires less than $250,000 direct labor costs per launch; the Shuttle requires almost $1.2 billion in direct labor costs per launch."

"So you save almost $1 billion per launch."

"That's right. Now we just have to prove it."

A BAP blue and white Sikorsky S-76 Spirit swooped by the launch pad and landed behind the farmhouse.

"Rolf's early." Max announced, checking his wristwatch.

Paul surveyed ground operations. "I want to stay here and push the ground crew. You go up and take care of my dad, okay?"

"Sure thing." Max rounded up Tyler and they drove back up the hill. They found Rolf sitting with Captain Rogers and Ted Winston in the dining room at a rough-hewn pine table, old as the farmhouse. Winston divvied up two boxes of Entenmann's strudel. Rolf smoked a breakfast cigarette. A flustered young woman rushed into the room with a bulbous glass coffee pot and three mugs. Out of breath and without a word, she disappeared back to the kitchen to fetch the cream, sugar, and more mugs.

Rolf rose to shake Max's hand. "I rushed down here fast as I could. You guys have already put Felix on her feet . . ."

"And we should be pumping fuel right now." Max looked again at his wristwatch.

Each man took a slice of strudel on a small plate, then sat down around the table. Rolf put four heaping teaspoons of sugar in his coffee. "Max."

"Yes?"

"Ted tells me you still don't want to put a crew aboard Felix. I thought we'd settled that issue long ago. Now, he says you tried to get Rogers here to opt out of taking her up. Is that right?"

Yeager glowered across the table at Ted. "We could use some more unmanned flights."

"Does Paul agree with you?"

"I don't know. He's not going to get between you and me about planning missions."

"I see." Rolf paused. "We've got to fly her manned. In terms of press and my ability to sell this program, the Marana bunny hop did us more harm than good. You should see the job the press did to us."

"I have." Yeager admitted.

"CNN showed the Shuttle roaring into space on one half the TV screen and our tethered bunny hop on the other. The Shuttle disappears into dark space; Felix just disappears behind a dust cloud. We've got the better technology, but let's face facts. The press (and I think with NASA's help) is selling the public that BAP just plays with model airplanes in the desert. They're painting the test as just another shameless grab for tax dollars to prop up an ailing defense contractor. There's even talk that after Congress finishes its investigation of Rockwell's B-1 bomber, they want to come have a close look at us. We don't need that kind of grief. I agree with Ted when he says that a big public relations boost like a manned Felix launch will prove that we deliver top quality goods, within budget, and ahead of schedule."

Ted nodded silent approval.

"But why manned?" Max asked Ted.

"Simple—sex appeal. From a public relations point of view, this could work. The press demands a human interest angle: 'Test Pilots Risk Fiery Death' in four-inch doomsday print has got a lot more zip than 'SSTO Passes Second Bunny Hop Trial.' TV stations want pictures of smiling, confident crew members climbing into the ship. Viewers identify with the pilot—the heroes. People fight over tickets to see a Shuttle launch. Why? Seven brave Americans strap themselves to five million pounds of high explosives, light the fuse, and wow! It's a thousand times better than a stock-car race. People don't give a damn about machines, they care about people. NASA figured that out in the sixties. Besides, you know the Air Force won't buy anything that doesn't have a pilot."

Rolf amplified, "Without a crew, we've just got another bunny hop—this time up to hundred thousand feet. What we really need is to put Felix and her crew into low earth orbit. We should have dispensed with the kerosene and gone straight to hydrogen."

"You'll have to take that up with Paul. I like propane." Max shrugged. "But then you wouldn't be able to launch so close to Washington. The bureaucrats would never let you fly liquid hydrogen near a populated area. Also, because we can't go over hundred thousand feet, we're not technically a space flight, therefore, we don't have to comply with the U.N. Space Treaty."

"Enough already." Rolf raised his hand. "We can thrash out fuel issues later. I'm more concerned about tomorrow's flight. Our manned launch loses a lot of its intended cachet if we prang the ship and kill the crew."

Rogers raised his mug of coffee, "A sentiment I wholeheartedly share."

"You are getting a big bonus."

"The boys and I truly believe we'll live to spend it."

"So," Rolf continued, "Rogers is comfortable. That leaves you Max. Are you worried because an early manned flight is bad procedure, or because Felix's not safe?"

Max looked across the table at Charles Rogers.

Rogers coaxed, "Would you take her up if you were me?"

"Oh, yes. With or without the hazardous flight pay. I'd take her up. I'd love to take her up—and I could too," Max volunteered. "But I can't speak for you and your crew. Right now, Felix-P is safer than the Shuttle, but that's not saying much."

"I've flown the Shuttle, thank you. I want to go up. I'm tired of sitting on the ground and letting the computer fly Felix. If God had wanted computers to fly, He would have given them wings."

Rolf took a last drag from his cigarette, then crushed it on the side of his plate. "Then it's settled. Rogers flies. Ted you make sure Carter Farm looks like our own little Paris Air Show. I want everybody who comes, to have a good time and learn something. When they go back to their offices, they're going to say, 'Shuttle launch? Why, that's small change. BAP sent their ship up and brought her back to the same spot. We saw a takeoff and landing for the price of one admission!' "

Bobby Tyler, who had been sitting quietly, sipping coffee, offered a note of caution. "I'm not so sure we want to promote a carnival atmosphere here. Security is lax enough. . . ."

"Speaking of security, Mr. Tyler . . ." Rolf only addressed Bobby as Mr. Tyler when a reprimand followed. "You've got a rather embarrassing situation brewing at the Pueblo site." He shoved a flimsy piece of fax paper across the table.

Tyler read the short message, folded it and slipped it into his pocket. "I'd better ride the chopper back to town with you."

After Rolf and Bobby had flown back to McLean, the helicopter returned with the rest of Rogers' flight crew, Dotz and Kazepis. Paul and Max stayed at Carter Farm to prepare Felix for launch. Ted Winston stayed to oversee preparations for the press: print media, radio, and television.

Dotz and Kazepis found Rogers, who gave them the preflight briefing. Straightforward enough—walk across the tarmac, smile at the cameras, climb into the ship, strap yourself in, enjoy the ride twenty-five miles straight up and back down again, climb out of the ship, and smile for the cameras. About $25,000 each—hazardous flight pay—for an hour's work, prepaid. Rogers, Dotz, and Kazepis accepted their fat checks and signed copious waivers, then ate a high protein dinner and went to bed.

Both Paul and Max worked through the night. Paul watched as Max pushed and prodded his engineers. They tweaked the onboard controls and environmental suite— old gear that didn't really fit. The techies cussed Yeager time and again for making them jerry-rig old gear into their new ship. Yeager purchased the old navigational set that Rockwell scrapped when NASA ordered the company to upgrade the Shuttle *Discovery*. Yeager got pleasure from paying ten cents on the dollar for proven technology, and he didn't mind the cussing. As far as he was concerned the whole ship was a kludge of castaway technologies and ideas either too old, too new, too simple, too complicated, too radical, or too boring for NASA. Paul walked behind Max and learned.

After Yeager's men finished bolting down gear, they tested and retested the onboard systems. They ran diagnostics on the sensors and the Crays. Everything checked out, yet, to a man, they put their trust not in the electronics, but in the eight aerospike rocket motors, or more precisely—any five of them, because Felix needed only five motors to land. Even so, they wished with all their hearts they'd put another two engines on the ship, even though they knew with all their math that the probability of three engines failing—let alone four—was statistically insignificant, unless of course you were in or under the spaceship.

The frenzy of work peaked with the approaching dawn. One could barely hear the cock crow over the hums and squeals of machines. The sun arrived and brought the first spectators driving down to Rixeyville to watch Felix-P take off and land.

The Culpepper County police, wearing bright orange vests, directed the line of cars to the solitary gate and makeshift parking lot, a flat, dry field of stubble from freshly mown hay. Signs, worn grass, and white tape guided the spectators two hundred meters, mostly uphill, to viewing stands.

Young women in crisp BAP-blue suits handed each person a folder containing a shiny four-color booklet entitled, "Meet BAP: Your Partner in the Future!", an agenda for the day's activities, a series of four articles (reprints from the *Journal of Practical Applications in Space*) explaining SSTO concepts, plus an 8½"x11" close-up color photo of Felix-P blasting three hundred feet above the Sonora Desert—the tie-down cables airbrushed out. The BAP hostesses coaxed the crowd up the hill with promises of coffee and danish—they'd get a full breakfast buffet at 8:00 AM. Thus fortified, the happy spectators trudged up the hill.

At the crest, the spectators found BAP's Research Center—a warehouse, really. Two acres of concrete slab, steel frame, heavy corrugated metal walls, and a flat black roof basking in the morning sun. Much earth had been shoved about the old Carter Farm, many trees cut down.

Seven of Ridgwell's distinctive plum-colored trucks were parked by a set of aluminum bleachers. Men and women in plum-colored uniforms set up tables, laid out white tablecloths, and wrestled great urns and trays from the trucks: food for five hundred. A man with chain saw and chisel carved a four-foot ice cube into a bald eagle facing the talons of war—Rolf's special request.

Further up the hill, under a canopy of ancient oaks, they saw the late eighteenth century farm house. The white portico peered out from the cool shade shyly regarding their al fresco breakfast. A pair of Sea Stallion helicopters landed behind the farmhouse, disgorged a dozen dignitaries, then took off.

From the warehouse and viewing stands, an unpaved but well-graded road curved through grassy hillocks to the launch platform and Felix-P standing beneath bright lights. The launch pad had once been a hill, since flattened and paved. Around the rim of the asphalt stood portable towers poking lights a hundred feet into the gray sky. An iridescent gold circle painted on the black pavement glowed beneath harsh lights. Trucks sat haphazardly outside the gold line. At the center of it all within the sanctuary, the spaceship Felix stood, a dull silver cone on five legs awash in artificial light. People in orange jumpsuits tended the sleek metal beast.

Dr. Paul Bernard wore his Redskins jacket over an orange jumpsuit. He cupped his hands around a cup of hot cocoa and watched the technicians make the final checks for Felix's first manned flight. She'd take a three-man crew to the edge of outer space. Paul brushed his hand over scorch marks on the composite tiles, just some carbon deposits left over from her bunny hops at Marana.

Looking down the valley road, he saw the procession of cars, headlights beaming, turning into the parking field. Max joined him, saying, "Good morning, Paul."

" 'Morning. Are you ready for this circus?"

"You're right about that. It's show time. But you've gotta

give the devil his due—Ted brought a big crowd. I don't like the man, but he's a damned good barker." Yeager craved a cigarette, but he stood within fifty meters of the liquid oxygen truck.

"Now it's up to us." Paul looked up at the spaceship. "We are the main act."

"We're the only act." Max put a stick of gum into his mouth. "I've never wanted to be the only act. I've got this sick feeling that while *Challenger* waited half frozen on the pad, some senior manager looked at bleachers filled with big shots and camera crews and said, 'The show must go on.'"

Paul sipped his cocoa. "Rogers is a bachelor, isn't he?" Max didn't hear the question.

An oddity to be sure, Felix-P looked too simple to fly— a plain cone with a slightly rounded nose, no external fuel tanks, no wings, just tiny, almost imperceptible stabilizing fins. An article in *Aviation Week* called Felix's hull design "technologically unaesthetic," a jibe that had raised Yeager's dander. He insisted, "Simple is elegant. After all, the first truly manned space ship, Planet Earth, has an even simpler design, a ball. God didn't put wings on His spacecraft. Why should we put wings on ours? Some engineers just refuse to learn from the Master."

The BAP meteorologist released a balloon, then copied data from instruments in his panel truck. He proclaimed an almost perfect day for the test flight, except that the wind was a brisk 12 to 14 knots. He passed the good news to Winston.

Ted Winston beamed confidence. Luck shined on him like the bright new sun. He'd chosen the perfect autumn day, one of those crisp mornings made for great beginnings. The press, foreign attaches, industrialists, congressmen, Pentagon brass, and scores of hangers-on arrived in droves near the west-end bleachers, set in front of the massive BAP Research Center doors. They gathered around the breakfast buffet of quiche, sausage, hash browns, bagels, cream cheese, and smoked salmon. Six men in tall white paper hats made omelets. The large ice eagle spread her wings over the pastries, blintzes, fruit, juice, coffee, tea, and milk. The guests stuffed brochures, press releases, and slick photos into their pockets to free their hands for eating.

The crowd gathered according to species—the underdressed press corps, laden with electronic gear, collected in clumps according to network, chatting among themselves, guessing the weight of the coming event. CNN claimed a choice bit of ground, laying cables back to a van with the satellite relay. Three distinct pools of green, blue and black uniforms marked the presence of the Army, Air Force and Navy invitees. Politicians in dark pinstriped suits stood around the periphery of the press corps. Corporate guests clung to politicians and military men they happened to know. Many used field binoculars or opera glasses to study the dull silver-gray cone standing four thousand feet away in the middle of a square concrete apron.

Ted Winston shoved his hands in his pockets. He wore his lucky yellow tie and his Naval Academy class of '64 tie tack. He was pleased to see the crowd growing back at the research center warehouse. In the distance, the Blue Ridge Mountains lay in a morning stupor, supremely indifferent to his good luck.

Ted's fifteen-dollar digital wristwatch beeped. He looked for the government sedan. *Ah, it just pulled away from the farmhouse.* Ted clicked his pen and put a little check on his time line. He ran his hand through his hair, moving a strand from his forehead where it didn't belong, to the top of his head where it was needed. He watched the bustle around the spaceship. He studied the flat silver finish, like the metallic sheen of the Delorean—*perish the thought.*

Forty-one engineers inspected the craft, checking

sensors and topping off fuel tanks. Men in baggy white suits with head gear and face masks finished loading the liquid oxygen from a series of bright white trucks, each bearing six-foot blue letters LOX. One of the LOX men wandered around the site with a clipboard, looking for a signature. Then, a soot-smudged silver tanker truck labeled Ogden Aviation, pulled up. Two guys in grubby gray jumpsuits and baseball caps hauled out hoses and rather casually pumped sixteen thousand pounds of fuel of RP-4 into the spaceship, packed up their hoses and drove away. Eighty-eight percent of the ship's weight was fuel.

From across the tarmac, Ted heard the ritualistic call, "Timekeeper! Mark eight thirty-one!" Ted glanced at his watch again to confirm the time, then walked back to the black stretch limousine waiting outside the gold circle. The driver got out to open the door, but Ted let himself in and pulled the door shut before the driver could reach him.

The limousine drove Ted to the tree line where BAP had invited the public to witness the flight. The crowd swelled with BAP employees from McLean, denizens of Rixeyville and Culpepper, space enthusiasts, and other hoi polloi. Rixeyville civilians, many sporting NRA belt buckles and John Deere caps cozied up to the BAP support staff, who wore tennis shorts and visors. The festive crowd stood around spindly card tables or sat on blankets. They ate cold fried chicken from plain white boxes. They drank coffee kept hot in tall stainless steel canisters and poured into styrofoam cups. Two men wearing BAP ball caps wrestled beer kegs into galvanized tubs filled halfway with ice. Others had brought cheap champagne. Most of the spectators had brought in some sort of binoculars or telescope, handheld or mounted. Everyone carried cameras, some with huge lenses. Ted's freelance camera crew—the blonde, the gaffer, and cameraman—stood by, ready to catch Rolf's "impromptu" remarks to the public.

A plain government sedan drove to the edge of the

public crowd. Out stepped Rolf Bernard, the chairman and chief operating officer of BAP, Inc., and Virginia's Senator Warner. Ted Winston stepped forward and gushed, "Senator!"

"Ted!" Senator Warner vigorously shook Ted's hand. "Tennis, next Saturday. I won't forget."

Rolf glanced at Ted with eyebrow raised. Two middle-management assistant-to types escorted Rolf and Senator Warner to a Chevy pickup truck, where they climbed onto the flatbed to address the crowd.

Ted Winston monitored his watch. It was all going well—the beat-up blue pickup, the beer, the Senator—just as he'd planned. Now, if Rolf would stick to the script!

Rolf raised his long arms. His gold cufflinks caught a glint of the rising sun. Workers and engineers cheered. Rolf had given them the day off; he had kept them in groceries throughout the recession; he bought the beer. The camera zoomed in on the crowd, making it seem huge.

Then the camera looked up to Rolf, a visual masterstroke. Standing in the bed of the old pickup truck, he looked so much in touch with the common man. And he looked so much in command, as he looked down into the camera's lens. The latter image held the truth. Mr. Bernard ran the show. He owned 17 percent of BAP, Inc. If necessary, he could exercise options to buy stock worth another 5 percent of the company. His wife, various aunts, uncles, nieces, nephews, and cousins controlled another 24 percent. So in one way or another, Rolf controlled the second largest and most advanced aerospace company on the face of the earth.

Yet, only the misinformed would say that Rolf managed BAP. Rolf ruled like a feudal baron. He looked like a feudal man: broad shoulders, long arms, strong neck. He got his oversized face, broad forehead, and thick straw-colored hair from his German forebears, a straight nose from the Scots, and wide-set gray eyes direct from his

Eastern European mother. He'd cultivated his own booming baritone voice. "Good morning!"

The BAP crowd led the antiphon. "Good morning, Mr. Bernard!"

Ted smiled. *Preparation is everything.*

"I want to welcome our neighbors from Rixeyville, my fellow space enthusiasts, my foresighted friends—welcome one and all to Carter Farm. But most of all, I want to welcome my fellow employees from BAP, especially the friends and family of the Felix project. Today is your day.

"In a couple of hours we'll open the railroad to the stars. Someday the history books will remember this day, just as we remember the day our forefathers drove the golden spike that opened the Pacific Railroad—their railroad to their frontier.

"The Felix spacecraft gives us the first true engine to operate on our railroad to space. Felix lowers the cost of putting a pound into orbit from $5,000 per pound to $200 per pound. What does that mean? It means we cut the cost of putting up the Space Station in half. Space Station *Freedom* should serve as our way station to further exploration. Most of you know better than I, that it takes more thrust to get *to* low earth orbit than it takes to get from low earth orbit *out* of the solar system.

"With cheap space transportation, we'll deliver cheap communications to the growing Third World. We'll feed our growing appetite for energy with cheap solar power. Just watch! In short order, BAP will use Felix to deploy our prototype solar power satellite for inexhaustible, clean electricity.

"I predict that within ten years of flying Felix, we'll get the cost per pound to orbit down to fifty dollars. Then you can fly into space for about the same cost of a round-trip Concorde ticket to Paris. You young people out there can go to the moon! How I envy you!

"But I salute you as well. You made this revolution possible—not the government, as you might think. The government is just a bit player in our Felix research and development. NASA doesn't want us to succeed, because we threaten the Shuttle and compete with their monstrous National Launch Vehicle. The Air Force would have nothing to do with Felix, because they're wed to NASA. Only the Strategic Defense Initiative Office—or SDIO to us—kicked in a few bucks in the early years; now SDIO doesn't exist. So what you see on the pad belongs to a private, capitalist corporation, my company, BAP. You built it; stockholders paid for it."

Ted began to sweat. Rolf had gotten off the script.

"And I predict . . ." Rolf took measure of the crowd. "I predict that after today, NASA and the rest of the United States government will realize they can't kill Felix; so they'll want to own it, or at least control it. Then, we'll set old disagreements aside and get on with the business of opening space for the twenty-first century!"

Applause!

Senator Warner raised Rolf's right hand high in the air and bellowed, "It's a great day, my fellow Virginians. Someday, our grandkids will come back to this farm just like we go to Kill Devil Hills, where the Wright brothers inaugurated modern aviation. I would be proud to offer a bill to build a monument to your great achievement today."

Applause!

The two men stepped down from the bed of the pickup truck and into the limousine, where Ted Winston waited. "You sounded good, sir, but you got off the script and I think you came down a bit hard on NASA and the Air Force."

"Oh?"

"The Air Force is our biggest customer; NASA's not far behind. . . ."

"Don't lecture me, Ted. I've sold a helluva lot more airplanes than you have."

"That's true, but—"

"But nothing. Let me tell you something about doing business with the bureaucrats. First, they want you to suck up to them, then despise you when you do. Second, they don't know how to do real work, so they pay you to do it for them. Third, they won't take any risks, but resent it if you won't. So, Ted, don't suck up to bureaucrats. Just do the real work and take the technical risks. And remember, we'll be here working long after the bureaucrats have retired to Florida."

"That might be true in the long run. . . ."

"In the long run, we're all dead."

"But, sir . . ."

"Are you going to argue with me, here in front of Senator Warner?"

"Don't let me interfere." Warner laughed.

Ted, caught in the middle, sighed. "I'm not arguing."

"Let me fill you in on some background. Ted, you haven't been around for all of this. Senator, you might find it interesting—off the record, of course."

"Of course, Rolf," Warner purred.

"Okay. Here's the short history. Rocket scientists have been kicking the single-stage-to-orbit idea around since the old X programs started in 1947, with not much promise until 1980. Then, it took nine years, but finally Max Yeager convinced me to build an SSTO. I went to NASA; NASA laughed me to scorn. I tried to raise my own R&D funds. The jealous bastards at NASA sabotaged my financing with stories in the *Wall Street Journal*, claiming our SSTO scheme was fantasy—that our crackpot ideas proved BAP didn't understand structures, fuels, engines, or the nation's space priorities. Banks backed off. BAP stock fell eight bucks. My own board of directors—remember Swanson and his guys?—turned me down flat. So I set up a general partnership: Cynthia's investment bank put up most of the money, Paul pledged his BAP stock, BAP bought in for some cash, plus facilities. SDIO kicked in a few bucks for a peek at our test data, but in the final outcome,

Cynthia, Paul, and I own that spaceship. And I'm not going to let NASA screw me again. I've got enough family problems without losing all their money on top of mine. So Ted, I appreciate you wanting to look out for the customer, but when it comes to NASA, you'd better remember whose team you're on."

"I see. Enough said." Ted changed the subject. "Where's Tyler? I expected to find him here with you."

"Tyler had to go to Pueblo. INSCOM's Special Security Office paid us a surprise visit, and we flunked the inspection. For what, God only knows. Tyler's got to straighten the mess out, jerk a knot, and somehow get those gumshoes out of our warehouse. I don't need another problem today."

"What do you guess Bobby will do?"

"Guess? I already know. He'll fire the site manager, which will impress the socks off the government agent. Nobody fires like Bobby. Most likely, the agent will agree to reinspect the site before filing a report. Bobby will promise to personally straighten out the mess. So he's stuck in Pueblo for a week. He'll pull it off: Bobby's a detail man. The details kill you every time. Right, Senator?"

"Every time, Rolf. Details and compromises." Warner nodded.

Chapter 5

Rolf tapped on the smoked glass. "Driver."

"Yes, sir."

"What's your name so I can stop calling you Driver."

"It's Henry, sir."

"Henry what?"

"Henry James, sir."

Rolf thought about that. "Mr. James, will you take us past the launch pad. Drive by slowly. I want the Senator to get a close look at the spaceship."

"Yes, sir." The driver turned the limo up the gravel road, and they cruised by Felix, where technicians finished checking seals for vapor leaks. Rolf saw his son, rolled down the window, and yelled, "Stay on schedule!"

Forty-eight straight hours of anxiety—the road trip, setup, fueling, and diagnostics had soured Paul's mood for his father's bit of posturing. Predictable, necessary perhaps, but aggravating. Without lifting his eyes from his clipboard, he gave a feeble wave.

Felix towered above the sedan. "Take a close look at her, Senator. Our prototype weights only seventy-five thousand pounds fully fueled. She can carry a six thousand-pound payload plus crew and life support, or she can carry fourteen thousand pounds unmanned. We're working on the full-scale production model, which is almost twice as big. Now look at the seamless skin. Know what it's made of?"

"Can't say that I do, Rolf."

"We made her a skin of a brushed gray epoxy carbon-carbide, and she can take a blistering three thousand degrees during reentry. Our simple—some might say radically modest—spaceship stands less than seventy-five feet high from its round nose to its five stubby legs. Look under her skirts. You see eight motors which, combined with her pair of Cray brains, gives her catlike reflexes. Felix will always land on her feet."

"Mighty impressive." Senator Warner added, "I'd like to have a lot of those built right here in Virginia."

The limousine took them behind the aluminum bleachers to the warehouse door. Senator Warner stepped out to meet some friends. As he disappeared into the crowd, he called, "Thanks for the private tour."

Ted Winston pulled out his schedule. "Mr. Bernard, breakfast lasts for another thirty-eight minutes. Most of the people will have arrived by then, and they will have had enough time to visit each of the information booths. Anyway, at 9:30, Paul and Max evacuate the pad. The meteorologist sends up a balloon—no big deal. At forty-five minutes after nine, you'll welcome the guests. Now, don't forget who's in this audience. We've got about twenty senior scientists from NASA in the crowd."

"Good."

"You've got a lot to cover in little time, so I hope you'll stick with the script."

Rolf grabbed a cigarette from his pocket. "I hate it when you tell me how to do my job."

"Just doing mine, sir. You introduce Paul, then Max, and you acknowledge anyone that comes to mind. You give a few remarks about the day's launch, then the blue and white van drives Rogers, Dotz, and Kazepis to the pad. They climb the steps into Felix. After that, the launch, the landing, then a champagne reception in the warehouse."

"I think I'll take my remaining thirty-eight minutes and see who's here." Rolf took out his thin gold butane lighter to light his cigarette, but the wind blew out the flame. Instinctively he turned his back to the wind, cupped his hands around the lighter, and succeeded on his second try.

Rolf walked into a group of Air Force blue and Army green uniforms. "Tom Marshall." Rolf stretched out his hand. "I haven't seen you since you got your second star. You still hanging out at CIA?"

"I'm flattered that you remember me. . . ."

"You're Bobby Tyler's friend. I remember."

"Right. Bobby and I did some work together near the Cambodian border in 1972."

"Which side?" Rolf winked.

"Pardon me?"

"Which side of the border?"

"Oh. We were looking for POW camps. Interesting work. We'll talk about it sometime."

"Of course. I met Bobby in Vietnam, too. The three of us should get together to swap lies. Do you play poker?"

Marshall laughed, "No. General Harchord, has already tried to lure me into your iniquitous band of gamblers."

Rolf stretched to look over the sea of bobbing heads. "Speaking of George, I expected to see him here. Did he come with you?"

"Matter of fact, he sent his regrets. The NSC grabbed him. They want him to drop leaflets, or food, or some foolishness into Bosnia."

"Bad luck. I wanted him to see this flight. You be sure to tell him what you see today. And you ought to consider that CIA could use a lot of the capability from our Felix system. You could plug gaps in any southern reconnaissance; you'll never need another U-2, SR-71, or stealth reconnaissance platform."

"And" —Marshall cleared his throat— "we could surge-deploy groups of satellites, especially with your ship's ability to move among orbital planes."

"That too." Rolf knew Marshall meant the Pebble antiballistic missile system. He wondered if Marshall was aware of the botched security inspection at the Pueblo site—he certainly hoped not. "Well, it's great to see you again, Tom. Enjoy the launch. If you can stay after for the reception, we'll talk some more."

Rolf walked to the edge of the crowd, shook hands with several people, and took a moment to gaze across the rolling farmland at Felix. All but two of the support trucks had left. The technicians had thinned out. Felix sat on her haunches, flexed, waiting to leap into the blue. The rising sun and artificial light cast a green hue around the ship.

A pert young BAP hostess approached. "Mr. Bernard? Mr. Winston says it's time for your speech."

"Oh, yes." Rolf checked his watch. "Get a big glass of ice water and meet me at the podium. Okay?"

"Yes, Mr. Bernard."

Rolf shook a few more hands on his way to the podium, where he found the ice water waiting. He put on his bifocals, then pulled out and unfolded a set of speaking notes, a mere adaptation of the sanitary speech he'd just given at a governors' conference—he'd jazz it up. He tapped the microphone, which sounded like the distant *krumph* of artillery fire. "Can everybody hear me?"

The crowd in the bleachers nodded like a barn full of owls.

"Distinguished guests. I want to thank each of you for coming out to Carter Farm, and I believe you'll leave today having witnessed an event that you'll love in the retelling. I'm going to keep this short and let Felix speak for herself, as it were. You've seen the information booths that explain the Pratt and Whitney aerospike rocket motor. Actually, it's our design and we licensed Pratt and Whitney to build them. You've seen the animation depicting likely Felix missions. And of course, in a few minutes, you'll see the real thing—our cone-shaped rocket will fly out of sight, then return. But let me, for a minute, tell you about the drama you didn't see.

"Only three days ago, the Felix ground crew—who number less than one hundred men and women—loaded Felix into the old Super Guppy, and flew her from Tucson, Arizona to Dulles. Then they loaded her on a truck and hauled her down the winding roads in the dark of night. They set her up on her launch pad, fueled her, tested her and otherwise got her ready to fly in two days. Think about it: two days! Can you imagine the people and the time it would take to bring a conventional rocket up to northern Virginia for a manned launch?

"Simple, rugged, economical, elegant. Felix is what we dreamed about when we built the original Space Shuttle. But in the sixties, we did not have the light composite materials, the powerful motors, the feather-light avionics, or the cryogenic fuels. Today, you who have known nothing but Shuttle missions will see twenty years of technical progress rise ever so gently to the edge of space, then return.

"Again, welcome. Enjoy your day with us at Carter Farm."

The crowd applauded warmly. Rolf left the podium and took a seat to the side. But the white van bearing the crew did not appear as planned.

They waited. Nothing happened, nothing but wind. The orange wind sock stuck out from the pole. A calming voice oozed over the public address system. "Ladies and gentlemen. We are experiencing a sudden and unexplained gust of westerly wind. Please stand by. We will resume launch operations shortly."

Paper napkins blew across the field. Wind gusts delayed the launch three times. The morning sun climbed toward noon. The crowd began to drift back to their cars as the food gave out. At fifteen minute intervals, a disembodied, earnest voice broadcast assurances that the countdown would resume momentarily. Each time the voice modulated a higher degree of earnestness, and each assurance shooed another wave of cynics to their cars. Another weather balloon rose from a green van near some trees and quickly disappeared east, following the cars back to Washington, D.C.

By three in the afternoon, the plum-colored catering trucks left, having not a crumb of food left to serve. Even Felix seemed to sag with slump-shouldered disappointment, stage fright, or simple embarrassment. Rolf paced the asphalt behind the bleachers. He stomped and fumed. The winds weren't brisk enough to cool him. He told the weatherman to loose another balloon. "And this time send the darn thing straight up!"

The weatherman did as he was told. The balloon did as it was told. Rolf beamed with satisfaction, taking some credit for the meteorological change of fortune. The disembodied voice cheerily announced: "Any moment now." The faithful remnant cheered anemically.

Ted Winston looked around to see trash barrels filled with promotional material, and television news crews sitting on the black boxes, guarding their gear. Rolf's opening remarks were five hours stale.

A small white van sped out to the cone-shaped spacecraft, and a crew of three men in flight suits stepped out without comment, and walked up a set of steps on loan from Dulles airport. The engineers secured the hatch, and the lot of them sped away in their trucks to the grandstands.

A monotone voice came over the loudspeakers with the final five minutes of system checks. Much relieved, Ted stood with his own camera, ready to capture a moment that would be greater than the opening of the transcontinental railroad.

A new voice patched through the loudspeaker system,

"This is Captain Rogers. We are in position. Request permission for takeoff."

Ground control responded, "Felix, you are cleared for takeoff. Have a safe flight."

Ted Winston looked around at the bewildered spectators. Everyone expected a countdown, but Felix was not a hunk of modified ammunition like a space shuttle, where you count down to zero, light the fuse, plug your ears, and run like hell. Felix worked more like a flying machine; so it needed a simple clearance for takeoff. Ted shook his head and muttered, "People like countdowns; they like to match their internal clock to the official clock. They like the measured expectation. They like that split second before success or failure. They like countdowns."

The crowd slowly rose to their feet. "What the . . ."

But as the spectators groped for answers, two of the eight engines roared to life. Felix shuddered in the center of its cloud. Two by two, the remaining engines roared as the pilot throttled them to life. Smoke and debris blew a quarter of a mile toward the stand. Captain Rogers blew the restraining bolts, and Felix rose nimbly from the scarred cement apron, straight up. The wind slid Felix slightly downrange to the east. Rogers leaned Felix into the wind to hold her above Rixeyville. The crowd whooped and cheered. Felix shrank to a speck atop a bright plume, then she disappeared from sight.

Paul and Max planned to fly Felix only twenty-five miles above the earth, well below the United Nations' mandated altitude defining a launch. Therefore, this pseudolaunch was, for the official record, called a flight demonstration that would incidentally test propulsion systems, aerodynamics of hull design, navigation, and control systems. Felix would hover to burn excess fuel, then land back at the same spot.

Twenty-five miles above Rixeyville and the greater Washington, D.C. metropolitan area, not everything went according to plan.

One of the eight green panel lights blinked yellow, then turned red, with an audible nudge from the computer. Felix stalled, dropped, then lurched forward. Propulsion engineer Kazepis said, "Damn, but that didn't take long. Engine seven dead. Engine five has throttled down for balance. Computers have throttled up the others."

Captain Rogers looked at the dials and the eight ball in front of him. "Pitch and yaw within tolerance. But I've got a bad feeling about this. If we lose another two engines, we're going to have to lighten the load. Kazepis, Dotz: you two fat guys decide which one jumps first."

No sooner had he spoken than another green light turned red. "Engine four failed. Don't—repeat—don't throttle down number two. Bring back number five. Adjust propulsion. We're going down."

Dotz reminded Rogers. "The computer knows that." He added, "You put the mouth on it, Charles."

Ground control broke in. "Felix, we show two engines red."

Rogers replied, "Affirmative, we're coming down. Other engines green, but two dead in eleven minutes looks bad. We're off-balance. We're sliding downrange. Do you guys have a clue as to what's wrong with these engines?"

"Negative."

"Ask Dr. Bernard. Is it the fuel? Did he buy rotten fuel?" Rogers turned around in his seat and said, "Kazepis, think of something."

Kazepis was rankled. "We never lost an engine before."

"I'm so happy for you." Rogers prodded, "So what now?"

"They're good engines. We'll make it. All we need is five engines to land."

Said Dotz, "I feel so much better. Spiffy. We can lose one more."

Rogers interrupted. "Shut up. You'll put the mouth on it." He switched his mike and asked ground control, "We're in trouble up here. The wind's pushing us east. I can't hold her over Rixeyville. Should we force her back?"

"We can try. Lean 268 degrees. Increase power to ninety percent."

Ground control: "It's not working, you're sliding east."

Rogers, an edge to his voice, said, "Find us a place to come down."

"We're looking."

"How about Dulles?"

"Negative. Winds are east-northeast at twenty-eight knots. You'll pass southeast of Dulles."

"Manassas airport?"

"Possible. No, check that. Negative on Manassas. You're going northeast of Manassas airport."

"Well, how about the White House lawn. That's east-northeast of here!" Rogers wiped the sweat out of his eyes. "Problem is, we don't know where we're going to land, because we don't know what we've got for engines. Dotz, you'll just have to pick something on the way down before we lose another one. Engaging landing sequence. Mark! Automatic to eight thousand feet."

Dotz switched on the tailsection camera to look for a place to land. The cameras looked aft through the flame and hot gases, and showed him a dark, double line—a highway that cut through the blur.

Rogers spoke. "Ground control. We're sliding east, toward Manassas with Interstate 66 below us. We'll put her down on 66. Get that highway cleared so nobody gets cooked. We've got to dump fuel."

"I wouldn't do that!" said the voice from ground control.

Rogers burst in, "Okay. We'll try to hold her at eight thousand feet and burn the fuel. But I say we're going down on Interstate 66, and that's it. Clear the road." He turned to Kazepis and said, "I used to commute on that awful highway; déjà vu."

"Cut the chatter."

Dotz asked, "Why 66?"

"Because I can see it, that's why." Rogers waved his hands over the nine-inch viewing screen. "You see anything you'd rather land on?"

Dotz glanced at the dark line jerking and weaving on the small screen and said, "No textbook landing today. I'm having a religious experience."

"Then you be chaplain, Dotz. I'm busy." Rogers looked out his starboard window, down the smooth gray skin of the ship. In the nose of the cone-shaped spaceship, he had a 360-degree view of the horizon. He could see everything but the ground below him—the place he most wanted to see. Fortunately I-66 stretched from horizon to horizon, giving him two points of reference that he could stay within. He could see the tiny cars zipping along the highway.

Ground control interrupted, "Rogers, increase thrust. We can't let you creep any further east. Too many people down there. Get to eight thousand feet. Burn fuel."

Another ninety seconds passed. The Felix crew practically held their breath as they made their descent. Rogers had kept her steady over I-66, pressing her slightly against the wind. The console gave another audible warning, and a third green light turned red. Felix shuddered and dropped as it tried to compensate for the lost power.

"Not another one." Rogers uncharacteristically slapped the console. He collected himself. "Kazepis, please tell me you over-engineered the engines and we can really land on four."

"If you say so: but it's really just a matter of how fast we land." Kazepis checked his shoulder straps and said, "Right now positive thrust is 0.88. We're going down hard." They began to fall.

Dotz silently alternated glances between his computer console and his starboard window. The computerized navigation control and the thousands of minute adjustments to the last five motors kept Felix steady. He marveled how silicon chips no bigger than his thumbnail could delicately tweak the hundreds of thousands of pounds of thrust. And he quietly calculated the odds of their survival—about one in three, which he thought reasonable, considering all that had gone wrong. He shifted back to his role as ad hoc chaplain.

Rogers spoke, "Control, we're at 8,700 feet and losing altitude at 54 feet per second. We can't maintain altitude. I've got to shed weight. Dumping fuel now." He didn't say what they all knew. If they lost another engine, Felix would fall like the wingless chunk of metal she was. Fuel would serve no purpose, except to scatter their mortal remains over northern Virginia. He flicked four black toggle switches, then looked out the port window.

Training, hope, and five rocket motors were all they had left. Yet there was no panic. Felix needed little fuel to set herself down. Should they run dry and fall like a stone, they still had a chance—the big titanium LOX tank and the thermoplastic kerosene tank would serve as giant air bags to cushion the fall. The massive aerospike rocket engines would absorb considerable impact. There was a chance they would live—if there was no fire.

Powerful pumps spewed the main tank's liquid oxygen— the bulk of Felix's weight—through an eight-inch nozzle on the port hull. At eighty-seven hundred feet, a groundling wouldn't notice spaceship Felix for her tiny profile. But the liquid oxygen instantly vaporized and built a giant upside-down mushroom cloud, bent at the stem by the hot engine gases. The instant cloud was seen from Rockville, Maryland to the West Virginia line. It was an odd, beautiful thing to see.

Twenty seconds later and a thousand feet lower, the main tank of kerosene fuel flushed out the leeward side and away from the ship. The wind scattered the fuel into droplets and the groundlings saw a strange prism in the sky. The droplets turned to mist, and that which did not evaporate on the way down showered several square miles

of Fair Oaks, with the heaviest concentration around the
Fairfax County Municipal Building.

Having shed 9,000 pounds of fuel, or 14 percent of
Felix's total weight, the ship achieved positive thrust and
Rogers could control their descent.

"We've got trouble," Dr. Dotz said with his face pressed
against his starboard window.

"Engine? Computer down? What now?" Captain Rogers
worried out loud.

"No," Dotz continued, "cars. Lots of them. All six lanes."

There was no sign of the local police or Virginia state
troopers. Motorists seemed oblivious to the spaceship
roaring less than two thousand feet above them.

Nevertheless, Rogers felt confident he'd get their
attention. A former Shuttle pilot, reputed to have a velvet
touch for docking maneuvers, Rogers earned his pay. He
backed Felix down with untold grace. As he took her
down to one thousand feet, the motorists below figured
it out; not details, but concept. Most pulled over to the
side of the road.

Kazepis guffawed, "Look! Someone's flashing his high
beams at us!"

Quite suddenly, a great traffic jam filled both sides of
the road, snarled into a herringbone pattern as some tried
to turn around. The drivers trapped near the front
abandoned their vehicles and fled. No one ventured
beneath the orange flames and clouds of white smoke.
Felix set out her five stout legs. Rogers set her down.

Interstate 66 was a bad choice, but there was no good
choice. The backwash of flame and hot gas chased
motorists farther back and ignited several cars. Car after
car burst into flame, and huge pillars of black smoke blew
toward the city.

Rogers called ground control. "We landed smack
center on westbound I-66, one quarter mile before
the turnoff to Haymarket. We're okay. Felix is safe,
but you'd better send fire equipment. We've cooked

a bunch of cars and we've started a brushfire. We're debarking just in case."

"We copy." The radio transmission crackled.

Kazepis pushed the hatch door opened and threw an aluminum escape ladder down the side of the spaceship. Then Kazepis, Dotz, and Rogers climbed out, in that order. Kazepis and Dotz stood gaping at the wall of charred cars, burning rubber and black smoke. Charles Rogers checked Felix's skin and legs. "Not half bad," he said. "Not bad at all. I still gots it."

Ground control at the BAP Rixeyville hangar caught hell for the rest of the day. The press churned itself into a feeding frenzy. Rolf withdrew from the fracas, nonchalantly shoving Winston into the press pool like a piece of chum. "Hey, you're the spin doctor. Earn your pay for a change," he said.

Fairfax County and the EPA went nuts about the kerosene dumped over two square miles. Virginia commuters suffered a spectacular rush hour. Adding to the misery on I-66, a truckload of chickens overturned on the American Legion Bridge, and the Wilson Drawbridge stuck open.

Rolf Bernard popped open a bottle of champagne, sat behind the glass walls of the small conference room, and watched the chaos. Paul sat at the other end of the table with his face cradled in his arms. "What do we do now, Max?"

Max sat across the table, "This is a new one on me." The phone rang. Max picked it up. "Yes?"

"Max? Is that you? It's me, Charles."

"Where're you calling from?"

"A nice lady let me use her car phone. We got a real mess out here."

"We know."

"How's Paul taking it."

"He's depressed."

"How's the old man taking it?"

"He's drinking champagne. Who can figure . . ."

"Tell Paul to follow the old man's lead."

"You sound in an expansive mood."

"Oh, I feel great—now." Rogers chortled, "I'm the happiest man alive. I just crash-landed a wingless rocket ship, and I'm sitting next to a good-looking woman, and she ain't no angel. And I'm talking to you on the phone. Like, I should be dead, but I'm not."

"Where are Dotz and Kazepis?"

"They can find their own. . . ." A background giggle interrupted Rogers. "Are you going to pick us up, or do we have to hire a cab?"

"You stay with the ship. We'll get something out to you. I'll save you some champagne. Good-bye."

Rolf handed Max a flute of pale amber champagne. Ted entered the room. Ted, who was disconsolate and badly needed a drink, didn't drink. "Today has been an utter disaster." He looked at his watch as if it could make the day go away.

"No, Ted. Once again you're wrong. An utter disaster is when you blow up on the pad. Not our best day, for sure, but you got to admit: She landed on her feet!"

Yeager tried to smile. He bolted the champagne and asked for another. He thought, *I might as well. Tomorrow's going to be one big headache anyway.*

Chapter 6

Bobby Tyler put his Bronco into four-wheel drive and maneuvered around debris strewn along the shoulder on Interstate 66. His wheels spit gravel from the many ruts cut by motorists fleeing the fireball that BAP had lowered into their midst the day before. Ahead, firefighters doused the smoldering remains of automobiles—the acrid stench of burning tires hung about. Men on foot extinguished lingering brushfires. Tow-truck crews hauled the black steel skeletons away. Felix stood above the fray. Hundreds stood on hillocks, watching.

Tyler drove through a flimsy strip of yellow tape, toward a Fairfax County police cruiser. Two policemen hopped out and waved Tyler down. "Hey! You can't drive through here. Didn't you see the barricade?"

"The yellow tape?"

"Yes, you drove right through a police line, mister."

Tyler showed the policeman his BAP credentials. "I'm chief of security for BAP. Our ground crew called and told me you forced them away from their ship. . . ."

"That's right, Mr. Tyler." The officer handed Tyler back his security badge. "Now, why don't you turn around and get your car out of here before we cite you."

"Hey, I'm trying to help. We can get the spaceship off

65

the highway as soon as we can get a heavy transport and a crane through this mess."

"You made the mess. We're just cleaning it up. Mr. Tyler, the county's going to save you the trouble. After we finish hauling these burnt cars away, we're going to bulldoze your spaceship to the side of the highway—or maybe use a winch—but in any case, we're getting it off the highway before the next rush hour. You can make arrangements with the county supervisor to pay your fines and remove your machine, or what's left of it."

Tyler muttered, "This is futile."

"What'd you say?" The larger officer unsnapped the leather strap that held his baton.

"Nothing, officer. Mind if I make a phone call?"

"Not at all, but first you'd better get your vehicle on the other side of that barricade." The officer pointed with his black baton.

Tyler climbed back in his car, grabbed his phone book, quickly flipped through the pages, then bound it open with a fat rubber band. He punched the numbers into his car phone as he started his engine.

A woman picked up on the first ring. "This is five one nine zero. Can I help you?"

"I need to speak with General Marshall. It's very important." Tyler drove slowly away, glancing at the cops and at Felix in his rearview mirror.

"He's in conference. . . ."

"Better get him out. Just slip him a note: 'Fairfax County about to wreck the Felix-P. Need your help.' "

"That spaceship? The one that crashed?" Suddenly the woman's voice indicated interest. "I'll put the general on."

Tyler heard a click, then Tom Marshall's voice.

"Bobby?"

"Yes, sir. The local police are going to bulldoze our spaceship off the highway."

"Can't you guys clean up your own mess?"

"We can't even get to the ship with a HET and a crane."

"Don't you guys have lawyers? Get an injunction."

"It's a little late for that."

There was a long pause on Marshall's end. "Oh, for crying out loud. . . . I'll call George Harchord. We'll think of something."

Tyler weaved around the debris where a group of men wearing BAP blue hard hats were keeping vigil. He called Rolf. Rolf called his platoon of lawyers and charged them to use every piece of paper known to litigious man to keep Fairfax County bulldozers from simply pushing the Felix off the highway. The county supervisors balked and consulted their lawyers, who were itching for a fight and some fat fee. Thus inspired, they passed emergency resolutions and dispatched orders to proceed clearing BAP's machine off Interstate 66.

Tyler paced the hill, watching the tow trucks haul wreckage away, clearing a path for the bulldozer. Men wearing county overalls hitched cable and chain to Felix to drag her from the highway. "What will that do to the ship?" Tyler asked one of the Felix crew.

"They'll pull her apart like a wishbone. She has no strength for side stress. They'll probably rupture the tanks. I figure we can save the engines. Can't you stop them, Mr. Tyler?"

Tyler stood up and tossed the man his handheld cellular phone. "Call Mr. Bernard—STAR 61. I'll need him to bail me out of jail." And he started down the hill toward the policeman.

The man caught the phone and pointed east. "Look!"

Tyler turned and saw three olive-drab buses caravaning down the highway. All of the buses drove through the yellow tape and squealed to a stop. Doors opened and a stream of young Marines wearing cammy fatigues, butt packs, and carrying M-16 rifles, ran from the bus to stand in parade formation. Tyler ran down the hill to meet the three platoons standing at parade rest. He found a tall, stern captain, who raised his hand to his soft cap and made a crisp salute. "Sir! You must be Mr. Tyler, sir."

Tyler instinctively returned the salute. "Thank God you're here, Captain. Secure the spaceship and keep those civilians away from it."

"Yes, sir!"

The captain made an abrupt about-face, snapped a few commands, and the platoons filed off in double time, squad by squad, to ring the spaceship. The senior county policeman, a lieutenant, stormed over to the Marine captain. "Hey! Get yourself and your soldiers out of here."

"They're not soldiers, they're marines."

"I don't care what you call 'em. We got a highway to clear. So put 'em back on your buses and get out of here. Or I'll arrest the lot of you."

The Marine captain looked down at the policeman, then over to his troops, and smiled. He took a deep breath and boomed, "Fix!" He took another breath. "Bayonets!" The captain rested his hands on his hips—more precisely, on his web belt and black leather holster, in which he kept a .45 caliber pistol. From the background, Tyler heard the distinct click—the hundred men from Henderson Hall, trained for ceremony, finally got to fix their chrome-plated ceremonial bayonets for something other than ceremony.

"Sir." This time, the marine captain addressed the Fairfax County police lieutenant. "We will extract the spaceship from your highway momentarily. The Military District of Washington and Marine Corps General Lynch appreciate your cooperation."

The policeman sputtered and stalked away to his squad car to consult his superiors. The bulldozer operator cut his engine and took a seat in some shade. The Marines stood at parade rest with their rifle butts on the ground, their gleaming bayonets pointed forward like a picket. They opened their ranks just enough to let the BAP ground crew unfasten the county's cables from Felix's legs.

Soon, a new sound, a discord of whine and thunder, slowly grew loud. Tyler searched the skies for the cause, then saw the insectlike Skycrane flying toward them, leaving a sagging trail of dark exhaust behind. They landed the olive-drab monster on the highway. The men wearing orange ear protection leapt from the helicopter's belly to the pavement. They hauled a large nylon web behind them, and with the BAP ground crew, configured a harness and collar. Within a half hour, the Skycrane rose back into the air just above Felix, beating everyone with her prop wash. They connected the Felix harness to the Skycrane's cables, and the huge helicopter deftly lifted Felix out of harm's way, and ferried her to Dulles Airport.

The Marines scrambled onto their buses and drove back to Henderson Barracks. Tyler jumped into his Bronco and headed for Rolf's McLean office. The BAP crew ran to their vehicles to pursue Felix, and make her ready her for the Super Guppy and her trip back to Marana.

By Saturday morning the scrambling had ceased. Max took Felix home to Tucson on the Super Guppy. Paul stayed behind to cope with the deep funk of failure hanging over BAP like a bad case of influenza.

Paul let himself into the empty BAP headquarters building and rode the elevator to the penthouse office suite where he found Herb Eckert, BAP's chief financial officer, sitting at the receptionist's desk, running a tape of numbers on a small calculator. Herb didn't look up. At the opposite end of the room, Ted Winston sat in a wingback chair, staring out of the floor-to-ceiling windows.

Paul walked over to Tyler, sitting alone on a love seat next to a Tiffany lamp, reading the business section of the *Post*. "Hi, Bob. What's up?"

"Not BAP stock—down twelve bucks in two days." Tyler thought, *I should have sold mine when Cynthia sold hers. Somehow she always knows.* He handed Paul the sports section and said, "Might as well relax, Paul."

"No thanks, I've got to make some calls."

Rolf was late.

Herb Eckert ripped a piece of white tape from his machine, studied it, and winced. He walked into the conference room where he rehearsed a few points before the mirror while he checked his graying hair. "What we have here, sir, is a probable $150 million R&D write-off, possible criminal charges carrying up to $100 million in fines, up to three thousand in personal injury and property damage lawsuits, canceled insurance, the loss of all new government contract business for at least five years, the probable cancellation of ten percent of our aircraft delivery contracts, the loss of key suppliers, and something like a twenty percent drop in the price of our stock—which may cause the banks to lower our A-rated bond to B-plus. In short, we have a situation that we financial specialists call the shit hitting the fan."

One must keep a sense of humor. According to the stress-reduction book Herb had read: *In crisis situations the effective manager must disengage from the event, and thereby insulate the creative mind from the consequences of failure.* What academic pencil neck wrote that?

Anyway, Herb *had* removed himself, but it was an out-of-body—perhaps kin to a near-death—experience. Herb delicately passed a comb over his head. He thought, *one shouldn't loose his hair because his company is on the rocks, because his career has hit the skids and his pension has most likely evaporated.* Leaning toward the mirror, he patted a loose hair into place. Herb had grown fond of his long, unusual face, having spent so much time in front of a mirror. Others, who had not studied Herb's face as thoroughly, thought his slack jaw, loose jowls, and wide eyes gave him the look of the perpetually astonished.

Paul took Eckert's place at the receptionist's credenza, where he argued into a phone, "I'm telling you, the problem was the fuel. I think Ogden Aviation slipped us bad fuel, but even if they knew, they wouldn't say. Yeah, we got about six hundred pounds of the Ogden fuel left when we drained Felix's tanks. . . . No, I don't want you to analyze it. I want Al to analyze it. . . . No, I'm not blaming you because you bought the Ogden fuel, although you are responsible for fuel quality. . . . No, I'm not looking for a scapegoat. Listen, don't take it personally. The reason I want Al to analyze the fuel is precisely because you have a vested interest. . . . Don't be so defensive. . . . Yeah, yeah, it could be the engines, but I doubt that. We'll know more when Dr. Yeager overhauls the engines. . . . Calm down. Let's just solve the problem. Okay? The sooner we get her back into the air, the sooner we'll be heroes. . . . Great. . . . Okay, Walter. You have a good day too. Bye."

Paul hung up the phone, turned on his pocket recorder, and said, "If fuel fails test, discharge Walter."

Ted Winston cleared a space on the coffee table. He turned the numbered cylinders to the lock on his leather portmanteau. The cylinders aligned—four, three, two, one. With a click, he popped the old beaten brass clasp and pried open the mouth of the big leather bag. Inside he grabbed a four-inch stack of news clippings. BAP Industries had been raked over the coals by every journalist who could spell spaceship. Having sprayed kerosene over Fairfax County and blown up, scorched, or otherwise cooked a couple of hundred cars on I-66, BAP had joined Three Mile Island, the Exxon Valdez, and Mount St. Helens in the "Ecological Disaster Hall of Fame." The Concerned Scientists of America instantly speculated that BAP's fiasco would blow a new hole in the ozone. Liberal Democrats demanded Rolf's head on a pike—and the Administration promised to deliver. Reacting in part to opinion polls, Congress authorized investigations and a special prosecutor; it demanded criminal charges, a trial, and a hanging—not necessarily in that order.

Suddenly, the world was awash with experts on single-stage-to-orbit spacecraft, eager to explain why Felix didn't work, and why BAP should have known better. Even consumer groups got into the act. Ted highlighted the *Washington Post* editorial entreating readers to boycott BAP products. Ted made a note: "Now politically correct Washington housewives will have to buy their wide-body jets from Boeing, and their weather satellites from TRW." But his favorite piece was the full-color, front page photo in the *Washington Times* showing an angry woman waving a placard emblazoned, DOWN WITH SPACE! "Heck, if we could get space down here, we wouldn't have to go to all the trouble to go up there. Would we?"

Ted pulled out a letter, sent by fax from the 3M Company, inquiring about rates. The company wanted to book passage on Felix's first commercial launch to low earth orbit. Ted stuffed that one in his pocket.

Ted looked at his watch. He saw himself—his reflection—staring through the glass wall, that fatuous barrier separating the elevators from the reception area. Few people haunted the building on Saturday. Some mechanical intelligence shuffled the six elevator doors. No one got off. No one got on.

Just as Ted got up to pace the floor, an elevator spit out a dozen men, led by a red-faced Rolf Bernard. He plowed through the double glass doors into the reception area where he said gruffly, "Let's get to it. We haven't got much time."

Rolf walked into the board room. Everyone, principals and horse holders, followed Rolf in and sat down.

Rolf reached across the table and poured himself a cup of coffee from the gold plastic thermos bottle. "We've got a problem—a big problem."

Everyone watched him load four spoonfuls of sugar into his coffee. Nobody was going to ask, "What problem?" or "Which problem?"

Rolf raised his cup to his lips, "Coffee's tepid."

Nobody moved.

Rolf drank half his cup and said, "I just finished a three-hour ass-chewing by a distinguished panel consisting of the Chairman of the Armed Services Committee, Senator Bailey, plus Senators Feinstein, Glenn, and Kerry. Meanwhile, my buddy, General George Harchord, sat in the back with his hands in his lap."

Tyler interjected, "He saved our bacon when he called the marines. He probably has to lie low for now."

"Perhaps. I sure could have used some marines this morning. Odems and Cummings were there. SPACECOM's Lt. General Bryce, and a roomful of GAO auditor types. The Department of Transportation sent some vicious little bastard from their brand new Office of Commercial Space Transportation to lecture us about their new, heretofore unpublished regulations for safety inspections, clearance permits, approval process—no wonder we're losing the space race. Did I miss anybody, Margaret?" Rolf turned to his aide.

Margaret looked at her notes. "Let's see. Dr. Fowley from NASA, some guy from the Justice Department—" Margaret adjusted her glasses. "I wrote his name down— Michael Sloan. Garvey from the FAA, and two gentlemen who wouldn't tell me their names or where they worked. I think they came with General Harchord." Margaret turned the page in her notebook and nodded.

Rolf settled back into his leather chair. "The meeting was interesting for several reasons. First, they had rehearsed— I know it. Fowley served as master of ceremonies. What a windbag! You'd think I'd dropped the atom bomb on the wrong city. After Fowley had his fun, each functionary took turns trying to outdo the other to teach me a lesson, inflict new and interesting pains, promise new humiliations. And good ol' George just sat there."

Tyler spoke again. "General Harchord won't use up his silver bullets so you can save face with a roomful of bureaucrats. But he'll be there when we need him."

Rolf took a deep breath. "I sure hope so." Rolf glanced around the table, taking the measure of his staff. "George could have offered a little sympathy."

Paul saw a brief flash of confusion cross his father's eyes—how bad could one meeting get? Was it confusion brought about by defeat? Or just the momentary paralysis when one loses both options: fight and flight. Paul saw reason to hope and tried to interrupt the gloom. "I realize I'm the junior member of this team—and I might not know how you all do business in Washington. . . ."

Rolf glanced sideways at Paul and muttered, "Count your blessings."

Paul ignored the comment. "Things aren't as bad as it looks. Felix took a three-man crew to the edge of outer space. The next step is to fly to low earth orbit. It's true we aborted because three engines failed, but we saved the aircraft and crew. Compare that to the *Challenger*. All of the other systems worked without flaw, although we need better visibility aft. I'm almost positive I know the cause of the engine failures—contaminated fuel."

"What!" Rolf rose from his chair.

"I can't prove it yet, but it appears that the fuel burned dirty, and our throttling failed to respond to the laser ignition. I hate to admit it, but it's time to shelve my dual-fuel dream for the near term, and burn hydrogen only. Hydrogen burns clean with much greater velocity. Hydrogen can get us to low earth orbit. It's a cheap, fast fix. Yeager's preliminary postflight reports suggest that we can change to larger fuel tanks to use slush hydrogen and take Felix-P up in twelve weeks. Rogers wants to go back up."

Paul looked around the table, and the group of tired faces looked back, puzzled. He had missed the whole point of the meeting. Nevertheless, he went back to the attack. "Pardon me, gentlemen, but we shouldn't sit here like a bunch of whipped dogs."

"See here, Son. That's uncalled for. . . ."

"No, Dad. Felix worked. You saw it with your own eyes. You thought everything would turn out just fine until your meeting this morning. And I don't see how an ass-chewing by a bunch of bureaucrats can change physical reality. We ought to finish our test flights at Marana, then get on with it. None of this flap would have happened if we'd stayed at Marana."

Rolf ground a cigarette butt into his empty coffee cup and scowled. "Physical reality and fiscal reality aren't the same thing, Son. You may know something about building spaceships, but you don't know zip about selling them."

Paul gritted his teeth. A rejoinder about the last week's marketing effort almost burst forth when Tyler summarized Paul's position. "I see Dr. Bernard's point. He's built a real spaceship—perhaps the only real spaceship ever built. We could own space if we wanted to."

"Precisely." Paul thumped the table. "We could put anything up there and who could stop us?"

Tyler turned to Rolf and added, "You two could be the biggest father-son team since Philip and Alexander."

Rolf put on his black-rimmed bifocals and pulled a set of notes from his shirt pocket. "You can get Felix-P up in twelve weeks, you say? You could fly her again in two weeks with kerosene."

"What's the point? Kerosene won't put us in orbit."

"Propane? Yeager prefers propane."

"Theoretically. But my dual-fuel problems aside, I'm the propulsion expert, not Max."

Herb Eckert cleared his throat. "Mr. and Dr. Bernard, I love it when you guys talk technical—gives me gooseflesh. But, could we move along? We've some horrendous short-term problems."

Everyone at the table braced themselves for the next exchange, but Rolf simply grumbled, "Herb's right. We'll discuss fuels and engines later when we have Max present. In the meantime, we've got to put a patch on our negative cashflow. This Rixeyville launch has backfired on us: I admit that. But whereas I expected a finger-pointing exercise, I didn't expect this big witch-hunt. The damnedest thing is, I'm the witch, and they know where to find me."

Rolf looked to his right. "Tyler, tell the Golden State plant manager to expect a visit from the Department of Labor. They're coming with an injunction to shut us down for some trumped up, two-year-old accident. They could delay our BP-3 plane deliveries to Qantas, Delta, JAL, and Thai Air by an average of sixty-five days."

A voice down the table interrupted, "Not the Thai order. Those are already certified to ship."

Rolf nodded and continued, "Also, the FAA intends to fine us for reckless endangerment, or some such nonsense. They say our flight plan at Rixeyville—straight up, straight down—was unprecedented. And therefore, criminally negligent. The Justice Department jumped on the bandwagon and more or less told me they are going to keep BAP in court long enough to bury us with legal fees, assuming we can get acquitted. The Defense Audit Agency plans to audit our government contracts."

Eckert sat upright. "That'll slow receivables." His wide eyes got wider. He whipped out his calculator and started punching the little rubber keys.

Rolf ignored the interruption. ". . . and Harchord officially ordered us to stop our Pueblo, Colorado work. Moreover, George said he has no choice but to suspend payments for the three hundred and twenty items we built until the audit is finished. Is that legal?"

Eckert looked up. "Does it matter? That $586 million installment was due in twenty-five days." He went back to his calculator, pausing to scribble notes in his black leather notebook.

Ted Winston asked, "Didn't General Harchord help at all?"

"Nothing. Zip. Nada. Zero. After the inquisition, George pulled me aside and told me to—and I quote—take my medicine like a man. But get a load of this: he told me to keep working on the Pueblo project—unofficially, of course. He assured me he'd have our first $586 million ready when the auditors finished. Then he had the gall to say that we've got to make the original schedule, just in case the government has to deploy the Pebbles in an emergency. He said that the Air Force has already allocated room on Delta rockets, and NASA needs our items to fill up some of its partial Shuttle loads—like I should care."

Ted Winston spoke up. "I can see why Harchord wants the Pueblo project on schedule. The Arabs can buy Russian physicists for a pittance, not to mention hardware. The Chinese just tested a device underground. The North Koreans . . ."

"Well, Harchord's crazy if he thinks we're going to work at risk to keep his pet project on schedule. When push comes to shove, he can't pay the invoice. Harchord told me the other night, he's on the way out. No offense to George, but I'm not going to bet my company on a lame duck, four star general."

"What did Dr. Fowley say?" Ted asked.

"In so many words, he claimed the Felix would never get to orbit, and his scientists could prove it. Otherwise, his people would be building an SSTO ship. You know, the typical NASA not-invented-here syndrome."

Paul asked, "Why would Dr. Fowley stick his nose into this mess? Felix is an SDIO and Air Force contract."

"Don't be naive, boy." Rolf lit another cigarette. "Dr. Fowley thinks he can use my SDI money to go to Mars. Well, he can skip Mars and go straight to hell."

After a moment of silence, Rolf looked over to where Eckert mashed his calculator and scribbled notes. "What are you working on?"

Eckert wanted to say, "Funeral arrangements", but that was too close to the truth. He said, "Rolf, I'll have my staff get you some real figures, but my guess is—give or take a week, BAP will fail to meet its obligations about ninety days from now. We've just finished one of the worst years in BAP's history. Ever since the Soviet Union unraveled, military aircraft sales have been in the toilet.

We're already down-sizing across the board. We've shown negative cash flow for three of the last five quarters. We couldn't even finance Felix without floating a separate class stock through your wife's investment bank."

"Don't remind me." Rolf glanced at Paul, regretting his loose tongue.

"You know, Rolf, Mrs. Bernard might consider it prudent to shore up our short-term problems with a line of credit from her bank."

"Forget that."

"Just throwing out options." Herb continued, "We financed the last quarter's operations on receivables, mostly the funds due from our Pueblo project contracts, which was supposed to make us whole for this quarter. Our combined debt runs us over $750,000 per day in interest, and interest rates are going up. Citicorp and Chase will roll our lines of credit, but they'll skin us for another 25 to 35 basis points. If the Department of Labor causes a 65-day shift in receipts of aircraft sales, we won't be able to meet payroll in January."

Eckert stopped talking; silence replaced the sound of his voice. Only the nervous creak of someone's new leather shoes offered to the fill the void. Rolf ran his fingers through his hair, and a long minute wasted away. "Ninety days?"

"Right. We counted on that Pueblo payment. Maybe we could stretch to 120 days, but I doubt it."

Rolf looked around the table. He wondered if the fight was already over. He turned to Paul. "I want Felix back in the sky as soon as possible—three weeks if you can manage it."

"Maybe in eight weeks with hydrogen."

Rolf snapped, "With Gatorade, if you want. I don't really care. Just put her into low earth orbit. We need a win, and we need it now."

The bright September sun poured through the venetian blinds, shining stripes across the cherrywood conference table. Herb caught one of those stripes with his solar-powered pocket calculator. He tried to offer some hope. "I'll think of something to buy time."

Nobody moved. Around the conference room stood a set of pedestals. Each supported a model of the great flying machines BAP had designed and built. Each pedestal bore a brass plaque that gave dates, names and numbers produced. Those numbers told the tale of BAP. The smallest model showed the BP-155, a small two-seater World War II fighter—over 145,000 copies made. World War II and the Korean conflict had been good to BAP. Around the room, the models on the pedestals grew in size, but the little brass plaques showed smaller numbers.

BAP's participation in supersonic passenger jets was a financial bath that remained a legend in the aerospace industry. Then BAP designed, tested, and built the giant C-17C air transport jet for the Air Force. The Air Force slashed the original order for 107 down to 18, as the mission for an air bridge to NATO evaporated.

In 1978, Rolf pushed BAP into building a prototype solar power satellite. They finished their satellite in 1982, just as oil prices collapsed back to ten dollars per barrel, and the alternative fuel development legislation fizzled. So the solar power satellite, or SPS, sat in a lab while its original inventor, Dr. Fenster tweaked the system, waiting for the next Mideast crisis to drive oil prices above forty dollars. But the Arabs proved to be more determined merchants than warriors, and the big crunch never came. The Iraqi invasion of Kuwait sent oil prices—and Fenster's heart—aflutter, but to no avail. The SPS model stood above a small plaque engraved with the number, One.

The National AeroSpace Plane, or NASP, made a great splash, but went the way of supersonic transport. BAP donated the life-size copy to the Smithsonian, who deposited it in their Dulles hangar. The small NASP model in the conference room had no plaque, no number.

BAP won a big piece of the Space Station Freedom

contract—crew living quarters. Congress squashed that dream. The crew living quarters sat mothballed in a BAP warehouse, but the research helped the Felix single-stage-to-orbit project develop a small, rugged, modular crew compartment.

The SDI black work for Harchord and Marshall promised to save BAP. At long last, BAP bent tin—and lots of it. A Brilliant Pebble model (an old, unclassified design) sat optimistically above a plaque that boasted 3,346—the number originally authorized, then canceled. BAP built less than ten percent under a kludge of black contracts.

Rolf doodled a picture of Felix on his yellow pad. He turned his mind off and waited. Nothing happened.

A bellicose sneeze ripped the silence, and the voice at the end of the table sniffled, "Ragweed," followed by some nose blowing.

"Gesundheit," Paul responded automatically.

Rolf shook himself out of his mental stupor and prodded his inner circle of advisors. "So, my trusted advisors, do you have any ideas, or do we pass out the cyanide capsules?"

Paul started to restate his case, when Herb Eckert cut him off, saying, "I'll get us an extension of credit."

"How?" Paul didn't doubt Herb.

"Dr. Bernard, the principle is simple. When you owe a bank a million dollars, the bank owns you. When you owe the bank a hundred million dollars, you own the bank. However, that works only once. We lack staying power. We need a big win."

Herb's right-hand man added, "We've got some good assets we could sell to raise cash. Most are profitable bits and pieces we kept after we bought up Analytics International. The data services company, Datek, would fetch a good price. Our car rental subsidiary has suitors. We own a profitable cable TV franchise in southwest Chicago. That would sell. And don't forget Roadrail, the intermodal trucking company we have in Alexandria. That's grown seventeen percent per year since we acquired it."

Herb glowered at his assistant. "Don't be ridiculous! We can't sell the service companies. They provide my only cashflow." Herb Eckert had fought Rolf for years to keep the service companies. Rolf considered them distractions.

Rolf rebuked Herb. "You'd have us all flippin' hamburgers if you had your way. Sell the service companies. Raise the cash."

Herb stiffened a bit in his chair. Rolf noticed. "You're too emotionally attached to your little darlings. Get rid of them. Raise the cash."

Another round of silence hung over the table, until a ruddy-complexioned salesman, part of Ted Winston's organization, spoke for the first time. "I'll move four BP-3 wide-bodies if you'll let me talk to my Chinese friends. They want them and they can pay cash."

Ted scolded his protégé. "You can't do that!"

"Paint and paperwork, Mr. Winston. We've got twelve on the way to Thailand in the next ninety days. We'll help them resell four of theirs to . . . Bulgaria. Bulgaria will sell them to China. Thailand orders another four planes at a hefty discount for their cooperation. China wires the funds through Thailand. We book another sale of four planes that we'll build later for the Thais. Technically, it's legal."

"But the new sanctions . . . we've got enough trouble without having State and Commerce after our butts!" Ted sputtered.

There was an unidentified snicker. "Butts?"

The salesman observed, "They'll have to wait in a long line, won't they? And it would be nice to have a butt when it's their turn."

"But the long-term . . ."

Rolf interrupted. "Do it. Sell those planes. Get the cash.

Make it happen. And Ted, we'll think about the long-term if and when it happens."

A rumpled old scientist at the end of the table put his hand up, which drew a smile from Rolf. "Yes, Dr. Iversen?"

Rolf looked around the table. The engineers revered Iversen, sort of a patron saint for rocket scientists. The support staff thought old Iversen extremely odd, but they would mind their manners. Throughout his adult life, Iversen had served as BAP's brilliant, albeit eccentric, structures engineer. Long since retired, he remained a member of the BAP board of directors, and he was a longtime friend of the Bernard family. Iversen had been a mentor to Rolf when Vincent Bernard died, and, in addition to engineering, Iversen taught Rolf to appreciate German culture.

Iversen had come to America after World War II, a refugee from Schleswig Holstein, and worked as a young draftsman for BAP while attending university. Iversen got Vincent Bernard interested in rockets and outer space, and Vincent Bernard put Dr. Iversen in charge of BAP's X program, the great-granddaddy of the Felix project. In fifty-five years, Iversen had not lost one particle of his accent, and after fifty-five years, he still failed to understand his adopted countrymen. He exaggerated American ambition, or perhaps he projected German mores onto his adopted country. Either way, Dr. Iversen considered America a latter-day Hanseatic League, and therefore held a deep conviction that America had a manifest destiny to manage the affairs of the world, the Hanseatic League having failed to do so. America must realize her destiny by controlling space.

Also, Dr. Iversen thought America was running out of time. Iversen certainly had few years left. Age had worn him down. Medicines, hearing aids, thick glasses, and insatiable curiosity kept him going day after day. With his round glasses and rumpled brown suit, Iversen appeared the archetypal old-world scientist.

His reticence about World War II, plus his cynical theories about the New World Order raised suspicions among the uninformed that Iversen must have been a Nazi—a bit of gossip he resented deeply. True, Iversen had been drafted into the Wehrmacht at age fourteen with the rest of his gymnasium class to carry messages and serve as cannon fodder in the last four weeks of the war. Iversen survived because he took his first message straight back to Lubeck, where he hid with his mother during the chaotic dissolution of the Third Reich.

In contrast, Rolf's German ancestors had fled Saxony during the late nineteenth-century famines. They settled in Texas as ersatz cowboys long before twentieth-century Europe unraveled.

Dr. Iversen put his hands together as if in prayer and said, "The long-term looks good if . . ." He made a dramatic pause, "If we will recognize what we in hand have got." Iversen blinked. He slowed his speech. "We have, or I should say, almost have a monopoly on space transportation. Felix has come through most of the tests. My colleague, Dr. Max Yeager, even now at Marana, is on the final tests working. We have built three more production models rated for 16,000- to 20,000-pound cargoes. We can put a pound into low earth orbit for a hundred dollars. Martin Marietta's Delta rocket can't put for less than five thousand dollars a pound into orbit. But I tell you truly, you mustn't sell Felix or any other SSTO-class spacecraft to anybody. Sell tickets. Put people and their cargoes into space. If you charge two thousand per pound, you will recover the cost of building a spaceship with three missions. Who would put cargo on a Delta rocket that might blow up on the launch pad, when they could pay much less for a rocket that can survive mechanical failure? Think of what that will mean to BAP. We become a service industry, like Herb's truck company—"

"It's called Intermodal Transportation," Herb corrected.

"Right, and it's a very nice truck company, too. But we will have the only truck company that goes into space. Nothing under twenty thousand pounds goes up that we do not send. And of course, we would give our projects big discounts. NASA would have to give us the space-station contract, because we would save the government twenty-two billion dollars putting it up. They'd have to keep us on the Pebbles contract, because we'd save them eighteen billion dollars putting the Pebbles up. We could put Dr. Fenster's solar power satellite up and give the United States electric power, much cleaner than coal and much cheaper than nuclear fission. That's just the icing on the cake."

Ted Winston patronized the little German. "You're being a bit naive. We just don't launch things. The U.S. signed the United Nations Space Launch Treaty. The government approves and monitors all launches. And don't forget, they're the competition. Do you think NASA and the Air Force are going to lay off twenty thousand of their people and give the whole show to BAP? Do you think the French and Russians are going to buy launches from BAP? The Chinese can and will underbid anybody to get business for their Long March program. All those governments—including ours—will launch for free if they have to. Then they'll retaliate and cut us to pieces. We'll never sell another plane to any government again. We've had enough pie-in-the-sky for a while. The reason we are having this meeting is because we got into the launch business, screwed up, and now we're talking about how to stay in any kind of business for the next year."

Dr. Iversen politely raised his hand. "Ted, this is backwards—what we've got here. You are a policy man. You are supposed to have vision. I'm an engineer. I'm supposed to be narrow-minded. We're backwards, you and me."

Ted opened his mouth, but Dr. Iversen politely raised his hand again. "Here is my vision. BAP keeps working on the Pueblo project—within financial reason. When the government comes to its senses, we put it up with our Felix ships. Thus, the United States ends the threat of nuclear ballistic missiles, and BAP saves the taxpayer eighteen billion dollars. After that demonstration, we put up the Space Station *Freedom* for a fraction of the cost. Then, perhaps a solar power satellite. The United States must control access to space, and fulfill her destiny. We can argue successfully that the United States must abrogate that stupid launch treaty Ted spoke of, if we ever were stupid enough to ratify it. Then, we let the market decide who's got the best spaceship."

Rolf took a couple notes in his peculiar code. He ripped the yellow sheet from the pad, folded it and stuffed into his pocket. Rolf didn't say a word and without his attention, the meeting atrophied into sideline conversations. When the noise grew loud enough to distract Rolf, he dismissed the group until Monday. He stood at his place and watched the room empty. With nothing but an empty house waiting for him, a big gaping wound of a house. He didn't feel like going home.

Tyler stood next to him and asked softly, "What did you think?"

Rolf said, "We're in deep, deep . . ."

Tyler glanced over his shoulder, then continued his hushed conversation with Rolf. "Iversen's an odd duck, isn't he?"

"He's a very useful engineer. At least he has vision." Rolf looked down at the sleek model of the BP-155 fighter.

Tyler continued. "Iversen's grand strategy could work, but for one flaw."

"What's that?"

"The government would cut us off at the knees like Ted said. They're doing it to us now. You've said it yourself. Government is the ultimate control-freak. Right now, they control access to space. They'll fight the private sector to keep control of space."

"You can't fight city hall."

"Not if you fight using their rules. Government makes the rules to ensure that government wins. If you were willing to break the rules, you could win."

"What do you mean, 'break the rules'?"

"Put Pebble System up as soon as you can. You take control of low earth orbit—unorthodox, to say the least, but you'd win."

Rolf grabbed Tyler's arm and turned him to face the wall. "You're nuttier than Iversen. I could lose everything."

"Rolf, you *are* losing everything. NASA knows what you've got with Felix—they know their days are numbered. There's no way NASA will roll over and let you have their business, and all of their jobs, their paychecks and perks. They'll stall you for three years with red tape, steal your customers with subsidized launch prices, then pirate your designs. They'll run you out of business, then take your technology to run their monopoly. According to the rules, right now you can't launch without NASA's permission. But, if you put up the Pebbles, *you* control access to space: NASA couldn't launch without your permission."

"That would be sweet."

"Wouldn't it? Furthermore, you'd control pricing. You'd have it all. It's just a thought."

Rolf stood for a moment staring at the wall. "Who would get involved in such a scheme?"

"You would. I would." Bobby whispered. "I'd bet Paul would."

"Paul? We can't have him involved. This is too risky."

Tyler looked through the door, where Paul waited. "I trust Paul, more than I trust Yeager. Think of it as a family venture: Rolf, Paul, and Uncle Bobby." Tyler grinned.

Rolf did not return Tyler's smile. "We'll discuss this lunacy later on. Right now, I want you to go to Paris and check on Cynthia. See if you can get her to come home. It would be good for Paul."

"First, I've got to go back to Pueblo. I fired the site manager and half the security staff." Tyler looked at the ceiling.

"So I heard. So when can you get to Paris?"

"Four days, a week maybe." Tyler nodded, and backed out of the room.

Rolf turned his attention to the last man there. Dr. Iversen carefully pulled one sheet of yellow paper along the perforation and laid the company pen back in the middle of the clean pad. He slid the big brown chair back into place, and returned his dirty coffee cup and saucer to the silver tray.

Rolf smiled at the old man and observed, "You've always had the grand vision, Dr. Iversen. So easy to say; so difficult to do."

The old man closed his gray eyes and sighed, "If you say so, sir. I'd hoped to live long enough to see our side win. Perhaps not." He clutched his small briefcase under his arm and left.

Rolf wondered, *Does Iversen know whose side he's on?*

Across the Potomac, in a small room nestled within the Old Executive Office Building, General Harchord sat at a long conference table with four intelligence reports spread before him. He sipped from a bottle of soda water, and read. An Air Force colonel from the National Security Council sat at the far end of the walnut table, nervously smoking a cigarette and blowing the smoke away from the general.

Searching in vain for an ashtray, the colonel crushed his cigarette against the side of a steel wastepaper basket. The smoke rose like a tiny mushroom cloud. "The White House Chief of Staff wants me to synthesize these four reports, then recommend some course of action he can take to the President. I'm supposed to write the draft. I'd like to know what the Air Force wants."

Harchord looked around the room, the fourteen-foot

ceilings, the thick molding, peeling paint. "You know, Nixon used this office."

"Pardon me?"

"Richard Nixon liked this room better than the Oval Office. I suppose he liked it because it didn't have any windows. What do you think?"

"I was in college then."

"Oh, yes." Harchord yawned. "You see the worn spot on the carpet, near your feet?"

"Yes, sir?"

"That's where Nixon kept his desk. You're sitting where Nixon sat. How's it feel?"

"Gee." The colonel laughed to himself. "I hope Nixon had a more comfortable chair."

"I don't think so." Harchord drummed his fingers on the current intelligence reports. He hadn't the heart to tell the young colonel that studies, reports, warnings, recommendations, interservice memoranda, and National Security Council appointments, for that matter, were nothing but a way to keep ambitious officers out of the way during the week, and busy on the weekends. Harchord flipped through the four reports. "Don't make me read this stuff. Just give me the bottom line."

"Yes, sir. NSA intercepted some traffic from Headquarters Strategic Rocket Forces to Moscow. They can't account for two ICBM warheads missing from a facility in Kazakhstan. Circumstances indicate theft. State Department resources say Yeltsin plans to publicize this nuclear weapons mishap, a Russian version of our BROKEN ARROW. The question before the National Security Council is, 'Will the missing warheads affect the multilateral arms talks scheduled in three months?' "

"It won't make any difference." Indeed, it made no difference when two hundred former Soviet nuclear scientists disappeared, emigrating to parts unknown to serve the highest bidders. It made no difference when both British and French intelligence speculated that Iran,

Syria, and Argentina had purchased nuclear devices in the Great Soviet Yard Sale. The nuclear genie was out of its bottle and would never be coaxed back in.

Harchord continued his thought. "The White House is interested in public relations, not national security. But if you insist, you can say that the Air Force wants an accelerated deployment of HEAD-I land-based ABMs, followed within two years by a deployment of the Pebbles ABM System. The White House won't let your analysis see the light of day."

General Harchord got up and the colonel asked, "How come you know so much about this room, sir?"

"Kissinger brought me in to the NSC. I was a hotshot major with a Ph.D. I had your job as a matter of fact; I worked next door." Harchord stood to leave. "Want some career advice?"

"Yes, sir."

"Punch your NSC ticket and get back into the Air Force. Hell, look at you: They don't even let you wear a uniform. And you need a haircut."

Harchord paused to look around the old room. "Good luck with your paper."

Chapter 7

Cynthia Bernard stepped out from under a faded awning onto wet cobblestones. Broken clouds, the remnants of an autumn storm, dappled the sky. She pulled her green paisley kerchief over her hair, turned her collar up, and slipped a pair of dark sunglasses over her eyes. She hadn't planned to spend the night, but she'd had too much wine on an empty stomach and Chip had been convenient, and seemed to want a reward for hauling her back and forth to Chartres. And the bitter blast of autumn wind and rain had offered a cold alternative to tacking on an extra night with Chip.

Must hurry, she thought, *shops close early on Saturday.* Cynthia had several errands, and she needed to study the Republic Gold deal. After a weekend of traveling and reveling with Chip, she sought the solitude of her flat, but she was out of everything, including toothpaste. She dodged puddles, stepping on dry spots of sidewalk. Stopping at a small corner market, she bought groceries, including a commercial pâté, a plastic two-liter bottle of table wine, and a liter of spring water. Like any Parisian housewife, she pulled a net bag from her purse to carry the load, and she paid cash.

The bottles weighed her down, and for once she wished that she had a car in Paris, or that it wasn't bad manners to hail a cab for less than four blocks. She walked across Pont Neuf, across the square in front of Notre Dame, and through a narrow side street toward her building, the bags tugging on her arm.

Despite her load, she detoured to her familiar newsstand to buy a copy of *Financial Times*, and stuffed it into her expanding tote. Her final errand took her to a *tabac* for a pack of Dunhill cigarettes, though she didn't smoke. She kept cigarettes in her purse for Chip to bum. She turned down an alley and stepped over a rusting bicycle that had fallen onto its side, kickstand pointlessly erect.

The narrow street led her to a weatherworn stone archway and a spotless marble hall guarded or perhaps merely occupied, by a fat tabby cat. "Bubo! You naughty cat." Cynthia smelled a mix of antiseptic cleanser and furniture polish in the air. The stair runner was ratty at the ends where Bubo had sharpened his claws. She set her purse and groceries down to open her mailbox and found a thick packet from the Harris Bank Trust Department and two letters, both from Rolf. The canceled stamps showed that Rolf had mailed them three days apart. She tucked her mail into the net bag.

Cynthia looked up the steep steps, braced herself and started the climb, muttering, "Chip is so thick. 'Nice windows for such an old church,' he says. I need to meet a man who reads books."

At the second landing she juggled her purse and net bag, shifting both to the crook of her left arm, and fumbled a key into the lock. She shoved the heavy walnut door open with her knee. Bubo rushed in between her legs, straight to a pair of bowls in the kitchen. Quickly, she inventoried her plants and noted which needed a drink. She placed her perishables and wine in a small refrigerator, plucking a container of rancid yogurt from the top shelf and pitching it into the empty garbage can. Then she put on a kettle for a cup of instant coffee, kicked off her shoes, and walked barefoot over flokati rugs to her bedroom.

She deftly unfastened the top button on her blouse as she walked through her open bedroom door, bowing slightly to dodge a coat hanger dangling from her chin-up bar. Instinct grabbed her. She froze. Someone was huddled beneath the covers on her side of the double bed. No face visible, but it was certainly a big person.

Her eyes scanned the room from right to left. A small, brown leather suitcase. Heavy, black, polished shoes that appeared to be American or British. Black socks, gray pants, gray suit coat, and white shirt draped over chair. Blue checkered tie, fat black wallet and cufflinks on dresser. A big man—asleep, but fitfully.

Cynthia's hair stood up on the nape of her neck. She refastened the button on her blouse and stepped back. She thought, *Not Rolf—much too big, wrong shoes. Couldn't be Chip.* With the stealth of a lynx, she slipped back into the living room, and to the hall closet. On the top shelf, buried behind a box of paintbrushes and ski mittens, she felt for and found her chrome-plated Beretta 9mm pistol. It fitted her hand nicely. She pressed the release, and the clip fell smoothly into her free hand, where she judged by the weight that she had four to six rounds. She'd need only one, maybe two. Never taking her eyes from her bedroom doorway, she slipped the clip into place, and with a tap to her palm, she heard the reassuring click.

She sought a corner of the room, where she could see the doorway, but where her unwanted visitor would fail to see her until it was too late. She crouched behind an overstuffed chair, with her back to the window. Then she chambered a bullet. The cat padded across the floor to nuzzle her leg.

Pausing to collect herself, the thought crossed her mind that she ought to walk into her bedroom and shoot the bastard where he lay. *A terrorist, probably a terrorist.* Sweat beaded on her brow and she felt a trickle from her underarm beneath her silk blouse. *What the hell kind*

of terrorist breaks in alone and takes a nap in your bed?
This was all wrong. Her hand was wet. She shifted the
pistol to her left hand and wiped her right hand dry on
the chair. And quite suddenly she thought, *Idiot, you've
got a phone! Call the gendarmes!* The phone was across
the room. She could make it.

But the kettle sputtered, whined, then shrieked.
Suddenly, no more time. No phone. No gendarmes. Her
heart pounded against her ribs. She yelled, "You, in there!
Come out with your hands up or I'll blow your head off."
She pulled back the hammer with her thumb and took a
deep breath. The big tabby cat crouched, ears back, sensing
the woman's fear.

Cynthia heard the covers rustle in the next room, then
a familiar but weak voice. "Cindy? Is that you? Oh, please,
shoot me in the head."

Cynthia carefully lowered the hammer, but kept the
gun ready as she peered around the doorjamb into her
bedroom. Bobby Tyler lay there, face down in the pillow.

"You bastard! I damn near shot you. . . . I ought to shoot
you now." Cynthia slipped the clip out of the pistol and
ejected the round from the chamber. She dropped the
live round in her pocket. As she stepped back to turn
the kettle off, she demanded, "How did you get in here?"

"I picked the lock," he mumbled into the pillow, and
added, "It's not much of a lock."

"Why?"

"Rolf sent me. I got here yesterday morning, already
feeling sick with the flu. You weren't here. I couldn't face
being sick in a hotel, so I let myself in."

"You broke in." She contradicted him.

"Your cat got away. I put myself to bed. I tried to clean
up after myself, but your bathroom . . ." He rolled over
and squinted at Cynthia.

"Oh, Bobby!" Cynthia walked over to take a closer look.
"You look awful." She pressed her cool hand against his
forehead. "You're burning up. What have you had to drink?"

"Nothing I could keep down. I'm afraid I messed up the bathroom. There's a plastic bag in the hamper."

"When the cleaning lady comes in on Monday, you can give her an extra two hundred francs. She'll forgive you." Cynthia went into the bathroom. On tiptoes, she reached high into a linen cabinet to a shoe box where she kept her medicines. She grabbed a thermometer, unscrewed a green bottle, poured a glass of tap water (okay for washing down aspirin), and returned to Bobby's side. He smelled sick. "Take these," she said. "I'll make you a cup of suma tea." She left him with his face buried in a goose down pillow, fighting to keep two small pills and a mouthful of water in his stomach.

Tyler's feverish mind wandered. He had first set eyes on Cynthia at her wedding, a merger, of sorts, between the Bernard and Dubois clans. He'd known Rolf Bernard long before, having met Rolf in Vietnam by chance, where he'd served as an infantry captain, prior enlisted, a product of the war's appetite for capable young men and Fort Benning's Officers Candidate School.

Bobby loathed the jungle when he was an enlisted man humping a radio on long-range patrols during his first tour in Vietnam. The loathing had kept him focused, and he survived. Then, the Army assigned Bobby, whose secondary specialty was intelligence, to the Phoenix Program. They gave him no unit patch and told him to hide his rank. They gave him one first lieutenant, a radioman, and a small mob of Southeast Asian mercenaries—thugs mostly, violent criminals. He got his choice of weapons, and he chose a .12 gauge shotgun—not for fear of Viet Cong or NVA, but fear of his own mercenaries. His predecessor had disappeared. Tyler took his mercenary band into a murky world near the Ho Chi Minh Trail to harass and interdict North Vietnamese supply lines.

On the day he met Rolf, he had waited in ambush where a secondary trail cut through a field cleared by forest fire. Bobby sat in the shade, swatting midges and opening a squat, olive drab can of peach jam with his lucky P-38, when a two-seater RF-4C reconnaissance jet roared over the tree tops and bellied into his killing zone. Tyler carefully set the jam aside, laying a dirty scarf over his food to keep bugs out. He grabbed the radioman and raced to the smoldering jet. He pulled a semiconscious pilot, face awash with bright, fresh blood, and lowered him to his radio man, who frantically pointed to the opposite side of the clearing. Bobby found the copilot dead, neck snapped like a dry stick, but not another mark on him. Bobby dropped the dead man out of the cockpit onto the ground. Then North Vietnamese regulars appeared at the wood line and peppered the burning jet with small-arms fire. As Tyler slid down the fuselage, a jagged piece of torn metal ripped his arm from the shoulder to the elbow. Blood dripped from his elbow, leaving black pockmarks in the dust. The burning hunk of metal and the black smoke covered their escape. Bobby dragged the groggy Air Force pilot into the brush just as the fuel tanks blew and fire consumed the crippled jet.

Bobby's company beat feet through the jungle to relative safety. The pilot trudged along, then swooned. Bobby ordered the mercenaries to carry him. Bobby and the lieutenant carried the dead copilot on a litter. The radioman called ahead for help. At their base, a chopper swooped down to collect the dead man and the pilot. The radioman, who doubled as a medic, opined that Tyler's wound would need about thirty stitches—which he could manage in the field, but he wouldn't guarantee against the wound turning septic. Bobby had smelled a septic wound before: some pathetic VC, maybe sixteen years old, left for dead with a piece of shrapnel in his side. They found the delirious boy by the smell of his putrefying wound. The wound was not mortal: the infection was. Without hesitation, Bobby put the lieutenant in charge and jumped aboard the Huey.

At the field hospital, a doctor sewed the cut on Rolf's

chin, and set his broken nose. The corpsman who stitched Bobby's arm and administered antibiotics, assured him thrice that sepsis, tetanus, or any other death by microbe was presently out of the question.

The two wounded men spent the day recuperating in the field hospital. For a time, Bobby forgot about the jungle. He spent an hour in the commode, butt glued to a real wooden toilet seat, reading a *Stars and Stripes* newspaper, instinctively tearing out the commentary before realizing a roll of soft paper hung from a bent wire by his side.

After a long visit from a rear echelon J-2 staff officer, Bobby ate a hot meal and wheedled an extra bowl of ice cream from the nurse. He took a couple pills for the pain in his arm, although the pain wasn't severe. He lay on top of the white sheets on his cot and watched the lazy fan above his bed.

Rolf lay in the next bed with a brace about his sprained neck, and orders not to move. "Are you the guy who saved my life?"

"Yep. That's me."

"I can't see you. They've got my head in some kind of vise. Can you come over, so I can see what you look like?"

Bobby slipped out of the smooth sheets and shuffled over to the pilot's bed. "Good-looking, aren't I?"

"I'll never forget what you did for me."

"Hey, we're even. You got me out of the bush for a couple of days."

Rolf volunteered the details of his hapless flight: how the engine failed, how he fell like a stone, and how he blacked out when he hit the ground.

Tyler interrupted, "Your copilot didn't make it."

"I didn't know. I assumed . . ." Rolf shut his eyes.

Bobby climbed back into his steel-spring bed, where he willed himself into quietude. Months in the jungle had taught Bobby to listen selectively. A twig snap rattled nerves more than cannon fire; distant cannons had no

effect. Tyler tuned out the sound of jets flying sorties
overhead. He tuned out the radio in the next room. He
tuned out the pilot snoring in the next bed, and the gecko
lizards chirping from the window screens. He watched
the fan. He kept his weight off his stitches and he let
the mild narcotic do its work.

Over the next few years, Rolf pursued a friendship with
Captain Tyler. Bobby liked the attention. Officers in the
Phoenix Program didn't make many friends, and Rolf
always bought the drinks. Tyler got a Bronze Star with
the "V" device and, thanks in part to Rolf's important
family, a mention in a *Wall Street Journal* article about
Rolf Bernard's narrow escape. Bobby figured he had a
leg up on promotion.

After one tour in Vietnam, Rolf left the Air Force and
went to work for his dad, the man who built BAP, Inc.
Tyler finished his second Vietnam tour, then attended
service schools in Fort Holabird, Maryland and Fort Bragg,
North Carolina. He married Mariam Houston from
Lagrange, Tennessee, got his new wife pregnant, and made
the majors' list—all in the same month. He lived in the
interim status of captain (P)—for promotable—and was
eligible to wait to become a major, which is sort of an
honor. While he waited for promotion, Mariam had a
girl, weaned her in eighteen months, and became pregnant
again. Bobby completed a tour in Europe and got his
RIF notice. The Army gave him fifteen thousand dollars,
an Army Commendation Medal and three airline tickets
back to Tennessee.

With a baby coming in four months, Bobby scrambled
to find work. His old buddies from the Phoenix Program
could find him immediate work plying his old trade for
the CIA, but the work meant travel, and considerable
personal risk for less money than he had made in the
Army. Then, Bobby visited Rolf at the BAP facility in
St. Louis. Rolf hired his old friend on the spot and put
him in charge of special projects and security, paying

him four times his captain's wage. That seemed like a lifetime ago.

A whiff of sassafras jostled Tyler's senses. The queasiness returned as he pulled his face out of the pillow, turned his head, and focused his eyes on Cynthia. She stood next to the bed with a tray bearing a cup and saucer and a pot of steeping herbal tea. She coaxed Bobby to sit, then set the tray before him, saying, "Don't you ever tire of fetching me? You should tell old Smurch to do his own dirty work."

"I've had worse assignments." Bobby sniffed the tea. "What is this stuff? Hot root beer?"

"Suma tea. Drink it. It's good for your respiratory system. Anyway, I'm not convinced you wouldn't be happier if you'd stayed in the Army."

"The Army tossed me out, I didn't quit." Bobby sipped the tea and stared past Cynthia's concerned look.

In point of fact, Bobby hadn't adjusted well to a peacetime Army. After his second tour in Vietnam, Bobby had gotten orders for Germany as executive officer of the woefully undermanned 1/15th Infantry Battalion, 3rd Infantry Division. He stood at freedom's frontier, a scant 65 kilometers from the East German border. Mariam had found a small apartment in Schweinfurt (German for Pigtown).

The Armed Forces had scavenged Europe clean to support the Vietnam War, and now that Bobby was in Europe, he resented that mightily. They didn't have enough ammunition to last six days, and they lacked the funds to train in the field, yet no one complained. Everyone was glad not to be in Vietnam—everyone except Tyler.

One 7th Army ritual was the perennial Noncombatants Evacuation Operations Plan inspection and briefing. Soldiers took their wives and sometimes their children, collectively known as dependents, to the post gymnasium where each family displayed their NEO kit: suitcase, identification papers, five-gallon gas can, and road map.

The division adjutant general briefed everyone on the plan—how, in case of World War III, all dependents would drive within the speed limit, in a calm and orderly fashion, to Frankfurt, where they would stand in tidy queues to catch empty supply planes returning to the States. Meanwhile, the indigenous population (Army talk for Germans) would remain in their homes to keep the roads free for military transport and the NEO Plan. People actually believed that.

Tyler didn't. He purposefully forgot to tell Mariam to prepare for the NEO briefing. Instead, he met her at the gym. He brought a brown paper bag, top curled into a ratty handle.

Conditioned by a 103-degree fever, Bobby's recollection of the gymnasium changed from black-and-white to living color.

The inspection team, led by the humorless division Chief of Staff, halted in front of Captain (forever waiting to be Major) Tyler, Mariam, and their rumpled bag. The Chief of Staff stood him at attention, pointed with his cigar, very Pattonesque, and barked, "What the hell is going on here, Captain? Where's your NEO kit?"

Verbal abuse didn't phase Tyler. "If you will allow me, sir—my wife's NEO kit."

Mariam started to interrupt but thought better of it.

"My wife shall not perish in the forthcoming war, for I have thought of everything." Tyler reached into the brown bag. "A negligee—featuring a brilliant, sheer, Soviet red, nylon cover with brassiere and panties to match." He handed the handful of cloth to Mariam. "A bottle of vodka! Imported from Sweden—the best I could find." He handed the bottle to Mariam. "And an English-Russian dictionary—indexed with common phrases."

The Chief of Staff took note of name tag, rank, and unit insignia, then turned to the colonel on his right and said, "Have this comedian in my office tomorrow at oh-six-hundred hours."

Bobby blinked and found himself staring up at Cynthia. "I suppose the Army and I were destined to part."

Cynthia centered the cup and saucer on the tray, then pulled the covers up to his chin and shoved a thermometer into his mouth. Bobby shut his eyes to focus his will on keeping medicine and tea in his stomach. He fell asleep. Cynthia picked up the phone and dialed a number she'd recorded in her little black book. The phone rang once.

"Hello?" The voice was matter-of-fact, edged with slight irritation, and a bit of Southern twang.

"Mariam, this is Cynthia. Did I wake you?"

"No, not at all. Excuse me just a sec'." The sound was muffled by a hand over the receiver. "Knock it off you guys. This here's long distance."

Cynthia asked, "How are the children?"

"The girls are at college. The boys, you probably heard, are home. How are you getting along?"

"I'm still here in Paris. I'm getting into Eastern European real estate. It's nuts, but it pays the rent." Cynthia never knew how much Mariam knew. And Mariam never, never let on. "Rolf sent Bobby over to bring me home."

"Are you comin'?"

"I might come back for a week. . . . Reason I called, Bobby's sick. He's got the flu. He's running a high fever, and I've got him in bed." Should she have put it that way?

Mariam cleared her throat. "Keep a bucket by the side of the bed. He's got a weak stomach. Make him some oatmeal if you have any."

"No, but I'll get some. Do you want me to call a doctor?" Cynthia did not want to make a mistake caring for Mariam's man.

"Well, if he asks for one, otherwise no. Don't worry, he'll ask. He's afraid of sickness."

"Okay. I'll have him call you when he feels up to it, and he can tell you when to expect us back in the States."

They said their good-byes, then Cynthia pulled out her

Petit Larousse: oats, oatmeal—*farine d'avoine*. She hustled out to catch the corner grocery shop before it closed.

Cynthia spent the night on a couch that was a bit too short. Twice she woke to hear Bobby convulsing with dry heaves, but she could tell from the resonance that he'd found his way to the bathroom. A toilet flush confirmed that her services were not needed, probably not wanted. Dozing back into a fitful sleep, she made a mental note to get a bigger sofa.

On Sunday morning, Cynthia made a colorless, tasteless, odorless bowl of hot cereal for Bobby, and a poached egg on toast for herself. Bobby stepped into the light, his skin pink from the hot shower, his cheeks and neck slightly raw from an overdue shave, his thin hair combed straight back, his head bowed. He shuffled into dining area and sat dutifully at his bowl. He sniffed the hot drink in the cup, which he recognized as suma tea. Across the table, Cynthia sat with the *Financial Times*, her plate of real food—meager as it was—and black coffee.

Cynthia opened her hand and dropped five fat capsules into a little pile next to Tyler's plate. "Now that you can keep your food down, we can help your body beat this flu." She separated the pills with her index finger.

"What is all this stuff?" He picked up a drab pill, sniffed, and made a face. "Smells like horse droppings."

"That's echinacea with goldenseal root. Those herbs boost your immune system. The dark capsule has got some burdock, which cleans the blood. A bad case of flu tends to trash the blood with toxins. The little pill is zinc— I forget why you're supposed to take it. The beige one is a thousand milligrams of time-release vitamin C. It also helps clean the blood. You'll take a set of these five pills four times a day." She laid a glass of water next to the pills.

"Do you take this stuff?"

"Yes, I do."

Tyler looked up at Cynthia and down at the assembly

of pills. Cynthia sipped her coffee and read an article about bartering in cash-strapped Eastern Europe. Uncapping a thick green pen that hung around her neck, she circled a couple paragraphs and snapped the pen back in place.

Bobby ate a spoonful of the cereal. "Cindy, what was this stuff before it crawled into my bowl?"

"Some kind of French oatmeal, I think." She replied without lowering her paper or reacting to his complaints.

"Am I boring you?"

"I'm sorry." She set her paper down. "I've never been much of a morning person—especially when I've been up all night. She glanced to her left at an antique wall clock. "I've got to go out for a while."

"Where to?"

"Notre Dame."

"To church? You're being sarcastic. You're going to see your young man." Bobby winked and smiled feebly.

Cynthia scowled. "I'll stand in the back if it pleases you." She slammed the door on her way out. Bobby stared at the door. He held a spoonful of warm *farine d'avoine* upside down over the bowl. His arm gave up before the farine.

Chapter 8

Rolf nodded awake, startled. He found himself sitting in his green leather chair in his study. The intercom buzzed. He stood up and spilled a month-old copy of *Aviation Week* from his lap to the floor. He'd been rereading an unflattering article about himself. The intercom buzzed again. He mashed the speaker button. "Yeah? What is it?"

"Rolf? Did I disturb you?"

"Oh, Margaret. You caught me napping."

"You got another one of those cryptic calls. The man simply said, 'Tell Rolf to watch TV at eight.' Then he hung up."

Rolf wiped his eyes, shoving his bifocals to his forehead. "Thank you." He made a mental note: Tyler called. He's posting a letter for Tony Valdez at eight o'clock.

"Do you need anything before I go home?"

Rolf looked at the old grandfather clock, the smiling enamel moon rising within the clock's face.

"Matter of fact, I do. Come here, please."

Rolf walked over to his double pedestal desk and sat down in the creaking old chair. He rose when Margaret Bergen entered the room. "Margaret, I need you to set up a little trip for me."

"Certainly."

"Cancel or move all my week's appointments—I won't be here."

"What about your Tuesday lunch with Senator Simpson?"

"I won't be here. I know you can sort it out."

"Okay."

"Put me on a commercial flight out of Dulles to Tucson, first thing Tuesday morning."

"You won't be taking the executive jet?"

"No, Margaret, a commercial flight. And I don't want anybody to know where I'm going, or what I'm doing. I won't even be taking you on this trip. It's business, but it's rather delicate. Put the bill on my personal credit card. If anyone asks, I'm out of town. That's all. . . . Where was I?"

"Tucson. Will you need a place to stay?"

"Hmm. Does Paul still have that coed living at his place?"

"I never inquired." A thin, satisfied smile turned the corners of her mouth.

"Find me a place. Call Max and ask him to pick me up at the airport. Then book me a Thursday hop to LAX. I'll fend for myself there. Then put me on the Saturday red-eye back to Dulles. I'll use my own car and drive myself back and forth from Dulles."

"Got it."

"Good night, Margaret."

"Good night, Rolf." She pulled the door as she left the room.

"Cindy?"

Cynthia studied a Citicorp report projecting the Deutschemark-dollar exchange rate, and how it would affect her cash flow from the Dresden shopping mall, and what it would cost to hedge that cash flow in the forward currency markets. She didn't hear Bobby.

He tried again, louder. "Cindy?"

She put a finger to mark her place. "Yes?"

"Can I borrow your office?"

"Just don't move any of my papers. Otherwise, help yourself."

Tyler shut himself in Cynthia's study. Pushpins held scraps of news articles and price charts to the walls. Buy-and-sell confirmations littered a burled ash and walnut lowboy. Two linear feet of unopened mail buried a gilt inbox. Cynthia had no desk; rather a large dining table, Greek revival or Empire—Tyler couldn't tell which. In front of the table sat one modern, armless swivel chair on a plastic mat. On the table sat an old reliable 486 computer of some mixed Japanese parentage.

Tyler flipped the red switch on the side of the computer. The oversized screen came to life and booted to a market data service. It being Sunday night in Paris, a screen for various Japanese securities presented itself. Tyler quit the data service, and to his relief found his subdirectory with familiar communications software. He composed a brief message to Rolf.

> Re: Project Green Lid. Count me in.
> Re: Cynthia. Someone's eavesdropping on Cynthia.
> I need more equipment to sweep her apartment.
> My handheld gear detects a tap on her phone. I
> need to determine motive. If you have some private
> dick working her case, get rid of him. If not, watch
> what you say and who you talk to, especially on
> the phone.

With a few more keystrokes, the machine encrypted the short message under the protocol "Mustang," compressed the text into binary form, dialed direct to a host computer somewhere in Cincinnati, found its way to the BIX online bulletin boards, and pumped the data down the line in a quick burst posted for "Tony Valdez" 's eyes only.

Rolf could retrieve and decrypt the file at his leisure.

Tyler rejoined Cynthia in the living room, where Cynthia

sat next to Bubo. "Cindy, someone's put a tap on your phone."

"I'll bet old Smurch did it."

"Rolf?" Bobby had forgotten Cynthia's irreverent pet name for Rolf.

"Yeah, old Smurch."

"Perhaps bug your apartment, but put a tap on a French phone? I don't think so. What are you doing to attract that kind of attention?"

Cynthia straightened her skirt. "Let me see. I'm syndicating a loan and getting a minority interest in a large Western-style shopping mall in Dresden. Some German skinheads don't like it, but it's a small deal really. What else? I'm factoring letters of credit out of the Bank of China—controversial in the UK, but legal here."

"Factoring what?"

"We help people and businesses get their money out of Hong Kong. The British don't like it, but most of my big Hong Kong clients *are* British. Let's see. . . ." She fiddled with her earring. "Through my Luxembourg subsidiary I made a sizable profit by shorting a bunch of US stock. The IRS disagrees with my position on tax treatment—which, by the way, is one reason I'm not too keen on going back with you to the States."

"How much are you worth?"

"Don't be rude. I never divulge my net worth or my weight." She chucked him under the chin and leaned back on the couch. "Care to guess?"

Max Yeager met Rolf at Tucson International Airport. Rolf peeled off his jacket and stripped the tie from his neck. Max took Rolf's small bag.

"First thing, we'll get you some lunch. Paul and Captain Rogers will meet us at Rosalinda's—best chili relleños in North America."

"Good—but first I'm going to smoke a cigarette." Rolf took a piece of gum out of his mouth and tossed it in a trashcan. He walked briskly toward the terminal doors. Rolf deftly juggled his briefcase and pack of cigarettes, timing the automatic doors to have a cigarette in his mouth and lighter lit as he stepped through. He took a deep drag. "Let's just wait here a minute, then we'll go back inside for my suitcase."

Max sat down on a stone bench. He looked over municipal lawns kept green with automatic sprinklers. "What's the surprise visit for?"

Rolf tossed the butt onto the pavement and crushed it underfoot. "We're going to map our future, Max. I'm going to bet my company on your spaceship." He looked Yeager in the eye.

Yeager's eyes got wide.

"What's the matter Max? Isn't that what you've been trying to get me to do for the last twenty years: ditch the old air breathers, take BAP into space where we belong—where untold wealth waits for enterprising man? Did I get your speech right?"

"Word for word."

"Let's get my bag. We've got a lot to talk about."

In the car, Rolf flipped the air-conditioning vents so that they blew onto his face. "We've had our first frost in Virginia."

"Not out here, Rolf. Tell me about your plans for Felix. If you're serious, I'll come out of semiretirement and work full time if you want."

"Absolutely." Rolf reached over and grabbed Max by the arm. "I wish my dad were alive to see this. He made you swear you wouldn't turn me into a space cadet, and you did it anyway."

"I think he'd approve."

"I know he would." Rolf settled back in the soft leather seat.

"So don't keep me in suspense. What's up?"

"Max, here's the problem. Thanks in large part to the government, BAP's out of money. If the government continues to withhold our funds, the banks will, in due course, refuse to extend our line of credit secured by those government receivables. You following me, so far?"

"The government has you by your fiscal manhood."

"Very poetic, Max. No one will ever mistake you for anything but an engineer."

"Thank you, sir."

Rolf seemed to talk to himself. "It's like a siege. We can hunker down and wait, but the government has unlimited staying power. We don't. The way we're operating now, either the government decides to keep us alive, or we just waste away. Or we can try to break out and seize the initiative. The risk is, the government might find out before we get the upper hand and they'll crush us."

"What's involved in hunkering down?" Yeager asked.

"We slow down defense work. We stop all space programs. We build commercial jets, write software, and I guess we flip some of Herb's hamburgers."

Yeager slowed at a stoplight, shaking his gray head.

"Or . . ." Rolf clenched his fist. "We break out. We use our technical advantage with Felix to set up a monopoly for space transportation. There's a $54 billion-per-year market out there. We could take it. All of it. But we get only one chance."

"I like it, so far."

"Yeah. I hope you can say that a year from now."

Yeager added, "We'll need to move fast. Technical advantage has a short life. In ten years, our patents on the engines, the fuels, and the bonding materials won't be worth a pitcher of warm spit. Most of Felix is off-the-shelf technology."

"I figured we've got a three-year lead." Rolf lit another cigarette.

"If we're lucky. Maybe only two." Max pulled into Rosalinda's parking lot. "Heck, I've got engineers on my payroll who could cross the street and build a Felix spacecraft in two years."

They stepped into the dark cafe and the smell of fajitas. Paul and Charles Rogers were waiting, side by side, in a booth with a red-checkered table. Rolf slid down the Naugahyde seat. "Hi, Charles. Paul." He examined the large plastic pitcher of ice water, the silk rose in the bud vase, and the thin tableware wrapped in white paper napkins. "Are we slumming it today, boys?"

"That was for my benefit." Paul put Yeager and Rogers at ease. "Dad doesn't like my taste in women or restaurants, but as I always say, you can't eat ambiance."

Rolf rolled his eyes. "You try to teach your kid to appreciate the finer things in life—good breeding, good schools, art, music. . . . What thanks do you get?"

"But restaurants and women?" Paul defended his tastes. "A man should be able to appreciate both with his eyes closed."

"He's just like his mother. God give me strength." Rolf shrugged his shoulders. "So what's good here beside chili rellenos—something so good I must eat with my eyes closed?"

Max laughed while Rogers nervously filled the water glasses.

Rolf abruptly changed the subject. "Max and I were talking as we drove here. I'm going to change the direction of BAP, Inc. We're getting into the space transportation business. But, as Max correctly observes, we have a short technical lead—short if measured in years. But we can stretch our technical lead. I'll tell you something my dad taught me. You take a two-year technical lead, use it to capture market share; then control pricing. That way, you turn market share into a twenty-year lead—maybe fifty years if your only competition is the government."

The news took Paul by surprise. He looked around the table for confirmation. His eyes settled on Max.

"Your dad's serious. He wants to build twenty Felix production models and haul cargo to space for a fat fee. I think we should go for it."

Rolf addressed Paul and Rogers. "Max seems eager enough. Me, I've got my own doubts. We've been put in a desperate situation. We've got to make sure we're not a bunch of desperate men about to do desperate deeds."

"It's destiny. . . ." Max opined.

"Destiny my ass. I feel like we're being *pushed* into the space transportation business."

"That's what destiny is, Rolf."

"Don't get metaphysical with me, Max. We've got to make sure we're going into this with our eyes open. We won't be dealing with a free market here. Governments don't want private enterprise in space. Even if what we're doing is not technically illegal today, you can bet your last dollar, the government will make it illegal tomorrow. So, somewhere along the line, we're going to find ourselves on the wrong side of the law. I don't know about you guys, but the Bernard fortune was made playing by the rules."

"Dad, the rules have changed so much since Granddad and you built the company. Seems to me, if we stay in the airplane business, we're going to become part of a nationalized industry, like European, Japanese, and Russian aviation. If that's the case, I'd just as soon cash out now."

"Max, Charles—somewhere down the line, we'd have to make unsanctioned launches and violate the international space treaty."

"I didn't sign it." Charles turned to Max. "Did you?"

"That stupid piece of paper was just the Soviet Union's first stab at galactic socialism. I think all of us at this table reject it completely. Anyway, if we don't start a space transportation industry, somebody else will. And I don't want to have to buy a ticket on someone else's spaceship when I could've ridden into space on my own."

The waitress nipped Max's space panegyric in the bud, took orders, refilled water glasses, and left. Rolf picked up the thread of conversation. "Would you fly for us as a privateer?"

"Sure. I suppose . . ."

Paul nudged Captain Rogers. "Charles, you sound as if you lack commitment."

"Hold on a second. This deal is like the chicken and the pig giving the farmer a Sunday brunch. You're like the chicken making a donation. I'm like the pig making a total commitment. And don't confuse caution with commitment. No offense, Paul, but you don't know what conviction is until you've strapped your butt to a space shuttle. When they fire the engines and blow the restraining bolts, the shuttle shakes, and the metal groans as she starts to fall over on her back. You think, 'You stupid ass—you're a lieutenant colonel in the Air Force. You've got a wife, three kids in college, and you could retire in eight months, making big bucks flying for the airlines, and you—you dumb, Cajun coonass—you're gonna die!' Then the solid rockets light, the sudden thrust presses you hard against your seat as the rockets shove the ship skyward. In that instant, you never want to do anything else with your life but fly rockets. I'll never get into space again if I don't fly for you. So yeah, I'm committed. I'll fly. I'm just practicing being cautious."

Paul could only manage, "Good."

Max interrupted, "You don't know the story, Paul. Rogers wasn't always so cautious. That's how he got—"

"I'll tell my own story, if you don't mind."

"Suits me. I like the way you tell it." Max withdrew.

"My astronaut career blew up shortly after the Challenger. I said some rash things about NASA, specifically that they based their hasty launch decision on budget and publicity considerations. A private company would never have let those minor irritations goad them into risking such a huge capital investment and crew. Then I made the unfortunate statement, quoted in *Aviation Week*, that I hoped the disaster would help NASA realize that the shuttle design was out-of-date.

"I received a thorough briefing on press protocols in Fowley's office. So, in the finest tradition of pilots, I tried to repair the damage, but made it worse. I defended NASA to an auditorium full of teenagers at a Prince William County high school. Some kid suggested NASA was liable for the deaths of the Challenger crew. I said, no way in hell—NASA was not in least liable for failing to disclose the risk of space flight to the Challenger crew. I said, 'You strap five million gallons of liquid hydrogen to your butt, then light the fuse—if you can't figure the risk in that, you're dumber than a box of rocks.'

"Dr. Fowley reprimanded me, and forbade me to speak at any gatherings. So I didn't. But I did go to a National Space Society reception the next week, where a young man asked if I'd fly the next shuttle mission if asked, and I said that I'd love to. But what if your shuttle blew up? the guy asks. We've all gotta go sometime, I said. I'd rather go out in a blaze over the Atlantic than rot at a desk at Goddard waiting for the bureaucrats to screw up the courage to resume shuttle flights. I didn't know the bum worked for the *Baltimore Sun*. When Fowley read the story, he didn't call me into his office; he didn't throw me out of the program; he just moved me to the end of the queue to get into space. I knew I'd never fly to space again, so I retired as a lieutenant colonel and found a job working as a test pilot for BAP."

"Their loss: our gain." Rolf shifted his water glass to make room for a Rosalinda house salad: a small pile of shredded lettuce topped with a dollop of guacamole and a solitary blue corn chip stuck in the green goo like a weather vane. He could hardly resist. "Gee, Paul, should I close my eyes, or what?"

Max deflected the barb. "At some point we'll need more pilots."

Charles boasted, "After we get rolling, I could get you two more pilots. I'm sort of a celebrity now. I'm the only astronaut to ever survive a failed launch. That's a very salable feature for astronauts. And not everybody in the program loves NASA."

The entrées arrived. Rolf said, "I'll count on you three to work out the details. For now, I can assure you that I've checked this with counsel, and so far, everything we're doing is legal. I know everything we're doing is moral. But I also know that if word of our intentions got out, we'd suffer a bigger public relations disaster than we suffered at Rixeyville. The government will cut our nuts off. If we're going to do this, we've got to work in total secrecy. You must promise me that no one—not even your families— will know that we're going to take the space transportation industry away from NASA, Ariane, Glavkosmos, and China."

Yeager nodded. "You know you can count on me."

"You know I'll fly as soon as you've got something to take me up."

Rolf asked, "So, Paul, how soon can you make the three production models ready?"

"We'll have Felix-P ready in six weeks. We're working three shifts to put in the hydrogen tanks."

"We're testing the larger Pratt and Whitney aerospikes now. We could put on a third shift, then launch the production models in four months—if we had a place to launch them from."

"Of course" —Rolf massaged his temples— "Ad hoc sites won't do. How's our Nevada spaceport coming?"

"At present, our Nevada spaceport is nothing but a bunch of surveyor stakes in the desert. We're looking at a $250 million investment and eighteen months to build it, if we can get the land-use permits. We've got Felix dressed up but with no place to go."

Max's face lit up. "It just happens that I know a place that is all dressed up with nothing to do—Cape York, Australia."

"It's a swamp." Rolf dismissed the idea with a wave of his hand. "You just want to get back with your Aussie space cadet, whats-his-name."

"Irwin Kirby. He gave me the idea for the aerospike. He'd be a great asset. . . ."

"Right, good ol' Kirby—like the overpriced vacuum cleaner. He tried to get me to finance his spaceport-in-the-swamp deal. Then, you wanted me to hire him, right? No, you wanted me to *buy* his whole damn company—I remember."

"No, Rolf. I tried to get you involved in the Cape York Spaceport, that's all. And Kirby had nothing to do with it."

"Apparently, it's a good thing you failed. So you're going to try again?"

"It's already built—almost—on somebody else's nickel."

"Cape York?"

"That's right, Rolf."

Rolf sighed. "That's a bit too far off Broadway, even for me."

"But isn't that what we need? I saw it after the 1990 Australian Space Development Conference. It's not really a swamp—more like a tropical bog. . . ."

"Oh, wonderful! A bog. Sort of a swamp with class?"

"I think so. Cape York's got rainforest, sky, and ocean. One big dirt road runs up the cape, then a little dirt road runs into Temple Bay, and to Kirby's spaceport."

"He should've stuck with his movies."

Max shook his head. "Don't write Kirby off just yet. He's had a bad run of luck—like you. I think you two would find yourselves with a lot in common. He's a good man, but he's practically out of business. Glavkosmos was supposed to furnish five Zenit boosters each year. In five years, they've delivered only one. Then, NASA screwed Kirby out of his main customer. They made sure United Technologies couldn't get licenses to launch satellites from Cape York. Kirby's only other big customer, the Japanese, pulled out as they accelerated their efforts to build their Sakishima Islands launch facility. You two were made for each other. Kirby loves space; he's mad at NASA; he can't stand communists. But getting to the bottom line, you could have Kirby's spaceport at a tenth of the cost of building the Nevada site."

"If—and only if—we can get the land-use permits." Paul reminded everybody.

Rogers added, "I toured Cape York two years ago. It's a rainforest, and I do mean rain. Add mud, rust, bloodsucking insects, and venomous critters. However, I must admit they had everything there but fuel and a place to billet a ground crew. They planned to truck in fuel, people, rockets, everything on their roadtrains."

Yeager added his bit to sell Rolf on the idea. "The Cape sits twelve degrees south of the equator, so we'd have good access to an equatorial orbit. We're talking the northern tip of Queensland: alligator and mosquito country—not a lot of press. I can't be sure, but I think it is the farthest point on the globe from Washington, D.C. Like Charles said, they planned to keep most of the Cape York staff in Cairns—which is a lot like Honolulu without a beach—then move them up on roadtrains for launches. I think Cape York could be had."

"How far from Washington?" Rolf scratched his chin. "That has some definite appeal. Max, why don't you take another trip to Australia."

Then Rolf threw his napkin on his plate. "Remember, the only souls who may know that we are accelerating Project Felix without a government contract shall be you three, me, and Tyler. Don't sink us with loose talk."

Yeager loosened his tie. "How am I going to keep it a secret from my people? I've got a thousand very smart people working on Felix. They figure things out. That's why we hired them—to figure things out."

Rolf leaned back in his chair and grinned. "The smarter the better. Engineers—present company excluded—are a gullible breed. Work them harder than they've ever worked before. Push the schedule. Keep them focused on their particular piece of the problem. If they ask questions, tell them it's compartmentalized TOP SECRET. Make up your own code word. Tyler can help you. He's good at that stuff. You make sure everyone is afraid to stop working. Tyler will make sure they are afraid to start talking. One hundred and twenty days, Max. We'll need three Felix ships plus the prototype, and we'll need a place to launch. Keep your trip to Australia short. We live or die in the next hundred and twenty days. Remember, a leak to the press kills us."

As they finished their meals, the conversation turned to small talk.

Paul drove his father up to Marana for a quick tour, where Rolf called Margaret Bergen to check for messages. He had one: Watch TV tonight. Tyler had left another missive for Tony Valdez.

At sunny Huntington Beach, in southern California, Dr. Ginny Abrahamson and Mark Holtz worked in the murky, secret world of the Pueblo project. Abrahamson's team built firmware for command and control, and onboard electronics. Holtz's team built and tested kinetic kill devices, IR sensors, and tested the power supply batteries. They shipped the parts to the BAP munitions warehouse in Pueblo, Colorado, where the parts waited unassembled in numbered crates. Nobody at Pueblo had the faintest idea what was stored in the warehouse. All the knowledge stayed behind at Huntington Beach. Both Abrahamson and Holtz knew each other's part in their black-world collaboration. They answered directly to Rolf Bernard, and no one else.

So neither thought it odd when Bernard called and said, "I need to see both of you, but not at Huntington Beach. The three of us must not be seen together—especially there. Meet me at a beach house—44 San Marcos Lane—off the coastal highway, eight miles north of Laguna. Be there by 2:00 PM tomorrow. Bring a bathing suit. Don't tell anybody anything."

Ginny looked across her desk, puzzled. "Mark, something's about to happen. Call it woman's intuition, but I think we're going to put them up." Ginny had a husky voice.

Mark wiped his brow with a linen handkerchief. "Doesn't seem possible."

"Why not?"

"We've been at it for over fifteen years. To tell the truth, I never thought we'd deploy when we updated the old BAMBI Project. I didn't think we'd deploy when we wrote the SDI white paper. We've built almost two hundred of the little buggers and I still don't think we're going to put them up."

"What a wet blanket you are."

"Maybe. Funny thing, though. While they're sitting in boxes in Pueblo, I never lose a wink of sleep wondering if they'll work. If they get up there" —Holtz pointed to the ceiling— "then, I'll worry all the time. I have this bad dream: Qaddafi shoots a nuke at New York. My Pebbles miss. A million people die, and their relatives come looking for me."

"I know what you mean, Mark. But my nightmare's different. Your Pebbles work perfectly, but my command and control system craps out, and we can't turn the Pebbles off. Then, your Pebbles sling around up there like smart mines, ready to attack upcoming rockets, be they civilian or military. We will have closed space for sixty years, until the batteries run down and the sensors quit."

"A hundred years. We just added the nuclear-powered batteries and solar cells on the sheath."

"Neat. So we can shut down space for a hundred years."

"That's if we choose to wait 'em out. We'd probably think of a way to clean 'em up—but we're talking very big dollars."

"Good Lord. You're starting to think like the Krupps."

Dr. Holtz found the Laguna Beach address easily. He recognized Dr. Abrahamson's red Chrysler convertible

bearing California vanity plates, KVETCH as he pulled into
the gravel driveway at the beach. When he knocked on
the door, he was greeted by a holler from behind an eight-
foot bamboo fence. "Come on in! We're in the jacuzzi."
Mark recognized Ginny's voice.

Mark Holtz found his way through the house to the
deck, where he stood looking down into the cauldron in
which Rolf and Ginny sat, like a pair of missionaries in a
stew.

"What are you staring at?" Dr. Abrahamson demanded.

"Nothing. It's just that I'm used to meetings with tables
and chairs. I'm from St. Louis, remember."

Rolf pointed to a small styrofoam cooler. "There's beer
if you want it."

Rolf leaned out of the jacuzzi and turned on a boom
box to the local soft rock station, and aimed it toward at
the beach. He commented in a hushed voice, "The security
people said that this special radio—and the noise from
the Jacuzzi—would defeat any eavesdropping attempts,
as long as we keep our voices down."

"It looks like any ordinary boom box to me." Dr. Holtz
peered around to look at the knobs.

"Don't touch it! It's a very delicate piece of gear, and I
signed for it. Geez, Mark."

"Sorry."

"Anyway the jacuzzi is just a civilian jacuzzi."

Dr. Holtz sat on the wooden deck.

"That won't work, Mark. You've got to get in." Rolf
shrugged his shoulders. "Hey, I don't make up these silly
rules. I just follow them."

Dr. Holtz raised his hands to surrender. He stepped
out of his flip-flops and took off his terrycloth robe. Then
he lowered his eggshell white body into the hot froth.
He probed the water with his feet and found an
underwater ledge to sit on. There he sat. He looked at
himself. His skin turned bright pink from the waterline
down and stayed pale white from the waterline up.

"That's better." Rolf took a sip of his beer and continued in hushed tones, "First of all, I want to congratulate both of you: You've been cleared for Project Green Lid. There are only twelve government officials and six BAP employees in the program. Each of the eighteen Green Lid operatives acts as his or her own special security officer. That's why we can't use any government or BAP secure facilities. By the way, you don't have a choice to be in or out. Just knowing about Green Lid makes you part of the team."

Mark recoiled slightly.

"If you don't like it, Mark, you can be angry with me, but like it or not, the responsibility is yours. I picked you both because I knew you'd want the job and that you could do it."

Ginny Abrahamson guessed the job. "Does this have anything to do with the Brilliant Pebbles?"

Rolf whispered over the bubbling water, "Yes! We are going to deploy three hundred and twenty Pebbles in a ten-day surge. We'll use the four BAP Felix ships, and deploy under the cover of flight tests. We deploy in four months if we can meet the schedule."

"I knew it! I knew it!" Ginny splashed the water and drew a disapproving look from Mark Holtz. She quieted herself. "I knew it."

"I thought you only had a Felix prototype?" Mark wiped his brow with a towel.

"One prototype and three full-size ships. Until now, you didn't need to know about the three big ships—just like the Felix people don't need to know that you're building three hundred and twenty Pebbles. By the time you two get your Pebbles finished, my son, Paul, and Dr. Yeager will have the Felix fleet ready to put them up."

Holtz nodded.

Dr. Abrahamson spoke. "The command and control is not up to spec. I thought we had another eighteen months. Why now?"

"I'm not privy to everything, but at a recent bidders' conference I got an earful. Apparently, competition in the Islamic world has gotten out of control. Each faction wants to get its hooks into the Islamic republics that spun off from the Soviet Union. The main prize is Kazakhstan— the first Islamic nuclear power. The ruling party in Kazakhstan is pro-Turk and pro-secular, but the Iranians have financed and trained significant opposition. Iran has been trying to radicalize Kazakhstan for twenty years. Uzbekistan and Tadzikistan have already set up pro-Iranian regimes. No one knows whether the Turks or Iranians will gain the upper hand in Kazakhstan. Meanwhile, the Syrians and Iraqis, caught in this vise, are trying to focus Moslem energies toward a common cause, or common enemy."

Ginny Abrahamson muttered, "Israel."

"Who else? The real kicker this time is that both sides are nuclear. Kazakhstan has ninety-four ICMBs we know of. We think they sold three nuclear devices to Iran. We are almost certain Iraq has a nuclear device. We know for certain that they have a missile that they can heave as far as Rome. Pakistan has the bomb, and their fundamentalist regime has new ties with Iraq. Unfortunately, the only lesson the Iraqis learned from Desert Storm was that Islamic countries can't compete with the West without nukes."

Dr. Abrahamson predicted, "Israel won't wait around to absorb the first strike."

"I wouldn't. Would you?" Rolf directed his question to Holtz.

"No."

"You're darn right, you wouldn't. And Israel won't place their fate in the hands of America without some hard evidence that we can and will protect them. They'll want to see more than Patriot and Arrow missiles to defend them from nuclear missiles."

Mark Holtz finished the thought, "So if we don't do

something soon—like in four months—the Israelis might try preemptive strikes?"

"Count on it."

Virginia Abrahamson had family in Israel. "Regardless of who fires the next round, we must neutralize those weapons. Winning will be small consolation to the few survivors." She paused to collect her thoughts. "I'd have to radically down-size the command and control to meet a four-month deployment. Mark's Pebbles are ready with their new micro-Cray, but we haven't even begun to install the gear with the National Command Authority. We haven't tested any software." She climbed out of the hot water and sat on the edge of the jacuzzi.

Rolf agreed, "Then, we'll down-size command and control. We go for the idiot-simple enabled option—the Pebbles stay armed and ready to intercept unless we—I mean, the President—turns them off. Ginny, you don't have to worry about doctrine: arm on impact, arm on launch, arm on warning. You don't have to worry about tying into DEWS, DSP, and other early warning systems, because we'll already be armed. And you don't have to talk to the U-and-S Commands or their airborne command posts. Simplicity also removes the political and technical problems of coordinating with Israel. Also, because we don't turn the system on or off depending on Israel's alert status, we can keep some semblance of neutrality."

"True, but if something happens to communications, those Pebbles would be armed. It could be a nightmare."

"And it will certainly be a nightmare if we don't get the Pebbles up soon."

"True."

"Also, Ginny, you won't need to run any threat-orientation software. You can allow double targeting, and we can still handle a regional war. You need employ only one up-link system. We'll get instructions where to put the up-link computer when we're closer to launch date. And because the Pebbles stay alert, a faulty computer can't shut down our defenses. Consequently, we won't need redundant systems."

Mark Holtz interrupted, "What about civilian launches?"

"They'd better coordinate with us, don't you think?" Rolf stopped to think. "Where was I?"

Ginny prompted him. "I need build only one up-link. Portable, I suppose."

"Right. You can kill the requirement for the AI software that we were going to use to help the Pebbles evade direct threats. Mark, tell her why."

Mark Holtz continued the thought. "Last spring we decided to use stealth material for the Pebble's shroud. To radar, a Pebble would look like a BB traveling 26,000 miles per hour, more than 150 miles above the earth. Radar can't track them. Pebbles rarely emit anything, except when they attack an oncoming missile. Then, it's too late."

Ginny added, "And the firmware already has logic that shifts Pebbles to fill gaps in coverage."

Rolf asked, "So can you do that much in four months?"

"Yes." Ginny ran her fingers through her wet hair. "All the hooks are in the code. I could have that much ready to test in two months. You know we're going to need to rebid the contract."

Rolf quickly corrected her. "No, Ginny. Don't worry about money, time cards, project reports, or any of that stuff. We're in a new ball game, like a Manhattan Project. Green Lid has its own funding; money is my problem. You don't talk to anybody about this—just Mark and me, nobody else. I can't even tell you who else is in the project, but I can tell you that you are the only two Green Lid personnel working in southern California."

Rolf drove a rental car down the coast to La Jolla to Dr. Fenster's lab. In the early seventies, the lab had been one of the largest clean rooms on the West Coast. There, Dr. Fenster had employed more than two hundred and thirty people to build his solar power satellite, or SPS. After the government's rush to alternative power had crawled to a stop, the bucks dried up, and Rolf lost interest in the technology. Soon thereafter, eccentric Fenster, who loathed anything nuclear, fell from grace, having gotten himself arrested demonstrating against the Diablo Canyon nuclear power plant.

Nevertheless, Fenster kept his security clearances and his job. A string of small follow-on contracts from the Navy and a handful of Department of Energy grants kept the lab and the satellite in stasis, plus they gave Fenster a few bucks to tinker with his satellite. Now the SPS staff numbered four. They'd converted the clean room into an expensive warehouse for Fenster's satellite.

Rolf's visit surprised and delighted Dr. Fenster, especially when Rolf volunteered, "I'm considering spending some company money to put the SPS over some remote part of the world—an equatorial site called Cape York, Australia."

"Then you'll be pleased with our progress!" Fenster shivered with excitement under his baggy lab coat. "Australia is good. Good choice, sir!"

"I can't have this idea talked about."

"Mum's the word. . . ."

"We plan to use our own Felix-class spacecraft to put the SPS up. We're limited to 18,000 pounds—12,000 if we send up a crew too. Is that a problem?"

"Have you already forgotten the specs—the weight of the satellite?"

Rolf tried to not look annoyed. "I've had a lot on my mind. Refresh my memory."

"Well forget what you knew about the old SPS: the new SPS is 6,087 pounds lighter!"

"Good. I'm hoping to prove that with Felix, we can cut the cost of launching SPS—or anything else for that matter—by two orders of magnitude. Treat these delicate price data as extremely proprietary, got that?"

"Yes, sir."

"No one can know that we would even consider putting up the SPS. If word gets out, I'll be forced to disprove the rumors by not putting SPS up. You understand that?"

"And that would be a catastrophe. We need to get SPS up and beaming power. I'm starting to see TV commercials for nuclear power—you know what that means!"

Rolf checked the red exit signs. "Right. Tell me about your work. It's been a couple of years."

"Nine, sir. You haven't been here for nine years. We've changed many components. One thing I've done is to make the microwave beam fully adjustable. When I determined that the government had no interest in an alternative to fossil fuels, I interested the Navy and SDIO in an alternative design for the SPS. I made the satellite into a high-energy laser, or HEL burner. I was able to fund my research for another three years with Defense money."

A forklift powered up at the end of the cavernous warehouse, then drove outside. Rolf had missed something. "A what? What did you do with the SDI money?"

"A HEL burner: thirteen megawatts of power in a four-inch beam. You can burn a hole through the deck of an aircraft carrier with it—carve your initials in Tienanmen Square if you want. Anyway, my idea is that the Air Force would deploy a bunch of my HEL-burner satellites, and when people discovered that HEL-burner satellites, like atom bombs, are good for nothing, the government need only build rectennas. . . ."

"Rectenna?"

"Yeah, a rectifier-antenna: a huge ten-acre grid to collect the microwave energy and convert it to electricity. A rectenna is a very thin, ten-acre diode."

"You were telling me about the HEL burner."

"Right. We can focus the microwave beam to kill, or we can spread it out over a rectenna to produce power:

a solar power satellite. Pretty novel idea, isn't it—a weapon that actually does some good."

"Practically unique."

"The real breakthrough was designing the beryllium metal optics to allow me to vary the beam from a four-inch circle out to a six thousand-meter ellipse. We also added a secure-communications link. You can't have the bad guys messing with your HEL burner."

"Of course not."

Dr. Fenster walked around the great folded arms of the satellite. "These new polycrystalline heterojunction panels are light as a feather, four times as efficient, and twice as durable. There's half of your weight savings. Because the panels bend easily, we'll have far fewer mishaps during deployment. Eventually, the cost for the panels will come down. GM is researching polycrystalline panels for its new electric car, and if they go to mass production, our cost to build an SPS will fall dramatically. Even now, we can build and deploy a gigawatt solar power satellite for less than it takes to build a gigawatt coal-fired power plant. Even cheaper, if what you say about Felix launch costs is true."

"Would I lie to you?"

"No, sir, not intentionally." Dr. Fenster reached into his shirt pocket and took out his silver pen to use as a pointer.

Rolf gently inquired, "You're going to give me the full briefing, aren't you?"

Fenster matter-of-factly responded, "Why, yes."

"Then I want to hear all of it. I didn't know you had made so many changes."

Dr. Fenster resumed his presentation. "We've tested this SPS prototype. On the ground, it puts out more than thirteen megawatts of power. The Schottky barrier diode rectenna, which we assembled in a corner of Edwards Air Force Base—here's a picture—significantly reduces the power loss from transmission. Now, we get 94.64

percent of the power to the end user. That's an improvement from our old efficiency of 85 percent. Simply remarkable!

"Some of the credit goes to the beryllium metal optics that focus the beam. We used to get between two and eight percent attenuation of the microwave beam, depending on weather conditions. Cloud cover or atmospheric dust could scatter some of the beam. Now the system automatically adjusts to get the optimum beam focus. The attenuation and scattering remains less than two percent in most conditions."

Rolf wrote a note: thirteen megawatts. He could do a lot with thirteen megawatts—for one, he could make cryogenic fuel. Rolf interrupted with a statement and a question. "My guess is that if I'm going to get the SPS over Cape York. The biggest level area in which to build the rectenna is Temple Bay—on a sandy bottom in shallow salt water. Am I going to run into any objections from the eco-fascists?"

"You shouldn't. The microwave is so dispersed that it has no effect whatsoever. It won't hurt the fish, the reef, the insects, the mammals. . . ."

"Okay. Do you foresee any problems putting the rectenna in the bay?"

"Maintenance would cost more, but that's the only problem. We ran tests underwater. What are the tides like?"

"I never thought about that."

Fenster pushed his glasses to the top of his nose. "We'll work it out." Then he continued with the lecture, "The rectenna changes the microwave to direct current, which travels a short distance—in our case two hundred meters, where we transfer it to sixty cycles alternating current. . . ."

Rolf had his answer. He politely tuned out the rest of Fenster's briefing. He walked though the cavernous warehouse gazing at large metal things: a giant scheduling diagram on a wall, more photos of experiments. Rolf nodded and smiled as if sitting through a slide show of a neighbor's European vacation.

From La Jolla, Rolf drove to San Diego where he dropped off the rental car and took a cab to the docks. In happier days, he and Cynthia had spent time boating, although she loved a brisk sail, and he preferred the luxury of a broad-beamed cruise. They had argued the merits of their nautical preferences. To prove his point, Rolf had given Cynthia a 62-foot cruiser that he christened *Terra Firma*. Cynthia retaliated by giving Rolf a 48-foot sloop that she christened, *Terra Incognita*. They docked the pair of boats in adjacent slips, side by side at the San Diego Yacht Club. For old times' sake, Rolf toured the docks. He thought he might spend the night on *Terra Firma*. From a distance he saw the cruiser's brightwork and polished chrome, and he knew that the maintenance was good. She'd be dry inside. When he walked to her side he saw a plain red and white sign—SOLD.

"The bitch sold her boat!" He went into the marina office and sold his.

Chapter 9

"I'm really glad you're going back to the States with me." Bobby meant it. He spoke little French, so he was happy to have Cynthia make the arrangements. She booked seats on the Concorde—an easy five hours to Dulles. She packed for both of them, and called the cab. As she tucked a few papers in her leather briefcase, she mused, "I'm intrigued. Smurch managed to tank BAP's stock another eight bucks."

"We had our share of problems at the Rixeyville test flight."

"Now that's an understatement! Someday Rolf's grandstanding will be the death of us all. Anyway, he vindicated my decision to divest a fourth of my BAP stock last month."

"How'd you know to sell?"

"Dumb luck, this time." Cynthia grabbed her briefcase when the taxi beeped. "Never underestimate the power of dumb luck."

"I wish I'd sold mine. What are you going to do with the rest of it?"

"I don't know. But I'm going to find out. That's part of my reason for flying back with you. Most likely, I'll dump it and sell short."

"Why?"

"Oh, I've got this funny feeling that Rolf's out of control, and BAP's stock has broken below a two-hundred-day trend line. . . ."

"Should I sell my stock?" Bobby asked.

"I just trade for my own account—I don't give advice. You see, Bobby, I'm not always right. But unlike Rolf, I know that, and I can afford to make mistakes. You can't."

Bobby did not relish getting back on a plane. His stomach remembered the last flight, even if he *had* put it out of his mind. "An airplane," he said, "is just a Petri dish with wings." He took two Dramamine and drank a wine spritzer while they waited to board.

Cindy wore a bulky wool skirt, a loose cotton blouse and her favorite, old, brown leather jacket—her good luck token. She looked like a graduate student who could afford to fly the Concorde.

Tyler waited till the plane took off before he said, "Did I tell you that Rolf will be out of town for a few days?"

Cindy turned to look out the window. "I would have come back anyway. I've got people to see in New York. I might catch a flight to Tucson and see Paul. There's more to do in the States than spend Friday night with old Smurch."

"I should have mentioned it. Anyway, Rolf's on the West Coast for a couple of days. We expect him back Saturday about 4:00 PM."

The champagne cart stopped by their seats. Bobby took two flutes and handed one to Cynthia. She observed Bobby over the rim of her glass as she drank. Bobby gazed back. The light from the window cast shadows around her high cheekbones, and her uncomfortably bright eyes looked into his. Cynthia turned away from Tyler to face the window and the stark blue sky. The Dramamine and champagne lulled him to sleep. The next thing he knew, he felt a jolt, a pat on the cheek, and he heard Cynthia's voice. "We're on the ground."

Tyler drove Cynthia to her house—part of his door-to-door service. The late autumn sun dropped a dim curtain of light behind the Blue Ridge Mountains, and a dry chill crept into their bones as they sat on the car's cold leather seats. Tyler took the back roads through Herndon, past horse farms toward the Bernard estate. In front of them, an old truck struggled under a load of pumpkins. Impatiently he looked for a straight piece of road where he might pass. Cynthia asked, "Would you kindly relax, I'm in no hurry to get home—certainly not inclined to take risks."

At last, Tyler turned off the state highway onto fresh blacktop. A simple black-on-white sign advised PRIVATE DRIVE. He drove another hundred feet to a massive iron gate barring entrance to the road, where he aimed a small remote control toward the trees to his left, and pressed a series of buttons. Pale artificial light came from sources hidden in the tall trees. The gate split away from the fence and rolled slowly to the left. He waved in the general direction of the hidden camera and drove the car onto the secure grounds.

The black asphalt driveway snaked through the trees. Exhausted maidenhair ferns lined the drive, nipped and burned from autumn's first frost. Patches of Christmas ferns boldly showed their hardier foliage. Dried leaves skittered behind the car. Tyler drove slowly, then slower still, as he eased his fat Ford Bronco over large speed bumps that Cynthia had forced Rolf to install soon after Rolf struck and killed a raccoon with his Mercedes.

When they drove out of the woods, they found themselves facing a Georgian mansion, a grander version of the Carlyle House. Cynthia fumbled through her purse to find a single key on a small ring, which she used to unlock the door. Tyler followed her in just long enough to show her the new combination on the security system. Then, Tyler brought her solitary bag from the back seat, and bid Cynthia good-night with a weary smile. She replied,

"Good night, Bobby. Call me tomorrow, when you know Rolf's schedule."

Bobby sped home to his wife, Mariam, pausing only for Cynthia's speed bumps and the gate.

Cynthia quickly surmised from the quiet that the household help had quit the main quarters for their small apartments. She carried her bag to the guest bedroom where she slept under a portrait of her paternal grandfather, Stephen Dubois. The mantel clock chimed eight times as she closed her eyes—early for Washington, but midnight in Paris.

She rose early, hours ahead of the alarm clock, hours before dawn. She wrapped herself in a man-size terrycloth bathrobe (each guest room had a set of towels, toiletries and a bathrobe), slinked down to the kitchen, steeped tea, peeled a grapefruit, and wrote her to-do list.

She took hot tea and a towel to the lap pool, a great wall of glass brick, blue-and-green tile around the cement deck, and exotic plants everywhere—her favorite room. Exercise always topped her list. She pulled her swim goggles from a deep pocket, then wriggled out of the bathrobe and tossed it onto a white wicker chair. Cynthia tensed, having thought she'd seen someone on the patio, but looking again saw the reflection of her firm body in the sliding glass door. She'd remembered her goggles but forgotten her swimsuit, and she could hear her mother now. "Cindy, you always overdress! Too much jewelry! Too many accessories!" What the heck, she'd wear the goggles anyway.

Cynthia lowered herself into the cold water: 71 degrees, a brisk temperature for laps. The fine hairs on her forearms rose, and gooseflesh textured her smooth skin. Quickly she adjusted her goggles, then churned through the water. She counted each flip-turn toward her goal of sixty-four lengths—one mile.

Cynthia finished her laps and prepared to spring out of the water onto the deck. She peeled the goggles from her wet face and saw a small woman wearing a gray smock standing in the doorway. The woman, slack-jawed and bewildered, held an armload of morning newspapers.

Cynthia demanded, "How long have you been standing there?"

The young woman clutched the newspapers to her chest like a shield. Already, the conversation was beyond the woman's grasp of English, but she understood her accuser's tone. She stammered, "I come do work. Just now. Who are you? Why are you in Mr. Bernard's house not have clothes on?" The house servant began to sense some advantage standing on dry land, fully clothed.

"I am Mrs. Bernard."

"Oh, I much sorry!" The woman looked for an escape. She clutched the papers tightly, then stood like one of the exotic plants on the blue-and-green tile.

"Where's Mrs. Bergen? Surely she told you I was coming?"

"*Que?* Oh! Mrs. Bergen, she no come here till ten o'clock."

"Very well. Please go. I want to get out of the pool. I want to get dressed. I'm cold."

The woman turned and fled toward the kitchen. Cynthia wrapped herself in the thick bathrobe and grabbed her towel. She retired to the guest bedroom where she could take a warm shower and dress in peace. She wondered who hired the young Latin girl, Rolf or Margaret. Certainly Rolf.

Once dressed, Cynthia returned to her to-do list, crossing out the word "exercise" and adding the word "swimsuit." After drying her hair and applying minimal makeup, she toured the main floor of her old house, conscious and slightly amused that the young woman had scurried to the lower level. It pleased Cynthia to find her shiny black Jaguar convertible where she'd left it. Even the keys were in the ignition where she'd left them. The engine started on the first turn of the key. The odometer showed several hundred more miles. Rolf had taken good care of her machine—Rolf always took good care of machines.

Cynthia put the top down and drove her car out into the crisp autumn air. She caught herself speeding, rather used to French and German superhighways. She sailed down Georgetown Pike and found her way to the George Washington Parkway, where maples and elms held onto their last red and gold leaves. The late-changing oaks broadcast their auburn hues. She first stopped at her bank to get some American cash, then drove to a shopping mall nestled next to the Pentagon, where she bought a swimsuit, a pair of walking shoes, and several pairs of cotton socks.

She had a strong urge to call some old friends, but reconsidered. She'd changed much in her four years as an expatriate, becoming more taciturn. She used to get well-intentioned letters from old friends, kindly chastising her for leaving old Smurch, who was so lonely, so unhappy, so blah-blah-blah . . . . She too often replied in cold, formal tones: Thanks for your letter and unsolicited advice; thinking of you, too; Sincerely, Cynthia. She could hardly ring them up now without picking an old scab.

She decided to call Chip. Then she decided against it. She decided to call Bobby. No, she should call Mariam instead. Even if Bobby answers, she should talk to Mariam first. She pressed a memory-dial number on her car phone. Mariam Tyler answered the phone, and Cynthia effectively invited herself to dinner. "Mariam, could I take you and Bobby to dinner tonight—my treat?" And Mariam predictably countered, "Why don't you come to our house? Six o'clock?"

Cynthia accepted.

At six o'clock sharp, Cynthia knocked on the Tylers' door. She held a large bouquet of flowers. A tall, adolescent girl with a blond ponytail opened the door and grinned.

"Oh!" The girl giggled. "I thought you were my date, but he's never on time. And he never brings flowers."

"Then you should get rid of him." Cynthia returned the smile, but the girl, intimidated by the older woman's harsh advice, backed into the foyer, beckoning Mrs. Bernard to follow. "You must be Ginger."

"Yes, I am."

"Please take these flowers to your mother." The girl took the flowers and nervously looked past Cynthia through the open door, hoping to intercept her date halfway up the walk before the important older woman could pass on more indelicate advice.

Cynthia, unaware of the girl's anxiety, corralled her back into the kitchen. She met Bobby, who stepped in from the deck with a beer bottle in one hand and barbecue tongs in the other. "I didn't hear you come in."

"Ginger—" Cynthia turned to thank the girl, but she'd already skulked away.

Bobby set his beer down and wiped his hand on his apron. "Let me pour you a drink. I made martinis for Mariam."

"A martini sounds wonderful, but no vegetables, please. Where is Mariam?"

"She's in the pantry hunting candles or mint jelly or something."

Mariam appeared on cue with a small green jar in hand. She set the jar on the counter. She paused to take the measure of the beautiful woman in her kitchen— the simple calico dress, low cut, gathered in the back to accentuate narrow hips, and flat stomach; modest makeup: close-filed, practical nails, the smallest trace of mascara, eye shadow, and rouge. Cynthia didn't need it. Her hair fell loose to her shoulders. And she wore the most unpretentious jewelry found on a rich woman: gold loops and a thin gold necklace, no watch, and an emerald ring with a fairly good size stone on her right hand. By any comparison, Mariam had overdressed, and she'd been taught always to dress a notch lower than the guest.

Mariam smiled. "You look lovely, Cynthia." She hauled her guest into the living room. "Bobby, dear, would you bring our drinks?"

Tyler brought the small pitcher of martinis from the freezer and dug another beer out of the refrigerator for himself. He found the women chatting, sitting side by side on the long sofa. Bobby sat on the navy blue upholstered rocking chair and deposited his bottle on the coffee table. Without a word, Mariam reached over the table, picked up a coaster, and flipped it to Bobby. The coaster bounced off his chest and into his lap. He, without comment, smeared the water ring across the polished cherrywood with his hand, dropped the little wood coaster, cork side down, and trapped it beneath his beer bottle—*thwack!* Cynthia leaned back into her corner of the couch. "Mariam was just asking me why I came back—to patch things up with dear old Smurch? Or what?"

"Mariam!" Bobby issued each syllable of her name in a low but threatening tone. "It's none of our business."

"Oh, it's all right." Cynthia defended Mariam. "It's not like you two are prying strangers."

"Prying friends, more like it." Bobby grumbled.

"If I were Mariam, I'd be justifiably curious. Rolf sends you to Paris to coax me back to Virginia. I come. Mariam draws the logical conclusion." Cynthia pivoted to face Mariam. "Rolf and I were never meant to be."

"Why don't you divorce him?"

"Mariam!" Bobby got up. "Oh, what's the use. I'm going out to cook the lamb chops." And he left.

Cynthia sipped her martini. "Divorce would cause more problems than it would solve. The Church would never annul the marriage, so . . ." She stopped midsentence, set her drink down. "And there are some advantages. Rolf is still generous with his contacts; I in turn, provide some financial stability. And Paul doesn't have to worry about getting a stepmother or stepfather thrown into the equation."

"Paul is what? Almost thirty? He's on his own now."

"Twenty-eight next September fourth. And no, Paul's not on his own. When you inherit a large family business, you're never on your own. And, Mariam, Rolf was thirty-four when his dad gave his mom the heave-ho: never quite got over it. Never. So I give you a bit of advice: Don't have this conversation with Rolf." She picked up her martini again.

Tyler's voice boomed from the next room. "Mariam? Check the rice, the squash, and make the salad!" The door slammed to punctuate the command.

"Looks like I've got work to do. Go out and keep the grump company. He thinks I meddle." Mariam led the way back to the kitchen. "I do take a personal interest in my friends."

"As do I." Cynthia took her drink and joined Bobby on the deck. Smoke poured from the seams on the gas grill. Bobby looked over his shoulder to where Mariam washed lettuce. Cynthia asked, "Should I go back in to help Mariam? Is it awkward, me being out here with you?"

"No. Mariam never says a word: Not about going to Paris to get you, not about staying in your apartment . . ."

"She said plenty." Cynthia sipped her martini and smiled.

"What do you mean?"

"Forget it."

Bobby opened the grill lid. The flames leapt high consuming fat from the lamb chops, and Bobby busily shuffled them right, then left, to dampen the conflagration. He asked, "Speaking of awkward, how's it going at the Bernard house?"

"I haven't run into Margaret Bergen yet, if that's what you mean."

"That's right. She used to work for you . . . ."

"I fired her, did you know that?"

"No, I thought she quit."

"She didn't quit. Of course, in those days, she was Margaret O'Hare. Soon thereafter, I left for Paris. She got a divorce, took her maiden name back, and Rolf rehired her to run the household."

"That *is* awkward."

"Worse for her than for me, I figure. I don't really care anymore how Rolf runs his life."

"Really?"

"Yes, Bobby. You see, the opposite of love is not hate: it's indifference. I cope much better now. Besides, I won't be around that much. I have some errands. I go to New York in a couple of days."

"Rolf's coming back tomorrow. I think he wants to make peace."

Cynthia swallowed a mouthful of her gin. Her blood rose until she realized that Bobby was just curious, perhaps concerned. She said, "Well, to be forewarned is to be forearmed."

Bobby turned the lamb chops and looked at Cynthia for more explanation. So she continued, "I just finished this conversation with Mariam; you should've stayed and listened. I'm not having this conversation twice in one night." She poured the rest of her gin over the deck railing. "I'd better cut down. Gin makes me talk too much."

She marched off the deck into the kitchen. Through the french doors, Bobby saw Cynthia smiling, chatting with Mariam, helping set dishes on the table.

After dinner, they took coffee in the living room. The phone rang and Bobby rose quickly saying, "I've been expecting a call." He walked into the study and grabbed the receiver on the fourth ring, just beating the answering machine. "Hello?"

"It's me. Tom. Got a minute?"

"Sure. Hold a second." Tyler pushed the hold button, then called into the living room. "I gotta take this call. Excuse me for five minutes." He punched the first line and spoke in soft tones. "We've got to make this crisp. We've got Rolf's wife over here for dinner."

"Mrs. Bernard? What the hell she doing at your house?"

"General, have you forgotten? They're friends of mine. I was best man at their wedding."

"Right. Don't get confused Bob. Don't forget whose side you're on."

"I'm on our side. This deal is good for Rolf, you, me, and the country. There are some win-win scenarios, you know."

"Sure. But when push comes to shove, don't forget whose side you're on." Tyler heard the steel edge in Tom Marshall's voice.

"Don't worry about me. Hell, I'm more worried about *you*. You have us way out on the limb. How do I know you won't just saw it off if things go south?"

"Bob, you know damned well, we'll saw it off: That's why you're running the operation and not me. That's why you're getting the big bucks and not me. I didn't call you up to discuss my theory of covert operations. Just tell me: Are we on or off?"

"We're on."

"Good. We've kept it contained within our threesome."

"We're contained on this side as well." Tyler looked at the small green light on the little black box next to his phone. "Which reminds me. Somebody's got a tap on Cynthia Bernard's phone in Paris. It's not ours, is it?"

"Can't be, but I'll check it out."

"Do that."

"Bob. One more thing. Scuttlebutt has it that the Administration has asked the Justice Department to turn up the heat on BAP, Inc. Lord only knows what they'll do, but for starters, you can expect surveillance. Be careful. Be damned careful."

"I understand."

"I'll see you at Fort Marcey park next Thursday."

"Two o'clock."

"Better make it four o'clock. And Bob . . ."

"Yes, sir?"

"Don't ever forget whose side you're on." Click.

Bobby set the receiver down and muttered, "Bunch of paranoids."

Tyler returned to the living room to hear Mariam tell Cynthia, "Wood sculpture keeps me busy. I'm almost finished making a replica of Tilman Riemenschneider's St. Elizabeth—one of the two Riemenschneider's outside Europe. It's pretty close. And I volunteer as a docent at the National Gallery to get access to poor old worm-eaten Elizabeth. Come down and I'll give you an after-hours tour of the LaFarge exhibit."

"I love stained glass. I'll call you and set a date." Cynthia got up. "I've got to go. My body still thinks I'm in France— I don't want to fall asleep on your couch."

Later that evening, as Mariam put the dirty dishes in the machine, Bobby chastised, "I can't believe you grilled Cynthia about her marital problems. It's none of our business."

"Yeah, but you know their story. I don't. I'd like to know a little more about the competition."

"The what?"

"You heard me, the competition."

"You don't think I . . ."

"I'd know if you did. But Cynthia's got her eye on you, so that makes Cynthia my business. What's the real story with Cynthia Bernard?"

"Mariam . . ."

"She didn't invite herself over to dinner to see me."

Tyler could see no way out of this marital conference. He brushed past Mariam to get a cold beer from the refrigerator, then sat down at the kitchen table. Mariam brought her cup of coffee and sat across from him. "Just consider this one of your debriefings."

Bobby took a deep breath. "I met Cynthia at her

wedding. Rolf had met her less than three months before in Hawaii and got her pregnant. Rolf found himself up to his neck in a mess. His mom howled entrapment and wanted Cynthia and the baby disposed of. Cynthia was raised a strict Catholic. . . ."

"Apparently not strict enough . . ."

"You want to hear this or not?"

"Sorry."

"Cynthia made it clear. She would have the baby, and raise it by herself if necessary. Her parents backed her. Old Vincent Bernard just about threw Rolf's mom out of the mansion. Nobody was going to kill his grandchild if he could help it. His grandchild was not going to be raised a bastard if he could help it. The old man told Rolf to marry Cynthia—or else. I know all of this because Rolf laid his case before me and asked my opinion."

"Really? What did you tell him?"

"Well, sure as anything, the Dubois heiress wasn't after his money. She was not some common wench Rolf could buy off or cast aside. And Vincent Bernard wouldn't allow it anyway. I told him to follow orders. Besides, Rolf showed me a picture of Cynthia. Frankly, I didn't see why it was such a hard decision. So Rolf called Hawaii, asked for Cynthia's hand, and the Dubois family ordered Cynthia to marry Rolf."

"So how was the wedding?"

"Huh? Oh, a great show—lovely stone cathedral in Wilmington, tents behind the Dubois mansion, white helicopter to fly the newlyweds away. The Duboises and Bernards collaborated on revisionist history: Cynthia would conceive in Bermuda."

"Paul knows?"

"Paul can do the math—of course he knows. Cynthia transferred to the University of Pennsylvania for her junior year. She bought a brownstone on Manning Street near Rittenhouse Square. She hired a nanny and went to school. Vincent kept Rolf on the road learning the ropes at BAP.

Rolf made it to Philadelphia every two or three weeks for a conjugal visit. When Cynthia graduated, she decided to stay for her masters in international finance at Wharton. To say the least, her decision infuriated Rolf."

"*You* would have dragged *me* out of there by my hair."

"Or maybe I would have moved to Philadelphia. But nobody tells Cynthia what to do, or where to go. Nobody." Bobby broke his monologue to toss the empty beer bottle into the trash. "Then Rolf met Ann, a voluptuous woman closer to his age. Now, I don't know what Ann did for a living. I don't know what happened between Ann and Rolf—maybe nothing; maybe everything. But somebody sent Cynthia an envelope full of black and white photos—candid shots of Ann with Rolf, poolside at the Eden Roc, Miami; a hot tub at Steamboat Springs, Colorado; in deck chairs on some cruise ship in the Caribbean."

"Hmm . . . how do you know that?"

"Rolf wanted me to find out where the photos came from."

"Did you?"

"Hell no. You'd just had Jack and we got orders for Germany. And I wasn't a gumshoe."

"So what did Cynthia do?"

"She forgave Rolf, or so he tells me. Who can be sure? She came into her inheritance at age twenty-five, moved back to McLean, bought the big house, then started a regional brokerage firm. She bought the ashes of a small investment company that collapsed in 1975, and renamed it Dubois Securities. She took advantage of Jimmy Carter's inflation and interest rates, and started the Dubois Money Market Fund. Later, in the eighties, she started various mutual funds. Dubois Securities grew into a major regional broker. She and Rolf tried to do some business together—a big mistake. Apparently, Cynthia tried to tell Rolf how to run BAP's finances; he tried to get her to finance some BAP's acquisitions. She balked."

Mariam observed, "They are both too competitive for their own good."

"Perhaps. Rolf wanted more kids right away. Cynthia wanted to wait. Cynthia's biological clock finally told her it was now or never. She decided to do right by her second and last child. She sold her interest in Dubois Securities— for a fortune, I might add. She got off the pill, but nothing happened."

"She must have been thirty-six. She was pushing it."

"It was a moot point. Cynthia had serious uterine fibroids, which required a hysterectomy. She could never have the second child. Rolf blamed her for waiting, and with a spectacular flare of insensitivity, seized the opportunity to tell her she deserved what she got. There was a fight—the details I don't know—but Cynthia left. She took an apartment at Harborplace in Georgetown for a year, and did nothing much. Rumor had it, she had a part-time roommate—a football player, I think. Then she took her fortune and went to Luxembourg to start her International Investment Bank of Dubois."

"She just left Paul?"

"By then Paul had started at MIT. Now Cynthia lives in Paris with her antiques, a semi-tame tabby cat, and she keeps a retired tennis pro in another apartment for her amusement. Rolf talks like he wants her back, but that would take a small miracle. Now you know what I know."

Mariam came around the table and sat in Bobby's lap. "Honey. . . ."

"Yes?"

"I still have that rusty straight razor hidden away."

"I know."

"Let's go to bed." Mariam pecked him on the cheek.

Chapter 10

Across the country on a sultry San Diego night, Rolf Bernard boarded a plane for the all-night flight to the East Coast. The big jet climbed above the desert, then slipped smoothly over mountains, thirty-seven thousand feet above forest and plain. He rattled the ice in his fresh scotch, and he wondered how it would be with Cynthia. *How have our lives grown so far apart? Had it all been so bad, that she should spurn my interests, live in Paris, sell her boat? She might not even be reliable for a proxy fight. And how does she explain our separation to her friends? Surely, I came off worse in the telling.*

The separation never ceased to be an embarrassment. Rolf hadn't seen his wife since the previous Christmas, when he lured her back from Paris with a house full of her blood relatives. Even then, she embarrassed him by taking the best guest bedroom for herself, forcing one brother and sister-in-law to stay at the Sheraton.

Rolf didn't like to read on planes. Fiction bored him. Nonfiction made him airsick. He liked to gaze out the window and think. Tomorrow, he'd see Cindy again. Would they have the same argument? Should he buy flowers? For certain he'd bring her up to date on the goings-on with beleaguered BAP, and he'd save the only good news for last: Paul's success at Marana. He'd never trust Cynthia with Project Green Lid.

He dreaded the first minutes alone with Cynthia—loose canon at best, malevolent at worst. Rolf swallowed the rest of his scotch, twisted the top off another miniature green bottle, and dumped its contents over the dwindling ice. A man was worthless at the end of the red-eye. One drink, more or less, couldn't hurt.

Again, Rolf gazed through his porthole into the night sky. He could see a sliver of moon rising. A few frost crystals caught the light. Frost reminded him of Christmas. Christmas reminded him of the first time he'd met Cynthia—strangely juxtaposed thoughts. There was no frost then.

After his tour in Vietnam, Rolf found himself marooned on Hawaii. The few buddies he knew at Hickam had brought their fiancées over for a little tropical R&R. But the lovebirds fled to the romantic seclusion of Maui or the Big Island.

Because everyone had taken Christmas leave, Rolf found himself stuck as duty officer four out of the next seven nights. The Air Force didn't love him any more, because two months earlier he'd turned down an assignment to instruct pilots for Tactical Air Command. Rolf had hit that fork in the road where he either stayed in the Air Force, or went back to BAP to earn his spurs. No contest: He'd done his patriotic duty as a captain in the Air Force, and now it was time to take his place as a captain of industry. He told the Air Force that he planned to leave military service as soon as he had fulfilled his obligation. Air Force Personnel took a cold attitude. "Who needs a short-timer? Might as well stick him on the duty roster." And they did. He joined the pool of short-timer gofers.

For the next three months Rolf found himself stuck in a holding pattern, nothing but fog below, and he was low on fuel. Pasty-faced clerks in Personnel chained him to a desk in the Material Airlift Command, Hawaii, where Rolf awaited orders for his terminal assignment in the States, and discharge. He inspected cargo tie-downs in the Globemasters, monitored airfield security, and proofread maintenance request forms going out under the base commander's signature.

The plunge from cockpit to desk practically rattled his teeth. He took some consolation in knowing that he'd soon find himself building the planes instead of babysitting them. He'd heard that the service sometimes tried to remotivate outgoing officers by treating them like dirt— another case of poor logic wrapped in a bad habit. Rolf didn't know whether to take it personally, or just wait out his last four months. In any case, he didn't want to be in tropical Hawaii on Christmas Eve—monsoon season. But there he was, wearing slacks, sandals, and the loudest luau shirt (bird of paradise motif) at the Hickam Air Base officers' club.

Rolf met Cynthia at a Christmas party there. He had gone to the officers' club Christmas party, because that's what pilots do on Christmas Eve: eat, drink, and forget that home is half a world away.

The party drew a large crowd—men with short hair in luau shirts, women with stiff hairdos, wearing moo-moos and high heels. The band played "White Christmas," "Mele Kalikimaka is the Thing to Say," and other peppy tunes. A blender whirred in the next room. Filipino waitresses, wearing skimpy red velvet skirts trimmed with puffy white fake fur, ferried trays of frozen drinks throughout the room. A wreath of ti leaves hung over the bar. A fifteen-foot spruce, flown in by the Alaska 55th Air Wing, stood above the crowd, decorated with twinkling lights, glass balls, shells, tinsel, and beads. A left-leaning angel looked down from the tree, onto the crowd. A crèche lay beneath a canopy of hibiscus flowers, on a table next to an eight-foot grimacing tiki carving. One was drawn for a closer look at Caspar, the black Magi. His paint had chipped, his turban rubbed round. He looked like one of the local women stepping off the beach in a bright floral robe, with a towel around her head. Nothing looked out of place to Rolf—or to anyone who'd spent a Christmas in Vietnam.

Rolf saw Cynthia at the buffet table and followed her from platter to platter. He told her his name, but she didn't reciprocate. While he picked shrimp, bits of teriyaki chicken and meatballs, the young woman chose cubes of mango, pineapple, papaya, and lichee nuts.

"Are you here alone?" he ventured.

Cynthia picked her mai tai up from the buffet table and replied, "You must be a pilot."

Rolf backed off. "What's the matter? You have a bad flight to Hawaii?"

"No, but my daddy warned me about pilots." She turned to spear another piece of pineapple. Her long black braid brushed Rolf's arm.

"Your daddy? What does he do?"

"He's a pilot."

"I'll bet he's a swell guy. We'd get along just fine."

"He's a Marine pilot."

"I'm flexible." Rolf pursued the woman, but didn't crowd her.

"Well, he used to be a pilot. He got hurt in Korea, but the Marines kept him. He hasn't flown anything since 1951, but he wears his combat wings, so he's a pilot."

"What's your name?" Rolf asked again.

"Cynthia Dubois."

"Well, Cynthia, I know you came here alone, because there's no guy around here staring me down. Don't you know it's dangerous coming all by yourself into this nest of pilots?"

"Hmm . . ." She raised an eyebrow. "Actually, I ducked out of my daddy's Christmas party. He's the Commandant of Marines at Pearl Harbor—the law, so to speak. God love him, he throws a dull party—Victorian England motif, dress uniforms, small brass ensemble—the ice-angel carving on the buffet table was having more fun than anybody there, so I ducked out. I heard about the party here, so here I am. Can I have another one of these mai tai things?"

Rolf obliged her, returning with a pair of drinks. Wanting to avoid the subject of pilots, Rolf kept the conversation moving with more questions about Cynthia. She, in turn, enjoyed the attention of the mature gentleman, who for once could talk about something other than himself. And she had ideas, being a rising junior at Brown University and a little drunk.

The food ran low. Cynthia set her last mai tai on a cluttered silver tray. "You want to get some air?"

"Lead the way!" Rolf followed her to her car—her mom's car, a Mustang convertible.

Cynthia knew the nooks and crannies around Pearl Harbor. She drove through Hickam's back gate to Fort Kamehameha. They drove beneath a canopy of banyan trees and coconut palms, turned onto a crushed-coral side road, then out onto a pier, where they sat in her mom's car and watched a sliver of moon gleaming over the mouth of Pearl Harbor. The waves broke on the reefs a thousand meters off shore. Behind them, a wall of vegetation hid the old officers' quarters, built at the turn of the century.

The dilapidated pier had once belonged to coastal artillery, who during World War II, had run a great chain across the narrow mouth of Pearl Harbor to keep Japanese subs out. Now, in the daytime, the pier belonged to kids with fishing poles.

"Very pretty out here. Very peaceful." Rolf stretched his legs as far as he could. "How'd you ever find this place?"

"Last summer I dated a guy. He used to bring me here, and we—" Cynthia turned, the faint moonlight flashed from her white teeth "—parked."

She slumped down in her seat and looked over the

Pacific, watching the moon slip behind tall clouds blowing in from the west. Rolf leaned over and kissed her. She didn't encourage him; neither did she reject him. "Let's just sit here a minute."

Rolf got out of the car and walked the length of the pier—made of concrete, creosoted pilings, and decked with crumbling asphalt. At the end of the pier he saw sun-dried fish guts and scorch marks where kids or fishermen had built a small fire. He stood at the end of the pier, his stomach churning with anticipation. *I'll bet she's watching, amused.* Then he felt a pair of small hands on his shoulders, and he turned. She rubbed up against his chest and raised her lips. Rolf kissed her and held her tight, pulling her hips into his. Nothing jiggled on this woman: her arms, back, legs, stomach, hips, breasts, lips—everything taut.

Cynthia broke the clutch, breathing heavily. "Oh, my." She stepped back, "We mustn't get carried away."

"Why the hell not?" He laughed and reached for her.

"I've got to go to midnight mass."

"You're kidding. You go drinking till ten—I'll bet you're not even eighteen. Then you come out here necking till eleven, then rush off to mass? What are you possibly going to do there, sit in a pew and daydream about sex?"

The stiff Pacific breeze and Rolf's insulting tone cleared her head. "Not tonight, flyboy."

She turned and walked back to the car. Rain clouds blustered from the west and swept away the moon and stars. The wind picked up a small chop in the Pearl Harbor Channel. Salt spray left white specks on the wind shield. "You'd better hurry up, Mr. Bernard. I'm the last ride you'll get back to Hickam."

Rolf rolled his eyes. "Sorry, Cynthia." He added sarcastically, "It would appear I got my signals crossed."

"I forgot about mass. Help me put the top up, will ya?"

Fat rain drops smacked the canvas top as they struggled to snap in down before the deluge. They barely made it, jumping into the car as a wall of rain pressed from the west, drenching everything.

"So, you're Catholic?"

"Very."

"So's my family, especially my dad. He's a fanatic."

"So's mine."

"Maybe I could go with you to midnight mass?"

"What are you going to daydream about?"

"You, babe."

"Forget it. I don't like pushy men." Cynthia drove him to the bachelor officers' quarters, where Rolf tried to kiss her—one last Christmas Eve kiss.

"I told you, I don't like pushy men!" She swiftly pressed the palm of her hand against his face, and shoved him toward his door. She laughed—a full-throated laugh. Rolf got out onto the sidewalk beneath a streetlight. The rain poured, soaking Rolf in seconds. Cynthia drove away. In the rearview mirror, she saw her mature gentleman staring back at her taillights, waving his fist, and yelling something—he told her later that he'd yelled, "Merry Christmas!"

Rolf slogged his way into the BOQ, leaving puddles down the hall. The TV in the next room flickered, the sound turned too low to hear. He fell asleep imagining what might have been, had the evening gone according to plan. He woke up the next morning expecting to see Cynthia nuzzled by his side, his dreams had been so real.

Rolf spent a string of days and nights as staff duty officer, checking arms rooms, safes, fuel storage, enlisted barracks, and the NCO club. He researched the whereabouts of the Dubois quarters and their phone number. During the light of day, he resolved not to call Cynthia. During the warm, humid nights, Rolf imagined her coming back to surrender that kiss, and maybe more.

He dialed the Dubois phone number, and Mrs. Dubois answered. *"Mele kalikimaka and a hauoli makahiki hou."*

"Wrong number." Rolf hung up and dialed again.

"Hello? Did you just call a second ago?"

"I don't know. I don't think so . . ."

"I said 'Merry Christmas' and 'Happy New Year' in Hawaiian."

"Oh! I didn't know! Gee, I'm sorry. I'm Captain Rolf Bernard. I didn't know who I'd called. I was trying to get in touch with Cynthia Dubois."

"I'm Mrs. Dubois. She drove to Fort Ruger to play tennis. Can I take a message?"

"Yes, ma'am. Tell her Rolf Bernard called. I'll try again later."

Mrs. Dubois wondered aloud, "Rolf Bernard? That's such a familiar name. We know the Bernards from St. Louis. They have a son named Rolf."

"That's me." Rolf felt his luck turn. "I'm Vince Bernard's son."

"What a small world. We know your family. My husband's brother—Dubois Plastics—does a fair amount of business with BAP. I met your father once at the Eisenhower farm."

"Oh! The Dubois family. Cynthia didn't let on."

"Neither did you. Imagine—Vince Bernard's son serving as a captain in the Air Force."

"Well, I had a choice, get drafted in the Army and walk, or take a commission in the Air Force and fly. I chose to fly. It added three years to my hitch, but worth it. And I got to meet your daughter."

Mrs. Dubois mewed, "Nice of you to say so."

"But I'm leaving the service in seventy-two days. I've got to take my place at BAP, or BAP will pass me by."

"I hope you'll come to our little New Year's Eve party. Maybe we can provide some of that home cheer you've been missing. I hope you're not already engaged."

The word "engaged" set him back, until he remembered that her generation meant "socially committed," nuptials not implied. "Not a thing to do, really. I'd love to come. I had called to ask Cynthia out, but I wouldn't take her away from your New Year's Eve party—especially when

I can meet you and Colonel Dubois in the bargain." *Boy, he laid it on thick.*

But it worked. Mrs. Dubois rejoiced. Cynthia, her eldest and wildest child, had brought some dreadful men by the house: rakes, scoundrels, fortune hunters, plus a few insipid, idle rich ones. Now, perhaps, Cynthia might show some interest in a man with social standing, manners, breeding, and promise.

"Mrs. Dubois, what's the dress?"

"Casual. Sports coat, four-in-hand tie. Some of Colonel Dubois's men will show up in mess jacket, but to tell the truth, I like to see the young men in civilian attire from time to time."

Cynthia returned from a long afternoon of tennis. She took the news of Rolf's invitation well, which surprised Mrs. Dubois. Cynthia usually howled "Mother!" whenever her mother tried a hand at matchmaking. This time Cynthia merely humphed and replied, "We'll just see how he handles Daddy. Rolf's an Air Force pilot."

"Not for long, dear. He's getting out in 72 days." Mrs. Dubois cooed, "You don't know the first thing about young Rolf Bernard."

Cynthia smirked. "Maybe a little more than you, Mother."

"Oh yes? Did you know that he is practically heir to the largest airplane manufacturer in the world?"

"Mom, he's a captain in the Air Force."

"For the time being, yes. There's a war on, you know. What should he be? A draft dodger?"

Cynthia paused to assess the information. "He didn't mention his family to me."

"Maybe he'd rather you like him as a human being. That speaks well for his character. I've seen too many spoiled, rich men try to bowl over a young lady with their prospective wealth."

"He's not bad-looking." Cynthia cut her eyes around.

"That's nice. Mind you, I'm not pushing young Bernard on you, but you ought to mix more with his class of people. The Bernards, like the Duboises, move in circles beyond those of ordinary folk. You'll need to bear these things in mind when you start courting."

"Yes, mother." Cynthia had the urge to giggle. Start courting, indeed. She thought her poor mother suffered from arrested development, stuck in a Victorian world.

On New Year's Eve, Rolf presented a bouquet of flowers to Mrs. Dubois when she opened the door. Mrs. Dubois promptly handed to flowers to a young Filipino wearing a white waistcoat; she handed Rolf to Cynthia. Cynthia wore a cocktail dress that conformed tightly to her body, and would have restricted her walk but for a generous slit up the right side. Cynthia took Rolf through an arched doorway to a large screened porch; there, a tall, Marine, Colonel Dubois, stood inspecting a flowering bromeliad. "Papa?"

Colonel Dubois turned and flashed a genuine, but lopsided smile. The right side of his face sagged slightly about the eye; the lips and the right ear hung to the side of his head like melting wax. Colonel Dubois offered his left hand for Rolf to shake. Dubois' right hand lacked a thumb, forefinger, and middle finger. "You must be Captain Bernard."

"Yes, sir."

"I am very pleased to meet you. How's your father?"

"He's not slowing down a bit."

"Good. Give him my regards. I used to fly your dad's planes in Korea—" He stopped in midthought. He managed a flute glass in his withered right hand and poured champagne with his left. "I should have asked if you drink champagne, or would you prefer some whiskey, a beer, or still wine?"

Rolf looked at the bottle. "That's excellent champagne, how could I refuse?" He took the glass and tasted it. "I haven't tasted Bollinger since my last trip to" —the place was Thailand— "San Diego. Cheers! Happy New Year, sir."

Colonel Dubois raised his glass. The weather-beaten, battle-scarred Marine smiled his half smile. Rolf contemplated the scars around the right half of his mouth, wonderfully repaired, hardly noticeable on the tan face, except for the lack of beard and the crumpled smile.

Colonel Dubois caught Rolf probing his old wounds with his eyes. "You're wondering what happened to me— I know the look." Dubois brushed the right side of his face with his crippled hand.

"I was just thinking you must have one helluva good war story."

Other guests filed into the room. Colonel Dubois shrugged his shoulders, "Duty calls." He lowered his voice, "Good to meet you, Captain. Usually, Cindy gets quite angry when Mrs. Dubois interferes in her social life, like inviting a young man over. Cindy must like you. You should be congratulated." He raised his glass and half smiled again and introduced Captain Bernard to his guests.

Rolf spent little time with Cynthia at the New Year's Eve party. As eldest daughter, Cynthia helped her mother hostess. Rolf Bernard attracted as much attention as the Prince of Wales; one guest recalled an article in the *Wall Street Journal*—how BAP's heir narrowly escaped death in the jungles of Vietnam while flying close combat support near the Cambodian border.

"Reconnaissance." Rolf corrected the record. "My Phantom took a lot of triple-A groundfire, and I went down. A grunt by the name of Tyler pulled me out."

"Thank God for that." The guests agreed.

Rolf cornered Cynthia at midnight for the ritualistic New Year's kiss—certainly antiseptic compared to the kiss on Kamehameha Pier. And having frittered away their evening, she playing perfect hostess, he the perfect guest, Rolf and Cynthia made a date to spend the second of January sightseeing.

❖   ❖   ❖

The rain stopped, and the sun made a rare appearance as Cynthia pulled up and found Rolf sitting on the curb in front of the Hickam BOQ. Rolf climbed into the Mustang, top up. "I'm so glad to see you."

"Let's spend the day in Honolulu."

Cynthia drove into the small city and parked the car on a side street near the city docks. They walked hand-in-hand up the beach facing Diamond Head, no particular destination in mind. They made short side trips off the beach to follow exotic sounds or smells. One such excursion led them to a small open-air charcoal grill, nestled under a bimini, where the purveyor cooked hamburgers on half the grill, mahi mahi on the other. Rolf ate the beef; Cynthia ate the fish.

They meandered down the beach, threatened by more rain clouds and relentless monsoon. They decided to stay close to shelter, so they took a table in the grand courtyard of the pink Royal Hawaiian Hotel. There they drank piña coladas and waited for the rain, which came in force. Grabbing their drinks, they hightailed it to the bar.

"Now what?" Rolf wiped the rain from his face with a napkin. "You hungry?"

"No."

"Want another drink?"

"It's a little early in the day . . . ."

"We could dash over to the International Marketplace."

"I've bought all the junk I need."

"Right. We could walk around in the rain. It's warm rain after all."

"Not warm enough for me, Rolf. I like my showers hot."

"I'll bet they've got hot showers in the Royal Hawaiian."

Cynthia looked across the small bar table. "I bet they do." She bit her lower lip. "Would be nice to get out of these wet clothes." She pulled a piece of the wet, cotton—now see-through—blouse from her skin.

"Very nice."

"Well, let's see." Cynthia averted her eyes. "Today's January the second. Thirty-one days has December . . . ." She counted back on her fingers, calculating her odds. She looked across the table again; her smile disappeared. "Why don't you get us a room."

"I'll be right back." Rolf reached across the table to squeeze her hand. "And if they're all booked up, I'll charter a boat, or buy a house."

The Royal Hawaiian let them a room looking down into the courtyard. Rolf bolted the door behind them, and he turned to see Cynthia peeling her wet clothes off: blouse, skirt, sandals. She stepped into the bathroom, then out again, naked, towel-drying her hair. Her tan line showed that she wore a one-piece bathing suit—a modest one at that. She sat on the side of the bed, rubbing her hair, pausing from time to time to catch a drop rolling down her back or chest. "Are you just going to stand there and watch?"

"I could. You're very beautiful." And he meant it.

"Well, don't." And she meant it.

A pocket of rough air jostled Rolf back to the present, and he saw a dark reflection of his face in the window. He tried to will himself back to his daydream, to relive the best, if not most costly, sex in his life. The plane banked hard left. The pilot steered the plane along a weather front, where a great line of cumulus clouds hunkered down beneath the pale moonlight. Then, white flashes of heat lightning lit the clouds with bursts and flickers, casting strange shadows among the pale giants, warning the jet plane to stay far away. Rolf tried to keep his eyes open to watch the lightning, but he leaned his head against a small white pillow and fell pleasantly asleep.

When Rolf got off the plane, he found a pay phone and called Margaret Bergen at home.

"Is Cynthia there?"

"She drove downtown."

"Nothing's open this early. When's she due back?"

"I don't know, Rolf. She doesn't speak to me—you know that."

Rolf groaned. "Okay. Why don't you take the rest of the day off. Tuesday, come to work at your BAP office."

"Yes, sir."

"And send someone to Dulles to pick up my bags. I'm coming straight home."

"Yes, Rolf. I can come in Monday if you need me."

"Take your day off. I'll need you fresh and ready to work Tuesday morning."

Rolf sped home. He didn't put his car in the garage, but left it in the driveway where one of the grounds-keepers would find it. He stepped up the walk, paused long enough to watch a man and woman, wearing green Merrifield Gardens shirts, dig out frostbitten mums and replace them with lavender and pale yellow ornamental cabbages. The woman stood up and pulled her leather gloves off. "Hi."

"Cabbages?"

"Yes. Mrs. Bergen ordered the cabbages. Very elegant. You know, sir, liriope would look good along this brick walk."

"Really? Then tell Mrs. Bergen. Did a black Jaguar drive in here?" He pointed toward the garage.

"No Jaguar. But Mrs. Bergen left in a small Mercedes about ten minutes ago."

"Thank you." Rolf nodded, then climbed the stone steps, and walked through the front door, stripping his tie off and throwing it and his jacket over the back of the couch. He peered into the living room. Rolf walked down a half flight to the lap pool. His footsteps echoed from the tile and glass. He retraced his steps, then trudged up the carpeted stairs to his bedroom. He saw a thin shadow pass by a doorway. "Cynthia?"

"Oh! It is you, Mr. Bernard." The young woman from Nicaragua stood at the end of the hall with a dust rag and a can of spray.

"Miss Escondido, where is Mrs. Bernard?"

"She is no here."

"I can see that. Where did she go? When do you expect her to return?"

"She no speak to me since she got here." She lowered her eyes as if admitting gross failure.

"Don't let that bother you." Rolf looked at a wall clock. *Where in the world would Cynthia go before ten o'clock in the morning?* "Did Mrs. Bernard know I was coming home today?"

"She no speak . . ."

"I forgot. Why don't you finish up and take the rest of the day off. I'll explain to Mrs. Bergen."

"Thank you."

The young woman disappeared quickly and Rolf could not help but wonder how relieved she must be to avoid Cynthia's homecoming. It made him wonder what had gone on at the Bernard mansion in his absence, and confirmed his suspicion that Cynthia had left him there to cool his heels. A quick tour of the house revealed Cynthia's gear in the guest bedroom. He retired to his study, a somber wood-panelled room, where he might at least cool his heels with a tumbler of twenty-year-old scotch, a wedge of Brie, and a row of crackers. He drifted off, asking himself, *What would it take to put my family together again?*

Rolf woke from a nap, hearing a commotion coming from the front of the house. The fog left his brain and he realized that Cynthia and the Nicaraguan girl had at last exchanged points of view. Rolf rubbed his eyes. He rose from his chair to find Cynthia standing in the doorway, a svelte shadow blocking the bright light from the next room, blocking any escape. The shadow spoke. "Well, well. It's eleven-thirty in the morning and the drinking lamp is lit."

"I was up all night on a plane." Rolf braced himself for the confrontation.

The backlight showed through the shadow's white cotton skirt where hips and legs shifted from left to right. But the shadow said no more. It approached, and the lamplight showed her cold, cheerless face. Cynthia would not speak; so Rolf did.

"Why did you sell the *Terra Firma?*"

"You gave it to me. It was mine; I never used it. It cost a fortune to leave it tied to that dock, so I sold it."

"You should have asked."

Cynthia crossed her arms over her chest and stood at her corner of the room. "I don't need your permission to sell what is mine."

"I see. Well, you definitely should not have sold eighty-five thousand shares of BAP last month!"

"You're right about that. I should have sold every share I owned, then sold BAP short. You managed to drive the price down eight bucks in a week—quite a feat, actually. I'd buy it back if I thought for a second you weren't about to sink it further."

"You drove the price down when you sold it. How else should the market react when they find out Rolf Bernard's wife is selling her shares?"

"They probably wonder, what does she know that we don't know?"

"Cynthia, there are laws against insider trading. Because you're my wife, the SEC will be all over our books like white on rice. They just might indict you. They're already crawling all over me. What's another line item in the indictment, eh? All I need is you giving them an excuse to investigate our stock sales. How bad would that look?"

"Look bad for whom? I think I can prove that I get no inside information from you. Is that why you asked me here—to lecture me on insider trading? *You* are going to tell *me* how to buy and sell securities? That's a laugh."

"What's the big argument about?" Rolf muttered.

"You started it, dear." Cynthia laced her voice with sarcasm. She added, "I thought husbands only got mad when wives bought things." She turned and walked out of the room.

Rolf picked up his scotch and shook his head and muttered, echoing Cynthia's sarcasm, "And it's great to see you, too. Lovely as ever."

Cynthia ate lunch alone on the patio. The bright sun and dry air put her at ease. She wore her darkest sunglasses, reclined on a lounge chair, pulled the straps of her sundress off her shoulders, swept her hair from her face, and pulled the skirt of her dress to the top of her long legs. Conscious of her skin, Cynthia never lay in the sun for a dark tan, but she prized the burnished tone that her skin took from spare moments of sunbathing—a soft color that made her look young when she wore pastels or white.

A shadow crossed her, blocking the sun. She sat up and found Rolf standing over her. She pushed the skirt down to her knees. "What do you want?"

"Why did you come back here, if all you're going to do is act rude to me and bully the household staff?"

"Curiosity, I suppose," she snapped back.

"I had hoped you might have wanted to come home." Rolf stepped into the shade of a palm. "You know what your problem is? You're angry. You're mad at me. You're mad at yourself. And I'll tell you why. You were out there making money you didn't need, when you should've been having the babies you wanted. Now you're angry because you can't have it all. But that's life, Cindy. Isn't it?"

Cynthia looked back with malice burning in her veins.

"I think your anger is bogus," Rolf continued. "You didn't really want children. Look at you. You're 48 years old and you look thirty-two. If you'd had kids, you'd look 48. Your narrow hips, they'd be a sight wider. Your 22-inch waist—add ten inches there. Travel, vacations, parties— my guess is that you'd have fobbed the kids off on a nanny like you did Paul. Then you would have gotten as schizophrenic as my mom was. No, I think you got it right the first time. And your fibroids saved you from second-guessing. You weren't fit to be a mother. You won't even stay at home for your husband! I was the one who wanted the kids, you didn't."

Cynthia's jaw quivered. "Get out! Get out!" she yelled. "Get out!"

Rolf calmly turned and walked back into the house.

Cynthia took her sunglasses off. She wiped a solitary tear from her face. She reached for the sweaty glass of iced tea waiting for her on a little table, knocking it onto the stone patio. The glass broke, and tea ran over the stones, collecting in little pools. She left the patio and went to her room to pack her bag.

Rolf followed Cynthia up the stairs. The guest bedroom door was open. He walked in as she zipped a garment bag closed. "Where do you think you're going?"

She didn't say a word. She stepped toward the door, but Rolf blocked her way. "I asked you a question. Where are you going?"

"I don't answer to you. Get out of my way." She grabbed her bag.

"Sorry to upset you, but it's the damn truth. You might as well face facts. Your place is here, not Paris. Most women would kill for the chance to be in your shoes."

Cynthia's eyes flashed. "Most men would kill to be in my shoes." She hefted her bag over her shoulder. "I'm leaving. And spare me the long-suffering husband schtick. And don't patronize me. It's so unbecoming." She elbowed her way past him and dragged her bag down the stairs.

Cynthia threw her bag into Rolf's car. She saw no sense in leaving her Jaguar stuck in some airport parking lot. She found the keys where he always left them, in the change cup by the seat. The car smelled of cigarette smoke and leather. She drove Rolf's car to the airport, took her bag, locked the keys inside. She bought a ticket on the next plane to New York.

✧   ✧   ✧

Ted Winston sat in his high-back leather chair behind his old, dark, oak desk. One of the collar buttons on his oxford-cloth shirt had popped off. He wore a blue paisley tie. Over that, he wore his faded, red Indiana University sweatshirt—a talisman from his grad-school days that he wore for really big games and election nights. He was drinking coffee from a large white mug that bore the presidential seal on one side, his name in gold leaf on the other.

His intercom buzzed. Ted swallowed quickly and answered the machine. "Yes?"

"Mr. Bernard will see you now."

"On my way." Ted grabbed a manila folder, stuffed a pen in his pocket, and left. As he walked down the hall, his assistant, Carla, matched him stride for stride. "We've got all the Felix clippings: twenty-six major papers."

"Put them on my desk."

"We can't find the unabridged text of Fowley's last press conference."

"You should have taped it—you know better."

"Yes, sir. Our mole at *Aviation Week* smuggled out an advance copy of Dr. Pendergast's article, 'Why Felix Will Never Fly.' Dr. Yeager can help us write the rebuttal piece to hit the street before *Aviation Week* hits the stands."

"Good work."

"Also, Senator Warner's office agreed to incorporate our changes into his floor speech."

"Good." Ted reached the elevators and punched the up arrow. "Tell the staff to tidy up any loose ends, because we're going to shift into high gear. Set up a meeting in the South conference room for five o'clock. The support staff needn't bother." The elevator door opened. He stepped in. "Got that?"

Carla scribbled a note, "Five o'clock today, tidy up, change gears—I got it." The doors closed as she finished her sentence.

Ted Winston walked into the antechamber outside Rolf's office and greeted Margaret Bergen, who sat at a desk with a check ledger. "What brings you to HQ?"

Margaret looked up from her pocket calculator. "I'm reconciling the Bernard household accounts." She glanced at Mr. Bernard's closed door. "We thought Mrs. Bernard might want the house to herself, but then, apparently, we were mistaken."

One would have to be six-days dead to miss the ire in Margaret's manner; so Ted didn't ask a follow-up question. He merely told her, "Rolf's expecting me."

"Then go in."

Ted wondered what the hell was wrong with Margaret. She'd never been anything but cordial before. He let himself into Rolf's office.

"Hey there, Ted. Come in. Sit down." Rolf noticed the red sweat shirt. "Too cold in here for you?"

"No. I wear my old alma mater's shirt to watch Bobby Knight kick ass—or when I kick ass. And if you approve my public relations plan, that's what we do, starting today."

"I read your plan. I'm not sure I see the kick-ass part of it." Rolf pulled out a couple sheets of paper.

"Really?" Ted sounded disappointed.

"Give me some examples of how you plan to deflect criticism aimed at BAP. Tell me how you expect to redirect it to government, especially NASA."

Ted opened his folder. "My strategy has two parts. First, we go on the attack, so they have to spend their resources defending themselves, instead of attacking us. Second, we always get someone else to do the dirty work. It's called a negative campaign in politics.

"I'll give you an example. I place a story through Congressman Bledsoe's office to the *New York Times*. The story claims first, NASA's big rockets launched from Canaveral and Vandenburg use ammonium perchlorate solid fuel, which, when burned, creates a great carcinogenic cloud wafting over an unsuspecting population. Second,

NASA knowingly subjects civilians to cancer risks, because they can't—or won't—design a big rocket using liquid fuels only. Third, the good guys, BAP, rejected ammonium perchlorate, in spite of its commercial benefits, to safeguard the people whom BAP serves—the taxpayers on the ground. Fourth, when BAP's new SSTO becomes a reality, the populations of Florida and California can finally rest; NASA will no longer rain carcinogens over their homes."

"Not bad."

"I call stories like that my little media grenades. I just pull the pin, toss it, and wait four or five days for the explosion."

Rolf rustled the paper before him. "This part about confusing the enemy . . ."

"I've got a couple angles on that. Throughout our campaign, we use third-party mouthpieces. Let me explain. I know every conservative or libertarian antigovernment lobbyist and think tank there is. I've got them in my database, programmed into my auto-dial fax machine. Their combined mailing lists reach more than twenty million politically active Americans. They're always on the lookout for fundraising ideas. I'll feed them stories; they'll carry our negative message to millions. Meanwhile, we stand above the fray, maybe even send sympathy cards.

"Also, I want to push hard to recruit the Green lobby to our cause."

Rolf balked. "We don't need those kooks."

"Kooks? Maybe, but they have a lot of pull with this Administration. Hear me out. Heretofore, the ecological gurus dismissed SPS because it was a big government project requiring huge capital investments. The same companies that owned and operated fossil fuel and nuclear power plants—their enemies—would also invest in and sell SPS-generated power. The Sierra Club and their ilk pushed solar power, but the small kind, like solar cells on the roof, a windmill in the back yard—the Walden

Pond approach to energy. The SPS approach needed big
bucks that only big power companies or the government
could raise. I'll concoct a story that DoD wanted to kill
SPS because it competed with nuclear power, and DoD
wanted more—not fewer—breeder reactors to provide
munitions-grade plutonium for continued upgrades on
our nuclear weapons. Nuclear power has become the
implacable foe of the solar power satellite. I can see the
headline: 'DoD to Kill Solar Power Satellite to Save Fuel
for Nukes!' "

"But that's not true at all."

"So? What's truth got to do with anything—this is politics,
Rolf. Besides, the story won't have BAP's fingerprints
on it."

"I don't know, Ted." Rolf scratched his chin. "What
else?"

"We hit 'em where they ain't. We blitz Congress when
they're out of session. I've got stuff planned for winter,
spring and summer. We hit NASA when they're preoccupied with a launch. The longer it takes them to react
to a barrage of negative press, the more damage we do."

"So do I have anything to do in this plan?"

"You won't have anything to do with the negative
campaign. In that respect, you're invisible. But you'll be
our point man to promote SSTO, spaceborne antiballistic
missile defense, and solar power satellites. I'll get Yeager,
Iversen, Paul, Holtz, and Fenster to ghost new talking
papers for you. You'll just do what you've always done,
but more. Since my negative campaign and your positive
campaign work concurrently, there's a danger the press
will try to suck you into the negative campaign. It's almost
impossible to resist piling on, but you have to ooze
sympathy for NASA as they get their skulls kicked in. In
1992, I watched them suck Quayle into the melee. It
was a mess."

"They won't suck me in."

"If you don't mind, I'll be standing at your side like

Jiminy Cricket, a little voice to warn you when they dangle the bait in front of you. In this kind of game, you've got to have at least two pairs of eyes and two pairs of ears."

"You really love this stuff, don't you?"

Ted laughed. "I haven't had so much fun since we savaged Dukakis. Yeah, I love it. You can't imagine what one man with a fax machine and phone can do."

"And a red sweatshirt."

"Yes, sir. My Indiana hardball sweatshirt. Have you ever gone toe-to-toe with Bobby Knight? You and Knight have a lot in common."

"I hope that's a compliment."

"Absolutely. At the Cuban games, he grabbed some little commie heckler, turned him upside down, and stuffed him into a garbage can. They threw Bobby out of the game—out of the coliseum, in fact, but we still won big. Great coaches make themselves expendable, and they always go out with a bang."

Rolf grinned. "Work your plan, Ted. But don't do anything to get me thrown out of the game. I'm not expendable."

"Very good." Ted stood, shook Rolf Bernard's hand, and left before Rolf could change his mind.

"And Ted . . ."

"Yes, sir?"

"You need to put some more resources toward selling Felix launches. I'd rather embarrass NASA by taking their customers than just calling them names."

"I'm way ahead of you, sir. I just pirated the best two sales reps from Orbital Science Corporation. They have the lead on payloads less than five thousand pounds."

"I want to meet them."

Ted rushed back to his office a happy man. As he walked by the cubicles to his office, he saw Carla again, flashed her a thumbs-up, then disappeared into his office, closing the door.

Ted organized his office like a bunker. He had his own PC and laser printer, his own direct phone lines, fax, and telex. Three walls bore his trophies: framed letters and photos from great and temporarily grateful men. The fourth wall held two floor-to-ceiling boards, one made of cork, the other glossy white, side by side. On the credenza behind his desk, next to his fax, Ted lined up twenty-three manila folders, each with an action in his plan of campaign.

On the white board, he'd drawn four columns with headings: layoffs, winter recess, spring recess, and deployment. He glanced at the digital clock mounted above his door—so much to do before five o'clock. He had to organize his staff, marketing majors from good schools, many with solid sales experience, but lacking the killer instinct. The newest addition to his little empire, Ben, had won awards writing direct mail copy, but none, except Carla, had lived through a for-real, nut-cutting, winner-take-all political campaign. Some things they don't teach in college.

Ted pressed the intercom button on his company phone and simply said, "Would you bring me a fresh coffee, thank you?" Then Ted pulled a brown bag from his lower drawer and inventoried its contents—admittedly strange behavior because he always made his own lunch, carried it to work in a brown paper bag, and stored it in his lower left-hand drawer. Nothing was ever missing. Today, Ted had made himself a tuna fish sandwich (soggy because he had used yogurt instead of mayonnaise), a Baggie filled with corn chips, and a Baggie filled with four Oreo cookies.

He hit the intercom again, "Belay that coffee order. Send Carla and Ben in here."

A moment later, Ted heard a tap at the door and his two senior assistants let themselves in. Ted got up. "I'm taking you to lunch. Ben, ready for a stress-filled lunch?"

"What sir?"

Carla smirked. "You're about to get a lesson titled, 'There Ain't No Such Thing as a Free Lunch.'"

"You guys mind executive dining-room food?"

"Sounds great!" Ben perked up.

Carla chortled, "Same as the food in the employee cafeteria, served on china instead of paper plates."

"Except the chili and cornbread." Ted corrected her. "I forgot."

Ted started walking toward the elevators. "Ben, I want you to take notes. Now here's how I want you two to organize your teams . . . ."

Bobby Tyler breezed past Margaret Bergen and let himself into Rolf's office. Margaret followed Tyler in. "Mr. Bernard is at lunch."

"I'll wait. Could you send in a cup of coffee?"

"There's a thermos and cups on the credenza. Help yourself." Margaret closed the door.

Bobby Tyler waited on the sofa, drinking his coffee and flipping through a book of satellite photography.

Rolf stepped through the door. "You're not on my list of people to see today."

"And I bet you didn't expect to get this either." Bobby said, tossing a brown envelope onto the black marble coffee table.

As Rolf opened the envelope, Bobby announced, "It's a subpoena. The Senate formed an ad hoc subcommittee to investigate fraud among defense aerospace contractors. You're the star. They want you the middle of January, just after they get back from their Christmas recess. Merry Christmas."

Rolf threw the envelope and its contents back to Tyler. "Give it to counsel. Have them translate it for me. What else is new?"

Tyler replied, "I'm working on a couple of ideas. Max left for Australia to see his friend Kirby. Eckert wants to see you about finances. This week we sent notices out to shareholders for the annual stockholders' meeting. Also, I ran into General Marshall—you met him at Rixeyville?"

"Yeah, I remember him."

"He gave me a message for you. He said, 'Keep your pecker up.' "

"That's it? That's his message?" Rolf arched his eyebrows.

"He heard through the grapevine that you got subpoenaed, and he said, 'Keep your pecker up.' "

"How odd." Rolf shook his head.

Chapter 11

Max Yeager sat at a small round table near a kiosk in the Brisbane International Airport. He rubbed his red eyes and fought back a yawn. Max passed the time reading the Saturday morning edition of the Australian tabloid *Truth*, which featured a front-page teaser about a man who claimed to have been swallowed by a twenty-five-foot, salty *crocodylus porosus*, details page C-6 in the Style section. Max grumbled, "I rather doubt that."

He studied the wisps of steam rising from his teacup. A wedge of lemon lay on the saucer, looking as if he'd brought it with him from Los Angeles. Max tried to recall why the citric acid in lemon juice turns tea from an earthy hue to clear golden brown. *How bothersome it is to forget so many things.*

Max set the paper down, too tired to read the lurid details about a twenty-five-foot, man-eating crocodile and the lucky fellow who was apparently swallowed, but escaped in the nick of time to make *Truth's* deadline. He slumped into his chair, chin on his chest; he closed his eyes and trusted that Irwin Kirby would find him. And Irwin did. Max jolted awake to a gentle hand on his shoulder.

"Gosh Max, we figured to find you in the taproom, not flaked out by a cup of tea. We been here half an hour already."

"Oh!" Max recovered. "I must have fallen asleep."

Irwin introduced his manservant, "You remember Archie—my driver, chef, and all-round helper."

"Yes. Pleased to meet you again." Max extended his hand.

"G'day, Dr. Yeager."

Irwin proposed, "We've been an hour in the car. Mind if we take a breather before we head back to Southport? Archie, bring Mr. Yeager's bags to the taproom. I'll shout you both a beer."

"Right, Mr. Kirby." Archie picked up the bags.

Max Yeager followed Irwin to a dim bar, decorated with large fans of coral, fishing nets, glass floats, and meticulously carved and brightly painted wooden fish. Above the teak bar, a twenty-foot great white shark bared its teeth. "You Australians certainly have a fascination with man-eaters—sharks and crocodiles in particular."

Irwin followed Yeager's wide eyes to the behemoth shark. "The fascination's universal, I suppose. We just happen to have an abundance of the big critters here."

Archie added, "You Yanks can have them all, providing you don't get nicked by the Greens."

Irwin translated. "As long as you don't get *caught* by the environmentalists. Most of our dangerous species are protected from hunters. By the way, Max, I got your cryptic fax yesterday morning."

"I'm sorry to rush in on such short notice."

"A special treat for me. Don't apologize. Your fax said BAP has some possible interest in the Temple Bay Spaceport."

"Yes. Very."

The pert waitress brought three large, frosty mugs of beer, Irwin lifted his mug. "To the first one today!"

"Goodo!" Archie replied.

"Cheers."

"Max, how long do you plan to stay?"

"I don't know." Max added awkwardly, "I need to learn

more about Temple Bay, and make you a proposal. I flew over assuming you might be interested."

"You've never had an idea I didn't just love to death, Max. You're staying as my guest as long as you like. I put you up at my house. Elizabeth made her cornflour spongecake and gooseberry custard just for you."

"I could do with some home cooking. Besides, I'm looking forward to seeing Elizabeth again."

Irwin turned to Archie. "Max stayed at our house for the weekend after the International Space Society Convention, two years ago."

"Before my time, sir."

"Well, then you don't know the grand master of rockets."

Max interrupted, "Here we go again. Irwin, you came up with the idea for the aerospike. I just found the money, did the heavy math, built a model, and tested it."

" 'Just,' he says."

Archie wiped a thin line of froth from his upper lip. "I recall now, boss. This here's your flush space cobber. You got that big antique frame with that little cocktail napkin with that little drawing, numbers and such."

"Max gave that to me at the convention—a really big do. Called me the Father of the Australian Journey to Space. You sure made me look good that night."

"I could not have been more sincere."

"Cor!" Irwin turned back to Archie. "After Max's big buildup, I raised the money for the Temple Bay Spaceport. Money sure was easy in the eighties. Laurie Connell—old Last Resort Laurie we call him—kicked in a sizable stake. Warwick Fairfax and Conrad Black, half a dozen small players—we all kicked in, then cosigned banknotes. The ten of us put up $58 million in cash, and borrowed another $360 million to build Temple Bay Spaceport, way up in Cape York. Nearly ruined us all."

Max interjected, "Last I heard, you were short cash and backing away from the venture."

Irwin laughed. "Backing off! More like running for the hills. Where you been, Max? We've been gut shot."

"But it seems like" —Max struggled to get his dates in order— "you had just started pouring cement. And I thought Australian Space Office agreed not to compete, so you had a lock on domestic business."

"That was two years ago."

"I'm sorry. I haven't been following that close."

"That's all right, mate. We haven't exactly been broadcasting our failures, and we sure as hell haven't had any successes to crow about. Here's how it happened. Queensland gave us a hundred-year lease on the land north of an abo reserve for next to nothing, but we had to fight our way through the red tape, the green tape, and the black tape."

"I don't understand."

Archie translated. "Red tape is the bloody bureaucrats, just like you got in your country. Green tape comes courtesy of our doughy ecology buffs. Mr. Kirby needed to cut down a couple of trees at Temple Bay, so he had to prove we weren't raping the land. Black tape is dealing with abo heritage stuff."

"Oh, aborigines." Max caught on.

"Right. We had to satisfy the state that we weren't conflicting with the aboriginal reserve. To move the story along, we got permission to build our spaceport. Then, we needed a rocket. Hawker de Havilland, Auspace, and British Space Australia were developing an indigenous Aussie rocket, but they couldn't deliver for five years. We shopped around, and about two years before the Soviet Union disintegrated we contracted to buy Zenit boosters from Glavkosmos."

"That much I remember."

"Before we turned the first shovel of dirt, we booked three years of launches. Our customers included United Telecom, Intelsat, General Electric, plus several small U.S. companies. Our biggest customer turned out to be the Japanese, who booked fourteen launches. We used the launch bookings as a big part of our collateral for the $360 million loan. At last, we started construction. You can see how the whole deal was interlocked—the advance bookings, government support, our cash, banks' financial support, the operations . . ."

Max interjected, "And not much in the way of corporate depth. I admire you for even attempting it."

"I thought it would be kin to building a big set to shoot a big movie: just bigger bucks—real instead of fake buildings. Anyway, we spent the next ten months cutting trees and brush. We moved dirt and poured cement. At one time we had eight hundred men building a little city in the middle of a jungle by the ocean. We built a small airstrip. We cut a connecting road to Bruce Highway—wait till you see Cape York's big highway. We built a dock for boats."

"How big a dock?" Max paused to scribble a note.

"Small. You can't get large boats into Temple Bay. Also, we built the launch apron, blockhouse, and a facility to store cryogenic fuels. We laid the foundation, four walls and a roof for a small power plant. We bought a huge diesel power generator but never hooked it up. We built one set of bungalows for permanent party. We billeted the rest of the men in trailers and tents. Archie spent a lot of time up there."

"It was fair dinkum stinkin' mess. Hot, wet, and buggy." Archie recalled.

"You didn't have to go there much. Anyway, we were just about to build the launch tower when the banks refused further draws on the construction loans. Why? Because a big piece of our collateral evaporated: Our customers bugged out."

Kirby paused to take a drink from his mug. The frost had melted away. "We lost our American customers because NASA persuaded them to break their contracts with us. The folks at NASA weren't too subtle about it either. They told Telecom that if they left NASA, they could never come back. And they gave the same lecture to General Electric, adding that they should also forget about bidding on future NASA projects."

"So then what happened?"

"When we thought things couldn't get worse, they did. Glavkosmos, now an agency of the Commonwealth of Independent States, had to renegotiate our old contract. Even after that haggling, we got only one Zenit booster, and we're afraid to use it. Funny thing about the Russians— what actually killed the deal was that some ex-communist nomenclatura, as they say, stood to make a buck from the deal, so the new, improved, capitalist Russians killed the deal rather than see some ex-communist make a buck from a capitalist transaction. All the pieces we so carefully wired together unraveled. Without our American customers, we couldn't get any additional financing. We couldn't get boosters, and without boosters, we couldn't attract new customers."

Max commiserated. "And I heard the Auspace booster won't be ready for at least two years by their schedule, but don't bet on anything sooner than four years."

"You heard right. Maybe I'm getting paranoid, but NASA helped get Auspace out of the booster-building business. They made Auspace a one-time, cut-rate deal for standby cargo, and guess what? They found standby room for Auspace on shuttle launches in 1995 and 1996. How the hell can anyone book standby space on launches planned eight years in advance?"

"You were bagged." Max shook his head. "I could probably guess the rest."

"I know. Then NASA gave Auspace the green light to put up Australia's next-generation telecommunications package, but only if Auspace could accelerate production of their twenty thousand-pound satellite. Of course, Auspace shifted priorities, pulled money out of the booster program, then poured it into finishing their big satellite to meet their standby launch date.

"So all you had left was a contract for fourteen launches for the Japanese, and no boosters to launch with."

"I wish. The Japanese reneged on their contract, citing their anxiety about using Zenit boosters. I think they'd planned to renege all along. You know why? Because they've started building their Sakishima Island launch facility. They committed 2.3 billion dollars for the project— makes our bootstrap operation look pretty shonky."

"I'm surprised the Japanese contracted with you in the first place."

Archie blurted out, "The Japs think us Aussies are the poor white trash of Asia."

"Enough of that, Archie." Irwin shook his head. "Archie's still living for the late seventies' White Australia Policy. And he's got uncommon cheek for a house servant."

"I do my job."

Irwin ignored the last bit. "The final chapter in my sad saga: The banks would disburse no more funds from our construction loan, and three months ago they accelerated the debt. They said, 'Go get the package refinanced somewhere else and take us out of first position.' But money got tight by the end of the decade. We can't attract foreign money. The Aussie dollar's weak. Our stock market's still thirty percent off its highs. Unemployment's stuck around ten percent. Rather sad, but our attempt at getting into the space industry is just what poor Australia needs to take her place in Asia."

"Didn't your banks insist on business insurance?"

"A surety bond, they call it. We used Lloyds, who refuses to pay. You could hear them laugh at us all the way from London when we sent our claim. I can eat my part of the deal, but my partners can't. And so they're suing me, because I'm the managing general partner. That's life. The only people making money out of this deal are lawyers."

Yeager concluded thoughtfully, "So Temple Bay would go forward, except that you lack capital, rockets, and customers."

Both Archie and Irwin laughed aloud. Irwin wheezed, "Too right! I told you my Yank friend had a dry sense of humor."

Max merely smiled at his companions' mirth. "Irwin, BAP can provide the rockets and customers. If necessary, Bernard can help with the capital."

The laughter stopped.

"True blue?" Archie broke the silence.

"Mr. Bernard needs a spaceport in three to four months. He hasn't got the time or the money to build one in the States."

"Well you've come to the right place. We got a spaceport with nothin' to do."

"I'll need a lot more information about Temple Bay Spaceport before we can make a proposal."

Irwin downed the last inch of his beer. "Well, what are we waiting for? Archie, settle the tab, please; then bring the car 'round to the taxi rank. And don't forget Dr. Yeager's bags."

"Yes, sir." And Archie left with Yeager's bags.

Yeager observed, "You don't seem too happy about our interest."

"Max, the Temple Bay Spaceport has been nothing but five years of pure hell. I lost a small fortune. Some of my friends lost more. When the banks foreclosed, frankly I was relieved. I could give up my intoxicating dream of space travel, I could bury this mistake and get on with my life, stick to the knitting—Canberra Studios' movies and TV. I feel like a tamed space larrikin."

"A what?"

"Like a reformed boozer or addict. Only, my addiction was space—you know that."

"An enthusiast yes, but not a what-did-you-call-it? Larrikin?"

"A space enthusiast reads books and goes to conferences. A space larrikin squanders his fortune, time, and last ounce of energy trying to climb out of this gravity well. I'm reformed now. I took the pledge. You're looking at a space enthusiast. Nothing more. I shall confine my enthusiasms for space to making profitable movies."

Max didn't believe a word of it. "I'm not asking for much, Irwin, just a good look at your spaceport and your promise to consider our unsolicited proposal. You'll find Mr. Bernard's offer irresistible. If you do, I'll want you to run our proposal by your limited partners."

"Don't have to. I'm the general partner. Anyway, they'll flog me if I miss any chance to salvage their investment. As soon as they hear about your offer, they go off like a bucket of prawns in the sun." Kirby looked across the table and winced. "You're a bit of a bad influence, Max. It's a damn good thing I didn't meet you in my wayward youth. We'll start with the blueprints at the house."

Like Rolf Bernard, Kirby had a lot to gain and a lot to lose. However, Irwin hadn't inherited a family fortune. He had inherited luck from his Irish mother, and a hit-or-miss business sense from his Scottish father. His father, Duncan Kirby, taught history and English at a secondary school for a pittance. Consequently, Irwin always felt that he wrote inadequately and lacked a true sense of history. But he did have advanced degrees in aerospace and chemical engineering.

Most people thought Irwin Kirby's passion for rockets came out of his lucrative work in action films. That was backward. Irwin's first company, Aussie Rockets, Ltd. operated from his father's garage. He sold his little rockets to hobbyists, then to Paramount and other Hollywood studios, who used the reliable rockets for their hi-tech, shoot-em-up films. Irwin dragged friends, including his future wife, Elizabeth, and prospective clients to the movies to watch helicopter gun ships, jet fighters, shoulder-fired antitank or anti-air missiles—his babies. He critiqued each launch. A bright flash and a straight trail of white smoke meant a good launch. Aussie Rockets, Ltd. made the best small rockets in the world—nobody doubted it. Irwin expanded into other special effects.

He purchased Canberra Movie Studios unintentionally. Canberra made a fortune rehashing American Westerns, then lost a fortune pursuing art. The studio tried to revive itself with a thinking-man's space adventure film called *The L5 Verdict*, an outer space rehash of *The Ox-Bow Incident*—painfully politically correct—something both Heinlein and Asimov would have approved. Aussie Rockets worked the special effects, which were considerable, and ran way over budget. The movie won major awards at the Cannes Film Festival, failed miserably at the box office, and dragged the studio under. Irwin Kirby, who was by far the largest creditor, rescued his receivables by plowing in more cash, and taking a large loan from Last Resort Laurie Connell to buy the studio.

Then, Irwin bet the farm on one movie—a mindless flurry of pyrotechnics based on a fictitious helicopter assault on Beruit to liberate hostages. There were more Aussie Rockets than words in the script. In the final scene, a disoriented martyr drove a panel truck into the wrong building, blowing up the Syrian Embassy . . . Irwin made a fortune. The Coca-Cola Company wanted to buy Canberra Studios; Irwin wouldn't sell. He found himself in the movie business, and he got rich. When *Rolling Stone* magazine asked him his secret for making hit movies, Irwin answered, "Movies, like rockets, need a high thrust-to-weight ratio."

Although Kirby devoted time and money to advance the Australian space program, he made his fortune in TV and movie production. His work at the Australian Space Office (NASA down under) went unnoticed. The public knew Irwin Kirby as the man who built Canberra Studios, whose action-packed movies had grossed more than 540 million Australian dollars in the past year. Most importantly he was the Australian Ted Turner, the man who brought cable TV to Australia with his satellite.

✧   ✧   ✧

Irwin and Max found Archie parked near the taxi rank. They piled into the back seat and Archie sped away. Max looked out the window. The sedan wound its way toward the coast past horses grazing on sunburned grass, in and out of a suburb, and up a steep ridge. They drove past a privet hedge separating the front lawn from a large vegetable garden and orchard. Sloe trees hung heavy with dark fruit. The driver pulled into a courtyard of a house with white stucco walls and red tile roof. Large ferns banked the south wall. A sun-bleached plastic tricycle sat in the middle of the driveway.

A small fluff of white dog bounced up and down behind a large plate-glass window. One could see the animal's breath fogging the glass and faintly hear the yap-yap-yap. Irwin Kirby said to the driver, "Archie, take Mr. Yeager's suitcase to the guest room overlooking the pool. Get rid of the dog."

"So, Liz forced you to buy a dog. I knew she'd get her way."

"A fait accompli—she brought home a puppy and gave it to the children. The wretched little beast piddles, barks, *and* scares the parrot."

"Where is Liz?"

"Christmas shopping. She'd better keep out of the pet store."

Irwin and Max walked into the house. The yapping sound trailed away as Archie dragged the dog deep into the basement. Irwin led Max into the dining room where they sat at the end of a large polished table. A shy face peered from the kitchen doorway. A small Asian woman presented herself.

"Pitsumi." Irwin waved her into the room. "Dr. Yeager will stay with us a few days."

She acknowledged with a slight bow.

"Please make some tea, and bring a plate of scones and jam."

The girl returned to the kitchen. Irwin explained, "Cambodian." He rolled his eyes. "Elizabeth's got a soft heart. Archie's worried she'll hire aborigines next, but he knows to mind his tongue around my wife. She'd skin him, then give him the sack for talkin' down to the help. Liz grew up on her dad's station by the Darling River, living in a little wattle-and-daub house with rough puncheon floors. She's used to animals and workhands about the house. Thank God the shire's got an ordinance to forbid her from lodging sheep."

Max drummed his fingers on the table. Talk of house servants and domesticated animals had no relevance for him. Irwin left to find his rolls of Temple Bay blue prints. Max studied the small etching that hung next to the china cabinet: a full-figured, sumptuously dressed, bejeweled woman lying on a divan, above the caption "Nouveau is better than no riche at all."

Irwin quickly returned with an armload of cardboard tubes filled with charts, mechanical drawings, land-use plans, and building blueprints. He selected the tube labeled "Temple Bay City Plan" and gently pulled the roll of paper out, flattening it on the table. He pulled out a red felt-tip pen. "More than half the buildings haven't been built."

"Are those exhaust vents on the launch pad?"

"Yes. But there's little more than cement. We left the tower stored in Cairns."

"We won't need a tower."

"Of course. You're going to build SSTOs, like your Felix prototype." Irwin drew a solid line around the launch pad.

Max started to tell about the three production models, but Irwin continued, "The blockhouse used to be ready." He shifted his pen to the blockhouse.

"You mean it isn't ready now?"

"We pulled out most of the electronics. The tropic's murder on electronics, especially near the ocean. You need the annual monsoon just to wash off the salt. Then, there's always some damned snake, lizard, spider, or bat living in the gear. My warehouse outside Brisbane is filled with the stuff."

"How soon could you put everything back together?"

"Six months, assuming we get the gear back before the banks auction it off."

Max rubbed his eyes. "We don't have six months. We could supplement your equipment. . . ."

"We need skilled men more than equipment."

While the two men stared at the blueprint, a linen-draped basket bearing scones slid onto the table. A small brown hand placed linen napkins and heavy Gorham silverware beside the two men. The Cambodian ghost poured two cups of Darjeeling tea, set the pot on a trivet, put a tea cozy over the pot, then disappeared.

"We've got to condense the schedule."

"It's possible." Irwin thought out loud. "We don't need a tower. We need to get our people back and finish some major systems: tracking radar, downrange security, fuel storage. . . ."

Max pointed at the marina. "Why don't you haul the fuel in by ocean barge and park it at the dock? Leave it stored on the barges?"

"We built the marina for small seaplanes and pleasure craft."

"Maybe we could build a bigger marina. . . ."

"Wouldn't do any good. We'd have to solve two big problems. First, it's not that easy hauling freight through the barrier reef. Even Captain Cook couldn't manage it without losing his ship to the reef. But the reefs are nothing compared with the Sydney wharfies. By law, all intercoastal transport must travel on ships registered in Australia, manned exclusively by Australians, and stevedored by Australians. And it don't matter a bit whether you're hauling pineapples or liquid hydrogen. Consequently, it's cheaper to buy the fuel in the States, ship it to Australia, and pay the import duties."

"That's ridiculous."

"Amen. That's why we planned to haul fuel up Bruce Highway in roadtrains, then store it. If business picked up to—say four launches a month—we contemplated making our own fuel, but that's far in the future."

Max took a note. "You give me an idea."

"About what?"

"About making our own fuel. BAP expects to start with four launches a month and work up to four a week by next July."

"With one SSTO prototype?" Irwin asked, surprised.

"You know about the Felix prototype. . . ."

"Even a tamed space larrikin can figure that much. I know Felix can fly much farther than her tests indicate."

"Well, you don't know everything, Irwin. We built three production models of the Felix. We've kept the project under wraps till now. Each production model can carry 16,500 pounds and a three-man crew. Paul Bernard has three shifts working to get those ships ready in four months." Max leaned back in his chair and grinned. "We have four ships."

"I'll be damned. How'd you guys do it? You can't keep stuff like that secret."

"Really? Who knew about the U-2? Or the Blackbird, the B-2 or the F-117A before they rolled out of their hangars?"

"I saw pictures."

"Yeah, but did you know how many they made?"

"Okay, Max. You win your point, but how'd you do it?"

Max smiled through his fatigue. "It's an inside joke—a little smoke, a couple mirrors. Actually, we started with spare parts. You know how engineers operate, we bid eight times what we needed. After all, we expected to crash a few, and the budgeters fully expected us to crash a few. But we bunny hopped and tested without burning or pranging a single ship. We bought used or obsolete avionics from Rockwell at ten cents on the dollar when they upgraded their Shuttle-D. Rolf raised an extra two hundred million dollars for labor and materials, and we built three more ships."

Max slathered sloe preserves on a scone. He smiled slyly. "I think I get it. Do you still expect to operate at a hundred dollars per pound to low earth orbit?"

"Thereabouts."

"So you can launch" —Irwin paused to do some mental calculations— "over a million pounds to orbit each year at a mere fraction of today's costs."

"Even more when we build more ships." Max shared Irwin's satisfaction.

Kirby nodded. "I see, now. BAP will have a virtual monopoly on space transportation. You'll raise hackles. So you want to get offshore."

"Exactly. We need a place to launch, somewhere NASA can't interfere. That's why I need to check out Temple Bay."

"Let's fly to Temple Bay tomorrow."

"I don't want to interrupt your plans," Max offered out of politeness.

"I'll change them." Irwin leaned back in his chair. An old Gustav Becker wall clock struck two hollow bongs. Irwin looked at his wristwatch, then said, "Why don't you go take a lie-down or hang about the pool or something. I'll make a few phone calls. We'll fly to Temple Bay tomorrow and you can look about." Irwin shooed Max upstairs.

Max sat on the soft bed and took off his shoes. The bed practically sucked him down. He could only plan his short descent to make sure his head hit the pillow and not the headboard. He stirred briefly to overhear the little dog yapping, kids squealing, and Elizabeth's voice. When the clock on the nightstand confirmed that he'd slept for five hours, Max washed his face and presented himself for dinner.

Elizabeth rushed to him and kissed his cheek. "Max!

Welcome back!" She led him to the stone patio overlooking a distant bay, a long crescent beach backed by hills of grass, low trees and occasional rooftops. The fading evening light turned the turquoise Pacific to lapis. Elizabeth pointed out the scenery and the slight haze in the north— the Brisbane lights. Citronella torches burned at the patio's corners. Small candles illuminated the patio table, set for three. Pitsumi brought a wicker tray, balancing tall glasses of sangria. Irwin followed, carrying the large pitcher of purple drink.

They sat at the table in the shade of Irwin's tall house. A southerly breeze refreshed them, as well as the sangria. Max looked up to see the faces of two children peering surreptitiously from a bedroom window, disappearing momentarily when Max wagged his fingers in a discreet wave.

Elizabeth broached the topic of Max's visit. "Irwin tells me you may revitalize his failed—excuse me, darling . . ." She offered a sympathetic glance to Irwin. "His spaceport."

"Yes. It's lucky for BAP that Irwin built it."

"Well—goodo! You'll have to emigrate to Australia to run BAP's launches."

Max chuckled. "I don't know about that."

"What's stopping you?"

What indeed, Max thought. A widower, Max had nothing tying him down to the States. "I recently read an article about the ten most venomous creatures in the world: Seven live in Australia. And the flies! You'd think the whole continent was one big, dead squirrel."

"Garbage!" Liz wrinkled her nose.

Irwin reached for the pitcher. "Can't deny it, Liz."

"You let me handle this, dear, I'm on the Board of Tourism. It won't do to say unflattering things about my country to me. I'm a trained protagonist. Do come live with us. As a scientist and engineer you'd feel right at home."

"Your hospitality has always—"

"That's not what I'm talking about. I'm talking science and engineering. Australia's got less than point naught three percent of the world's population, we publish two percent of all scientific papers—proportionately more than America. We earn one point three percent of Nobel Prizes—proportionately more than America. We file point seven percent of all patents for new inventions. In the brains department we carry our own weight. Plus, we've got industry: Three car manufacturers in fact. Your GM exports our car motors to Opel in Germany and Vauxhall in Britain. We make steel. We've got electronics. We've spectacular minerals, including oil, gas and coal. The point is, Max, you could build your spaceships here in Australia."

"She's right, Max."

Max looked out at the deepening blue sky and the early stars. "It's a lovely place."

"Fair dinkum gorgeous!" Elizabeth gushed. "I warned you, I'm a trained protagonist. Besides, we need people like you here, Max. Australia needs a boost. We're barely seventeen million souls. Just to our north, we face Indonesia with two hundred million people. If we don't capture some unique niche in Asia, something to give us influence way beyond our numbers, I fear we'll be sucked into the pit of the Asian Third World. To be blunt, Max, we've been backsliding for fifteen years with the mining industry. We can't compete head-to-head with the Japanese in manufacturing."

Max looked at Irwin. Irwin shrugged. "She's got herself into politics, mate. Come election time, it's awful. She walks like a don, talks like a don."

Max tossed her a challenge. "Really? Why don't you see if you can get rid of Australia's asinine departure tax. It's a damned nuisance—twenty dollars just to leave."

"See, Max, we want you to stay."

Pitsumi returned with platters of food—grilled shark steaks, bearnaise sauce, saffron rice, side dish of curried spinach, papaya spritzed with fresh lime—all prepared

by Archie—and Elizabeth's own gooseberries and custard
with a side slice of her cornflour spongecake for desert.
The long trip, delectable meal, and three glasses of fortified
sangria elevated Max to a peak of festive energy, then
dropped him into a torpor. Irwin promised to wake him
in time for their flight to Temple Bay. Max put himself
to bed.

The next morning, Max woke to a soft tapping at his
bedroom door. Archie called, "Dr. Yeager?"

"Yes." For a second Max thought he'd fallen asleep at
his desk in Marana, Arizona. His subconscious mind had
worked all night while he slept. He quickly inventoried
his senses: the soft pillow against his cheek, the smell of
French-roast coffee, the Kirby dog yapping, the heavy
vegetation outside his open window.

"Mr. Kirby asked me to wake you. We'll serve breakfast
in forty-five minutes."

"Thank you, Archie." A hot shower, shave, and coffee
aroma raised Yeager's spirits. His imagination ran circles
around his conscious mind as he wondered about his new
home—for Elizabeth was right. Felix would fly in and
out of Temple Bay, and he would live there in the
Queensland wilderness—or commute from Cairns—
tending to and improving the technology that would carry
Man to the pristine wilderness above.

Nevertheless, Max sang in the shower. He was happy.
And happiness can shake fatigue better than food, or sleep,
or even a hot shower.

Irwin Kirby rushed Max through breakfast and thirty
minutes of polite chitchat with the Kirby kids. Liz kissed
her husband on the cheek and promised to have a babysitter
for the night of their return from Temple Bay. Then Archie
drove Irwin and Max to a small private airfield.

Irwin led the way into the hangar. Archie pushed a dolly
with some provisions and two overnight bags to a
Beechcraft Airstream. Irwin followed with a picnic basket,

which he handed to Max as he joined his mechanic to make the preflight checks. Irwin Kirby didn't trust machines, and there just weren't many places to put a plane down on Cape York.

They took off, rose above the trees and houses, turned northeast to avoid the clouds building over the mountains. Almost immediately they left civilization behind.

Max looked down on the rainforest. He felt like a time traveler gazing down upon the primordial forests. Muddy rivers flowed to a shoreline of intermittent rocks and wide beaches, belching brown water into crystal blue. He imagined that below the canopy of trees, a multitude of creatures stalked each other, the small fleeing the large. He looked down at a solitary stork, large black-on-white wings spread to catch a thermal updraft. Occasionally he saw a building or road, but after the jet flew past Cairns, there were few signs of man.

Neither Irwin nor Max talked much. Max looked down at the land the way a tourist might look up at an ancient cathedral. Irwin left Max to his thoughts. From the left side of the plane, Max saw the Great Dividing Range, a peculiar spine of rock more modest than its name—a pile of stones, and oddly enough, not a volcano among them. Australia, for all her mass, had no volcano, the only continent without one. From the right side of the plane, Max saw the bands of color in the land and sea, from green forest to golden sand to various light and dark shades of blue water reaching out to the Great Barrier Reef, the world's largest living thing, much grander than its name.

In time, Max's thoughts turned to the heavy picnic basket. Max gave up his seat as copilot to become flight attendant. The basket offered four bulky chicken salad sandwiches, crisps, fruit salad, cookies, two bottles of beer, and a large thermos of coffee. Max held up a plate of swirled pastries. "What are these?"

Irwin peeked over his shoulder and said, "Vegemite pinwheels, one of Liz's specialities."

While they ate their sandwiches, Irwin abruptly turned the conversation to Temple Bay, asking, "I can't help but wonder what's in the deal for me?"

"I'm not the numbers man. You'll need to work the details with Rolf Bernard or with our numbers guy, Herb Eckert. But I'm sure it will be worth your while—we're working with a huge profit margin. You'll do much better than shooting Russian boosters."

"Something's better than nothing."

"And I think we can do much better than just something. We figure each ship is good for a hundred launches before metal fatigue takes it out of service. Personally, I think we'll find that the number of launches will reach two hundred per ship. Fuel costs aren't bad. The components and composite materials in the ship keep it very light— microelectronics and new carbon-carbon graphite materials. The aerospike engines' thrust-to-weight is eighty percent better than the old bell-nozzle design. So, with direct labor, fuel, and depreciation, we can fly for less than five million dollars a pop."

"No one would believe it."

"In fact, it's so good we stopped advertising the fact. We'd just as well have no one believe it. We don't need competitors trying to beat us into production."

"I could see Mitsubishi running with your SSTO design—you want to talk about a monopoly in space!"

Max carefully unwrapped the plastic wrap from his sandwich. "That's certain. The Japanese know how to capture and imprison market share. We'll take that chapter from their book for a change. Sweeter still, we can capture market share while making big money. Let's assume we charge a thousand dollars per pound to put payloads into low earth orbit. At that price, we'd cut our nearest competitor's price by eighty percent. But that's just the beginning of the customer's savings. Ever tried to buy insurance for a Delta rocket cargo?"

"Expensive, I know."

"Exactly. Insurance for a Felix launch would be dirt cheap by comparison, because we've cut the chance of catastrophic failure next to nil. Truth be known, we can probably put a pound into orbit for about the same cost as purchasing insurance for shuttle cargo."

Irwin amplified the thought. "Lower costs will generate demand. And we won't have to worry about our customers canceling out so they can pay five times our price and take five times the risk to stay with NASA, Ariane, or the Chinese."

"So we know the Felix earns a good profit per launch."

"Absolutely." Irwin agreed.

"Now add volume. Originally, your Temple Bay operation planned how many Zenit launches?"

"Three the first year, six the second year, with a capacity of nine per year."

"With our Felix fleet, we could launch nine per month— nine per *week*, if we had to. Heck, we can make money on a flight that's half full. Let's assume BAP contracts all ground support from your partnership and pays twenty percent of gross revenue to your partnership, plus BAP pays for fuel. And let's be ultraconservative. Let's say we do four launches per month. Your share of the gross revenue would be . . . over $13 million per month, or $156 million in the first year." Max didn't need a calculator.

Irwin turned and looked at Yeager. The plane banked slightly to the right.

Max prompted him. "You fly. I'll talk and work the figures. Quite simply, our numbers work. The profits are real. It took the railroads a hundred years to realize that they were in the transportation business, not the train business. With Felix we've got to understand that we are in the space transportation business, not the rocket business." Max, excited by his own argument, made a punctuating gesture with his sandwich, losing a small chunk of chicken that flew past Irwin and adhered to the instrument panel.

"I believe you. I believe you."

"Oh, I'm sorry. All over your altimeter." Max fumbled a napkin from the basket.

"Don't bother. I'll clean it later. Anyway, if the needle gets down to the chicken, we're in deep trouble."

"I got carried away. I didn't mean to toss the chicken salad."

"I forgive you. We've had worse tossed up here." Kirby turned and grinned. "I can't be coy: A hundred and fifty-six million per year! Are you serious? That's a three-year payback for the spaceport. Max, that's beyond our wildest dreams."

As they approached Temple Bay, a thin blanket of clouds settled over the land. Irwin Kirby set the jet down on a thin runway cut from thick vegetation and covered with crushed coral and limestone, kicking up a great white cloud behind the jet. They saw two men, one in a jeep, the other in a Range Rover, waiting at the end of the runway near a row of tin sheds. Irwin taxied to a stop, cut the jet engines, and said "Excuse, please, my back teeth are treading water." He quickly let himself out of the plane, and disappeared into a small shed.

A moment later, Max poked his head out the doorway. The two sunburned men grinned. The smaller man spoke, "G'day! I'm Bonser Pratt and this here's my mate, Kyle Weedham."

"And I'm Max Yeager." Max looked around. "Where's Mr. Kirby?"

"He's in the dunney. Man's got a four-hour bladder—like a clock, a precision instrument."

The quiet Kyle Weedham said, "Mind your manners, Mr. Kirby's your boss, you no-hoper."

"I am the personification of hope." Bonser winked at Max Yeager and added, "Don't pay attention to Kyle, Mr. Yeager. He takes things too literally; he's an engineer, you know. Can't help himself."

Max raised an eyebrow. "I'm an engineer."

Kyle poked Bonser. "See there. What a hoon you're makin' yourself to be."

"Sorry, Mr. Yeager. I figured you were just up here for a bit of troppo." Pratt shrugged his shoulders.

Max didn't understand.

Kyle translated. "A bit of the tropics."

"No vacation for me this trip. My company wants to resuscitate your spaceport."

"You see, ya big galah? You better treat Mr. Yeager with more reserve. We'd better get about our work. You tether the plane. I'll pump the petrol." He turned to Max and said, "You and Mr. Kirby take the Rover." He touched the brim of his hat, a brusque courtesy, then walked back to the petrol shed, while Bonser Pratt secured the plane.

Max mopped his forehead with a handkerchief. The panorama before him looked serene, even cultivated. With his briefcase in hand, Max stood looking across Temple Bay, a quiet pool of eternal blue. He looked back toward the high ground that stood above the scarred land, the corrugated steel Quonset huts, and the concrete and steel pad with short houses built like pillboxes. He looked at the unpaved roads cut through seething jade-green vegetation. Nature would take back anything Man didn't fight to keep. His shoes were already covered with fine white dust.

Bonser called out, "Mr. Kirby, sir. We've got electric power in the blockhouse, dormitory, and machine shop."

Kirby reappeared from the shed and answered with a wave, adding "There's a case of lager in the plane—bring it, will you?"

Bonser effused, "Much appreciated, boss."

Irwin and Max threw their bags into the Rover and drove away, leaving the two hired hands to tend to the plane. Max asked, "Those are your two caretakers?"

"Right. Bonser and Kyle run the place. Kyle's my civil engineer—a good mechanic, too. He's shy, but he worked

with us through most of the excavation and building. I
wanted to keep him on to mind things till we sort out
our money problems. Plus, he needed the job."

Irwin drove over a deep rut where rainwater had cut a
ditch through the road. Irwin refused to slow down, letting
the Rover and their backsides absorb the punishment.
"I hired Bonser out of Cookland. He used to drive
roadtrains up Bruce Highway. He knows most everybody
on the Cape—most of the roughnecks from Cairns to
Cookland—and he gets along with the aborigines. There's
one reservation south of here, another on the west coast
of the peninsula. And Bonser can handle the ratbag gold
diggers running about. He knows the territory."

Irwin reckoned he had five hours of daylight left, and
he hurried to start the tour of Temple Bay Spaceport.
Heavy clouds rolled down the coast. Max asked to see
the pad first. It was reinforced cement, slightly grooved
for foot traffic. They had molded a great trough to shunt
rocket blasts seaward. Large iron footings, primed with
orange paint, stuck an inch or so from the huge concrete
table. Irwin pointed to the beams that had been driven
thirty feet into granite—they would hold the tower steady
through a typhoon. Max gently reminded Irwin that Felix
did not need a tower, just a flat, solid piece of cement.

The blockhouse offered few creature comforts. The
stale air smelled faintly of gasoline and mildew. Electric
generators lined the walls, their gas tanks drained and
filters laid out to dry. Max heard one generator humming
outside. It accounted for the ceiling lights and the
dehumidifier. Tables and desks lay empty except for odd
notes taped to beige Formica tops. Cables poked out from
holes, and empty metal casings stood where displays were
supposed to go. Irwin explained that the black cables
served data and communication links; the blue cables
brought in video from unattended observation cameras,
plus a satellite TV signal.

Five metal folding chairs sat in a circle as if continuing

some conversation. Heavy cork, the kind that Irwin might have used in Canberra Studios, covered the rear wall. The other walls were gray concrete, streaked where lime had leached through fissures. A white synthetic tile covered the raised floor. Irwin's boots made a hollow sound as he walked around the dimly lit, unfurnished room. A single door marked "Lavatory" led to a small tiled room, empty except for a single toilet with the lid taped securely shut, and a set of capped pipes where a washbasin would go. Max took notes.

"We still dig dunneys because we never got 'round to hooking things up to the septic tank. We don't have potable running water either. We got stream water for bathin' and washin' up, but we got to use halizone pills, or drink bottled water," Irwin explained.

Irwin pushed open the heavy steel door and let in a bright flood of sunlight that poured through a gap in the gathering clouds. Out they stumbled, squinting and shielding their eyes. Max asked, "You built from a Russian design, didn't you?"

"Basically, yes," Irwin answered frankly. "I figured they've had more live tests of their blockhouses than anyone, and we were planning to use their boosters. Is that a problem?"

"No, no," Max assured Irwin. "I just noticed that it's . . . it's so . . ." Max groped for the right word. "Thick." Max noticed Irwin's concern and added, "Thick is good."

Irwin and Max walked through the remainder of the launch complex. In a separate shed they visited a diesel locomotive engine—French design—stripped from its carriage and bolted to a concrete slab. "That's our electrical power plant." Irwin walked over to wipe a bit of rust from the radiator fan. "We run her twice a month to keep her seals wet."

Max believed he could launch Felix from Cape York in less than three months. He needed to airlift four trailers filled with electronics, find adequate fuel, and add to the electric power plant. "I think we're going to want to make our own fuel."

Irwin shook his head. "I don't understand, Max. Either you'll have to haul liquid rocket fuel to Temple Bay, or you'll have to haul natural gas or something up here to drive a turbine and break down into hydrogen and oxygen."

"Perhaps. But you've abundant hydrogen and oxygen in the water. I just need you to find us a cryogenics plant."

"That part's easy. Sishumi in Melbourne will sell you their plant, but you don't have the electrical power to run it. I doubt there's enough capacity this side of Cairns. And you'd go broke lining up enough diesel generators to run a cryogenics plant. Even then, you'd have to haul in diesel by roadtrain, unless, of course, you prefer to tangle with the wharfies and the Great Barrier Reef."

"You let me worry about getting power." Max pulled out a card and jotted a note. "We're contemplating launching our own solar power satellite to beam about thirteen megawatts down to Temple Bay."

Irwin's eyes got wide.

Max grinned. "Right. Just think what SPS technology could do for Australia."

"You could run for prime minister, Yank or no."

Rain pecked at the Range Rover's metal shell, warning Irwin to get to shelter. They drove toward the empty dormitories, located on higher ground. In the distance Max saw an island—not a slab of dry reef, but a shard of rock lying outside the bay at the edge of the reef. Max recovered his card and scribbled another note. Thunder grumbled from the mountains, and a soft, steady, warm rain followed.

Kyle met them at Dormitory #1. He stood for a moment on the wide porch to catch his breath. Bonser had taken an umbrella and a fishing pole down to the beach. It was Sunday, after all, Bonser's official day off. Bonser spent a fair amount of time fishing on his official days on, too, but Kyle didn't mind. He'd never know one day from the next if it weren't for his calendar, and an occasional lock at the TV. Kyle thawed a box of lamb chops. He put the meat on a propane broiler that was set on the leeward side of the porch. The heavy rain blew under the rafters and drops of it hissed as they hit the broiler. Kyle announced that he'd boiled some frozen greens and opened a tin of Queensland pineapple. "Too bad we can't get the genuine article."

The dormitory still smelled of fresh paint and new carpet. Each of the four standing dormitories was built as a square. The common area—sitting room, and kitchenette and scullery—filled the middle third of the square. There were ten suites, five on either side of the common area. Each suite slept four men in bunk beds. Each suite had four closets, four chests of drawers, a common bath and toilet. Each dormitory could house one hundred and sixty men, except for the dormitory Kyle and Bonser stayed in. There, they converted one suite into an arms room and another into a small jail. Kyle's crews had poured footings for three more dormitories and a set of bungalows for the upper crust, but the money ran out, and the footings sat like white grave markers on a muddy, weed-infested field.

They built no separate facilities for women. The women—the dozen or so who came to work at Temple Bay in its heyday—shared trailers close to the bay. None of the trailers remained.

One of the more poetic limited partners had christened the set of dormitories. Stellarville, extolling the theme that they lived at the gateway to the stars. The workers thought Stellarville a bit pretentious—they called their piece of the world Lizard City, or Bug Burg, democratically named for the majority of inhabitants. As the unofficial mayor of the dormitories, Bonser Pratt had chosen Lizard City because lizards were relatively high on the city's food chain—and it stuck.

Rain fell harder. Rivulets poured from the roof, creating a curtain of water around the porch.

Max and Irwin made themselves at home. Inasmuch as the building was nearly empty, each got his own large room with a screened window facing the ocean. Max found his overnight bag and a set of clean towels sitting at the foot of a steel bunk. He dried his hair and changed his shirt, then joined Irwin and Kyle for dinner.

As Kyle finished setting a table for four, the front door flew open, and there, filling the door frame, stood Bonser Pratt, Lord Mayor of Lizard City, drenched, half-naked, holding an armful of sodden clothes, a pair of boots slung over his shoulder. " 'Scuse me, mates. I'll try not to track too much water. Got me jersey wet, me trousers . . ."

"Ya should've taken your oilskin."

"You're not me mum." Bonser Pratt walked past the table, slowing long enough to survey the menu. "I'll be right back," he promised as he disappeared into his private suite, leaving a trail of small puddles behind. Max looked at Irwin. Irwin looked at Kyle. Kyle just shook his head. "Shall we wait for Bonser before we say grace?"

They waited till Pratt returned. Torrential rain beat the roof, and the constant drumming forced everyone to raise his voice for dinner conversation. Pratt persuaded Max to forsake his tea for beer, saying, "We don't want any Pommification happenin' this far beyond the Black Stump."

"In the wilderness." Kyle translated for Max.

Bonser and Kyle took turns putting questions to Max, and they liked the answers they heard. Lizard City would again fill up with people and payroll. Not only would they see spaceships leave the cape, they would watch them return! They would help maintain the craft, care for the crews, and somehow—Max didn't explain—they would make their own rocket fuel if Max could make enough electricity. Because they had nothing to lose, they felt no reason to be cynical.

After dinner, Kyle escorted the guests to the television room. He had assembled a dish antenna, then rigged some leftover electronics to access Irwin Kirby's TV broadcast satellite and break the scramble code. "You stinker, you bloody pirate!" Kirby rebuked Kyle. "You nicked my satellite signal, didn't you?"

"Shall I turn it off?" Kyle inquired sincerely, and Bonser fumed, "I told you not to show it to Mr. Kirby, you bloody galah!" He paced the floor waiting for Kirby's verdict.

The rain beat the roof. Kirby said, "Keep it on, please. To whom shall I send the bill, Kyle?"

Chapter 12

In the southwest corner of Arizona, the predawn black puts on a world-class show of stars. Sixty miles west of Gila Bend, at the rest stop outside the small town of Dateland, a man wearing a BAP-blue hardhat, stepped out of small pickup truck, looked up at the canopy of stars, then lit a bright red flare. The light spooked a group of mule deer that disappeared into the gloom. The man faced east over a blank stretch of Interstate 8, which disappeared down a gentle slope, leaving nothing but the darkest patch of star-speckled sky.

A yellow glow became plain over the ridge, then slowly rose, flashing—the lead car in the caravan, and behind it the first behemoth cargo—the bottom third of a Felix spacecraft, the production model—squat upon a special trailer, and draped in a silver tarpaulin, rolling the prescribed thirty-five miles per hour through the desert. After her hindquarters, a chase car followed, yellow lights flashing. Then a second trailer came bearing the nose section laid into a great wooden cradle and tethered on its side, nose forward, shrouded. Then another chase car with yellow lights blazing.

The man with the flare waved the caravan into the rest area. Ten minutes later the scene repeated. A second bisected Felix lined up in the rest area. Then the third lumbered into the lot. Trucks and cars opened doors and disgorged tired men. Bright white headlights and yellow beacons blinked off. A tan Range Rover drove to the head of the column. Out stepped Max Yeager. Paul Bernard followed, stepped to the side, and bent over to touch his toes. "That's it for the night."

Max poured espresso from a thermos into the silver cap, then offered it to Paul. "You don't have to ride shotgun all the way to San Diego."

"These babies aren't going anywhere without me. You know Murphy's Law." Paul started to walk down the line of trailers, watching crewmen test heavy chains and canvas straps, looking for any signs of shifting loads. The custom-built trailers were BAP's property now: three axles front, three axles back, twenty-four wheels.

Max retorted, "Well, they won't be going anywhere for another seventeen hours. I booked us a couple of rooms in a motel outside the Yuma Marine Air Station. I need to make some calls and get some work done. You *are* coming aren't you? Or are you going to sit here?"

"I need a shower."

The foreman approached waving a flashlight, "Dr. Bernard?"

"Yes."

"We've got a chuck wagon showing up with a hot breakfast. We're putting up some shade. We're leaving a quarter of the crew here to secure the vehicles and the rest are driving an hour to Yuma for rest. We'll have them back by eight in the evening, and we'll be back on the road at eleven tonight."

"Good."

The foreman spit what looked like black treacle. "We got word from the California highway patrol. They'll monitor us from Yuma to San Diego. They want us to stay tomorrow night at a rest stop west of El Centro. I checked the extended weather report—no problems." He spit again, expertly.

"Good. Make sure that container ship . . ." Paul fumbled for the name. "I must be tired."

"The *Skalhorne*, sir."

"Yes. Call ahead to make sure the *Skalhorne* is ready and waiting for us to load."

The foreman unscrewed the lid from a small can and took a generous pinch of snuff. "I wouldn't worry. Mr. Tyler chartered it. He said the *Skalhorne* is a very special ship: efficient, reliable, especially for moving oversized military cargo."

Paul cocked his head and stared back at the foreman disapprovingly.

"But of course, I'll call Mr. Tyler just to be sure." A noise caught the foreman's attention. Crew members drove tent stakes for awnings. Gas lanterns set off white glares. Folding tables and chairs appeared. He spit. "Why don't you and Dr. Yeager go get some breakfast. I'll be here when you get back."

Paul drank his espresso, climbed back into the Range Rover, and started the engine. Max took the passenger side, reaching back through the suitcases and boxes for a bag of cookies, asking, "Why on earth did you bring all this crap? Ever heard of UPS?"

Paul answered with a silent side glance.

"Oh, no. Don't tell me you're still going to take that stinking freighter to Australia. We've got men assigned to travel with the Felix craft."

Paul set the cruise control. "I'm not so keen about this whole deal. You cut my spaceships in half. You're hauling them to God knows where."

"Temple Bay. . . ."

"Yeah, but does God know where Temple Bay is?"

"I'm sure He does. What's eating you?"

"You know Max, when we put them back together, we're going to need a dust-free, humidity-controlled hangar."

"I told you. Irwin Kirby's people are building the hangar. In two weeks we'll have our own BAP technicians in their own bunny suits, assembling the Felix ships in a giant dehumidified, air-filtered hangar, complete with laminar airflow. When my guys get finished, you won't be able to find the seam on the titanium silicon skin. They're more artist than engineer."

"In two months we could have flown them out."

"If we could have gotten permission." Max changed the subject. "You let me worry about putting the ships together. You start thinking about making cryogenic hydrogen and oxygen fuel. You've got an old Sishumi factory, all the water you need, and all the electricity you can get from Fenster's solar power satellite. But you've got to put the stuff together. Can you?"

"I'll have to see the Sishumi equipment, but yes, I'm sure I can manage."

"Good. Because you'll need to figure out how to make enough fuel to support eight to ten launches in a four-week window."

"That's a lot of slush hydrogen . . ."

After breakfast and a short nap, Max dragged Paul to his room. Max had pushed small bits of furniture aside, stripped the wall of several cheap prints, then taped up long paper banners—a computer-generated PERT chart. He lead Paul to the wall, then traced the thicker line with a red pen. "This is the critical path, which says we can get there from here on schedule. We've got to prep the solar power satellite, build and test the rectenna, install the cryogenics plant, build a fuel storage, ship in the first eighty thousand pounds of fuel, put up the SPS with Felix-P—"

"Whoa. Each milestone represents a couple dozen tasks."

"Wrong. Hundreds of tasks. You couldn't fit a PERT showing individual tasks in this entire motel."

"Have you run the detailed PERT?"

"Not yet." Max betrayed his frustration. "I don't have a decent handle on fuel production. That's why we're spending this quality time together. I've got to brief your father about our plan next week."

"We need more help."

"That's not an option. You and I drive this train, Paul. Get used to that—or you'll find yourself working for the employees."

"Hmm." Paul studied the chart. "Why did you make fuel storage dependent upon SPS operation?"

Max shrugged. "I guessed. It takes a lot of power to keep slush hydrogen cold and under pressure—more power than we can squeeze out of that diesel-powered generator."

Paul rubbed the back of his neck. "We'll get a lithium sponge which cuts the amount of power needed. Then we can run fuel storage off your diesel generator. We can buy General Motor's sponge."

"You sure about that?"

"I helped build the GM sponge, remember?"

"Right." Max squinted at the chart. "That cuts a week from the path. Good."

Paul traced the line with his finger. "What's this task up here labeled 'Deliver cargo'?"

"Your dad just said he'd deliver a cargo ready to put into low earth orbit by April fifteen."

"What cargo?"

"He wouldn't, or maybe couldn't say. The customer wants four launches, back-to-back. That's all we know."

"But we've got to know."

"He might tell you, Paul. He sure as hell wouldn't tell me."

"Hmm." Paul scratched the two-day stubble on his chin. "That smells . . . ."

After a long day standing in front of the motel wall, adding a couple hundred tasks to Max's PERT chart, Paul drove Max back to the caravan and they made the second leg of their three-day road trip to San Diego. Max and Paul spent a second day mashing the schedule, sweating the details, recalculating the PERT chart's critical path. While Paul napped in preparation for the night's drive, Max typed his notes in Hypertext. While Paul drove the Rover at the back of the caravan, Max took short naps.

The BAP caravan suffered little traffic until they passed Palm Springs on the third day. The traffic thickened as they approached San Diego, even at four o'clock in the morning. They skulked through town, effecting a torturous maneuver to get into the docks.

The *Skalhorne* waited at the dock. Four hundred and eighty feet long, she was rigged to carry containers in a gaping square hold, then stacked sky-high on the decks. She showed little rust, just enough about her skirts to prove she worked for a living. She flew a Liberian flag, sailed for a Danish captain, and carried a crew of mixed breed.

Long gin poles hung over the sides ready to hoist BAP's unusual cargo. Sailors with measuring tapes scampered about the trailers containing the Felix nose sections: they could fit in the hold. The three fat ends of the Felix craft would travel on deck. The crew worked quickly using the last couple hours of darkness. Part of their special skills included loading and unloading oversize cargoes without attracting attention.

The ship's captain greeted Paul with the Nordic reverence for titles, "Mr. Dr. Bernard, we have the pleasure to invite you aboard. Your letter of credit is in order, and we may proceed." He bowed and sent a pair of Estonian seamen to haul Paul's baggage aboard.

Paul went back to the dock to nervously watch the crew load the three Felix craft aboard the ship. Moments thereafter, a trio of Nordic seamen set a sling around Paul's Range Rover, connected it to a cable hook dangling from a gin pole, then hoisted it up, slipping it into a hold. With similar dexterity the crews detached the customized trailers from the large Peterbilt tractors. They nimbly hoisted each trailer and Felix nose section into the air over a yawning hatch and lowered them into the hold. Having finished securing the nose sections below, the *Skalhorne*'s large crane hauled the big sections— trailer and all—onto the deck, where the crew secured them amidships. Thick steel cable and chain bound the trailers to the deck. They stretched a thick black nylon web over the bulk, adding yet another assurance that nothing would slip. As a finishing touch, the crew built a screen of empty containers around the unusual deck cargo.

Before the sun rose over San Diego, the BAP caravan had disappeared, half in the *Skalhorne*'s hold, half on deck hidden by a wall of containers. The large cylinders in the middle looked like nothing but standard tanks for a refinery. The Peterbilt tractors drove away.

Max stood next to Paul on the docks. The first rays of the sun lit the ship's superstructure, and the captain called down, "We have permission to leave port: Come aboard now, if you please, Dr. Bernard."

Max bid Paul bon voyage, and rebuked him by adding, "You should stay behind and help me cut another twenty days from the schedule. Right now, our plan assumes that nothing goes wrong. Now how realistic is that?"

"Our plan assumes that our three spaceships make it to Australia."

"You can't affect the trip by riding with them."

"Who says? Besides, we don't even know what we're planning for. We don't even know who the customer is or what kind of satellite they want to put up, what kind of orbits to plan. It's more likely the schedule will slip another sixty days. I'll call from Australia and see if I can't get some answers."

"Do that." Max shook the younger man's hand. "Give my warmest regards to Irwin and his wife, Liz. You'll like them both. I'll be seeing all of you within the month."

Paul scampered up the gangplank. As Paul stepped on

deck, the *Skalhorne* slipped her lines and left the dock for open sea.

Max waved once, then left to pay a short visit to a friend at the U.S. Space Surveillance Station at Brown Field; the next day he was back in Washington, D.C.

Chapter 13

Winter hunkered down on Washington, D.C. The cold and damp crawled under the skin, and people who'd complained about July's oppressive heat now complained about January's relentless chill.

Max Yeager drove to the Bernard mansion to deliver a late-night briefing, subject: Temple Bay Spaceport Operations. Only Rolf Bernard and Bobby Tyler attended. Max concluded the presentation of his detailed plan. "At present, Paul, Felix A, B, and C are aboard the *Skalhorne* bound for Cairns Harbor. Bruce Highway—the only highway up Cape York—practically runs through Cairns Harbor. They'll simply put the trailers ashore, hook them up to six tractors, and haul them straight to Temple Bay."

"I take it you're flying the Felix prototype in with the Super Guppy."

"Yes, sir."

"And the solar power satellite?"

"We shipped the rectenna a couple of weeks ago, ordinary freight. It's stacked like a giant erector set on the beach at Temple Bay. Fenster plans to transport the satellite on one of our BP-17s, land in Brisbane, and haul it north by roadtrain. No doubt he'll make schedule with his deliveries."

"Good."

"Fenster will need six weeks just to assemble the rectenna in the bay. Maybe a little longer. He says it's just pouring out there, and that the ground has turned to slop. They've already got six inches of rain in January with a week to go."

Rolf said, "My money's on Fenster, that he'll make schedule. I'm pleased, Max."

"We can't get too cocky. We could still slip badly. Paul and I are trying to do too many things at once. It's chaotic."

Rolf waved off Max's doubts. "Don't worry about the chaos, it serves as our camouflage, our hiding place, our plausible denial. Let your engineers make their own order; you just adjust their timing so that all their chaotic schedules come into order at once. You and Paul have never let me down before."

"Thank you, I guess."

Tyler interjected, "Dr. Yeager, there is one thing, one little adjustment I'd like to see in your schedule."

"What?"

"Just a small but potentially significant item. Rolf appears before a Senate committee next Thursday. You must get everything you need out of the country before then."

"Why?"

Tyler shrugged. "Just to be on the safe side."

Rolf echoed, "The safe side—how true. Those pols could do something crazy—freeze assets, commandeer property, pass some retroactive resolution, who knows? So get Fenster's satellite out of country pronto. After you get our gear stowed at Temple Bay, I'll feel a lot safer."

"Fenster doesn't answer to me," Max reminded Rolf.

"I'll see to it then." Rolf faced Tyler. "I really need to get to Australia and check things out."

"No, sir—bad idea." Tyler leaned forward in his seat. "Temple Bay is still a sideshow, and we need to keep it that way for as long as possible. If you go to Temple Bay all eyes will follow. We need you to stay here and keep the wolves busy."

"I'm not sure how I ought to take that."

"A compliment, of course."

Max raised a finger. "One last item. Just what are we launching next April?"

"Pardon me?" Rolf delayed answering.

"You know what I'm asking: four launches in less than ten days. Just what should I plan for?"

Tyler took over. "Dr. Yeager. I shall see if I can get permission from the client to give you the details."

"See that you do."

Tyler stiffened and added sardonically, "Frankly, I don't think the client will give a damn whether you know about the cargo in advance, but I'll ask."

Max's cheeks burned a shade redder. "Please tell them that my foreknowledge would reduce the risk of the schedule slipping."

"I promise to tell them." Tyler nodded to Rolf, who brought the meeting to a close.

With business out of the way, Rolf invited Yeager and Tyler to his study. He set three short crystal tumblers on the cherrywood bar, added ice, then produced what looked like a wine bottle with a musty yellow label. "I've been saving this particular bottle of scotch for a moment like this—I wish Paul were here. I feel like we've crossed the Rubicon."

Rolf peeled a thin lead cover from the neck of the bottle. While twisting a corkscrew, he commented, "General Rommel owned this scotch. He captured a huge store of British liquor during his African campaign and hauled the great barrels around with him, finally back to Germany, where he stored it in his castle cellar near Ulm. There, it stayed lost for years, a source of speculation and litigation. The Brits wanted their booze back, but they lost. . . ." Rolf affected a British accent. "Spoils of war and all that tommyrot!"

He pulled at the stubborn cork, and with strained voice he continued, "Found by Americans in the early 1970s, the liquor was bottled, sold, and for the most part consumed."

He popped the cork and poured scotch into the tumblers. Tyler looked on. "Field Marshal Erwin Rommel?"

Rolf tasted the scotch and pronounced it "Drinkable. Not remarkable. Rommel, who sought only to defend his homeland, had problems with his government, too."

Tyler mused, "And when he crossed his Rubicon, to use your analogy, his last option was poison or *The People's Court*."

"No!" Rolf barked. "No, Bobby. Rommel could have, and he should have, fought to the last breath. He was in the right, after all." Rolf downed his glass of scotch. "I'll drink Rommel's scotch, I'll share in his predicament, but I won't share his poison."

"Good for you." Tyler drank his glass. "I can't abide fatalists."

Max Yeager emptied his glass and Rolf filled all three again. "A truly indifferent whiskey."

"Perhaps this poor scotch traveled too much." Max decided, sniffing his glass.

Rolf shoved a glass toward Tyler. "Then, for God's sake, let's put it out of its misery."

"Hear, hear!" Tyler took his glass.

Max drank half of his scotch and wished aloud, "We could really use Paul right about now."

Max hustled back to Australia to work on the Felix spacecraft. Dr. Fenster packed up his satellite and took it to Temple Bay in time to watch his rectenna grow like a spiderweb in shallow saltwater.

Rolf steeled himself for Thursday, his turn before the Senate Select Committee on the National and Defense Aerospace Programs Procurement. Winston rehearsed him on questions, admonishing him, "Don't take the bait. This is not your garden-variety brief on the defense budget, aviation, and space. They'll try to suck you into a confrontation. But whatever happens, don't take the bait. My mole on the Hill tells me they're going to try to nail you for building the production models at the same time you were delivering a mere prototype."

"That's just the way the contract worked out."

"Doesn't matter. If they can make you look like a chiseler, they make points as warriors against waste, fraud, and abuse. So you have to emphasize the value that was added to the prototype through BAP's initiatives."

"Gotcha."

"Next, my mole tells me they're going to try to hang you for smuggling technology out of the country."

"We didn't do anything illegal."

"Doesn't matter."

"I can see where this is going." Rolf shook his head. He and Winston stayed the night.

Herb Eckert rode with Rolf to Capitol Hill and they walked together quietly, tight-jawed to the Senate hearing room. A pair of BAP lawyers waited for them outside the room. The four men walked inside and took their places at a table elevated on an small platform—an uncomfortable dock, a hotbox. Ted Winston and Bobby Tyler sat at the back of the room.

At the front of the room, Rolf could see senators and staff milled around swapping war stories and comparing questions. Who would set him up? Who would deliver the coup de grace? Behind Rolf, the press adjusted equipment, cameras, klieg lights, and sound-recording gear. A handful of Air Force officers sat in a pack to the side. General Harchord's aide sat near the front. Harchord, scheduled to testify the next day, did not attend.

Herb tried to take some of the tension out of the air with small talk. "I just got back from Atlanta. I restructured our debt with Universe Bank. So, I was walking back to Peachtree Plaza, and guess what I saw?"

"What?"

"Atlanta puts its steam grates in the middle of their streets—a bit hard on homeless people, don't you think?"

Rolf turned and looked over his bifocals. "What's the point?"

"You used to say New York was a tough town."

Rolf blinked. "Washington's tougher. In Washington we beat our own so others will fear us." Rolf slowly turned to face the commotion on the dais.

Herb settled down for a long Thursday with the boss. "I was just trying a little humor—you know, let out some of the pregame jitters."

"I'm not jittery."

"Well, I'm nervous enough for both of us," Herb admitted. "Or maybe I'm just weary of bad news, the surprises. I get tired of telling you each day that we're out of cash."

"And I get tired of hearing it, Herb."

"I know. We need a win, and here we are, about to get a beating from a bunch of politicians."

Rolf tapped his pen on the table, leaned away from the lawyers, and whispered, "Our big win is coming. I'm working on a deal that will either fix things or . . ." Rolf paused.

"Or what?"

"Can't say just yet. Never mind. In another three months I could have told the Senate where to stuff their subpoena, but at present, I've got to play their game. So do you."

Herb looked wide-eyed at his boss.

The senators—six Democrats and four Republicans— took their seats. From their high-back leather chairs, perched on their stage behind their crescent table, they looked down on Mr. Bernard and grinned for the TV cameras. Defense contractors were always fair game.

With a single tap of a gavel, the chairman spoke in a calculated business-as-usual tone. "Please come to order. My esteemed colleagues and I want to welcome you—

Mr. Bernard and your staff from BAP—and we'd like to extend our welcome to the visitors in the gallery and to our esteemed members of the press. And before we begin these proceedings, I'd like to go over the procedures that we . . ."

Rolf felt as if he was stuck on a crowded elevator between floors. The room temperature hit seventy-eight degrees—thanks to a hyperactive furnace and sluggish ventilation. The klieg lights raised the temperature at the witness table even more. Rolf felt small beads of sweat forming along his hairline. Finally, the preliminary gab stopped and oaths sworn. Rolf waived his opportunity to make an opening statement in a vain hope that the politicians would likewise be brief.

Rolf was disappointed. The big senator from Alabama used ten minutes coughing up some furball about his love for space ("I hope everybody in Huntsville is list'nin'!"). He concluded with a question that could be paraphrased as, "Mr. Bernard, would you explain to this committee how you happened to come by four SSTO spacecraft, when your SDIO contract specified one Felix prototype?"

"Well, Senator, we built them," Rolf answered, well rehearsed. "My Chief Financial Officer, Mr. Herb Eckert, will submit, if you wish, an entire accounting of the time and materials used for the Felix prototype and the three production models." Herb rustled around in his fat briefcase and fished out an inch-thick document. A young woman came around from behind the dais, retrieved the document, and carried it up to the senator from Alabama.

Rolf added, "Those internal BAP documents have passed your GAO audit."

"Very forthcoming. Please sum up for the committee, if you don't mind, how BAP paid for the three extra spaceships—or more precisely, with whose money."

"We're still paying for them. We established a partnership with some European investors. . . ."

"Foreigners?"

"No, family connections that I'd rather not get into at this forum. The partnership, filed under Regulation D of the Securities Act of 1935, permits us to limit public disclosure. Anyway, we used BAP retained earnings and our own capital sources. The Defense Audit Agency and GAO satisfied themselves that only the prototype received government funding."

"Don't go tryin' to hide yourself behind the DAA or the GAO. . . ."

There was a tap of the gavel and the chairman interrupted, "Time. With no objections, I'll yield another ten minutes to the senator from Alabama."

"I thank you." The Southerner was scrupulously polite to his fellow senators. Rolf took a deep breath. He'd have to endure another ten minutes of an itch one ought not to scratch. "What I'm trying to get at, Mr. Bernard, is that BAP used the government's R&D money to develop a prototype when, at the same time, you had the ability to build a production model—three of them in fact. It just seems to me that you took advantage of the taxpayer to front your R&D so you could profit from production. Maybe we need to look into how this whole Felix procurement came about, but I know most of my constituents are going to wonder how come we got the one prototype and you got the three production models."

Rolf jumped on the last question to stop the banter. "You may tell your constituents that the government paid in round numbers, fifteen million dollars to build an unmanned prototype that the contract required us to fly one thousand feet up, maneuver side-to-side, then land. We added about twenty-five million of our R & D money to accelerate the program. Plus parts of the design go back to the early sixties. We share the patent for the aerospike motor with an Australian inventor. In short, the design still belongs to us; we own the patents. The taxpayer got a prototype SSTO spaceship that exceeded government requirements. Whereas the contract called for an unmanned ship, we made it a manned ship at our own expense and with the approval of SDIO and the Air Force. Frankly, we learned so much so fast, that we started building the production models. Unfortunately, we have not been able to interest NASA in using our ships in lieu of shuttle launches. The taxpayers got the bargain of the century."

"That's a matter of speculation." The big Alabaman surrendered the microphone.

Senator Reinhart tapped the working end of the microphone. "I'm not sure we all agree on how BAP ought to pay for the three production models."

Rolf looked sideways at Herb and the lawyers, then faced the dais. "Do you want me to comment?"

"No." Senator Reinhart rustled a couple sheets of paper. "Tell us, if you will, Mr. Bernard, *why* did you build those other three spaceships?"

Rolf forced a smile. "Senator, I'm glad you asked me that question." It was one he'd rehearsed with Winston. "Frankly, I'm flattered that you've taken such an interest in our little experimental spaceships. We've been trying to get the government interested in our work for over twelve years now."

"Well, we're all ears now, Mr. Bernard," the senator added with a note of sarcasm.

"We've been working on the Felix concept, well frankly, ever since man thought of rockets. The first Buck Rogers rockets were all single stage. We had good reasons for using the old disintegrating totem poles, our multistaged rockets—technological obstacles that I think we've finally overcome with stronger and lighter materials, more efficient rocket motors, and cryogenic fuels. I remember when we made the decision to build the three ships. We were driven in part by necessity, and in part by opportunity. I'll explain."

Rolf paused to take a sip of ice water. The hot klieg lights oppressed him. "Necessity first. We built the three spaceships as a reaction to a soft world economy that hurt orders for civilian aircraft. Orders for military systems fell off sharply after the Iraq war. Congress canceled large parts of the space program that BAP had contracts for. In short, I was faced with laying off the best and brightest aerospace engineers and technicians in the world. It takes years and a lot of money to put good teams together. I kept them on the payroll building three spaceships. It seemed a reasonable investment. I figured we'd find a buyer after the prototype proved itself."

"Could you get to the point?"

"We saw tremendous opportunities in pursuing SSTO technology—much of which has been well documented by numerous scientists writing for the *Journal of Practical Applications in Space.* I can have reprints sent to your office."

"That won't be necessary. . . ."

"Without getting into the fine details, our Felix ship, with its multiple motors, is more forgiving than conventional rockets, where a launch is either perfect or catastrophic. Big conventional rocket boosters are *so* unforgiving that you must put an army of expensive engineers on the payroll to make sure everything happens perfectly. In contrast, a BP-3 or a Boeing 747 has four engines. If things don't go perfectly, if one engine fails, we simply land the jet and fix the engine. On the other hand, a faulty rocket either blows up on the pad, or we make it self-destruct to keep it from flying off course where civilians might get hurt. Can you imagine a jumbo jet with a self-destruct mechanism?"

"That's absurd."

"Of course it's absurd. Consequently, NASA prudently keeps more than fourteen thousand highly paid technicians on-site to launch a shuttle. In contrast, Delta Airlines probably has fifty people preparing one of their flights. Also, the Delta crew of fifty may turn around six flights in one day. The shuttle ground crew of fourteen thousand may launch one bird every thirteen weeks.

"To make the math easy, and compare apples to apples, let's assume each support person costs $100,000 per year in salary, benefits, and training. Delta Airlines would pay ground crews about $3,300 per flight. NASA, on the other hand, pays their ground crews over $325 million per flight. In round numbers, NASA spends about a hundred thousand times more money for ground crew operations per flight than does an airline. The point of all this is, we believe we can operate Felix more like an airplane. Some have even speculated that a fleet of Felix spacecraft could operate at a cost less than $100 per pound to low earth orbit. That's about five percent of the cost of using the shuttle or conventional rockets."

Rolf let that much sink in, then added, "To put those numbers in a different perspective, if you fly round-trip from Washington to Tokyo on the Concorde with one suitcase, you pay about $5,000, or about $25 per pound for 200 pounds. If our numbers hold up, we can put people into low earth orbit for about four times the cost of flying on the Concorde, maybe less. People would pay to fly on Felix."

"NASA doesn't concur with your numbers."

"NASA has committed itself to build their National Launch System to carry a sixty-seven-ton cargo. Our concept competes with their vision."

"I don't see the competition, Mr. Bernard. You address small payloads, NASA figures to handle the large ones."

"Senator, I've already lost that argument with NASA. We believe there shouldn't be any sixty-seven-ton cargoes: not until we can build a big enough SSTO. But NASA's certain I'll fail, so in that sense, I guess there's no harm in my trying. It's my money, so to speak. We're going to determine the true cost of operations. If I'm right, everybody wins."

"Everybody?" Senator Reinhart pressed.

"Yes, everybody." Rolf bit his tongue and thought, *Everybody but NASA. They lose big.* NASA's National

Launch System with its huge payload was—as far as Rolf
was concerned—designed to keep private enterprise out
of space and NASA in control. What private sector
company would ever need to put sixty-seven tons into
space to the same orbit all at once? A commercial fleet
of Felix craft would cut NASA's financial throat.

The microphone passed to Senator Hocking, who
continued his colleague's line of questioning. "So you want
to operate your spaceship like an airplane?"

"Yes, sir. We can do it, too."

"That does take some of the sex appeal out of it, doesn't
it?"

"Quite the opposite. Just think, Senator. You and I, men
our age, could fly into space for about twice the price of
a plane ticket around the world. We don't even have to
be particularly brave. In spite of the grief we caused with
the Rixeyville flight, we proved our point. We had a
mechanical failure, and the crew came back safely to the
ground, ready to go back up in a month. Think of it,
Senator: mechanics in greasy overalls, working out on
the tarmac or in a hangar, preparing routinely scheduled
spaceflights—not an army of technicians in sterile rooms.
With eight throttled aerospike motors, we can control
Felix's climb just like an airplane. You don't have to build
your cargo and train your crew to live through eight *g*'s.
Like I said, gray-haired men like you and me could go
into space. Haven't you ever wanted to fly into outer space
and look back on the earth?"

The room caught Rolf's enthusiasm. The microphones
caught the audible "Yes! Yes!" from the crowd. The
chairman rapped the gavel and Senator Hocking changed
the subject. "One of the things that greatly concerns me,
Mr. Bernard, is why you would take these powerful
technologies—as you described your spaceships—out of
the country to foreign soil, under the cover of darkness."

Herb whispered something in Rolf's ear. The lawyers
leaned over and conferred. Then Rolf asked with a bit

of false naiveté, "I don't understand what you mean by under cover of darkness?"

"I think you do. You did move your ships from Arizona to San Diego on trucks through the desert at night, covered in dark cloths, or do you deny that?"

"Bright silver cloths, actually."

"Well you snuck them out at night. Do you deny that?"

Rolf steamed, "Of course I don't deny that. Local municipal ordinances prescribe oversize loads be moved at night. There's no secret here. One doesn't secretly move three spaceships that stand a hundred and ten feet tall through open country. They sat in ordinary rest stops each day for all the world to see. What are you driving at, Senator?"

"I don't think you were straightforward about the means you used to get your equipment out of the country."

Rolf's ears turned red. The BAP lawyers whispered to Rolf, who controlled his rising anger. "We followed the law to the letter. The State Department approved our applications."

"You didn't inform the State Department that you were sending space ships to Australia."

Again the lawyers whispered, and Rolf spoke. "We sent components to be assembled in Australia. Not one component violates any tech-transfer covenant we have as far as Australia goes."

"What about that new rocket motor?"

"Sir, we share that patent with an Australian, a Mr. Irwin Kirby."

"What about the cryogenics?"

"We're using Japanese technology."

The senator glowered. "So what are you going to do with your three spaceships in Australia? Land them on our highways, like you did on Interstate 66?"

Rolf sloughed off that cheap shot. "I'm going to fly cargo for profit. As for landing on highways . . ." Herb nudged him, and Rolf reconsidered. "We got a tankful of bad fuel."

The rest of the senators remained quiet until the senator from Illinois volunteered, "I have nothing further at this time."

A small, acerbic liberal from Washington state, home of BAP's biggest rival, switched on his microphone and said, "We have information that shows you are building an antenna at your foreign base of operations at Cape York. Is that right?"

"No. We're building a rectenna."

"Whatever. There are some concerns in the intelligence community that you've built an antenna to monitor our submarine communications. How do you respond?"

Rolf turned to his lawyer and whispered, "Is he suggesting I'm a damned spy?"

The lawyer shook his head and whispered, "Who knows what he's fishing for?"

The senator pressed, "How do you respond, Mr. Bernard?"

"It's a rectenna."

The senator snapped, "Are you listening to submarine communications?"

"Not with a rectenna. I may be out of my field, but I don't think that's how one monitors a submarine fleet. Give me a second and I'll explain . . ."

"Then explain the purpose of your huge antenna."

Rolf snapped, "A rectenna is short for rectifier-antenna."

"Aha! You admit it's an antenna."

Rolf felt his blood rise. "A rectenna," Rolf pronounced each syllable slowly, "receives microwave energy and converts the energy into alternating electric current. Our rectenna—which is in no way an antenna—is tied to research, and does not concern the National Security Agency or the Department of the Navy."

The senator from Washington muttered into his microphone, "I don't believe that rectenna story for a second."

"What'd you say?" Rolf demanded loudly.

The gavel thwacked. Herb grabbed Rolf by the elbow and whispered, "Don't lose your temper. It's a sucker's game. These guys are experts. They'll tear you apart."

Rolf settled back into his chair. The morning dragged on. Rolf switched from ice water to black coffee. The questions shifted from BAP's SSTO to its civilian aircraft sales. The committee chairman led the discussion. "I have an article from the *Wall Street Journal* that I would like to submit for the record. There's a copy in your packet, Mr. Bernard. The article says that BAP paid a bribe to the Minister of Transportation in Nigeria to win a bid to sell four planes. Did BAP pay a bribe?"

"I investigated the matter. It wasn't a bribe; rather, it was a sales commission. For a whole year I was able to employ five hundred men and women from the great state of California with that Nigerian order. I paid a lot of federal taxes with that order, some of which probably ended up in your pocket."

The room snickered. "How can you call it a sales commission?" The senator raised his voice. "You pay a senior Nigerian government official a large sum of money. He arranges to purchase four planes. Where I come from, Mr. Bernard, that's a bribe."

Herb's voice, even in a whisper, carried a sense of urgency. "Don't take the bait."

Rolf jerked his elbow away from Herb, a slight maneuver unseen by all but the senators on the dais. In his controlled baritone voice, Rolf addressed the chairman. "In Nigeria, they call such payment a commission, or *dash*. Where you come from, Senator, it's called a PAC contribution. And Senator—I know you're intimately familiar with those, because your fundraiser practically lives on my doorstep, rattling his tin cup."

"Are you trying to show contempt for this committee?"

Rolf couldn't resist. Herb, Ted—even Bobby knew it was coming. "No, Senator, I'm trying my hardest not to show my contempt."

The room erupted with laughter. The gavel pounded their laughs into murmurs, then murmurs into silence. The ancient Senator Symington leaned toward his microphone and croaked, "You walked into that one, Bert."

The chairman flashed an angry look at his distinguished colleague. "I move we hold Mr. Bernard in contempt."

Rolf piped up again. "For heaven's sake, let's not waste time on that procedure just yet. I'm not through."

"I advise you to mind your tongue, Mr. Bernard." The chairman rapped the gavel.

Senator Hatch from Utah interrupted. "Let the man speak. You dragged him up here to speak. Let him say what's on his mind." He smirked and sat back in his leather chair to enjoy the fireworks.

Before another senator could confirm or withdraw Hatch's invitation, Rolf launched another salvo. "I've figured out your game. You're gunning for my integrity, my reputation, so let's go all the way. I'll match my integrity, my reputation for honesty, for paying my lunch tab, for keeping straight with my local post office, for keeping my stock transactions above board, for covering my checks, for keeping my zipper zipped, for anything you want—" Rolf paused to catch his breath. "I'll match my good name to Congress' any day. You exempt yourselves from the laws you impose on us; then you haul people like me in here for a little daytime soap opera!"

Herb pulled at Rolf's jacket and Rolf sat down, having finished his tirade. Then he drew an invisible line above his head and spoke into his microphone again. "I've had it up to here with you guys. I'm going to just get out of the government business. It's too big a pain. And you know what? You're a lousy customer. Just ask your questions so I can get out of this kangaroo court."

The room fell silent. One could hear the cameras hum, and a slight rattle in the ventilation. Senator Hatch grinned. "I move we take a brief recess."

Another rap of the gavel concurred. The heavy double

doors in the back of the room opened, and the crowd shuffled out. Ted Winston, who had been sitting in the back, fought his way against the human tide. Rolf saw him coming and expected Ted to admonish him for losing his temper with the senators.

But Ted said, "Don't let up now. For good or ill, you're in it now. You've got to make them think you're too hot to handle."

"How's that?"

"Just remember what Sonny Liston said after he fought Cassius Clay: 'Yo cain't fight no crazy man.'"

Rolf didn't always see the wisdom in Ted's advice, but this tidbit he turned over in his mind, *you can't fight no crazy man.*

Throughout the afternoon session, Rolf stayed on the offensive. For the better part of two hours, the questions stayed closer to fact and farther from rhetoric. The committee asked specific questions about BAP's partnership with the Australian citizen, Irwin Kirby, and they cautioned Rolf about technology transfer. The details embedded in their questions astonished Rolf, and he asked himself, "How can they know so much about Cape York and the three Felix craft? For that matter, what don't they know?"

Then the Democrats grilled Rolf about cost overruns at BAP, and Rolf blistered them about pork barrel and hopeless government procurement policies that cost the taxpayers hundreds of billions of dollars. The Republicans nervously enjoyed the pyrotechnics, occasionally throwing more gasoline on the fire. At one point, Senator Hatch asked Rolf, "What do you think we ought to do with NASA?"

"NASA used to be the best-run agency in government, but that was when they were poor. Now look at their price tags, and look at the waste. How much did they squander on the Hubble telescope? Heck, they invented that boondoggle to create a 22,000-pound payload for the shuttle.

Now they want $400 million for the multicultural mission to Mars. Who do they think they're kidding?"

Then Rolf made CNN's day with a frigid blast. "NASA's just hanging on with massive infusions of tax dollars. But you want to know something? I don't blame the people at NASA. They're good people. Pork barrels and politicians are killing NASA. Just look who controls their budget: the Department of Health and Human Services, for heaven's sake! That's the stupidest arrangement imaginable. I suppose you could make an argument, however thin, for putting NASA under any other cabinet, but Health and Human Services? Ridiculous! As it is, you experts on the dole—Freudian slip—I mean, you social-welfare experts can't possibly do a credible job managing the resources for the cutting edge of the nation's technologies. It would be laughable if it were not so tragic. You have squandered our lead in aerospace technologies, which was our only hope to compete in this world. You abandoned tomorrow's breadwinner for today's handouts. If I ran my company the way you run the country, I'd be thrown in jail. The public has not a clue as to the damage you've done. Although I never attribute to treason what can be attributed to stupidity, I've got to say your results have been the same."

The gavel came down with a loud thwack. "I've heard about all the impertinence I can stand, Mr. Bernard. You can make your points without the cheap insults. I will cite you for contempt!"

The committee hastily called another recess during which the majority and minority leaders decided to call the next witness and dismiss Mr. Bernard. That evening, the major networks ran the Bernard-versus-Congress bout over and over. Almost everybody, including the President, took sides—*he* actually took both sides. Institutional investors sold BAP's stock down 4¼ dollars, down to $48—· BAP's stock had traded as high as $88 just two months earlier.

✧　　✧　　✧

Rolf brooded in the back seat of his car. He watched the Washington Memorial slip by, then the hidden Vietnam Memorial—he called it "the grotto." Through leafless trees, he saw a group of joggers wearing Marine Corps red. The driver sped by the Lincoln Memorial, and over Memorial Bridge. Ice crusted the shoreline along the Potomac River. The afternoon sun glared through a thin veil of clouds that threatened snow. The driver sped past Arlington Cemetery and onto the George Washington Parkway toward McLean.

Rolf tapped on the glass. "Change of plans. Driver, take me home."

Then Rolf picked up the car phone, punched a number, and Margaret Bergen answered, "Ms. Bergen speaking."

"Margaret, I'm coming straight home from the Hill. I'm too agitated to—"

"I watched the whole thing on CNN. It looked rough."

"Rough? Yeah, I'd call it rough. Call the office and tell them I won't be coming in."

"Okay."

"Are you free this evening?" Rolf thought it polite to ask. Barring a death in the Bergen family, she'd be free.

"Why, yes. I am." Her voice raised a half tone.

"Let me take you to dinner. Pick a restaurant and make reservations for seven-thirty. I should arrive home in about twenty minutes. Oh, would you ask Escondido to build a fire in the study?"

"Yes, sir. Good-bye." Click.

The driver stopped in front of the Bernard mansion. Rolf grabbed his thin leather briefcase, let himself out of the car, and walked up the stairs looking over his shoulder at the thickening clouds. He let himself into the foyer and draped his suit coat over the banister rail.

He walked quietly to the study and paused at the door where he watched the young woman from Nicaragua working on her knees, carefully poking kindling beneath a stack of logs. Her skirt hiked up slightly as she leaned forward, showing her long legs, a white sheen from her stockings that disappeared up her green skirt—a heart-shaped figure. Rolf caught himself staring, then announced himself. *"Buenas tardes,* Escondido."

She turned her head, seemingly unaffected by her compromised position, and worked faster. "Mr. Bernard. I almos' finish." She turned to light a piece of newspaper, raising it into the flue to heat the chimney, leaning far forward, speaking into the chimney. "I see you on TV. You are a bery famous man."

Rolf went to his bar and prepared himself a short, dark scotch. "Your English gets better every day."

"Thank you."

Rolf turned to see the fire consume the kindling, crackle, and catch the split logs. Escondido stood before him. "I tell Mrs. Bergen you at home."

Rolf nodded and the girl left Rolf sitting at his desk with his scotch. He pressed buttons on a remote control wand and watched as the walnut panels slid apart, a large glass TV screen blinked, then came to life. Rolf turned the sound low and found the news, watching snippets of himself on TV, and glancing periodically at his notes. The detailed questions still bothered him. The Senate Select Committee knew too much. How did they find out? *How much more do they know?*

Just as he clicked off the television, Margaret poked her head in the door, staying only long enough to say, "I made reservations for two at Madeleine's, seven-thirty, smoking section. I'm going to freshen up, then come back to pick you up at seven." She left him in quiet.

Rolf contemplated his future. The cold moonlight glowed against the sheer curtains pulled across the tall windows. The night made no sound, not even a whisper of wind to keep him company. A tomb might be as quiet. He took another sip of his scotch. Again he mashed a button on the remote control, bringing to life WGMS, the classical music station, and a live performance of the Philadelphia Philharmonic. They began the evening by playing Delibes's "La Roi S'Amuse."

So much of his future lay in the hands of other men, all of whom he trusted—all but Ted Winston. Perhaps he had judged Winston unfairly, but the man was foisted on him by an outsider, then White House Chief of Staff Sununu, and Winston loved brass-knuckle politics. Winston had too many close ties to the Hill—too many. Although Ted seemed ready to use his contacts for BAP, one had to wonder about Ted's obligations to his political buddies— the payback. What would Ted do to get back into politics?

Rolf took a big swallow of scotch. He thought again, *the senators knew too much, too soon. Something's not right.*

Rolf quit the study and took his scotch to his bedroom, where he showered and changed into fresh clothes, brooding over the consequences of a leak in his security: financial ruin, disgrace, prison. Fortunately, if there was a leak, Rolf had the best man in the business for finding it and plugging it—Bobby Tyler. He resolved to share his fears with Tyler, and with that decision behind him, Rolf enjoyed his evening, dining with Margaret Bergen.

Next morning, a pale, wintry sun woke Rolf. He had a slight crick in his neck. On his way to a hot shower, he paused by the phone, called Tyler's house, and asked Bobby to meet him at the Washington Golf and Country Club for breakfast.

With no commuter traffic on Saturday to contend with, Rolf beat Tyler to the club. He sat next to a floor-to-ceiling picture window, looking over the first tee past a long stretch of green dusted with snow. A solitary golf cart and bundled duffer rolled down a wet asphalt path into the trees. On the other side of the river, on the opposite hill, stood the Washington Cathedral.

A waiter in a white jacket refilled Rolf's cup and left the pitcher of coffee. Rolf ordered two breakfasts. He spread pieces of the *Post* and the *Times* out on the table to compare stories about his performance before the Senate committee.

Bobby Tyler approached the table. Rolf rose stiffly to shake Bobby's hand. "Bobby, I think we've got a leak."

Bobby glanced from side to side. "A leak?"

"Those senators alluded to things about our Australian operation that they shouldn't have known—couldn't have known! They knew that the *Skalhorne* was due to dock at Cairns. A coincidence? They knew all about Kirby's piece of the deal. How? If they piece together the rest of Green Lid, we're going to prison."

"Don't jump to conclusions. I'll check our security at both ends."

"Go ahead, check it out. But meanwhile, tell me, if you can, how did they know?"

"I can't."

"Then we have a leak, don't we?"

Bobby looked at the ceiling. "Could be."

"What about Winston? We should watch that man." Rolf prodded.

"Ted? What about him?" Tyler avoided Rolf's question and poured himself a cup of coffee. "Can we order?"

"I ordered for both of us—the big ham-and-eggs breakfast."

"Good." Tyler reached for the cream and sugar.

Rolf continued in a low voice. "I've been thinking about the whole bunch: Yeager, Iversen, Rogers, and now Kirby—but most of all Winston."

"I don't believe what I'm hearing. You're not getting paranoid on me, are you?"

"Don't insult me. I want you to keep an eye on Winston. He's the only outsider."

"Ted's reliable and you know it."

"There's more at stake than you, me, and BAP. I can see that clearly now, especially after yesterday. Space is up for grabs, a bigger opportunity than Columbus ever dreamed of. And who's going to take the prize? Not America—not the way we're headed. No, I'd put my money on the Japanese. Did you know the Japanese have already copied our design for the aerospike engine?"

"That's not confirmed."

"Then speculate, Bobby. Do you think they've got it?"

Tyler's silence conceded Rolf's point.

Rolf pressed him. "Right. We're about to get aced by the Japanese. That's one thing on which I whole-heartedly agree with Irwin Kirby. Japanese sci-fi animators already draw a biconic variant of the Felix design that every Japanese school-aged child can see on their Saturday morning cartoon shows. The Japanese are pouring hundred of millions of dollars into their Sakishima Island launch facility. What do you suppose they plan to launch?"

Tyler sipped his coffee and shook his head.

"Then I'll tell you. I've seen their plans for a moon colony. Do you think they're just goosing ghosts? Just romancing a bunch of sci-fi enthusiasts? I'm telling you, we're in a race. I've got enough problems trying to cope with the bureaucrats in my own government. And if I get sidetracked by some stupid leak in my own organization, I'll lose my lead, and the Japanese will beat me into space with my own invention."

Tyler studied Rolf's anxious face, as one might check a fine teacup for cracks. Then he answered, "Calm down, Rolf. If there's a leak, I'll find it. You know that."

"I know you will. I guess I'm still a bit wound up from yesterday."

"You were in rare form, I'll grant you that." Bobby smiled.

The waiter brought two large plates and a full pot of coffee. Rolf acknowledged with a thin smile and a nod. He put his napkin in his lap, waited until the waiter retired to the kitchen, and cut into his eggs, letting the yolk run into his grits. "Now that I've got this Senate hearing behind me, I can think about getting over to Australia. Herb needs me to close some financing in New York next Tuesday. Then I want to take a look at Cape York."

"You can go in February for a couple days, but make it part of a some broader itinerary. We can't risk the attention, especially after March tenth."

"That's when you move the—" Rolf caught the word in his teeth.

"Yes. That's when we move them."

When Ted Winston reached his desk, he found it littered with pink "While You Were Out" slips. Carla caught up with him in the office and handed him a list of offers. "*Good Morning America* wants Mr. Bernard."

"No."

"How about McLaughlin *One on One*?"

"No. Give me the list."

Carla surrendered the list. "Mr. Winston, I thought we were supposed to get exposure for Mr. Bernard and BAP? This should be a gold mine."

"Carla, you need to learn the difference between press exposure and a firefight. What we've got here is a firefight, and we're not going to shove our boss out there to get shot. Understand?"

"Yes, sir."

"Good. Now, using the same warfare analogy—does the war thing make you uncomfortable?"

"No, sir."

"Good. Because the analogy is apt. I'm going to show you how we mobilize and arm the press guerrillas. You're about to learn that the best PR is the PR that seems to come from nowhere, like sniper fire."

Carla stepped into Ted's office and shut the door. "What's first?"

"Produce and mail a transcript of the committee hearings to my A list."

"A for activists?"

"Yes, that's the one. Then have the staff prepare a background briefing on Rolf. Put the rugged individual, Vietnam veteran, patriot spin on it. Ditch the silver spoon and intellectual stuff. Do not put the background story on the wires, but offer it on a nonattribution basis to news organizations who request it. Do not offer them archived photos. I'd just as soon not get any credit for any Rolf Bernard stories for the time being. Got that?"

"Yes sir." Carla scribbled notes furiously.

"Then you and Ben script me a story lionizing the defiant Rolf Bernard standing up to the Senate Special Committee. I'll approve your story line. Then I want you to produce another script from recent news clips. Patch together a story using nothing but outside sources. Cite the sources. I'll find a way to introduce the tape. Get that ex-boyfriend, ex-tabloid copywriter you talk about."

"Oh, him." Carla wrinkled her nose.

"This is his big shot. I want the most sensational story he can dream up. Vitriol, pictures—the wilder the better—and I want the story placed in foreign tabloids. Let the translators mangle the story."

Carla, Ben, and crew pumped information through third parties into the press. What should have been a nonevent took on a life of its own because it had a certain dramatic interest, and as luck would have it, there was nothing—absolutely nothing—happening in the world that week. The media puffed the story into the biggest bang since Krakatoa, and the people who rely on news naturally agreed. Scores of foreign magazines and tabloids ran the story with pictures. Most flattered quixotic citizen Rolf Bernard—all except *The Economist*. They wrote a short but satirical piece about the spoiled American industrialist who, having supped at the government's table, pouted because there was no dessert. The cartoonist pictured a petulant baby Rolf in a government high chair, bawling with infantile outrage and banging his government spoon on his government tray. Ted clipped the piece for his scrapbook.

If controversy is mother's milk to public relations, then it is meat and potatoes for direct mail political fundraising. In the eight weeks that followed the now famous Bernard hearings, over twenty-two million pieces of direct mail dropped, using the Bernard vs Congress angle as part of the pitch asking for donations for their particular project. "Rolf Bernard proves that people can stand up to big government! You, too, can stand up to Congress. Send fifty bucks!" Nearly one hundred cause-oriented organizations got into the act. They bashed Congress. They bashed NASA. They bashed the White House. They bashed the National Endowment for the Arts, and they bashed the Food and Drug Administration. Who knows why? Who cares? Rolf Bernard's stand against Congress loosened the purse strings of little old ladies across America.

The massive response pleased Ted Winston; it didn't surprise him. Everyone knows that television coverage and collateral press increase the amount and frequency of donations, regardless of the issue. People in the direct mail business refer to the hot issue as the "hook." The best two direct mailing events in recent history had been the Oliver North testimony and trial, and the war against Saddam Hussein. But the direct mail deluge gave way to a direct mail drought—until the Bernard hearings. With every organization cashing in on the Bernard hearings— all one day of it—politicians found Rolf Bernard too hot to handle. Ted had no higher hope than that Rolf Bernard should be left alone.

Chapter 14

Rolf and Herb spent two days in New York securing BAP's line of credit with Citicorp. In a separate deal, they guaranteed Chemical Bank's part of a loan syndication to Temple Bay spaceport. The terms hurt. On the helicopter back to La Guardia, Rolf reached into his breast pocket and fingered his passport and Australian visa. He asked, "You got anything for me for the next couple days?"

"No big action. Ernst & Young will present our audit report Thursday. You need to sign off on their numbers before we send them to the printer for the annual report."

Rolf cleared his throat. "You sign for me. I'm not going back to D.C., I'm going to take a side trip to Australia and see what's cooking at Temple Bay. I just signed a loan guarantee for two hundred million dollars we don't have—for a construction project I haven't seen. And Paul hinted that they might not make schedule."

"Any messages?"

"No, thanks. Before I catch the flight to Cairns, I'll call Margaret from the airport lounge. She can patch me through our satellite link to Temple Bay, and I'll talk with Paul direct."

"So no messages? You've got everything you need?"

"I think so. Let's be sure." Rolf pulled out his thin wallet. He had forty-three dollars in cash, a plastic security key, two credit cards, and a faded picture of a young Cynthia and a two-year-old Paul sitting on a painted merry-go-round horse.

At La Guardia, Rolf waved good-bye to Herb and sought the United Airlines ticket counter, where he began his trip to Cairns, Australia: six hours, one movie and one meal to Los Angeles, a nine-hour layover at LAX—long enough to find, purchase, and use a set of toiletries, fresh socks, undershirt, and shoulder bag; then back on the jumbo jet for fourteen hours, two movies, and three meals to Cairns.

Despite his new purchases, by the time he stepped out of the jet in Australia and felt the warm moist air, he felt like he needed to be disinfected. Paul met him at the small customs booth.

"Welcome to the tropics. You here for a surprise inspection?"

"Of sorts." Rolf sagged from fatigue.

"How was your flight?"

Rolf handed Paul his briefcase, but held on to his small shoulder bag. "The thrill is gone."

"We bought you some clothes, and we booked you a room at the Hilton."

The thought of a shower revived Rolf. "Good thinking. A shower, a beer, and a catnap."

"Take a long, hot shower and eat a big, hot meal. It's still a bit rough up at Lizard City."

"What did you call it?"

"The men named the barracks area Lizard City. You can't miss the lizards, but you do miss other things like hot water under pressure, fresh meat, fresh vegetables, fresh bread, fresh newspapers, and flush toilets."

"That's not the picture I had." Rolf dropped his bag. "Well, give me the bottom line, Paul. Are you going to make the April fifteenth launch date?"

Paul stopped dead in his tracks. "I don't think so." He waited for his father's reaction.

"Why not?"

"We've got a thousand little reasons. Not one amounts to an excuse. The constant rain keeps us from pouring cement when we want to pour cement. If a piece of equipment breaks, we lose a day—maybe two—flying all over the Pacific looking for parts. Your typical Skip—"

"Typical what?"

"—native Australian."

"Talk in English, will you?"

"Your typical Australian doesn't work at the pace we do, but they work well enough that we ought not complain."

Rolf grumbled, "So when will you be ready to launch?"

"Late May or early June."

Rolf raised his hands to massage his temples. "You'd better be sure. When I get the cargo over here, we can't sit around and offer excuses. We've got to fly."

"I feel good about a late May launch date."

"Feeling good won't hack it, Paul. We've got our nuts in a vise. It may not bother you now, but—"

"Okay. I promise we'll put the SPS up in late May; the other launches should start within a week of turning on the power to the cryogenics plant. You'll see." Paul pointed the way to the taxi rank, where they caught a ride to the Hilton. Paul left his father at the desk. "I've got a shopping list a mile long. I'll come back to get you for a late dinner. In the meantime, if you need anything, our pilot's staying in room two-twelve. His name is Stouffer."

"What's his first name?"

"I never asked. We just call him Stouffer. If you're interested, take a look at this." Paul dug a magazine out of the side pocket of his khaki jacket. "We made the cover of *Aviation Week*."

Rolf unfolded the magazine and held it at arm's length. The headline read "Temple Bay Resurrected." The front cover featured a high-altitude picture of lovely Temple

Bay scarred with new construction—the re-invigorated spaceport. Twelve pages of text with color photos waited inside. Rolf shook his head, let himself into his room, and tossed the magazine onto the double bed.

Rolf carried the *Aviation Week* magazine to dinner, where he joined Paul. They sat on a balmy patio listening to the waves slap a small stretch of man-made beach. After brief assurances that the project had progressed on schedule toward the April launches, Rolf demanded, "Where did *Aviation Week* get these pictures?"

"We don't know."

"Well, some of the photos are ground shots. Somebody took them."

"We use some casual labor. They do get some tourists up there, though none I saw."

Rolf tossed the magazine onto the table. "This is awful."

Paul picked it up. "I don't know. They only reported what anybody with two eyes could have seen. And they're already about four weeks out-of-date. And, I might add, they got half of it wrong. Look at this." Paul flipped to a subhead and read from the article. " 'One of the most curious activities occurred near the tranquil shores of Temple Bay's shallow lagoon. Technicians spent a great deal of time uncrating, inspecting, and cataloging what seemed to be a giant erector set but was more likely an antenna for sending and receiving signals to submarines— a suspicion somewhat confirmed by the crew's heightened security.' "

"Hmm. So now I know where that jackass got his bad data about the rectenna."

"Who?"

"We're hearing all kinds of speculating about what's going on here. I don't like it, Paul. The security around here stinks."

"There are practical limits to what we can hide, Dad. Max sealed the big hangar. Nobody but our Marana crew goes in or out. The Felix-P just sits on the launch apron for everyone to see, but that's never been a secret. But we can't hide the fact that we're building a rectenna out in the water. And we are shoving dirt, or mud, all over the place. Anyway, you'll see for yourself tomorrow."

And Rolf did. He stepped from Stouffer's plane onto the pasty dirt of Temple Bay. The monsoon had dropped another quarter inch of rain the night before. They drove in Paul's mud-speckled Range Rover to Lizard City, a mere mile away, and parked in front of a new bungalow. Paul announced, "Your future home at Temple Bay. In three weeks we'll have flush toilets and hot showers."

Rolf looked around at the mud and the vegetation creeping back to reclaim spots torn by excavation. Paul pitched Rolf's bag onto the porch and began the walking tour. Rolf slid with his first step. "Steady, Dad. This mud's slipperier than fish guts on a doorknob."

Rolf gave a Paul a quizzical stare. "Very colorful."

They walked past freshly poured platforms for eight small buildings, then to the big hangar. Max greeted them and sent them to the dressing room, where they stripped to their skivvies, donned BAP-blue bunny suits, and stepped through a plastic-strip curtain to an air-conditioned hall. Two Felix ships lay head-to-toe on long flatbed cars that were set on rails. Max showed the seamless skin where his men had rejoined the ships' halves. Men with respirators worked on scaffolds repairing the third Felix. Max steered Paul and Rolf away from the toxic gases.

They dressed back into their street clothes and left the hangar, following two pairs of steel rails. One turned to the left toward a great slab of asphalt; another turned to the right toward the concrete launch pad. Paul handed Rolf a pair of binoculars and directed his attention to the bay. Rolf saw a crew of electrical engineers setting up radar on a spit of land. Others laid cable. In the water, some forty men worked, neck-deep, constructing the vast array, a weblike grid, the rectenna, or—Rolf chuckled to himself—Senator Kern's nefarious submarine antenna derived from bad data in *Aviation Week*'s inaccurate article. Then a sobering thought crossed his mind. *Perhaps* Aviation Week *got the antenna story from Kern. If so, where did Kern get his intel?*

Paul pointed out the bunker to the left, then took Rolf back toward the hangar. Felix-P stood like a shy sentinel, hiding by the hangar's left side, just the barest tip stretched higher than the hangar's roof. "I saved the best for last," Paul boasted.

They stepped over the hill behind the hangar and looked down on a crew that was bolting down a steel corrugated roof on Temple Bay's new cryogenics factory. "You'll note that we put the plant on the reverse slope of land spur. It would act like a thick berm if something went wrong with the fuel plant. Ours is just a small to midsize plant, but it'll produce enough liquid oxygen and hydrogen to support forty launches per year. I figure we can add capacity if we need it."

"Oh, we'll need more capacity within two years."

Paul took Rolf inside the plant. "Over here we perform electrolysis. We're fortunate that we have a very clean artesian well about two miles from here toward Iron Mountain. We pump the water here and break it into hydrogen and oxygen. We had to make some fairly radical adjustments. Most cryogenics labs used chemical processes to capture hydrogen and oxygen from natural gas or propane. We altered the plant design to use nothing but electric energy. We have a magnetically powered turbine pump to pressurize the gases and cool them."

Paul pointed to a large blank area on the cement slab. "Over there, we're setting up the world's largest lithium sponge to hold the liquid hydrogen, a technology pioneered at General Motors for a hydrogen powered automobile."

"The largest?"

"Absolutely. Shortly after GM Laboratory built their lithium sponge, they abandoned the hydrogen car in favor of the more politically correct electric car, because the hydrogen car involves combustion. Which, of course, is ironic, because hydrogen exhaust is nothing but water, and most electricity comes from fossil-fuel fired plants—"

Rolf interrupted, "How did you hear about this sponge thing?"

"A team of us at MIT helped GM with the design. GM tried to sell the sponge to MIT, but MIT couldn't afford it, and we're damned lucky they couldn't."

Rolf raised an eyebrow. "Can we afford it?"

"It's expensive, but we can't afford to do without. The sponge reduces power needed to store the fuel. We can keep the sponge cool enough with the power generated by the auxiliary diesel. That's crucial."

"In case the SPS shuts down?"

"No, Dad—when the SPS shuts down. We put SPS in geosynchronous orbit. We get uninterrupted solar power every day except twenty-two days before and after each equinox. Then the earth eclipses the sun up to seventy-two minutes each day around local midnight. No sunlight means no thirteen megawatts of power, and we have to live on the auxiliary diesel. In fact, I want to purchase another diesel power plant—an auxiliary for the auxiliary, so to speak."

Rolf spent three days wearing a BAP-blue hard hat and watching the machines shove dirt, watching sparks fly from welding torches, watching Max's men in bunny suits patch the third Felix ship. And he would have stayed longer, but he got a terse phone call from Tyler: "You've got to come back right now. 'Bye."

Rolf flew back to Washington on a frigid February morning. He stopped by his house long enough to change his clothes, then drove himself to the office. Tyler met him at his office door, ushered Rolf inside, then held his finger to his lips to signal silence. He handed Rolf a piece of paper that read, "Don't talk here. Follow me."

Tyler led Rolf out of his office to the elevator hall, where in a hushed voice he introduced Rolf to a middle-aged Chinese woman. "Rolf, you've met Theresa Chung before, haven't you?"

"I'm sure I have." Rolf wasn't sure of anything at the moment, and he would never admit that he forgot peoples' names.

Theresa smiled. Tyler added, "She's going to sweep your office for electronic devices. She's already checked the outside phone lines and internal PBX." He turned to the woman and said, "Theresa, if you find a bug or anything, don't remove it; don't use countermeasures. We'll decide what to do later."

"Right, Mr. Tyler." She gathered her metal case of equipment and let herself into Rolf's office.

Bobby took Rolf to his car. "You like country music?"

"No, not really."

"Well, keep an open mind. I'm buying." Tyler drove to the entrance of the underground garage. "Get down, out of sight." Rolf complied without comment, and Tyler drove straight for the Beltway, where he said, "You can get up now. Next time you go to work, notice the white Chevy van in the bank parking lot across the street made up as Queen's Steam Carpet Cleaner. There's no such company. They're FBI, I'm sure."

"What? Why?"

"That I don't know, but they put eight devices in your house, tapped your phone, and they're reading your fax machine. They'd need a federal warrant to do that. Either they think you're breaking the law, or they think you are a serious security risk."

"How much do you think they know?"

"Let me finish. Our Australian partner, Irwin Kirby, told me that the CIA contacted his friends in Australia, and Temple Bay has had a few unlikely tourists poking around. It's curious how the CIA and FBI work together. By law, CIA can't spy on people in the U.S., and FBI can't work outside the U.S. Nevertheless, when they've got a big problem like a major security breach, and they have the Administration's blessing, they set up a special coordination cell where they divvy up surveillance and share data. Apparently, you've got both FBI and CIA on your tail, which means you've attracted the attention of the National Security Council. In other words, they think you're dirty."

"What do you mean, dirty?"

"That you're selling technology to bad guys, spying."

"That's outrageous. Besides, they keep telling the public that there aren't any more bad guys. Hell, they want to give our technology to the Russians, and I'm trying to keep them from doing it." Rolf paced the floor, frustrated and exhausted. "Why don't they just pull my tickets if they think I'm dirty?"

"They want to catch you in the act. They need a case and a conviction to get enough leverage to pry out all your past sins, real or imagined. They might even get you to admit that you leaked the stealth technology. By the time they're through with you, you'd confess to stealing the Lindbergh baby."

"How long have they been listening in?" Rolf wiped his brow.

"Probably about the time Kirby got a visit from his bogus tourists. Two weeks, maybe."

Rolf fidgeted. "I'd bet four weeks."

"It would be unwise to try to find out precisely."

"So, what do you think they know?"

Tyler paused to consider the damage. "That's a tough question. They know we're planning to use Temple Bay at Cape York as a launch facility. And they know we've moved our spaceships there. They know we're designing the facility to be self-sufficient. I don't think they know everything we intend to do. I'm confident they don't suspect that we plan to take 320 Pebbles from Pueblo, Colorado to Cape York. If they knew that, we'd be having this conversation in the basement of some building at Vint Hill Farms."

Rolf rubbed his hands nervously, "Damnation. This could all go south. We could end up in prison."

"Not for long. So we stole a bunch of our own Pebbles that the government wouldn't buy. Screw 'em—we'd do six months, maybe a year. And you could never run for president. So what?"

Rolf shook his head. "I wish we'd never started down this path. You seem pretty relaxed, given our situation."

"I figure I'm in for a penny, in for a pound. It's like every other tactical situation I've been in. There comes a time when it's more dangerous to go back than it is to forge ahead."

"Just great. Just what I need to hear. So what do we do now?"

"First of all, don't underestimate our advantage. They don't know that we know they're listening. Also, their intelligence requirements are skewed. I mean, they're listening for the wrong information. They think you're in cahoots with the bad guys. Hell, we are the bad guys! We just have to make sure they keep hearing what they want to hear. They'll never figure us out."

"You're pretty confident, aren't you?"

"The Bureau here in D.C. is good, very good, but they've put their best people against the drug traffic from Central America. Nevertheless, I've got to believe they'll stay a step ahead of us. We'll need to make them work hard for their misinformation or they won't believe it. On the other hand, CIA's operation in Australia is laughable. What sort of career spy signs up for duty in Australia? What a cush job! I'd take it if I didn't work for you."

Bobby took I-95 South, made a quick exit into a snarl of new road construction and traffic barriers, then onto a small two-lane road. He announced, "If we had a tail, we don't have one now." He smiled without turning his eyes from the road, and added, "Don't you just love it?"

"No."

Ten minutes later, Bobby turned into a gravel parking lot and parked between a pair of shiny new Toyota pickup trucks. A flashing neon sign bragged about Carolina barbecue and live music. A hand-written sign on the door told them they needed proof that they were twenty-one years old, and to find their own table.

Rolf surveyed the room. Cigarette smoke hung in a gray haze a few inches below the yellow lights. Five older guys and a woman, wearing matching cowboy shirts and string ties, sat at a table next to the stage guarding their instruments and a round of drinks. An old jukebox played a ballad posing the rhetorical question, "Will there be any boxcars in heaven?" Rolf poked Bobby and whispered, "This had better be awfully good barbecue."

Bobby found an empty table. He brushed a few crumbs of food and cigarette ash onto the floor. "This is my kind of place."

A waitress wearing a red calico shirt, black slacks, and running shoes, came to take their order. Bobby ordered a pitcher of Bud, a platter of baby back ribs wet, and extra napkins. The beer arrived. Rolf poured. "So what are we going to do about our listeners?"

"I've got the basic plan worked out. I'll prepare a detailed script, but the idea is simple: We overload their circuits. We've got about forty-five days to screw with their minds. First, you'll accept an invitation to go to the Aerospace Expo in Moscow. You can set up at the Metropol and you'll meet all kinds of major players at the International Center. Talk shop, make friends. Take Ted along, he's done his bit here. And he knows some of the conservative politicians in Eastern Europe."

"Figures. . . ."

"Don't knock it. He can get you a dinner with Karl Bruder, head of Die Republicaner Party. Bruder will tell you why Germany should become a nuclear power and how he'll get Poland back without firing a shot. You'll be noticed in his company, I'm sure. If you pick up a tail, improvise. Split up. Send Winston south. You go west. We'll tell everybody you're just out there selling airplanes and rockets. The more contacts you make, the better. You'll stretch the CIA so thin, you could see through them. Maybe we can get you up to Japan."

Bobby paused to sip some beer. "In the meantime, I'll get Herb to open accounts in Malta and the Caymans. We'll churn enough funds to attract some attention. We should send Paul for a little rest in Singapore." Bobby raised his glass for a toast. "You've got to admit, this could be lots of fun."

"I'm not amused."

"I need two weeks, Rolf. I need two weeks when everybody is watching you, Ted, Paul, and any other decoy we can push out the door. I need two weeks so that I can slip in and get the stuff."

Rolf whispered, "It's risky and I don't like it. You've got friends who still work in the Agency. You've got to find a way to track their progress. This spy-versus-spy nonsense will blow up in my face."

"You've been watching too much TV. Theoretically, Green Lid could blow up in our face, but only if they get lucky—very lucky. I'll tell you how it will go. They'll follow you all over the place, collect thousands of pages of notes, analyze the crap out of them, figure out the politically correct thing to write, then shuffle the data to fit their report—if they have enough time, which they never have. The CIA specializes in revisionist history. Rolf, all I need is two weeks to get the stuff. Then if we can keep them guessing for another thirty days, we win. Just keep them busy chasing leads—the wrong leads. They won't start putting pieces together until it's too late. Then, they'll just bury twenty man-years of surveillance in a vault, because they're not going to admit they got sucked into a wild-goose chase."

"But—"

"But nothing. The CIA is big, slow, and usually wrong. Remember their reports about troop strength in Vietnam? The CIA fought for decades defending their point of view, which stated that the Soviet economy was better than it was. Likewise they argued that Soviets spent only twelve percent of the GNP on their military when it later proved that they spent upwards of twenty-five percent of the GNP. They told the world that Iraq was decades away from a nuclear device. Those examples are big mistakes on big issues. By comparison, we're barely a nuisance. The way we handle the CIA is to overload their HUMINT collection with irrelevant data, then let their analysts tie the data into knots. If you've got to worry about something, worry about the FBI. Even so, we can keep you out of their sight by keeping you out of the country as much as possible. You see, Rolf, the way to beat these guys is to keep surveillance offshore."

"That's great advice, worry about the FBI instead of the CIA. Are you nuts?" Rolf poured another glass of beer for himself. Bobby held his glass forward, pleading for a refill. Rolf reached for the pitcher saying, "I'll have to get a bunch of shots if I'm going to be traveling."

Bobby sipped his beer. "Rolf, I need you as a decoy. I've got the men lined up to grab the Pebbles, but we need a strategic diversion."

"The launch schedule slipped to late May. Shouldn't we postpone grabbing the payload?"

"No, I've got our five specialists scheduled for the grab. They're very expert, but rather suspicious men. We can't book these guys for the grab, then put the operation on ice for six weeks. They'll get nervous. I want to get those Pebbles out of country as soon as possible and send our five specialists packing."

"You know I don't like the risk of introducing five strangers," Rolf held up a handful of fingers, "five individuals who can put us away for the rest of our natural lives."

"Don't worry. I know these guys. The leader's a refugee from Seal Team Delta. They're not strangers to me. And they have tremendous incentive to stay far away from U.S. authorities. Let's just say they got on the wrong side of a small popular movement in Central America. You're going to have to trust me on this one."

"I'm not convinced. Your guys might just sell us to the government to patch up their problem. I don't like the risk."

Bobby turned on his boss with a glint of anger in his eyes. "You agreed to this plan two months ago. I couldn't just turn it off if I wanted to."

"I still have some reservations. . . ."

"And I still can't think of a safer plan. Maybe you can, but consider: We cannot simply break in and steal the Pebbles. Someone would discover the theft within twelve hours. Also, I don't need a confrontation with our guards. And I'm going to have to hire some outsiders unless you want to try to smuggle forty thousand pounds of satellites through customs in your briefcase."

Rolf started to rebut, but Bobby cut him off. "Rolf, the best thing you can do now is act as my decoy. And please don't tell me how to do my job."

"Oh, all right, Bobby. I'll make some propositions to the Russians that will keep the CIA busy."

"Good."

Rolf dug his pack of cigarettes out of his shirt pocket. "That means I'll have to go to Moscow—when?"

"The Expo runs March 16th to March 21st."

"Just two weeks away." Rolf lit the cigarette. "I ought to fly out to Huntington Beach and check on Dr. Abrahamson."

"Why? I thought she was ahead of schedule."

"She says she is, so I suppose she is. I just don't get the same warm fuzzy feeling dealing with black boxes and software. What do I know about encryption? Not much. Now, take Holtz's Pebble: I've seen it fly. I've seen the little IR sensors track a hot cigarette a thousand feet away. I've seen the little sucker simulate attack. But, I've never seen software demonstrated that could not just as well have been artful collusion. You've got to look programmers in the eye and trust them, or sit down to read a million lines of code, assuming you could understand the algorithms, which I can't. I trust Ginny Abrahamson, don't get me wrong. I just want to see it in her eyes."

"I tell you what. You make your plans for Moscow. I'll go to Huntington Beach," Tyler volunteered. "You just logged a round-trip to Australia. You need the rest."

"Can't argue with that. I haven't slept well. Adrenalin and caffeine, perhaps."

"So catch up on things here and get some rest. Besides, I ought to haul some gear out there to check Abrahamson's and Holtz's security."

"Good point." Rolf's eyes lit up. "Hey, you never told me who put the tap on my wife's phone."

"There's no way to be sure. The tap originates in the central switch."

"What does that mean."

"It means the telephone company knows about the tap, so it's a safe bet that the French government ordered the surveillance. My guess is, Cindy's found a way to avoid paying French taxes."

Rolf shook his head, rebuking his absent wife. "If she's got their attention now, just wait till we deploy the Green Lid and tell Ariane they can't launch their rockets. They'll run her out of France and seize her properties."

"*Au contraire*, they'll seize her person." Bobby tossed out the cold fact.

"Then she'd better get out of France while she can. Bobby, short of telling her our plans—we can't have her blabbing our plans over her tapped phone, for crying out loud—persuade her to get out of France for a while."

"Why don't you tell her, Rolf?"

"You know darn well she suspects anything I say or

do. I want you to get her out of there, Bobby—as a special favor to me. You can tell her I'm about to do something that will greatly irritate the French government."

"That's an understatement."

"It'll have to do. Just get her out of harm's way if you can. I don't owe her much . . ." Rolf stopped.

"But what?"

"I owe her some kind of warning."

Chapter 15

"Did you buzz me?"

"Yes, Margaret. We've got to go to Moscow for a week. There's an Aerospace Expo at the Armand Hammer Center—you remember, the Mezh. We're going to see if we can't sell them some Felix launches—maybe barter some technology. Here's the itinerary." Rolf handed Margaret a brochure annotated in his handwriting.

She studied the paper. "Do you want me to book rooms in the Metropol or the Mezh?"

"Try to put us on the fifth floor of the Metropol. Then, check out the conference schedule, and set up a cocktail party. Invite everybody over the rank of full colonel, and include senior U.S. Embassy staff—I want the damn Russians to think the Czar's back in town. Bring a couple cases of Johnny Walker Black if you have to. Throw one of those two hundred dollars per person spreads. And you might as well let it be known that's it'll be the best free meal at the conference."

"Yes, sir." Margaret smiled.

"Also, I asked Mr. Winston to bring his Russian foreign affairs guy along for me and a sales rep from each division, so you'll need to get with Winston to see how many will come in his party."

"Shall I book flights on Lufthansa?"

"No," Rolf sighed. "Russians consider it a snub if you don't fly Scare-flot. See if you can get our assigned seats together this time."

"Would it matter? They've never gotten the seat assignment right before. I'll warn the others, and I'll bring plenty of dramamine, and plenty to read."

"Check my visa. Send one of the clinic staff up to give you, me, Ted and Ted's people shots at my office tomorrow—" Rolf flipped through a small black day planner "—at five-forty in the afternoon. Got that?"

"Yes, Rolf." Margaret jotted notes on the brochure. "I'd better get on this right away. I have only thirteen days to do two months' work." Margaret was simply pointing out her scheduling challenge the way a gourmand might comment on a spice, and in doing so, ensure that everyone appreciate the culinary art—or in this case, her incomparable task management skills. Rolf understood this about Margaret. And he knew that the correct response was neither concern nor compliment, but confidence, polished with commitment. "Do whatever you need to do."

Tyler walked into the BAP Huntington Beach Office Building, confirmed his tickets with the special security officer—who incidentally worked for Tyler. Then he walked into Dr. Ginny Abrahamson's office unannounced.

"Good morning, Dr. Abrahamson."

"Mr. Tyler!" She got up from her desk to close the door. "What can I do for you?"

"I'm out here on Green Lid business."

"I figured."

"Somebody put a tap on Mr. Bernard's phone."

"Oh, dear."

"So we thought it might be prudent if I came out to check your phones and have a little face-to-face with you and Dr. Holtz. We'd just as soon not have anyone see Rolf, you and Holtz together."

"We? You and Rolf?"

Tyler ignored her last question and sat on the small sofa. "How's it coming?"

Ginny sat down at her desk. "Essentially, we're done. We've finished the code, cut the ROMs—how much detail do you want, Mr. Tyler?"

"As much as you think an old retread infantryman can understand."

Ginny chuckled. "We've set the Pebbles to keep track of each other's location within a cubic meter of space, and they're linked with a pulse code modulated, or PCM shot. Each Pebble is always in line of sight with at least five other Pebbles. The redundancy in the system is terrific. Of course, that's pretty much the way we'd always designed it."

"How does the ground talk to the Pebbles?"

"The ground link actually talks to a geosynchronous satellite that talks down to the nearest Pebble, which then shares the command with the others. It takes about three seconds to transmit a command to all the Pebbles, and to get an acknowledgment."

"Which satellite?"

"We modified the telemetry package on Fenster's solar power satellite. Rolf says we'll put it above Temple Bay and manage the Pebbles from there until that National Security Agency sends up their next bird."

"Have you tested everything?"

"Yes. In fact, we sent and received a signal patched through BAP's corporate comsat to Fenster's SPS sitting on the ground. The way Rolf down-scoped the specs, the commands are pretty basic: initiate access code, change access code, enable, disable, and a couple of housekeeping commands. After you guys initiate the access code, you won't need me. It's that simple."

"Have you built in a fail-safe—you know—just in case we lose the code?"

"You know what NSA would do to us if we built a mechanism to circumvent the encryption. No, we built a simple, down-and-dirty, single key system. Two or more people had better know the key. As with every other good encryption device, you end up relying on good people."

Tyler wanted to be sure on the point. "So once armed, the Pebbles stay armed until somebody uses the access code to send a command to disarm."

"Right."

"And if for some gosh-awful reason the code were lost by technical or human catastrophe, we'd effectively close low earth orbit."

"Most effectively, and for a long, long time."

Bobby looked at the ceiling and thought: there would be a short time in the near future when he and Rolf would be the only living souls who could let mankind into space, or keep mankind out—an awesome power, and even more awesome responsibility, that he would be eager to transfer.

Tyler finished a sweep of Holtz's office, found nothing, then returned to his hotel. He gathered his things, ate a quick dinner, and debated whether he should call ahead to Cynthia. Her phone was tapped for sure. He decided against it, but he did not want to waste three days on a useless round-trip to Paris.

Early next morning, Tyler took a cab to LAX. A moment before he bought his ticket, he dialed Cynthia's number . . . breakfast time in California, late afternoon for Cynthia. She picked up on the third ring, but before she could finish saying "hello," Bobby hung up.

Twenty hours later, Bobby stood on the sidewalk below Cynthia's apartment building. A light shone through her window. Bobby paid the cab driver, a refugee from some Balkan hellhole, with a handful of dollars. The cab driver said prudently, "*Moment*, if you please," as he counted out the bills and nimbly calculated the exchange rate. His face softened as he figured out that this awkward transaction would net about a hundred francs more than the meter required. "Okay, buddy." He unlocked the trunk and handed Bobby the small garment bag, and said, "I pick you up?"

Tyler shook his head no. He saw a shadow—a slight woman's shape—pass behind the sheer drapes across Cynthia's lit window. And he was surprised how relieved he felt to find her home. Indeed, he wanted to see her. He wondered, *What's the harm in that?* At the top of the stairs, Bobby knocked on Cynthia's door. He was about to knock a second time when a shadow passed over the peephole, and a voice inquired, "Bobby?"

"Yes. May I come in?"

Locks turned, a dead bolt clicked back, and the door swung open. Cynthia stood in a Delft blue satin robe. Her hair hung straight and wet. She wore glasses. She held a fresh white towel in the crook of her arm. The robe stuck to her skin in places. "Have I caught you at a bad time?"

Cynthia grinned. "No, no. Come in. It's good to see you. I was getting ready for a dinner date." Cynthia waved him into the living room and she retired to her bedroom. "I'll just dry my hair, put my eyes in, and slip into a dress. You'll find a bottle of wine in the fridge."

"I can come back tomorrow," Bobby spoke down the hall.

"Nonsense! I'm taking you to dinner. I've already got reservations for two. You like Greek food—of course you do."

"What about your date?"

"He'll get over it."

A hair blower roared and whined from the bedroom. Bobby asked, "Three of us?" Oh, she'd like that: two men competing.

But Cynthia did not hear the question. "What did you say?" She turned off the hair dryer.

"I said that I don't think it's a good idea adding me to your little party. Three's a crowd."

"No, Bobby. I'll take you out. I'll cancel the other guy. I prefer my men one at a time."

"Just an old-fashioned girl, aren't you?"

"You might say that." The hair dryer roared, and Cynthia recalled dinner parties where she'd been trapped between two competitive men eyeing her as they might a trophy. She'd much rather compete with a second woman for the solitary man. Even better, she preferred to compete with the man for his other affections.

Bobby relaxed on the couch with yesterday's copy of the *Wall Street Journal*. Several stories had been cut from the pages, leaving awkward tatters. A pile of news clippings sat in a heap on an old mahogany ball-and-claw Chippendale secretary. On a large corkboard over a desk, Bobby saw a large price chart for BAP, Inc., with red lines resembling a large skewed triangle, poking into the future at the lower right-hand corner. A note in her handwriting read, "Buy at 18."

Bobby couldn't make out the other margin notes written in Cynthia's hand, so he turned his attention toward overhearing Cynthia's end of a phone conversation. "I've got to cancel our dinner date. I'm sorry. . . . No, I feel fine. A friend of mine popped in from the States quite unexpectedly. . . . Of course it's a he. You know I don't have any girlfriends. . . . His name is Tyler. He works for Smurch. . . . Yes, he's the man Smurch sends to check up on me. Call me Monday. . . . You, too. Bye."

Moments later, Cynthia walked into the living room looking like she'd stepped out of a Greek travel poster, like Persephone bringing spring back to Paris. Her black hair was pulled back into a short pony tail. Her face, neck, and shoulders cast an olive glow against the simple white cotton dress. Her red coral earrings and necklace shined like an August sunset over the Aegean Sea. She smiled upon seeing her effect on Bobby; then she went to the closet and pulled a long wool coat from a hanger. It was, after all, Paris—damp and cold outside, but inside the long wool coat everything was hot and bright like a Grecian beach. She grabbed her fat leather purse and said, "Let's walk. The Taverna Samos in the Latin Quarter sits about eight blocks from here."

As they stepped onto the street, Cynthia asked, "Mind if we talk business?"

"Sure, Cindy, what's on your mind?"

"What are you guys doing to BAP? Your common stock has plummeted to $28. That's a 66 percent drop in eight months!"

"You should ask Rolf."

"He's never given me a straight answer in his life. His stock only goes down because 'stupid' people sell it—or it won't go up because 'stupid' people won't buy it. You tell me what's going on."

"I don't know where to begin."

"Okay. Why did BAP sell Freedom Car Rental?"

"Herb needed to raise cash."

"I thought so. Why?"

"There are several reasons. First, the government won't release funds to a half dozen of our biggest contracts. They owe us three billion dollars which they won't pay until the Defense Audit Agency reviews our operations, and they're taking their sweet time. We can't get any relief from the courts. Our banks refuse to increase our lines of credit. They'll only roll our previous lines at exorbitant interest rates. According to Herb, our cost of money has increased eighty basis points. We've laid off twelve thousand people in eight months."

"I knew that. But I can't figure out why the institutional investors are dumping BAP. BAP's breakup value is around thirty-eight dollars. They know something I don't. And Bobby . . ."

"Yes?"

"I hate getting aced by institutional hacks."

"Maybe they're wrong."

"Perhaps. But they don't usually dump stock twenty-five percent below break up value. What's really going on? What's the story behind the Defense Audit Agency?

You've got to level with me." Cynthia stopped at a corner as some traffic rolled by.

"I'll tell you what I think. Rolf started a rather nasty little war with the United States government, his main customer."

"Oh, dear. What has Old Smurch done?"

Cynthia led Bobby across the busy street, and Bobby replied, "You know about the Senate hearings. Rolf ended by really dishing it out to Congress in general, and NASA in particular."

"I can't believe that."

"Believe it, Cindy. Congress called Rolf up for a ceremonial whipping. He wouldn't sit there and take it this time. Now they feel obliged to teach him and all other defense contractors a lesson."

"Rolf should just make peace and get on with business."

"I suppose. But he's got Ted Winston running a semicovert public relations campaign to tar and feather the government."

"Fat chance. Those old pols aren't stupid, and Rolf knows the government won't trade insults with him. They'll crush him like an insect. I'll bet I know why the banks won't increase your lines of credit: Someone from the White House tells someone from the FDIC to suggest to a couple of banks that BAP loans may be subject to extra loan-loss reserves because of special circumstances, and *voilà tout*—that's all folks. A banker will cut you off for less than that, I assure you. I'm surprised the banks didn't accelerate your existing loans. Then someone from the Administration whispers that the SEC may discuss BAP with the Justice Department." Cynthia laughed. "You guys don't know the rules, do you?"

"Can you make some money with that information?" Bobby asked.

"Oh, you've made me some nice change with your shenanigans already. I bought put options for 225,000 shares when I sold my BAP common stock last year at

$86. Those puts are presently worth almost twelve million dollars."

"Goodness."

"It's just money, Bobby. And money is just information on the move. Right now my information says BAP's in a world of hurt. I've just got to figure out if BAP's going to come back. What do you think?"

"I think things will get worse for Rolf before they get better. Then, I think business will turn around and Rolf will own the monopoly for space transportation."

"I'm intrigued. That almost sounds planned."

They turned onto a gaily lit street and walked past a line of ethnic restaurants, turning into a white stucco doorway where they were greeted by the smells of kalamaria, roast lamb, and ouzo. In the artificial atmosphere of sunny Greece, all talk of business stopped. At their table, Bobby raised his small glass of retsina wine and made a toast. "I toast you. Charm deceives. Beauty fades. Money talks."

"I'm positively insulted! I won't drink to that."

Bobby straightened up. "I meant it as a compliment. It's a proverb from the Bible—I think."

"A lousy compliment, biblical or not. You'd better try again."

Bobby raised his glass again. "If I may stick to my theme—maybe I can stay out of trouble this time."

"Let's hope so."

"I toast you, Cindy. Your charm exceeds your beauty, your beauty exceeds your money, and you are the richest person I know."

"Much better. I'll drink to that!"

The bottle of retsina lasted halfway through their meal. As Bobby was about to order a second, Cynthia countermanded him. "Save yourself, dear. We've a full night ahead."

Guitar and bouzoukia filled the small restaurant with music. Students rose from their tables and stumbled through an inebriated dance they called a tsamikos, bouncing off tables and walls, crying "Oppa!" and pretending they were Greek. A burly maitre d' placed himself among the young men and women, signaling with a dour glare that they had better not break the plates. Cynthia explained, "French students misbehave. We should leave now. It will get worse."

When the waiter returned with the check, Cynthia rattled off a barrage of French. The waiter raised an eyebrow, smiled and presented Cynthia the bill. Bobby simply snatched the paper from the man's hand and, without so much as a glance at the figures, handed him a credit card. He turned to Cynthia and apologized, "I'm afraid I'm just an old-fashioned boy from Tennessee." The retsina lit his cheeks.

"Then I thank you for dinner, although it was supposed to be my treat."

They donned their coats and stepped into the gloom. Ignoring the cold mist, they walked upstream through the Saturday night crowds that poured down the narrow, well-lit streets through the Latin Quarter. Cindy navigated through the quays around Ile de la Cité. She followed the sound of Chicago jazz toward a small neon sign that even Tyler understood: THE JAZZ BAR. Cynthia asked, "Have you ever had a Kir?"

"No, just American girls, thank you."

Cynthia grinned. "It's a drink. Shame on you, Bobby."

"I know what a Kir is—I've never had one, that's all."

"Then you must let me buy you a Kir."

Bobby let Cynthia pay the cover as he reached into his pocket and realized his wallet carried no French money. Cynthia introduced Bobby to a Royal Kir: a large quarter-liter tulip glass filled with mediocre champagne charged with creme de cassis—fairly potent on the heels of retsina. They listened to the jazz. The quartet took a break and Cynthia took advantage of the silence to say, "This is fun, don't you think?"

Bobby looked back into Cynthia's steel-blue eyes. "You are fun, Cindy. You know how to have fun."

"I wish I'd met you twenty-nine years ago instead of Rolf." Cynthia leaned back in her chair and cradled her glass of Kir in her hands. Bobby looked at the ceiling. Cynthia continued, "It's true. How complicated we have become. Nevertheless . . ."

Bobby interrupted, "We should not have this conversation, Cindy. I work for your husband."

"So? I said life was complicated, didn't I? Life is full of compromises."

"More than you think, dear girl." Hoping to change the topic of conversation, Bobby added, "My life would be far less complicated if you hadn't left Rolf. I wish you two would patch it up or get divorced."

Cynthia set her glass back onto the table with some force. The smile left her face. The laugh lines about the eyes turned down. Worry and care replaced them, and Cynthia aged a decade. Then as suddenly, the transformation reversed itself. Her lips turned from a pout to a self-satisfied smile set in tight jaws, and she answered with measured words. "It would appear that you don't know how to have a good time."

Bobby felt cornered, and Cynthia's blood rose at his discomfort. She added, "You know something, Bobby, I've only gotten to know two types of men: the first type wants to get me on a bed for some high-impact aerobics, and the second type wants to get me on a couch to ask me a bunch of foolish questions. Unfortunately, Bobby, you are one of the latter."

"Or maybe I'm a third type." Bobby defended himself.

Cynthia smiled and took Bobby's right hand, "No, Bobby. I know men. There are only two types." She squeezed his hand, pondering whether perhaps he was both types. "But . . . we're getting a bit ahead of ourselves. I'm fond of you—you know that. You are fond of me, aren't you."

"I am." Bobby loosened his grip on her hand.

"I dream about you."

"Oh, God." Bobby set his drink down. "Cindy—"

"So where will you stay tonight?" She withdrew her hand and sipped her Kir.

Tyler felt his resolve buckle. He stammered, "I don't know. I haven't booked a room at a hotel. I should have taken care of that. . . ." He wiped his brow with a cocktail napkin. "Gee, it's warm." He laughed halfheartedly and said, "Cindy, Cindy. . . ."

"What?" She prompted him.

"I wish we *had* met twenty-nine years ago, but we didn't."

Cynthia reassured him with a wink and a nod. "I can't blame you for that. Pity. We'll get you into the Hôtel Régency. Close to my flat. I guess we'll toss and turn tonight without the benefit of each other's company."

Cynthia and Bobby talked about inconsequential things as they strolled back to her neighborhood. Bobby was relieved to find a vacancy at the hotel. He signed the register. Cynthia smiled like a cat at the old man behind the desk, daring him to say, "Any luggage, monsieur?" Bobby walked Cynthia back to her apartment, where he collected his garment bag and briefcase.

"Cindy."

"Yes?" A flicker of hope flashed through her eyes.

"You must get out of Paris . . . out of France."

Cynthia sighed. "It won't work this time, Bobby. You won't get me back to the States."

"I don't care where you go. Just get out of France."

"But I've got work to do."

"Just for a couple months."

"What on earth for?"

"Rolf's about to finish a deal in Australia that will put Ariane out of business. We're afraid the French will consider Rolf's monopoly of space transportation a threat to French national security. They might try to get to Rolf through you."

"That's absurd!" Cynthia laughed out loud.

Tyler knew he'd told a bad lie—a half-truth, but a bad lie nonetheless. Still, the truth wouldn't do. "I'm serious. For your own good, get away."

"Well," she purred, "I've got a two-week sailing trip coming up in mid-Spring. Join me and I'll stay at sea for a month."

Tyler shook his head.

"Then it can't be too serious." She kissed Tyler on the cheek and ushered him out the door. He quickly marched himself back to the hotel, where he could not fall asleep.

After a brutal day rattling around inside an Aeroflot jet, Rolf retired to his room in the Metropol. He sent Ted Winston, plus entourage, to the International Hotel to scope out the conference and confirm his itinerary. Margaret Bergen attached herself to the efficient young German woman who ran the Metropol's catering services, the same woman who had taken Margaret's telephoned instructions. Rolf escaped to his room to shed some of the fatigue building up like a thick crust over body and mind.

Rolf Bernard pulled the heavy drapes aside and pulled a cushioned wing chair to the window where he sat to nurse his jet lag and gaze down from the Metropol window onto gray Lubyanka, the jaws of death for so many unfortunates, especially during Stalin's reign— torture or quick bullet to the base of skull depending on accidents of birth or politics. Lubyanka still served as home to the new state security. He noticed that the street running in front of Lubyanka had changed its name: once it was named for Cherninski, godfather and architect of Lubyanka's terror—a street name steeped in history, associated with sounds, smells, viscera, and cunning—now it was called New Square, a nothing name, bland and tasteless, a placeless name, the kind of street name that causes people to lose their way. Rolf saw the spot where a small alley bent past

Lubyanka to the only Catholic church in Moscow. How
it stood unmolested all these many years, Rolf could
only guess. But on a previous visit during Brezhnev's
time, Rolf had gone inside the church, mostly out of
curiosity, and had noticed the cameras hanging from
Lubyanka's walls, watching the church door and
everyone who entered and exited.

Sitting in his comfortable chair in the Metropol and
remembering, Rolf muttered the Savior's promise
regarding His Church, "The gates of Hell shall not prevail
against it" —to which Rolf embellished scripture adding,
"and if Lubyanka's gates were not the gates of Hell, they
were a damned close second."

Rolf fingered a couple of tickets he had procured for
the Bolshoi Ballet—a little bit of Russian heaven, a temple
façade, again ironically next to Lubyanka. He considered
the ironies: Russians wearing Western-style business suits,
exuding hope and cynicism, locked in a struggle to keep
or break industry's partnership with the State. Rolf
sympathized with that struggle. Was their struggle so
different than his? Was he not trying to break away from
U.S. government control of his business? Soon he, for
his leading part in Project Green Lid, would find himself
reviled by his government's apparatchiks. Would he not
become the U.S. government's enemy? Or perhaps now,
just competition. Is there a difference? Perhaps, he
thought, he must develop a sense of irony to appreciate
his predicament, just the way one must develop a sense
of irony to appreciate Moscow.

Rolf looked around the room, elegant European—in
fact Finnish—decor, as tasteful as any found in New York.
He looked at the gray phone on the desk: another irony.
*My home phone in Washington is tapped. My hotel phone
in Moscow is safe.* He laughed a short loud burst, then
chewed an antacid tablet and laid down on the king-size
bed for a nap.

❖   ❖   ❖

Each day at the conference began with a ministaff briefing and breakfast, wherein Ted laid forth the day's events. "Today, I take my cadre to the International Hotel and haunt the convention. We're making a presentation to representatives of Aeroflot that we try to break Lufthansa's stranglehold on airline maintenance. BAP trains Aeroflot mechanics how to maintain Western technology. They'll position themselves to maintain most of the Third World airfield for both Aeroflot and Western jets. The Minister of Air Transport in Belarus is particularly interested. Our State Department might object, but what's the harm in talking about it?"

"Good."

"Mr. Bernard, today you're the guest of Lt. General Provnostov, head of PVO Strany. You're going to see a demonstration of their newest radar technology. Apparently, they've gotten their radar to recognize incoming missiles—like from our Wild Weasel—and it puts out some potent countermeasures, or so they say."

"Who is they?"

"Provnostov's office."

"What do we know about General Provnostov?"

"The little State Department blurb describes him as a Soviet War hero—Afghanistan. He has advanced degrees in electrical engineering and psychology. He advanced steadily through various regimes. . . ." Ted added his own assessment. "He seems to have a knack for picking the winning side in politics. Yeltsin loves the guy."

Rolf poured a second cup of thick coffee from the sleek stainless steel pitcher. He dropped two small cubes of sugar into the tar-black and aromatic drink. "I really want to see Dr. Varrinyev from Energiya."

"He's not at the conference. He's not in town." Ted shrugged.

"But he will be!" Margaret let loose her good news. "And he's coming to our party Thursday evening!"

"That's wonderful, Margaret."

"Thank you, sir. I spoke with Dr. Varrinyev myself. He said he wants especially to meet you, and he'd like to see Dr. Yeager again."

"What did you tell him about Yeager?"

"I told him we'd try to get Dr. Yeager here for the event, but that he was presently engaged with launch preparation at Cape York, and so forth."

"Clever girl. Leave Dr. Yeager be: I'll take good care of Varrinyev. How goes your plans for the cocktail party?"

"Better than I would have imagined. We've got the room. They're going to move the grand piano from the mezzanine to our ballroom for some background music. We opted for Seagram's whiskey, Stolichnaya, and Zolotoye Shampanskovo."

Ted asked, "Shampanskovo is Champagne?"

"Yes, Gold Champagne—their indigenous sparkling wine. The Russians are very proud of it." Margaret pointed to herself. "I haven't tried it yet."

"Why not?" Ted teased.

"I prefer Stolichnaya." Margaret continued with her report. "We've procured the room, food, drink, and music. Now I'm rounding up the guests. I got a list of Russian and American must-haves from our embassy, and I've started at the top. Rolf, you'll have your two hundred people."

"I'll personally invite General Provnostov."

When Rolf poked his head inside the black limousine, a stretch Zil—he'd expected the more modest Volga sedan—he was relieved, indeed delighted to find General Provnostov waiting. The general, who had been reading a fat black, leather-bound book, dropped a bookmark into his place, took the bifocals from his nose, and said in lightly accented English, "Good morning, Mr. Bernard. You have a reputation that is bigger than both of us."

Rolf smiled as he tried to decipher the odd compliment.

He shook hands with the big Russian, who practically pulled Rolf into the car. "Sit. Sit. Make yourself comfortable. We have an hour drive to Domodedovo Airfield."

Rolf complied. General Provnostov bluntly observed, "You didn't bring anything to read, Mr. Bernard, so I propose we make a conversation."

Rolf felt intrusive. "You can read if you wish. I won't be offended. What is that book, anyway?"

Provnostov held up the thick book. Chipped gold-leaf Cyrillic letters and an Orthodox cross emblazoned the cover. "It is my mother's Bible. She forced me into promise to read it—a dying wish. Of course I don't believe these stories, but only a dog would deny a mother's dying wish. Do you agree?"

"Completely. About the wish."

"Also"—the general ran his hand over the rough cover— "it has become fashion to quote scripture instead of Lenin, and I am a progressive fellow." He kept a straight face. "So what to talk about, you and me? Religion? Politics? Economics? Arts? Technology? Women?"

Rolf looked at the scenery through the limousine window. They'd already left the polish of the old city within the Garden Ring and the city grew more and more drab. The soot-stained snow stood in long ridges on the sides of the road. "Perhaps we should talk about politics on the trip out, and women on the trip back."

"So," General Provnostov broke ground, "what do you think of democratic Russia?"

Rolf looked at Provnostov's weathered face, wrinkled skin and crooked teeth, red-splotched, closely shaved cheeks, square jaw, straight nose, and gray eyes—gray as the March sky. Provnostov waited for Rolf's answer with slightly arched eyebrows. "Tell me the truth. You can't offend an old Communist like me, a relic in a post-communist world. What do you think?"

Rolf spoke as plainly as the Russian. "It won't last."

The general smiled. His front teeth had worn down

on the right, where he had held a pipe for so many years. "What won't last: Russia, or Russian democracy?"

"Oh, Russia will outlast her flirtation with democracy."

The smile brightened into a sunbeam. "I like you Mr. Bernard. An honest American. How refreshing! You make more sense than half the Russians in Moscow." He gestured with a back-handed wave to the tall brown buildings behind them.

"Thank you." Rolf dredged up a return compliment. "I admire people with such a command of language. Your English is perfect."

"I look forward to the day when I can forget how to speak it." General Provnostov's blunt retort caught Rolf off guard. Rolf could think of no response, so he remained mute. The silence annoyed Provnostov. The General looked out the car window and said wistfully, "Communism is dead as an economic system. Do you agree?"

"I certainly do." Rolf sat up.

"Economics does not respond to state planning. We Russians know that better than anybody. The wretched five-year plan will never come back, and . . ." he turned to face Rolf, "I won't miss it. I used to consider the communist economy the sacrifice we had to make to have the many benefits of communism."

"Like what?"

"A strong central government to rule so many disreputable people."

Rolf left that last sentiment alone. Provnostov continued, "We are going through a painful transition now. Thanks to our new Western-style liberties, Moscow now has the sixth highest murder rate among the world's capital cities— although I doubt we can ever eclipse the depravity of Washington, D.C. A small consolation. However, I have confidence that in the long run, the Russian people will reject your American democratic model and select a model closer to state socialism. Some prefer the Swedish model. I detest it. I believe we will use the Chilean model,

Pinochet's adaptation of the German state socialism. You know, Marx was right about one thing . . ."

"And what was that?"

"The first successful communist state would be in Germany."

Rolf laughed.

"That's so funny?"

"Just ironic. Please continue. Tell me how you will run your new state socialism."

"Oh, it is already done, and quite successfully too. Simply put, the State promotes capitalism, then bends it according to State policy. The State promotes religion, then steers it to support State ethics. We take the best of your system, capitalism, and bind it to the best of our system, authoritarian rule."

"Which could finance your formidable Russian Army, eh?"

"Of course, we need to continue to defend our borders from aggressors, especially your avowed first use of nuclear missiles. It takes discipline to maintain the peace. I see little discipline in the West lately. But don't misunderstand this old Russian soldier. I and my comrades have no taste for conquest. No, we are contented to instill discipline in our people while the West debauches its vigor away."

"I think the American press makes our problems look bigger than they are."

"Oh, I believe your free press. I see in my own country the consequences your Western-style liberties brought to us in a few short years. We have prostitutes by the hundreds. We have hooligans committing theft and murder. We have the vilest kind of profiteering. We have drugs. But not to overlook the bright side: We now have pizza, hamburgers, and earrings for our boys. And now they want to do away with conscription and put together a mercenary army like yours."

"We prefer to call it a volunteer army."

"Do they really volunteer, or do you pay them?" Provnostov asked a purely rhetorical question.

Rolf forced a thin smile. For the rest of the drive, Provnostov speculated that Yeltsin, whose health was not good, would not run for office when his term expired, and that the ensuing election would be "how do you Americans say—one for the history books. When we get a strong leader, we dispense with our shameful bilateral relationships within the CIS and reestablish some political and military order. Then, we finish the economic reforms started by Count Vito a hundred years ago."

Rolf struggled to remember what he'd learned of Russian history, but could not recall a Count Vito, so he let the matter drop.

"We need another Count Vito, and a strong government to back him. He built the Trans Siberian Railway, and he set up a banking system. He fathered industry in Russia."

"What happened to him?"

"Vito was too good. Nick feared Vito, who had mixed Russian-German parentage, might usurp his authority; so Nick dismissed Vito. A truly strong political leader accepts success like Vito's."

Rolf felt nothing but sympathy for the defeated Vito. "Take this bit of advice from a practiced capitalist: government always resents successful business—politics aside. Why? Simple competition. Both compete for capital, talent, resources, and—most crucial of all—popular support. I think the natural competition between government and business will thwart your vision."

"Then you did not understand my meaning, or perhaps my English is not so good." Provnostov turned slightly to face Rolf more directly. "In my future, there is no silly competition between business and the State. Businesses may compete with each other, but the State manages the competition. Any business who presumes to compete with the State for capital, workers—anything—violates the rules, so to speak, and finds itself very quickly out of business. In that sense, we just do more efficiently what the Japanese already practice."

Before long, the Zil limo pulled onto the airfield, and drove past the civilian terminal to a set of military hangars at the deserted end of the field. Rolf peeked into the hangars and saw a line of Mig-29 Fulcrums—near replicas of the American F-15 Eagle. The Russians knew a good idea when they stole one. They'd copied the old B-29 Superfortress screw by screw in 1944, and called their copy the Tupolev TU-4. And they built thousands. They copied the B-1 bomber and called it their Backfire, and thanks to a squishy Congress, the Russians even beat the Americans to deployment. They copied the Space Shuttle with their Buran spacecraft. Rolf would not have been shocked to have seen a Russian copy of his Felix SSTO sitting on the tarmac; he half-expected that somewhere in Russia there was a lab building something very much like a Brilliant Pebble. And Rolf firmly believed that men of stern discipline like Provnostov would not hesitate to deploy a strategic defense of the Motherland.

Rolf got a semiprivate, three-hour demonstration of the radar. Semiprivate because a separate gaggle of Third Worlders also witnessed the demonstration—prospective buyers and guests of the factory. The demonstration highlighted a fly-by of an SU-17 attack jet simulating an attack on the radar site. The radar sensed the threat, flashed a light and sounded a shrill klaxon, then automatically began countermeasures which included dummy emissions to draw the air-to-ground missiles from the radar. And the briefer assured the spectators that the surface-to-air missile (unseen and presently not for sale) would chase the aggressor plane. Rolf thought back to his pilot days, when small-arms fire brought down his Phantom in Vietnam. He would not have survived the system he saw demonstrated at Domodedovo airfield.

During the trip back to Moscow, Rolf invited General

Provnostov to Thursday's cocktail party at the Metropol. The general accepted.

Margaret Bergen, Ted Winston and Ted's Russian specialist greeted the guests at the BAP cocktail party. After quick hellos, guests breezed briskly to the bars and ordered whiskey for the most part. Margaret followed some guests around the food table and watched what they ate and how. She had never made a study of the art of eating caviar. Here, the experienced guest took a slice of bread—a small round disc with chewy edges—and, with a silver knife, probed the little butter sculptures, clever little yellow bas-reliefs shaped as flowers, stars, the Tsar's Bell (which looked a lot like the American Liberty Bell, except there was a cross on top) and the cone-shaped spacecraft over the letters F-E-L-I-X. The caviar-eating guest either speared or scooped an artistic pad of butter onto the bread and mashed it around, where it served as a bonding agent for little shovelfuls of red or black caviar.

Flanking the caviar, a small silver platter held a crowd of shot glasses filled with vodka. Beside the vodka sat little china plates covered with lemon slices. Margaret assumed that the lemons were somehow connected with the vodka—something akin to tequila and limes—yet for all the vodka consumed, the lemons remained unmolested, so she abandoned the theory. Some of the more prudent imbibers alternated between a shot of vodka, and a green bottle of Narzan, the local mineral water served at room temperature.

The room soon filled to capacity. One could barely hear the grand piano over the buzz of conversation. The whole smoked salmon attracted much attention, as did the trays of thinly sliced roast pork. Guests whittled away at rounds of Brie and other cheeses. Boxes of empty champagne bottles, empty Stolichnaya bottles, and Seagram's scotch bottles lined the walls behind the mahogany bars. The tables laden with food and the multiple bars ensured that no guest stood in or even observed a queue. The room rippled from small outbursts of cheer, but for the most part Margaret, who understood no Russian, thought the conversations seemed serious, earnest, maybe even intense.

Rolf posted himself near the main entrance and he personally and warmly greeted dignitaries as they entered. As he surveyed the room he noticed a pair of Americans hanging back, carrying around champagne glasses but not drinking, occasionally making notes, sometimes splitting up: one to keep an eye on Rolf, the other to catch the name of the Russian guest. Rolf knew he'd achieved the undivided attention of the CIA in Moscow, and that amused him. When General Provnostov arrived with a small entourage, Rolf lavished a greeting on the old Soviet warrior and escorted him to the bar for a whiskey, which set the CIA men into a dither. Within moments a third nondescript American showed up to help monitor Rolf and his guests.

A lanky, spectacled gentleman walked through the front door flanked by two colleagues. Dr. Varrinyev—Minister of Intercosmos, father of Mir Space Station, the human force behind Energiya and the Russian's Buran Shuttle—straightened his tie and looked about the room for familiar faces. Rolf recognized Varrinyev from photographs. He excused himself from a conversation about Russian flying boats, and hustled over to meet Dr. Varrinyev.

"I'm so glad you came. I'm Rolf Bernard, your host."

Dr. Varrinyev politely extended his hand to shake, somewhat reserved. Rolf's enthusiasm seemed out of character for such a renowned American industrialist. "I am glad to meet you, too. Let me introduce you to my associates—Dr. Alegrei Yakovlev . . ."

"Pleased to meet you."

" . . . and Dr. Nicholas Dedjer."

They shook hands. "Come. Let's get you gentlemen something to drink and eat. We need to discuss some mutual interests." Rolf led the trio to the bar, then purposefully steered them toward the two CIA men. "Dr. Varrinyev, I have always admired your space program. However, gentlemen—" Rolf paused for dramatic effect "—I hope you will forgive me for being blunt."

"Go on, Mr. Bernard. We shall not be offended, I'm sure." Varrinyev spoke and his colleagues nodded.

"Very well. I think your Mir program has great promise, but it also has great problems. I'll address the problems, then tell you how I may be able to help. First, you are having problems with your Progress launches to reman and reprovision Mir." The Russian Ph.D. in physics, Dedjer, started to protest, but Varrinyev raised a hand to quell the controversy.

"We know that your Star City workers have periodically gone on strike. . . ."

Dr. Dedjer strained, then spoke. "No, not strikes. My Russian workers have protested the lack of pay. We work in Kazakhstan, you must understand. In the political confusion, Russia says Kazakhstan should pay our wages, Kazakhstan refuses."

Dr. Yakovlev added, "However, you must admit, the protests have practically turned to riots."

"Enough." Varrinyev gave each man a look which conveyed his unspoken message: Listen more, talk less.

Rolf summed up his last point. "Whatever the cause, it appears that you cannot confidently say you shall get your Progress launches to Mir on schedule. The other problem I see with the Mir Space Station is the deployment times: you leave those poor bastards up there for a hundred-twenty days at a stretch. In part, I know you use long deployments to cut your costs, but consider the consequences. We've all seen your brave cosmonauts wheeled around on couches because weightlessness has robbed their strength and they cannot cope with gravity. We know that they suffer terribly from osteoporosis. For some yet unknown reason, weightlessness causes loss of bone mass. We suspect that your crew efficiency drops considerably the longer your men stay in space. They have to spend more time exercising and they suffer greater depression. We've overheard your staff psychiatrists talking over the radio with despondent cosmonauts. And your poor spacemen—if something goes terribly wrong, all they can do is strap themselves into the Soyuz and drop themselves down to earth to auger into some patch of soft dirt, if they're lucky."

Dedjer bristled. "When we build our big space station, we'll use the wheel design and create a gravity with centripetal force."

"Gentleman, I'm not criticizing your Mir program. For Pete's sake, you have a space station and we don't. I think you've done everything you can to make your program succeed well despite infrequent launches. You can be proud of yourselves."

Varrinyev bowed slightly.

"How would you like to make weekly trips to Mir?" Rolf asked.

Dedjer laughed. "Of course! If shrimp could whistle . . ."

"Truthfully." Rolf stanched Dedjer's sarcasm. "I'll fly you to Mir each week for less than a thousand dollars per kilogram. You figure out what it costs you to launch a Progress mission. My guess is that you spend ten times my price. I can solve your Mir problems. . . ."

Dedjer blushed. "This is embarrassing."

"Nicholas, hush. I see advantage in Mr. Bernard's proposal. I know much about Dr. Yeager's work with the SSTO. I always thought your claims about costs were outrageous, but perhaps not. You seem to be willing enough to back your claims with action. Very admirable."

"Thank you, Dr. Varrinyev. I simply wanted to broach the concept with you face-to-face. At present, we plan to launch our SSTO ships from Cape York, Australia."

Dr. Yakovlev speculated, "That's an inefficient point from which to access the orbit for Mir."

"True. Either we burn more fuel or find a more suitable place to launch. I'm sure those details can be managed."

A pretty young woman arrived with a tray full of champagne glasses filled with Zolotoye Shampanskovo. Dr. Varrinyev swapped his empty for a fresh glass and thanked the girl in Russian. He raised his glass to Rolf and said, "I am, to say the least, intrigued."

"Good. We'll talk further. There are some things you can do for me, Dr. Varrinyev. We need launch sites at various latitudes so we can achieve high inclination orbits. Unfortunately, my own government's policies have forced me offshore. I need a sympathetic, space-faring country in the northern hemisphere who will cooperate with me to run spaceports." Rolf turned as if to lead his guests to the food table. He took a good look at the two CIA operatives, who immediately, with practiced nonchalance, turned and melted into the crowd.

Chapter 16

Rolf and his BAP contingent did not stay for the last day of the Expo. Rolf phoned Herb Eckert, who described with some trepidation the shenanigans he pulled at the behest of Mr. Tyler: setting up an offshore corporation on the Cayman Islands and pumping cash through it. Herb also reported that Tyler had left abruptly in the middle of the week to check security at the Pueblo storage facility. Rolf took a deep breath, thanked Herb and hung up the phone.

Rolf intended that his exit from Moscow appear hasty. "Ted, send your people as home soon as possible. However, I want you to hang around Moscow a couple of days. Arrange a trip for me to Star City in Kazakhstan. Broadcast that I'll haul cargo into space for anybody, and that I'll even fly for barter. Tell Verrinyev's people to grow some gallium arsenide chips in Mir. Be creative." Rolf turned to Margaret. "Right now, I'm going to Berlin, then to Vienna for a couple of days rest and relaxation. You can come too."

Bobby Tyler carried his garment bag off the midday flight at Denver International Airport. He sat beneath a United Airlines poster of a Caribbean beach and looked through the floor-to-ceiling plateglass over the runway.

Tall clouds piled up on the mountains in the west—just a squall-line tossing a few snow flurries around the high mountains, and rain showers in Denver proper.

A man wearing a cowboy hat with a snakeskin band took the seat beside Tyler. He handed Tyler a small plastic cup of frozen yogurt. "Macadamia white chocolate. Dig in."

Tyler took the cup and spoon. He looked the man over from the tip of his brown Lucchese boots, faded jeans, and goosedown vest, to the top of his Stetson hat. "Ed, I haven't seen you for seven years, and you haven't changed a bit."

"I thank you for that, Bobby. However, it looks like you've gotten a little soft." Ed patted his own flat stomach.

"I work smart." Tyler took a bit of the frozen yogurt. "Surprised the hell out of me to find you working in the States."

"We're in between jobs, you might say."

"Oh? I thought the Feds were after you."

"That! No big deal. We grabbed the wrong guy, that's all. Our client set us up."

Tyler gave a sideways glance and a wry smile. "I heard you and your fellow refugee Seals started an exciting new concept: preemptive bodyguards. Right so far?"

"Close enough." Ed looked around to satisfy himself that they sat in the privacy of an anonymous crowd, but out of anyone's earshot. "We describe ourselves as personal security specialists from the Vince Lombardi school. A good offensive is the best defense—a more dynamic approach."

"So your client set you up and you grabbed the wrong guy?"

"Sort of. A wealthy importer, who shall remain nameless and who is—according to reports—presently missing, engaged our services because he was being staked out for what he told us was a kidnapping attempt. We cased the would-be kidnapper who, we soon discovered, had made the necessary preparations: surveillance, transportation, weapons. . . ."

"So you grabbed the would-be kidnapper?"

"Such is our preemptive strategy."

"Let me guess. You applied some of your old Seal Team Delta charms on him. . . ."

"In a manner of speaking, yes. Unfortunately, it turns out the so-called kidnapper worked for the DEA and our client—mucho dirty. So we let the poor sap go."

"One lucky fellow."

"We have ethics. We figured we could get some help upstairs to straighten out this little misunderstanding. But so far, it's still a mess, blown completely out of proportion. The DEA agent is taking the whole thing much too personally."

"Why's that?"

Ed stifled a laugh, "The poor guy told us straight out that he worked for the DEA, but Deloney broke four of the guy's fingers before we believed him."

Tyler winced. "Geez, Ed."

"Yeah. It's so important these days to know your clients." Ed finished a last spoonful of yogurt. "Let's get out of here. Why don't you rent a car and I'll take you to Idaho Springs to see our stuff."

"Idaho Springs?"

"Right. It's off the main highway. The men take turns skiing. Fritz and Deloney are skiing in Breckinridge today while Doc and Joe take their turn babysitting the truck and the gear. We've spent a lovely five days cooling our heels waiting for you."

"I got sidetracked running a personal errand for Bernard. Day after tomorrow, we grab the stuff."

Tyler rented a Cadillac and drove Big Ed to Idaho Springs. As they climbed into the mountains on Interstate 70, the large patches of white snow grew broader and thicker. Clumps of clouds, seemed to be lost in the valleys, hemmed in, claustrophobic, looking for the way out. An occasional patch of turquoise-blue sky and a bolt of sunlight showed the way and restored the sense of great distances between mountains.

Bobby had never been to Idaho Springs before. One look around quickly dispelled the notion that Ed and crew had nestled into the lap of luxury. Idaho Springs was a truck stop with a few old buildings on a main street that sold or rented ski equipment, peddled semiprecious stones, showcased handcrafted gewgaws—feather and clay bead necklaces, pots, wool wall hangings. One restaurant served basic Italian, the other served basic dry buffalo meat.

Ed guided Tyler to a motel with an Alpine motif and a large sign boasting the best all-you-can-eat breakfast buffet in the Rockies. They drove around back where Tyler parked beside a long eighteen-wheel rig—a brushed aluminum trailer and black cab, both caked with road salt, no other markings. Ed waved toward a second-story window. A shadow waved back.

Ed unlocked the trailer door, cracked the door open slightly and motioned Tyler in. He followed, flicked a light switch and closed the door behind them. The light shown down upon an Air Force blue sedan. Tyler walked around the sedan inspecting the white stencils and proofreading the words. They'd spelled Peterson Air Force Base correctly. "Fritz made the license plates. We didn't have to steal a thing for this job."

"Good. We don't want any attention."

"Look here." Ed opened a pair of padlocks and lifted the lid of a steel box.

Tyler peeked inside: three pairs of spit-shined boots, three sets of Air Force fatigues, belts, buckles, socks, and black berets with insignia—a steel fist full of lightning bolts—three sets of dog tags, three M-16 assault rifles with the short twenty-round clips, one pair of black patent leather, low-quarter shoes, one garment bag, one Air Force baseball cap with a major's gold leaf, one web belt with a

Colt .45 pistol snugged in the holster. Tyler looked over the heavy starch, spit and polish. "Your guys all got haircuts?"

"The buzz, just like mine." Ed took off his Stetson. A half inch of stiff hair stood up from a stingy crew cut.

"Good. Did you have any trouble telling Deloney to get rid of the earring?"

Ed laughed. "For fifty thousand dollars per man! We'd have cut his ear off. . . ."

"Let me see the paperwork."

Ed pulled a stainless steel briefcase from the blue sedan. He turned the tumblers on the cylinder locks and opened the lid. "Here are our TDY orders to billet at Peterson— we won't need them."

"You never know."

"And here are the orders to evacuate the cargo, with the list of lot numbers and description. What are we moving? Stingers?"

Tyler gave Ed a dirty look.

"Never mind. In this envelope, we've got our military ID cards. I've got one set of B-and-C's for me."

"What about the fax?" Tyler looked in the briefcase.

Ed slipped a crisp piece of letterhead from a manila folder. "We got a piece of Defense Munitions Agency's letterhead and a copy of General Krowstowski's signature. Deloney wrote the text. We even got a blank fax transmittal sheet we can fill out when we send it."

Tyler read the message. "This will do. Don't let Joe forget to add the date. And don't forget to program your fax machine with the DMA's tag and phone number. I want the fax heading to make it look like the call came from Washington."

"Joe knows what to do."

"Okay. I'll give the final go when our BP-17 sets down at Colorado and tells me we're ready for pickup. Then, you guys arrive outside the Pueblo Army Depot at 1300 hours on Friday. I'll control the inside; you control the outside. If anything looks funny from the inside, I won't let you take the stuff. If anything looks funny from the outside, you simply won't show up and we'll regroup. Now promise me you guys are going to look like real airmen."

Ed ignored the comment. "How do we reach you in the meantime."

"I'll stay at the Sheraton in Lakewood tonight. I'll find something in Pueblo Thursday night, but I'll call at 2100 hours. Don't call me."

Bobby Tyler rolled into the BAP Pueblo warehouse and launched into a surprise inspection. He laid out their building access logs and document destruction logs. He inspected the Wackenhut robot that toured the facility with camera and motion detector. Bobby sent a man to stand in front of every remote camera. Finally, he ran a series of rapid response drills, until the BAP security force halved their time. Everyone but Bobby mopped sweat from their brows and tugged at their uniforms to pump cool air next to their wet skin. No one complained. Everyone knew Mr. Tyler was a fanatic for security. They'd seen him fire the last security chief, Smiley's predecessor and former boss.

"Smiley?"

"Yes, sir?"

"After lunch I want to see the rest of the facility. I want to see the locker rooms, the ready room, the kitchenette. Then, we'll walk the fence."

"Yes, sir."

"And you might as well call Mrs. Smiley and tell her you've got to work tonight. Meet me at the gate at midnight: We're going to watch the night shift. And don't warn them. I'll know if they've been prepped."

"Yes, sir."

Smiley reconvened his staff after lunch and they had just begun a walkthrough of the men's locker room when a woman hustled in to report, "Mr. Smiley. There's a Major Smith and an armed escort with a huge truck outside. He asked for you."

"For me?"

"Yes, sir."

Tyler chimed in, "See? I told you we'd get an unannounced inspection before year's end. But I never thought this soon."

Smiley sent the rest of staff back to their duties. He and Tyler walked to the antechamber leading to the warehouse, where they confronted four large Air Force personnel: Major Ed Smith, a pair of sergeants and a driver.

Smiley held out his hand, "What can I do for you gentlemen?"

Major Smith handed Smiley a set of orders and said brusquely, "We've come to transfer certain munitions listed on the manifest. The order directs your staff to assist us in loading the trailer. According to the manifest, you have thirty-two pallets, each with ten pod-like casings, each pod weighing approximately eighty pounds."

Smiley turned to Tyler. "I . . . I don't know?"

The major directed his next comment to Tyler. "Sir, we'll have to ask civilians to clear the area."

Tyler stiffened. "I'm BAP's special security officer and Mr. Smiley's boss." Tyler handed the major his red and white striped badge.

"Oh." Major "Ed" Smith handed the badge back. "Please show us the palletized munitions listed in the manifest."

"They're in the vault."

"Then open it, please."

Tyler stepped forward, almost toe-to-toe with the large major. "Something doesn't fit. Why weren't we notified about the transfer?"

"It's top secret. You don't have a need to know, sir."

"Smiley!"

The guard stepped up. "Yes, Mr. Tyler."

"Don't open the vault until I check these guys out."
Bobby stomped into the glass-enclosed office. He left
the door wide open so everyone could listen to his fictitious
tirade. Suddenly Bobby raised his voice. "Then get me
his exec!"

Pause. Bobby looked through the glass at the small group
and shrugged his shoulders, then he returned to the phone,
animated. "Yes. They're here, but they could be anybody,
now couldn't they?" Short pause. "I couldn't give a rat's
ass who you say they are, or what piece of paper they
show me!"

The voice at the other end, heard only by Bobby Tyler,
said, "I think you're overacting."

"What! Well, I'm not opening the vault until I get the
word directly from General Krowstowski."

Another short pause.

"Then, we'll just wait here until hell freezes over." Tyler
looked through the glass window at his audience. Everyone
looked resigned to a long wait.

"What?" Bobby gesticulated with his free hand. "He
won't come to the phone? Then he'd better send a fax
or something, or send his troops some rations. We're not
moving!" Then Tyler set the receiver down and stuck his
head out of the glass cage. "Hey, Smiley. What's your fax
number?"

"7-1-9, 5-5-5, 2-5-8-7."

Tyler scribbled a note to himself, picked up the phone
receiver and repeated the number, said a terse good-bye,
then hung up. He stepped out of the glass booth.

The guard asked, "What do we do now?"

"Where's your fax machine?"

"Upstairs in my office."

Major Smith interrupted, "We don't have all day, sir.
We have our orders. . . ."

"Screw your orders, Major. I've got my orders, which
is to safeguard the contents of these premises. And I don't
like the way this whole transfer is being handled. I'm

not going to cut corners just because you don't have all day." Tyler seemed most agitated and the guard stepped back to give Tyler and Major Smith plenty of room. Tyler turned. "Smiley?"

"Yes, sir?"

"You go wait by the fax machine. I'll guard the vault."

"What if the general doesn't send a fax? My shift's over in an hour."

"You're not going anywhere, Smiley. If you're hungry, you can order a pizza and we'll sit down to eat it in front of these men."

"Okay." Smiley scudded up the steps to watch the fax machine.

Staying in his role as Major Smith, Ed picked a speck of lint off his blue wool-blend uniform. The new patent leather shoes pinched. Tyler went back into the glass-enclosed office to sit down.

Ten minutes later, Smiley lumbered down the wooden steps reading a curled sheet of fax paper. Tyler and the major went out to hear the verdict as if they didn't already know. "We got Krowstowski's fax."

"Let me see that." Tyler reached for the fax. "I don't get it. Listen to this: failure to comply with the commissioned officer's lawful orders to remove the itemized munitions will put BAP in gross violation of the Defense Munitions Act, etc., etc. What's the big deal, Major Smith?"

"Sir, I don't even know what's on your pallets. All I know is, I got to put those pallets under armed guard and deliver them to . . ."

"Ahem." Sergeant Deloney cleared his throat. "Sir, we noncoms ain't supposed to know what the cargo is. And the civilians ain't supposed to know their destination. Those is orders, sir."

"Very good, Sergeant."

Tyler took a deep breath. "Okay, Smiley. Get a man and a forklift to put the pallets on the truck."

"Yes, Mr. Tyler." Smiley started to leave.

"And you check each pallet number against the these orders. If their paperwork isn't correct, the pallets don't go." Tyler sneered at the major. "They're just as likely to ream us out for cooperating too much as for not cooperating at all."

Major Smith rolled his eyes.

When the last pallet rolled into the truck and the last strap cinched tight, Major Smith produced three pain-of-death disclosure documents for Tyler, Smiley, and the forklift operator to sign. "What's this?"

"Mr. Tyler, its a form in which you promise not to tell even your mother that we moved these top secret whatever-they-are from Pueblo."

"We don't have to sign these."

"Quite right. I'm just supposed to offer you the forms. I can just as well report that you refused to sign. No skin off my nose, sir. Of course, General Krowstowski might want to watch you more closely since you're disinclined to guarantee your silence."

Smiley seized a sheet. "I'll sign."

The forklift operator followed suit. Tyler grudgingly took a form, scrawled a signature, and shoved it back at the major, who ended the conversation. "We'll be off now. Sorry to interrupt your day."

Smiley and Tyler watched two uniformed men climb into the rig. The other two slid into the sedan. They drove away. Tyler turned with feigned disgust. "Cancel the rest of the inspection. I'm going back to Washington to get to the bottom of this mess."

"Mr. Tyler, sir. Do you think we should interfere like that?"

"You can trust the government to screw up now and then. We got to keep them honest, know what I mean, Smiley?"

"Yes, sir. What was on those pallets, anyway?"

Tyler looked at the tractor trailer driving west toward Highway 25. "A new kind of Stinger ground-to-air missile. You'd better wait to hear from me before you breath a word of this."

"Yes, sir."

Tyler caught up with the trailer south of Colorado Springs. Fritz, Deloney, Doc and Joe worked in the back of the truck stenciling D O O P S on the pallets. They wrapped each pallet in a tough, clear plastic wrap, then covered each with an orange web which they bolted to the pallets. Tyler produced forged documents from the Department of Customs and a Customs seal to show that the contents had been inspected at BAP's site.

As the sun slipped behind the white-crested mountains and the badlands slid under a shadow, the team finished their packing job. They peeled the white stencils from their blue sedan and swapped license plates. They shed their uniforms and donned truck driver attire. Ed set his Stetson hat on his head, then they all hit the road. They drove straight through to Denver International, to the far side where they park the old Caribous. A commercial BP-3 rigged for cargo sat waiting. The BAP flight crew plus Tyler's burly ex-Seals manhandled and winched the pallets up roller-ramps into the plane's cargo bay—some thirty-two thousand pounds. Bobby bid Ed and crew good-bye. All payment had been prearranged, therefore, no mention of pay was necessary. The big BP-3 waited its turn for departure. Bobby sat in the cargo bay with the Pebbles with his Glock-17 pistol loaded at his side.

Although the field at Cairns was too small for the BP-3, they landed there anyway. They scared the Aussie traffic controllers half to death when the big jet rolled two hundred feet off the tarmac, within ten feet of the tall chain-link fence. Bobby watched an Australian crew load the pallets onto one of the large Australian roadtrains, a heavy-duty double-trailer truck. Tyler sat with the driver on the long, bumpy, dusty drive up Bruce Highway. He slept in the trailer with the mysterious cargo at a rest area where a half dozen other roadtrains nestled together for the night. The next day, Tyler timed his arrival at Temple Bay Spaceport for nighttime to avoid surveillance. A ground guide led the massive truck past three Felix ships parked on the tarmac.

Bonser Pratt welcomed Tyler's return with a fat tinny of cold lager beer. Tyler cheerfully accepted the beer and gave orders to unload and store the crates marked DOOPS immediately—tonight. The ground guide led the truck into the cavernous hangar where men with forklifts removed the pallets and stored them in a room that Tyler sealed with a pair of padlocks. As he clicked the second latch on the locks that secured the large steel doors, Tyler exhaled. Had he held his breath since Colorado? He took one long drink from the can, excused himself, went to his small room and sent an electronic message to Tony Valdez. "Arrived with all my bags. Thanks for entertaining my friends during my absence. The wife decided to stay abroad. See you soon."

Bobby pulled his heavy shoes off and lay down on his bed for a catnap, but he couldn't keep his eyes shut. Noises, in and out of his head, kept him awake. From inside his head, the memory of the roadtrain's big diesel engine rang in his ears. Outside, generators hummed throughout Lizard City. Suddenly, a piercing whine, a metal-on-metal grind, ripped the air—worse than fingernails on a blackboard, a nerve-tearing screech. Tyler put his shoes back on. He followed the awful noise to a Quonset hut where he found Max Yeager wearing red plastic earmuffs, standing by a metal lathe, prodding the operator to work faster.

"What's going on here?" Tyler tapped Yeager on the shoulder.

Yeager turned and said, "Oh. It's you."

Tyler recoiled slightly, "What's eating you?"

"Give me an ounce of credit, will you? I've already figured out your truckload of DOOPS," he yelled above the screaming lathe. "You mean dupes, like in fools, don't you?"

Tyler motioned toward the door with his eyes. "Let's get away from this noise."

They walked to the hangar where the unmanned Felix-B lay on her side. A dozen technicians tested her bay doors. Inside the womb of the ship, the solar power satellite sat dormant but strangely anxious to spread its eighty-meter panels. Max stopped to peer into the ship at the satellite, but Tyler coaxed him forward, saying "What kind of parts do you think I brought up here?"

"Think? I know what the secret cargo is. First of all, Paul won't talk about it, which in a strange way, I find comforting, so I presume he knows what's going on. Second, Mark Holtz, BAP's longtime engineer for the spaceborne kinetic kill device known as the Brilliant Pebble, gives me the specs for transport racks to load small but identical packages—a size and weight very familiar to me, I might add. A week later, Ginny Abrahamson, BAP's command and control specialist for the old Pebble project, arrives with two technicians and an old communications hut filled with computers, a secure laser transmitter, and three small antenna dishes. The only pieces missing were the Pebbles themselves. Then you showed up with thirty-two pallets of DOOPS."

"Who else knows?"

"Nobody? Everybody? I don't know, but it's not hard to put the pieces together, if you know what the pieces are. I presume Rolf, Mark, and Ginny know what's going on. I'm sure Rolf told Paul. Why don't I know?"

Tyler's face turned to stone. "We ran out of billets."

"That's a lame excuse, even for the government."

"Max, I'll get you cleared for the whole show."

Yeager shook his head cynically. "They won't bother."

"Oh, they'll give you the clearance just so they can hold

a prison sentence over your head. In the meantime, if your people start to wonder out loud about our operation, just tell them DOOPS stands for Disposable Orbiting Ozone Probes. And you can tell them the client—a very big and important client—demands a confidential launch."

"So when do I get the whole briefing about the Pebble deployment?"

Tyler stopped. "Don't even say the word Pebbles out loud again. Call it Project Green Lid. I'll contact the Special Security Office and get official permission to brief you— not that there's much you haven't figured out. In the meantime, the only cleared personnel are myself, Rolf, Paul, Holtz, and Abrahamson."

Yeager nodded with self-satisfaction. He chided gently, "You should have brought me in from the beginning."

"You know I don't make those decisions. Neither does Rolf."

"I understand."

Yeager walked Tyler to the middle of the launch pad. Tyler sat down on one of the steel footings and noticed the orange paint had been burned away. Yeager commented, "We've hopped all four ships over the launch pad." Yeager pointed to the round scars on the great cement slab. "In two days we launch the solar power satellite in the Felix-B."

"I saw some of your people loading the SPS."

"Correct. If all goes well, we'll have SPS up and working within the week, beaming 13.2 megawatts of power to the rectenna. Look down into the bay. Can you see the rectenna?"

Tyler strained his eyes through the night. From their place on the cement table overlooking Temple Bay, Tyler saw glassy water reflecting a half-moon. He saw a necklace of sand around the black water and a lonely shard of rock in the distance. "See what?"

Yeager squinted his eyes. "It must be high tide. You can't see Fenster's rectenna at high tide. If he had to do it over again, he said he would have figured a way to make it float, like a six-acre lily pad, but he had to build it in the shallows of the bay. The rectenna rests on a bed of coral and sand. If you sat here for a half hour, you'd see it seem to rise from the water like a spiked disc. According to Fenster, the seawater doesn't affect the power."

Yeager turned slightly and pointed to the beach. He continued, "Can you see the shed about two hundred feet from the shore."

"On stilts, is it?"

"Right. There, Fenster's transformers change the direct current from the rectenna into the alternating current we use. We've come a long way in just sixty days."

Tyler agreed, and the rest of his midnight tour proved the point. He saw a diesel locomotive lying on its belly, no wheels or track, just a slab of concrete beneath it. The humming blue hulk generated enough electric power to light Lizard City and run the small liquid fuel plant at two percent capacity.

"That seems hardly worth the effort—making a trickle of liquid hydrogen."

"Oh, but it is." Max explained. "Making fuel is one of the most delicate processes we handle at Temple Bay. Paul needed to run his plant for the last three weeks just to tweak the machines and ensure that the lithium sponge works. At the present rate, it would take a year to make enough fuel to launch the prototype. We've had to haul fuel up Bruce Highway in the meantime. When we get the SPS cooking, we should be able to make enough fuel for forty launches a year. And we'll have enough power so that later on Paul can quadruple his fuel plant."

Dr. Paul Bernard stepped out of a small office with an assistant—the cryogenics plant manager-in-training—one Jake McCullough. Paul held a clipboard and trainee Jake held a flashlight. Neither noticed Max or Tyler, whose presence was masked by the amber light and loud mechanical rumblings. Paul and the trainee rooted around the plant equipment, looking at dials, recording numbers which Paul checked against a computer printout. Beside the big diesel, two men sat in folding chairs watching the great engine go nowhere. They listened for the slightest sputter, because they'd have less than ten minutes to react to a loss of power: the electric power from the locomotive maintained the pressure and temperature of the lithium sponge, which held the liquid hydrogen. Everyone looked forward to the day SPS would send more than enough energy to Temple Bay, and the reliable diesel would retire to auxiliary duty. Max and Tyler did not disturb Paul's work, but quietly left the cryogenics plant.

For the last stop on the tour, Yeager took Tyler to the blockhouse. The bright empty room boasted one ten-foot viewing screen, a wall of smallish but powerful computers, a pair of large paper plotters to track orbital mechanics, and two rows of desks with phones and consoles. Six men worked at the far end of the room laying out blue coaxial cable, which they would stuff under the floor. Tyler complimented Yeager on the functional room, neat in every detail, not a scrap of paper to spoil the aura of hi-tech. Tyler said, "You may be the first man to ever design, build, and operate a truly paperless office."

Yeager congratulated himself. "That's the general idea."

The door to the lavatory swung open with a crash. An agitated man stood in the door frame with his bib overalls half undone. He bellowed, "There's no garsh-darn paper in the bloody men's room again! Hey, you with the broom. Git me a roll." The man turned and walked back into the men's room. His mutterings and swearings echoed from the tiled walls.

The next day, Fenster's people secured the SPS in the Felix-B cargo bay. They checked the satellite's motor and fuel, simulated deployment for the last time, then sealed the bay doors. The Felix-B rolled slowly out of the hangar.

She lay atop a flatcar that rolled along standard gauge rails. A small tractor pulled her to the edge of the launch pad. A large portable crane lifted Felix-B and moved her the last fifty feet to the launch pad, set her stubby legs onto the steel footings, and bolted her down.

There she stood, slightly singed from reentry from her tests, but no worse for the wear. The BAP ground crew crawled over her, shined lights on her looking for any blemish or pock mark on her skin. Finally, they filled her tanks with liquid oxygen and slush hydrogen that had been hauled up a treacherous thousand miles of rough road.

The weather behaved. The sun burned off the little bit of morning fog. The wind barely whispered. The Temple Bay occupants still considered launches and landings a novelty to witness and celebrate, so they clamored for space in the bunker, or took folding chairs to the hillside overlooking the launch pad.

With no fanfare, Felix-B's engines roared. Spectators shielded their eyes from the blinding white light, or held their hands over their ears. Felix-B shot into the air and out of sight over the blue Pacific. In many ways, the Temple Bay staff agreed that the straight launches offered far less entertainment than the test hovers.

One hundred and fifty miles above the Earth in an elliptical orbit, the dual Crays aboard Felix-B found the ship's precise position, then issued the preprogrammed commands. A flood of telemetry poured down to Temple Bay each ninety minutes as Felix flew overhead. She opened her bay doors; slipped the SPS from her bay into the cold, black void, and with a spring-loaded mechanical arm, shoved it gently from her. From the blockhouse at Temple Bay, Dr. Fenster gave the command to fire the SPS's onboard rocket motor that pushed the SPS into a geosynchronous orbit—twenty-four thousand miles above Temple Bay. Dr. Fenster studied the return telemetry and adjusted SPS's station, tweaking the eight-ton satellite with tiny puffs of forced air— "a little mouse fart here, a little mouse fart there. . . ."

The Temple Bay blockhouse sent a signal to the Felix-B, "Come home." The Cray brains required data from Felix-B sensors, mechanical eyes and feelers that could affix precise location, relative speed, pitch and yaw. She took her measurements, processed the data, and turned herself around on one pass; then with preprogrammed commands, she fired three of her eight motors, breaking her speed, sending her down into the atmosphere somewhere over Africa. Felix used the hot gases from her rockets to create a shield, a buffer against the even hotter result of atmospheric friction. She descended over Australia.

The blockhouse caught her on their radar screens to confirm her descent. Everything flawless so far. She fired the remaining five motors. The blockhouse computer aimed the large tracking telescope and the video screen showed a bright speck grow larger, indeed a plume of white light and a trailing white cloud.

Yeager, Paul, Tyler and a dozen or so bunker rats—or so they called themselves—left the video screen to walk outside and see the landing. Rogers stayed behind to man the remote controls, if necessary. Fenster stayed behind to tend to his satellite.

The outdoor public address system broadcast the chatter inside the bunker: data, mostly. The Temple Bay radar watched the Felix-B approach and the ground computers monitored pitch and yaw, speed and angle—comparing data from ground sensors to data sent from above. The midsize Cray on the ground shared data with the two small Crays in the Felix-B. Together they brought the ship over Temple Bay.

Felix showed herself overhead like a midday star. As she closed in, the groundlings could see the lateral motion. She looked more like a slow meteor dragging its own billowing white cloud behind itself. In a short time, the sound of the engines reached Temple Bay. Felix approached, roared, and shook the ground. She hovered above the tarmac, sidestepped a couple meters, then stepped onto the concrete surface with as much grace as a lady stepping from a train to the platform. The Australians cheered. Yeager mopped the sweat from his brow and grinned. Charles Rogers stepped out from the bunker shadows and muttered, "I'd rather fly the ship from the inside."

The flatcar didn't haul Felix-B back to the launch pad. Rather, they rolled her back to her place between the Felix-prototype and Felix-C. She wore her singe marks like chevrons won in combat.

Fenster and crew worked to take the tiniest wobble out of the solar power satellite, which finally assured all concerned that she sat riveted above them. Then, Dr. Fenster sent the command through the ether, telling the machine to unfurl its solar panels, and twenty thousand miles away, the SPS obeyed. She began to unfold like a silver flower with twelve giant petals—a heliotrope for certain—staring directly at the source of all life's energy.

Two days later, Dr. Fenster sat at his console, told everybody to cross their fingers, then transmitted the order for the SPS to send microwave energy to the rectenna he had built in the shallows of Temple Bay. Ten seconds passed. Then, in the same instant that the satellite acknowledged Fenster's order, a deafening explosion sent a shock through Lizard City. Fenster nearly fell out of his chair as he scrambled from the blockhouse in time to see charred pieces of the transformer shed raining down around the blue ball of vaporized copper, and flaming, sputtering inverters. Fenster jumped up and down, a picture of infantile rage. He shook his fist at the sky: "Why! Why!"

Later he found out why. A three-foot thick copper buss bar had vaporized in a blue flash—simply turned to mist when the 13.2 megawatts of direct current hit an imperfection—or perhaps several—fruit bats clinging upside down to the buss bar. The copper vapor condensed around the remaining inverters, shorting them out as well, setting off the second, third, and fourth explosions. Among the debris, Dr. Fenster and his crew found fruit bats— hapless residents of the transformer shed, frozen in death, burnished in copper. Like gilded gargoyles tossed from their cathedral perch, the bats lay on the ground, grimacing. The fine detail showed tufts of fur, small pointed teeth, and tiny claws plated in copper.

Chapter 17

Rolf sat at his familiar desk. He hit the escape key on his computer, which cleared the screen and cut the phone link. He considered the Tony Valdez message: "SPS burned out the transformers. Repairs under way." *Damn.*

His intercom beeped. "What?"

"Sir, our security office got a call from the CIA. They want you to come down to Langley and submit to the standard debriefing for your Moscow trip."

"Have the security office call me. No, check that. Tell security to do nothing until Tyler returns. He'll handle it." Rolf recalled the panel truck across the street listening to his conversations. "Get me Ms. Bergen on the phone, please. And book me a couple of hours with Herb."

"Yes, sir."

Rolf pressed a button to end the conversation. He looked at the two stacks of correspondence on his desk— one stack to read, the other to sign. He pulled the cap from his fountain pen and pulled a folder from the stack. He struggled to keep his mind on the mundane, but Temple Bay beckoned and the Government threatened. The two stacks of correspondence shrank in significance. Nevertheless, Rolf put a dent in one stack. Ted Winston rushed into his office unannounced, shut the door, and in a hushed voice, said, "Mr. Bernard, I got a visit from a pair of FBI agents."

"Where?"

"At my house! Scared my wife half to death."

"Why?"

"Oh, she grew up in Indonesia. There, when a couple G-men knock on your door, that's very bad—very bad."

"What did they want?"

"They wanted to know about our trip to Moscow—where we went, who we saw, and why we went. They want to know what you did in Berlin and Vienna."

"What did you tell them?"

"I told them we'd been shut out of the U.S. market, so we were selling our services abroad. I told them about your visit to the PVO Strany. I told them about our return date to see Dr. Varrinyev. What else could I tell them?"

"You talk too much, Ted."

"What? We're not doing anything illegal. Are we?"

"Our business is none of their business."

"Then why are they poking around?"

"They don't want us to take our technology offshore. We must be getting to them. Tough, isn't it?"

"Well, I'm not too crazy about having the FBI snooping around."

"At least they're not the Bureau of Alcohol, Tobacco and Firearms. We'd have to increase your fire and life insurance." Rolf smirked.

"That's not funny."

"What else did the FBI want?"

"Nothing, really."

Rolf raised an eyebrow. "They didn't tell you to keep an eye on me?"

Ted backpedaled. "Well, actually they did."

"So what are you going to do?"

Ted set his jaw. "I told them they could keep tabs on you without my help. That's the point of this meeting, sir. I just wanted you to know that the FBI asked me questions about us. What do you want me to do?"

"Just do your job, Ted. I'll inform Tyler. We'll follow his advice."

That evening in his den, Rolf took a large snifter of brandy onto his patio where he found Margaret Bergen. "I don't know how long I'll be in Australia. You'll have to run the household while I'm away."

She looked pained. "Yes, sir."

"Herb's going to run the McLean headquarters, while I'm away."

"Something's wrong. I can tell."

"Things have been a little crazy . . . ."

"A little? We haven't entertained for six months. We haven't accepted a single invitation to a single engagement since Christmas. You don't read your mail. . . ."

"I really haven't had the time."

Ted Winston sat next to Rolf Bernard in the first-class cabin of a United Airlines jumbo jet. Ted pushed his glasses back onto his nose and opened a thick novel. A dried four-leaf clover slid off the page onto the tray-table. With thumb and forefinger, Ted carefully picked up the fragile green flake and held it to the light and smiled. Rolf watched Ted slowly twirl the translucent piece of luck. "I see you've got a four-leaf clover. That's good luck."

"My wife picked it from a patch of clover near our driveway. I didn't know she'd pressed it in my book."

Rolf looked back at his inflight magazine and muttered, "Don't lose it. We could use some luck."

Ted carefully placed his wife's remembrance deeper into the novel where he would rediscover it. He quit the Navy because he couldn't stand the long deployments. This latest one to Australia for BAP, Inc. seemed as restrictive as any carrier deployment he'd known: no leave, no visitors, limited outside communications. Ted counted the weeks on his fingers. He'd miss his youngest son's high school graduation. Neither Rolf, the book, the small tray of sushi, nor the tea—not even memories of his wife, children, and home filled the empty space inside. Ted dug through the book and found the four leaf clover again. He wondered how he could pay the next onslaught of college bills if he quit BAP.

Paul Bernard and Max Yeager met Rolf and Ted at the Cairns airport. BAP's pilot, Stouffer, found their bags and threw them aboard his Learjet, the Temple Bay shuttle. They flew to Temple Bay and landed at dusk amidst a carnival of lights and music: the mayor of Lizard City, Bonser Pratt, had proclaimed the day a holiday to celebrate the long-awaited arrival of Temple Bay's benefactor, Mr. Rolf H. Bernard, and as Rolf stepped from the plane, four hundred denizens sang "For He's a Jolly Good Fellow!" Paul sent Rolf's bags to a private bungalow. Ted disappeared with his own bags. Then Paul joined his father in the revelry. He and Rolf soaked up the praise and a couple lagers.

Rolf found Bobby Tyler nestled between Jake and Angie McCullough, the husband-wife team whom Paul hired from Mitsubishi Cryogenics. Jake ran the swing shift for the cryogenics plant. A row of empty beer bottles lined the middle of the table. Rib bones and inedible bits of prawns lay about in small piles. Bobby started to get up to greet Rolf, but fell back into his seat. "Rolf!"

Rolf laughed at his friend. "I haven't seen you this drunk—ever!"

"Then you've forgotten our weekend in Bangkok."

"Oh, yes. I try to forget Bangkok every chance I get."

Bobby waved an arm. "Introductions are in order." He set another empty bottle in the line, then looked at Angie McCullough's name tag stuck to her bosom—he had to look very closely in the fading light. Tyler and the woman burst into raucous laughter. Mr. McCullough, whose work shift started in an hour and had to stay sober, tried to look amused. Bobby flourished. "Rolf, these two people, John and Angie McCullough . . ." Tyler checked his thought. "They make liquid oxygen and liquid hydrogen for your spaceships."

Tyler faced the man on his left. "John . . ."

"Jake, if you please."

"Oh, Jake. Sorry. Isn't Jake a nickname for John?"

"Hardly." Mr. McCullough tried to signal his wife to leave. "Darling, we should go. You're full as a goog."

"Oh, don't be a wowser." Angie turned and prodded Bobby. "He's just sore that you called him John. He hates the name John. Loves the name Jake."

"Really?" Tyler held Jake to keep him from getting away. "Jake's slang for crapper. Crapper means john. A jake is a john. So I can call you John."

Nobody commented.

"Well that's the way it is in Tennessee. Jake or John: there's no difference. What do they call jakes in Australia?"

Angie McCullough squealed with laughter. "Dunneys. Maybe instead of Jake, I'll start calling you Dunney, honey." She and Tyler howled. "It rhymes!"

Rolf intervened. "Angie, Jake. Would you mind terribly if I tear Mr. Tyler away from your party?"

Jake helped Bobby to his feet and bid him good evening.

Bobby forced a large tinny of strong beer into Rolf's hands, and he dragged him from table to table. Paul interceded and asked with jovial and false concern, "Mr. Tyler, are you trying to get my dad drunk?"

"Someone's got to do it, boy."

"At least he's in the hands of a professional." Paul scored. The table erupted with approval.

They settled into a long evening of drinking cold beer, nibbling on ribs, and telling war stories. Tyler warmed the small audience. "Back in 1980—about this time of the year—I attended a meeting in the National Security Council. I consulted on the Manzariyev piece of Carter's hostage rescue attempt. So, there I attended this critical briefing. American lives and our nation's prestige lay on the line. President Carter, Hamilton Jordan, Vice President Mondale, and Dr. Brzezinski sat in the front row for the briefing. General Vaught, General 'Roundheel' Jones, Colonel Beckwith, and a gaggle of us minor support weenies sat behind them. Beckwith laid out on the table some of the equipment he'd use when he stormed the American Embassy in Teheran. Then Beckwith explained the operation. He told the President his men would storm into the compound—armed guards they'd shoot in the head, unarmed guards they'd handcuff. Mondale asked, 'Do you mean you're going to kill them?'

"Beckwith answered, 'We hadn't planned to stop to take their pulse, sir.' "

The Aussies hooted.

"As Beckwith continued his briefing, Mondale started playing with the set of handcuffs Beckwith put on the table for show-and-tell. Mondale put on one bracelet— click; then the other—click. You could see the smile in Beckwith's eyes. Mondale tugged at the handcuffs throughout the briefing, then finally asked, 'Where's the key to these handcuffs?"

"You just knew Beckwith wanted to gloat, but he couldn't. 'There aren't any keys, Mr. Vice President.' We had to put an overcoat over the Vice President and escort him to a machine shop to cut the handcuffs off."

They drank to Walter Mondale. They drank to the Queen Mother. They drank to everybody they could think of. The last toast Rolf remembered was a ripping hurrah for Ned Kelly.

And he remembered nothing after that.

The next day, Ted Winston and Paul, rousted the near dead for breakfast. They conjured up Yeager, Rogers, Dr. Fenster, Holtz, Abrahamson, and Tyler for a late brunch on a screened porch overlooking serene Temple Bay. Rolf Bernard did not attend breakfast. From their shady perch, they saw a lone man sitting on a fallen palm tree at the water's edge.

"Is that Mr. Bernard?" Rogers asked.

"I think so." Yeager squinted into the morning light.

"He's praying, isn't he? It's Sunday morning and he's praying." Holtz guessed.

"He's meditating. You can tell by the way he has his hands covering his face. And he's dovening like my old uncle. That's a meditating thing to do." Abrahamson speculated.

Dr. Fenster added, "Meditating relieves stress. Many captains of industry meditate. Henry Ford meditated, just like that, I wager." He pointed toward the lone figure rocking to and fro on the palm log.

Ted Winston asked, "Bobby, is Rolf praying, or meditating?"

Tyler held his head. "He's hung over." Tyler closed his eyes. "I should know."

A long, flatbed truck brought four new electric current inverters to Temple Bay. Within the week, Dr. Fenster delivered solar electric power to Temple Bay, and the faithful diesel engine that provided Temple Bay's power rested. Paul pushed Temple Bay's cryogenics plant to full tilt, making enough fuel for a launch every nine days. The large lithium sponge could store enough hydrogen fuel for another launch.

Rolf spent the week with Ginny Abrahamson, working through simulated communications with the Pebbles System. She gave him a diskette holding the software for the security access codes, saying, "I know we've been over this, but I want to be absolutely clear about the flaw in the command and control." She pointed to the diskette and added, "This system is not what I had intended to build, but I guess it will have to do for now."

"Yes, I know."

Dr. Abrahamson pulled a cigarette from a pack in her

pocketbook. The power of suggestion sent Rolf's hand groping at his shirt pocket for a cigarette, too. "When we arm the Pebble System, we cut off access to outer space. Therefore, we must disarm the Pebble System before any friendly launch."

"Yes, I know." Rolf flicked his ancient Zippo lighter, offered the flame to Abrahamson, then lit his own.

"Thank you. And because we can't have the Russian GRU turning off our Pebble System, we've developed a rather sophisticated encryption technique. The only way to break the access code is trial and error. And it would take a supercomputer with a direct comm-link to the Pebbles sixty days to break the access code. And of course, with our laser comm-link we'd know if they had direct access to the system."

"That's good," Rolf assured her.

"Not really. If, for whatever reason, the access code gets screwed up, scrambled, or if the receivers on the Pebbles get damaged and can't accept the disarming code—space is closed. You can't go up to repair the system for the obvious reason that the Pebbles will shoot down the repairman on his way up. The risk here, Mr. Bernard, is that the Pebbles could keep Man out of space until their batteries run down. The batteries last eighty to one hundred years. Or we could spend huge sums of money clearing them out."

"I know." Rolf looked at the diskette. "Is this the only copy?"

"Of course not, but that doesn't make a bit of difference. You could give the software to the Russians. It would only help them a little."

"Can we be sure there's no override?"

"Yes, I'm sure. I reviewed the software myself. My team wrote it in Ada, if you care. And I compiled it myself. One doesn't build an override in an encryption device— sort of defeats the purpose, doesn't it? You have my only compiled copy. You can have my source code if you want.

Frankly, I don't want to be the one carrying around the disarming code."

"Why's that?" Rolf asked.

Dr. Abrahamson pulled hard on her cigarette. She filled her lungs with smoke, thinking of an answer. She gave up, blowing smoke away from Rolf. "I don't know. I just wouldn't want to be the one with my finger on the button— if you'll forgive the analogy."

Rolf put the diskette in his pocket, thanked her, and left. He walked into the canteen, an adjunct to the dining hall. Men in white aprons cleaned tables and mopped the floor to prepare for the supper meal. At the far end of the room near a coffee urn, Ted Winston sat with a pad of paper and a cup of coffee. Rolf peered over his shoulder. Ted laid his forearm over the words. "It's a letter to my wife."

"Hmm. Well say hi from all of us. You know, you can bring her out here if you're homesick. Buy her a flat in Cairns—probably a lot like her home in Indonesia. She could take up scuba diving."

Ted sat there like a school boy guarding a love note from a surly teacher. Rolf broke the awkward silence. "See you around, I guess." And Rolf left.

That night, Bobby Tyler officially inducted Max Yeager and Captain Rogers into Project Green Lid, the clandestine deployment of the Brilliant Pebbles, spaceborne, missile defense system. They met in the blockhouse with Rolf, Paul, Dr. Abrahamson, and Mark Holtz. Rolf looked each member of the team in the eye and said, "We have our orders. In four days, we send up the first eighty Pebbles in the Felix-P. We'll deploy eighty Pebbles in each of four flights—one flight every three days for twelve days. Our cover story is that we're launching the first set of DOOPS to study the effect of the SPS beam on the ozone layer."

Mark Holtz shook his fist like a hammer. "Great idea."

Dr. Abrahamson echoed quietly, "This is a good thing we're doing."

Charles Rogers said nothing. Tyler slapped Holtz on the back.

Max Yeager observed, "I see you've built racks in Felix-C and the prototype. I assume the flights will be manned?"

Rogers quickly defended his chance to fly. "We've got but one irreplaceable set of Pebbles. Someone's got to go up to handle contingencies. So Dr. Holtz will fly with me to supervise deploying the Pebble satellites. He knows more about the equipment than anyone. We could use another hand, if someone wants to volunteer. How about it, Dr. Abrahamson?"

"Not me!" She put her hands out to fend off the suggestion. "I'll just stay down here in my swivel chair. I can run all my tests down here."

"I want to go." Max Yeager stood up. Years melted away from his face. He looked at Rolf and expected affirmation.

"No, Max. No offense, but you're too old."

Yeager suddenly looked older. He sat down. Yeager's colleagues watched the old inventor and former test pilot sit in his folding metal chair with hands clasped to his knees, his eyes cast down. Tyler flashed Rolf a hard look.

Then Max Yeager stirred. "Rolf?"

"Don't argue with me, Max. We've got too much going on and I need you on the ground."

"I am going up with Rogers and Holtz. Paul can handle the ground operations. Isn't that right, Paul?"

"Sure, I can."

"What is this, a conspiracy? Did you guys rehearse or something?" Rolf turned to Max. "Do me a favor. Forget this nonsense."

Max looked up from his seat. "No. I won't forget it. I've wanted to go up in the Felix-C ever since she was just a wild idea in the back of my skull. And in a way, you're right—I am too old. I'm too old to wait around to get your permission to fly in my own spaceship."

Bobby saw where this was going. He interrupted Rolf,

saying, "I think Max should go. You could use the help, couldn't you Charles?"

Charles Rogers' sympathies lay with Yeager. "Absolutely. Yeager could fly the Felix if something happened to me."

"I could, couldn't I!" Max agreed.

"Oh, that's just great! You guys did rehearse. What else have you decided to tell me?" Rolf snapped.

Tyler took Rolf by the arm and told the group, "Excuse us for a minute." He pulled Rolf aside and whispered, "Lighten up. Let the old fart ride on his spaceship."

"Don't tell me how to run my company." Rolf whispered back.

"Listen, Rolf. In three weeks, you're going to need all the friends you can get—not employees, not vendors, not customers—but friends that would risk going into a burning building to drag your butt out. Because, Rolf, in three weeks when you arm those Pebbles, it could get mighty hot around here."

"This whole business is driving me crazy."

"Now, let the old guy have his joyride." Tyler started to lead Rolf back to the group.

Rolf spoke loud enough for all to hear. "What the hell. Although I need you down here, Max, if you're bound and determined to have a heart attack in your very own spaceship, so be it. But don't say I didn't warn you."

Yeager nodded. "I'll take that as a yes."

"And Max," he nodded toward his son. "You'd better make absolutely sure Paul can handle Ground Ops."

"Don't worry about me, Dad."

"Then don't give me anything else to talk about tonight."

Tyler adjourned the meeting to the canteen where he bought pitchers of beer for the cadre. They found Ted Winston alone in the canteen, writing another letter on his yellow pad. Rogers and Holtz coaxed him into joining the small party, and Ted put his writing materials away, and brought his tall glass of iced tea to the line of tables Tyler had pushed together.

Ginny Abrahamson raised her glass. "Gentlemen, I think we should toast the United States government."

Rolf rapped the table with his knuckles. "For heaven's sake, why?"

Ginny hadn't expected to defend her patriotic sentiment. "I suppose" —she lowered her arm and rested her glass on the table— "we owe some debt of gratitude for the DOOPS system we are about to deploy, and the people they may save." She drank.

Rolf softened. "Okay. I'd rather drink to the United States of America." He up-ended his glass. The others followed. Then Rolf stood to lecture the small gathering about government. "I hope I'm not splitting hairs when I put my country ahead of my government."

"I understand." Dr. Abrahamson admitted.

"When I think of government, do you know what I think of?"

Everyone had the good sense to keep quiet, except Ted Winston who had rapidly tired of the whole Temple Bay operation. He guessed, "A checkbook."

"No!"

"A big refrigerator?"

"No, no." Rolf, who stood while the others sat, glared down at Ted. "Government is simply organized crime with better public relations. You take a rat, and add a little tail fur. Now, you have a cute squirrel. A little tail fur can do a lot for a politician's image. Don't you agree, Ted?"

"Oh, yes. We all benefit from a little tail fur."

Rolf cleared his throat. "I can defend the proposition that government is organized crime. Consider how they've raised extortion to a fine art. They take forty percent of everything you make to cover their overhead—most of it interest on money they borrow and never intend to repay. They extort another seventeen percent to pay somebody else's retirement. And if you kowtow to the government, they'll steal from your children to pay for some of your retirement, too. Then, they grab another seven percent of everything you buy or own—much of which goes to create subsidies, like education grants. And if you kowtow to the government, you might qualify for some of those bennies. All in all, they extort two thirds of everything you have. And if you do what they say—if you genuflect to them—they might give you some of your money back less overhead. Al Capone could never have gotten away with that."

Ted interjected, "Of course, one way to avoid suffering taxes is to work as a contractor for the government and raise your rates enough so that the government pays your taxes for you. There's the genius in defense contracting—you help government guard the pie, and they let you keep your piece."

Rolf added, "In fact, government is the epitome—the very essence, indeed the dream—of every crime syndicate! Government really does own the cops and the judges! And what does government do with all the money they take from you and me? Just like organized crime, they offer protection. Protection from whom?"

Ted couldn't resist. "Communists?"

"Only partially correct, Ted. Governments protect us from other governments. It's like the Gambini Family protecting us from the Corleone Family. When they can't agree on a common enemy, they protect us from our fellow citizens—the other guy—all the petty thugs trying to do you in, petty thugs just like you and me trying to make enough to pay our damned tax bill. If that isn't enough, government claims to protect us from accidents, old age, and death. It's a pity we can't sue them for false advertising."

Rolf paused to take a drink from his beer. "I've studied governments far back through the ages. I've made one startling discovery! Robin Hood and the Sheriff of Nottingham were the same man. For therein lies the purest form of government, the symbiotic nature of law and lawlessness, where every poor bastard has a choice, but can't see that it's the same choice," Rolf finished.

Ted added, "I knew that."

Rolf lost his temper, "How could you know that, Ted? You worked for the government, the very worst branches of government in fact: Congress and the White House. In fact, I think you're working for the damned government even now. Aren't you?"

"That's ridiculous."

"I think you've been leaking stuff to your cronies on the Hill. I think you sit around drinking your iced tea, watching what we do, then send back your reports to our political enemies. I think the FBI got hold of you to keep tabs on me."

"You're drunk."

"Oh, yeah? What's on your yellow pad? Notes for your handlers?"

"A letter to my wife." Ted rose from his chair. "I'm not going to take any more crap from you, Mr. Bernard."

Rolf blew up. "Winston, you're fired."

"Suits me." Ted turned to leave the room.

Rolf's face turned red. "Tyler!"

"What?" Bobby was thoroughly disgusted by the scene.

"I told you Winston was the snitch." Rolf lowered his voice to a gruff whisper. "I want you to hold him here for the next two days, then get him out of here. And he doesn't send a single scrap of paper out of here unless you read it."

Tyler snarled, "That was uncalled for. That was most counterproductive."

Tyler followed Ted out of the room. He followed Ted's shadow toward the barracks and caught up with him. "Ted!"

Ted Winston turned and faced Bobby Tyler. "What?"

"Don't make a big thing of it. Rolf's under terrific stress. Lord, I think the man's cracking up. If he fails at Temple Bay, he'll lose BAP, he's done for, ruined, disgraced. He will have sunk the largest aerospace company on earth. He reads the paper. He knows the terrible things written about him impugning his integrity. . . ."

"Thanks for the pep talk, but I'm out of here. He meant every word he said. He doesn't trust me, and I don't want to work for a man who doesn't trust me."

"Well, don't take it personally."

"How else should I take it?"

Bobby took a deep breath. "We need you. Stick around for a couple days. I'll smooth things over with Rolf. You're not really fired. Heck, I think he's fired me a couple times," Bobby lied. "We'll send you back to McLean. You can help Herb keep a lid on things. We should have left you in McLean in the first place."

"When does Stouffer fly down to Cairns?"

"I'll ground the plane if I have to, Ted. I want you to cool down and think this through for at least two days. Promise me that. Then I'll send you back to McLean— and if you want, you can look for your next job while you're on payroll."

Ted glowered. "I don't want to owe Mr. Bernard anything."

"You won't, Ted. You owe it to yourself to be cool, even when Rolf gets out of line."

"Good night, Bobby. In any case, I don't blame you."

Ted left Tyler and walked to his room. Tyler returned to the canteen, but everyone had left. A full pitcher of beer sat at the end of the table. Bobby filled a glass and took it out into the tropical night. A sliver of moon rose from the Pacific, and for a moment, it took the shape of a sail heading straight for the rock in Temple Bay. But it sailed effortlessly over the rock, into the sky among the stars.

Tyler sat on a chunk of rock with his back to Lizard City. He sipped his beer and gazed out to the water and night sky. He found no frame of reference there, no human scale. Wisps of fog blew over his head from the thick vegetation toward the vacant sea. He shook his head and looked into the void.

Bright sunshine and the sounds of heavy machinery wrestled Tyler out of bed. Smells from the Lizard City Food Palace tweaked his appetite. The smell of bacon, biscuits, eggs, and coffee drew unshaven men from their barracks, up the gentle slope to the dining hall. Tyler found the Green Lid party reassembled at a long table, all chatting smartly, except Ginny Abrahamson, who stoically avoided the cholesterol-laden meal in favor of a cigarette. Likewise she avoided the disapproving glances from several nonsmokers. *What do they know? After all, cigarette smoke enhances—it does not clash with—the smell of bacon, biscuits, eggs, and coffee. It's a matter of taste.*

Mark Holtz left breakfast early. He joined his team of four technicians, and together they installed the R902 nuclear batteries into the small satellites. They tested circuits and repacked the Pebbles back into their protective pods. Holtz satisfied his helpers' curiosity, telling them he was building a geodesic dome of powerful sensors (a half-truth) to monitor the environment and lay to rest the controversy about global warming and ozone holes (a big lie). Tyler and Yeager supervised crews who worked through the morning loading hundred-pound pods, like bombs, into racks fitted into the Felix-C. Rolf Bernard pointed to the stencils on the pods and told the men that the pods contained the Disposable Orbiting Ozone Probes—DOOPS. The men believed the story about the ozone.

By midday, the great hangar doors opened. The tractor towed the Felix-C, which lay on a flatbed railcar. The railcar looked like an old-fashioned roller skate beneath the huge hollow cone. But the great bulk slid effortlessly along the standard-gauge rails. Without fuel, the spaceship weighed less than a midsize commercial jet.

The Felix-C rolled into the sunshine and out to the tarmac, where a set of hydraulics in the flatcar tilted the Felix-C upright. The massive crane hoisted her a few feet above the tarmac and carefully lowered her onto the orange metal footings, where the ground crew bolted her feet to the cement. Before the crane could disengage the cables, a crew of men in lime green jumpsuits hauled fat hoses from pill-shaped trucks and pumped in Temple Bay's home-brewed liquid oxygen and slush hydrogen— over sixty thousand pounds of fuel.

Some younger men from the night crew played volleyball on the beach.

Rolf Bernard and Mark Holtz spent their day in the blockhouse rechecking the programming for the orbital mechanics to deploy the Pebbles System. Tyler stayed with the Felix-C, spending hours squatting in her cargo bay looking at the pods, each stenciled DOOPS plus a four-digit number. Like a serpent guarding her eggs, Tyler sat by the pods. Technicians carefully walked around Tyler making their preflight checks.

Charles Rogers took Mark Holtz and Max Yeager into the ship to try their suits, harnesses, and communications gear. They rehearsed takeoff, in flight, and landing procedures. Rogers discussed space sickness and space hygiene. They planned to be in space for less than fifty-six hours. Rogers eschewed tube food, the staple of astronauts and mountain climbers. He preferred granola bars, bananas, and other high-energy, high-fiber delights. He claimed that his diet helped ensure a quick turn around. Rogers described, but refused to demonstrate, an Apollo-vintage apparatus euphemistically known as the trucker's friend. Felix had no toilet. They practiced the takeoff one last time, then Rogers ushered Holtz and Yeager to the barracks, where they tried to get some sleep.

The ground crew pumped fuel into Felix's belly until midnight, Paul supervising. Felix stood ready. The night crew mingled around the giant cone like so many chauffeurs with not much to do but polish the fenders. Occasionally a man with a white hard hat walked beneath the aerospike rocket motors and peered into their innards with a blinding white light.

At two-thirty in the morning, lights went on throughout the compound. Regardless of assigned shifts, men and women rose, dressed, and went to safer ground on the ridge a thousand feet behind the blockhouse. Max Yeager had wondered out loud if the barracks and dining hall were not a bit too close to withstand an explosion on the pad. Most of the launch crew had stayed up through the night monitoring the perfect weather and practicing their duties.

With a pat on the back from Rolf Bernard and a handshake from various crewmen—Charles Rogers, Mark Holtz, and Max Yeager walked up a set of aluminum stairs, each holding a helmet in one hand and something like an umbilical cord draped over a shoulder. Max turned and waved at the shadows of men standing beyond the glare of the artificial lights. They shut the door from the inside. A pair of technicians inspected the seal on the door, then rolled the aluminum steps back toward the hangar some three hundred fifty meters away. A voice came over the loudspeaker. "Clear the launch area. Ten minutes to launch."

Forty men climbed aboard a bus which drove out of sight. Rolf and Ginny rode to the blockhouse in a golf cart, leaving Tyler behind. Tyler walked briskly behind to the blockhouse, where he stood behind the thick glass and watched.

The Felix-C engines flickered, then burst into white light and billowing smoke. The roar deafened; the light blinded. The shuddering numbed. Tyler stood senseless before the window, shielding his eyes, unable to see the cone-shaped ship, just a painful white light rising overhead, downrange.

For security reasons, Temple Bay and Felix-C talked

only fifteen minutes each hour. Felix transmitted a narrow, low-power, high-frequency signal to the solar power satellite that relayed a pencil-width beam to a one-meter dish on top of the blockhouse. Temple Bay responded in kind. The reticent crew of Felix-C sent short messages, such as "DOOPS zero five niner out." The equally reticent Temple Bay ground crew replied, "Copy."

Rolf, Bobby, and Ginny stayed awake, keeping vigil in the blockhouse. The ground crew asked them why they cheered each "DOOPS out" message. They got no answer. They asked who collected the data from the Disposable Orbiting Ozone Probes—still no answer. They wanted to suggest that Bernard, Tyler, and Abrahamson take a break, eat a meal, get some sleep, and take a bath.

With Max Yeager aloft, Paul worked double duty: He ran his cryogenics plant and managed ground operations—both essential for a crisp turnaround. With so little slack in the schedule, Paul walked circles around the Felix prototype, exhorting—even annoying—the hangar crews to work faster with greater care. The men in their identical lime green jumpsuits looked like ants carrying foodstuffs through the hole in the side of the spaceship: loading racks, then life-support gear, then a long line of DOOPS pods, four ants to a pod. A large digital clock on the wall counted the minutes and hours the crew had to make the Felix prototype ready to take to the launch pad. Only twenty-eight hours, thirty-seven minutes remained. Judging by the rows of racks and pods lying on the hangar floor, Paul Bernard guessed they were six hours behind schedule.

Paul fussed, "Quick turnaround: That's what makes the Felix system the best in the world. Hey, you. Where are you going?"

The halfdozen men turned around, looked at each other for a spokesman. A fellow with a yellow beard raised his voice. "It's the end of our shift, mate. Besides, we works for Dr. Yeager."

"But you're behind schedule. You can't go."

"We can't go?" several echoed back in a sarcastic chorus. An anonymous voice complained, "I'm a cot case."

The noise of work in the hangar stopped. At the moment, the men in the hangar could not have cared less. Sweat dripped from their matted hair, stinging their eyes; their arms and backs ached.

"All right, all right. Listen up. I need you guys. I'll make it worth your while. I'll pay triple overtime and there's a thousand dollar bonus for every man, but if—and only if—you put her on the pad on schedule." Paul tried his hand at peer pressure, adding, "Here's the catch. Either you all get the bonus, or none of you get it. I just want results. There's no A for effort."

The men huddled briefly. Voices echoed in the cavernous hangar. "Overtime plus bonus: That's two weeks pay in one day. I'm for it." Another voice spoke, "Count me in. There's not much else to do in Lizard City 'cept work. Even the women . . . what women?" The group guffawed.

The man with the yellow heard approached Paul. "You sure your dad'll go along with this?"

Paul glowered back, his sense of humor drained by fatigue.

"Okay, we'll do it. Get your checkbook ready, Dr. Bernard."

Paul took the measure of the wiry Australian. "I'll expect you to keep everyone on the job."

"No problem. We're all mates, and no one bugs out on his mates. You Yanks don't quite understand that, do you?" He walked past Paul to resume his place among the pods.

Chapter 18

Major Arnold Colgate didn't wait for the NORAD shuttle bus. He walked briskly past the blast doors, down the winding asphalt road into the mountain. The air cooled by fifteen degrees and, after the bend in the road, all light was artificial. Colgate recalled the familiar smell of the ever-present molds. He walked into the man-made cavern with the four-story, windowless buildings. Gray cubes sitting on steel springs—each spring almost as big as a man—office buildings on shock absorbers.

In theory, the quarter mile of solid rock would withstand the PSI and the thermonuclear heat; the springs would save the structures and inhabitants from being shaken to bits. Far from confident, most of the Hole's inhabitants remained fatalistic, because they expected that such a juicy target as NORAD would get a triple helping of Russia's twenty-five-megaton warheads, which would bury them alive under a quarter mile of gravel and blow away their antennas. Everyone always wanted to know if they had on staff an officer commissioned from the Colorado School of Mines. Those would be the skills needed in NORAD after the attack. Colgate remembered speculating that their underground lake of drinking water and food stores would keep a motivated crew of amateur miners going long enough to pick and shovel a shaft to daylight.

Major Colgate showed his badge to a guard who looked up his name on a computer screen.

"DIA passed your tickets this morning, sir. Who are you going to see today?"

"Colonel O'Reilly."

"Oh, yes, I see. She requested your tickets. And the note says you can go unescorted, sir. Sure you won't get lost?"

"I used to work here."

"Then welcome back." The guard pressed a black button and an audible click announced that the door was open. Colgate climbed a metal staircase to the watch center. It had grown since his last visit three years ago. The dim honeycomb of rooms housed various screens and technicians passively watching, some typing messages or reports. Arnold looked for a familiar face. He stopped a navy lieutenant JG in the companionway. "Excuse me."

"Yes, sir."

"I'm Major Colgate."

"From DIA? We get your reports every day."

"I'm a little lost. Is this the NORAD Watch or the SPACECOM Watch? I hate to admit it, but I haven't been out here in a couple years."

"Actually both, sir. But most of the SPACECOM personnel work on the west set of offices."

"Which way is west?"

"Through that corridor, sir."

Colgate looked down the narrow passage. Two oncoming travelers would have to turn their shoulders slightly to pass. While he had a knowledgeable denizen of the Hole at hand, Colgate asked, "I'm looking for Colonel O'Reilly. I assume her office is next to the SPACECOM Watch."

"Yes, sir. I think you'll find her in the briefing theater right now. Same way."

"Thank you." Major Colgate wound his way through the maze and found the briefing theater. That hadn't changed. He stepped into the empty room on the balcony section and looked down at the large plastic screen and a row of theater-style chairs. He saw a shadow move behind the screen. Colonel O'Reilly stepped out to the podium with a handful of viewgraphs and saw Major Colgate.

"Arnie!" She greeted him with genuine, collegial warmth. "I called your office yesterday evening and they told me you were already out here."

"Yes. I gave a lecture at the Air Force Academy about the Air Force Intelligence Service. Your message said you have something you want me to look at."

"Right. Follow me." Colonel O'Reilly beckoned Colgate down to the briefing pit, then led him through a back way to the SPACECOM watch. She pulled up a chart, drew her finger over a trajectory and asked, "You see this launch?"

"Northern Australia? I thought they launched from Woomera?"

"Yes, but these aren't Australians. America's BAP sent up several rockets in rapid succession from Queensland, Australia. Do you know anything about it?"

"We don't process ephemeris data on American launches, whether land- or sea-based. I guess NSA would classify BAP's Australian launches as American. What's the problem?"

"We want to know what's going on. It's just too much activity, and BAP hasn't given us any forewarning. And get this—they put up a geosynchronous bird almost five weeks ago. And it's huge. Our radar and telescopes confirm what BAP says: It's a satellite for collecting and transmitting solar power. If so, why not tell the world about it? Isn't BAP in the business of selling satellites?"

"BAP has never been shy before. Very odd."

"You haven't seen odd, yet, Arnie. Yesterday, they launched again. This time, they cut telemetry."

"I don't understand."

Colonel O'Reilly explained. "They stayed up there for almost two days. They shifted orbits six times—"

"That takes a helluva lot of fuel," Colgate interjected.

"True. And their total transmissions amount to two hundred and eighteen seconds."

"That's odd. They must be deploying satellites."

"No, we looked for that. We detect nothing of the sort. Not with radar, no signals, nothing."

"If they're not deploying satellites, why change orbits?" Arnold muttered.

"We think they're practicing for some operation. But that's pretty darned expensive practice, don't you think?"

"Practice for what?" Arnold spiked that hypothesis and offered his own. "Maybe they're just demonstrating a capability."

"I doubt it. BAP's been totally secretive about their Australian launches. If they wanted to demonstrate their new rocket, they'd have invited the whole world like they did at the Rixeyville launch."

"True." Major Colgate stared at the plot, especially the marks where the spaceship burned fuel to shift orbit. "This looks strangely familiar . . . ."

O'Reilly stood up. "I wish you'd look into it. We're supposed to keep track of the junk up there, and right now if somebody asks, we don't have a clue. Besides, I'm curious."

"So am I, Colonel."

"I don't have the necessary analysts down here in the Hole or at ADCOM. And you are the expert."

"Sure. You don't have to butter me up, Colonel. You've given me a neat puzzle. I'll see what we can figure out. You can help me get the data?"

"Absolutely, we'll endorse your request to NSA. In fact, we'll compose and send the request before you leave. How's that?"

Major Colgate returned to northern Virginia, to the man-made caverns beneath the Pentagon. He added the Temple Bay ephemeris data to his daily computer runs and assigned the analysis of those data to himself. His small three-man office studied the telemetry of anything and everything put into orbit by a foreign power, plotting maps from ephemeris data. Believing that it was easier to get forgiveness than permission, Colgate kept his research project to himself. He sidestepped internal policies to study these peculiar American commercial launches. Colgate had followed Felix technology since his days in the Academy, ten years ago when Felix, just a generic concept for single-stage-to-orbit, or SSTO, was a set of line drawings and exaggerated claims. These flights fascinated him.

Arnold Colgate studied the orbits. They jogged his memory, but nothing specific fell into place, except that those vaguely familiar plots seemed to predate his stint at DIA. Colgate decided to try a hunch. He pulled the computerized drawing from the old plotter, folded it to the size of a handkerchief and carried it upstairs to the skunk works, where a colleague maintained the SDIO deployment plans.

"Look at this." Colgate spread his sheet of plotter paper over a light table. "Have you ever seen a 5-degree, west-walking orbit, shifted 2 degrees right, every forty-two minutes?"

"No. Should I?"

Major Colgate led his young colleague into the vault and to a large map case filled with maps and plotter paper. He said, "I hope it's still here . . . aha!" He pulled out a drawer and carefully slid a dozen sheets of plotter paper from the flat drawer. "I made these plots when I worked up here in the skunk works—oh, you weren't here then. These are plots of six options to deploy the Brilliant Pebbles System."

Colgate leafed through the six sheets and selected one, laying it over the fresh plot on the light table. He carefully aligned them, smoothed the creases, and taped them onto the glass. "They match perfectly."

The younger captain agreed, but showed no other signs of comprehending. Colgate prodded him, "The ephemeris-data plot I just brought up here comes from an odd telemetry source—a private company that launched something from Cape York, Australia made this plot."

"What does that mean?"

"First of all, it means that the Temple Bay launch has the same—and I mean exact—orbital mechanics as the SDI Limited Surge Deployment Plan. Lord only knows what they're really doing up there. They went through a lot of trouble to limit their telemetry signals, and it makes one wonder. Can I borrow your old SDI deployment plot? I want to show this to my boss."

"Sure." As they peeled off the masking tape, the captain asked, "You don't think our people are actually deploying SDI and nobody told me?"

Colgate smiled. "That would take some nerve." He rolled the papers, stuffed them into a cardboard tube and returned to the dusty basement, where he passed a series of friendly guards and ciphered doors. He threw the rolled charts of orbits onto his light table and returned to his desk, where he logged onto the central computer that handled messages and served as the word processor for classified reports. Major Colgate cracked his knuckles, then quickly typed a defense intelligence note, or DIN, for tomorrow's edition. In it, he merely stated the facts, then he added his opinion that someone was rehearsing to deploy the spacebased Brilliant Pebbles Antiballistic Missile System. He offered, then rejected, the idea that the Temple Bay operators had somehow stolen the Pebbles' deployment plan and were fooling around. He titled his DIN with the question, "SDI Deployment Dress Rehearsal?" He saved the text to his personal read-file, then he left his cubicle, stepped out to the grassy courtyard in the middle of the Pentagon, where he bought a box of popcorn and sat on a park bench beneath an ancient elm. He pondered the DIN he'd just written. He tried to recall the credo of the intelligence community. Was it publish or perish? Or was it publish and perish?

He threw a handful of popcorn as far as he could, hoping to dislodge a herd of pushy pigeons gathered at his feet, begging. Pentagon pigeons—especially the courtyard pigeons—had to be the most brazen creatures on earth. They worked in gangs. Where begging failed, they'd intimidate. The black woman who ran the cash register at the courtyard food concession told Major Colgate that she once saw two pigeons tie a lieutenant colonel's shoestrings together. "They tripped that poor man and took his bag of popcorn!"

Major Colgate decided to send his DIN up the chain for approval. He returned to his desk, mashed the necessary keys, and sent his DIN to Colonel Morris, his boss. Before the end of the day, a message flashed on his computer screen: Approved—SDI Deployment Dress Rehearsal. Colgate worked late to prepare background information in case someone called him into the Chief of Staff's morning brief. More telemetry from another Temple Bay launch arrived. He poked the ephemeris data into his computer and it, too, matched the SDI deployment plan exactly. What did it mean? Why Temple Bay?

Major Colgate pulled his crumpled leather chair in front of a heavy, gray, four-drawer filing cabinet. There he plowed through six linear feet of the *Yellow Bird*, the Pentagon's own news clipping service, so called for its yellow cover sheet. He pulled editions that carried articles about the resurrected Temple Bay Spaceport, and began to see references to BAP's many political and technical problems. He started pulling articles about BAP's single-stage-to-orbit spacecraft. He chanced upon a Janes' *Space Week* article about BAP's Dr. Holtz, who they supposed continued his research into spaceborne kinetic kill devices with old colleague Dr. Ginny Abrahamson, the SDI command and control guru. "Good Lord," he muttered. "They really are putting the Pebbles System up."

Major Colgate used a secure phone—the gray one—
to call the night editor. He dialed. He recognized the
voice that answered. With five different shifts, five possible
night editors, he had managed to get Lockwood. "This
is Major Colgate speaking."

"Oh, it's you. What do you want?"

Arnie Colgate had once inadvertently caused Lockwood
grief, but there was no sense apologizing. Two years earlier,
while Colgate waited for his billet to open in Current
Space Analysis, the powers assigned Colgate to the Third
World desk—the Caribbean and sub-Saharan Africa, to
be precise—a crushing bore. Arnold's blank existence had
been sparked with a glimmer of life when riots broke
out in a small trio of Caribbean islands—three miniscule
dots missing on most maps. Arnie thought the issue
fascinating because the islands operated under the joint
administration of the Dutch, French, and British. The
Caribbean brouhaha put an interesting strain in the
administration of the island specks, known collectively
as the Condominiums. Arnie wrote a DIN. His coworkers
told him he'd wasted his time— that nobody would read
a DIN about civil riots in the heretofore unknown island
kingdom, so thoroughly insignificant that even the
European powers had agreed that they were too
insignificant to compete for. And if the Europeans, who
owned the islands, didn't care, why should DIA?

Arnie rose to the challenge to attract an audience. He
titled his DIN, "Pandemonium in the Condominiums!"
He got his audience, and the DIN editor, Mr. Lockwood,
got a reprimand for allowing the ridiculous title to get
through.

Lockwood attacked the problem with policy. He engaged
the senior briefer, a Marine full colonel, to issue a policy
that stated, "No DIN title will use three-syllable words
other than proper names." Arnie felt abused by the
draconian policy, but kept his own counsel on the matter.

Then, Central Africa flared up. Its latest potentate, one

Sergeant David Dako, faced a coup by one of the many self-proclaimed and armed plenipotentiaries. Arnie wrote the DIN, then titled it, scrupulously avoiding three syllable words. The title read "Dark Days for David Dako." Eyebrows raised. Arnie got a few winks as he wandered the halls of the National Military Intelligence Center, but nothing serious. As it happens with most Central African coup attempts, nothing happened. And in a week, Arnie penned a follow-up DIN to close the episode. Again he chose an appropriate title: "David Dako's Downfall Doubtful." The analysts thought it great fun. The junior readership throughout the community, CIA, State, and NSA, enjoyed the sport. But Director of DIA didn't catch the full flavor of the Colgate's wit, and said so colorfully. And the stuff rolled downhill until it came to rest in Lockwood's lap.

So Colgate expected no favors from Lockwood. He heard the hurly-burly of the document production room. "I wrote the DIN called 'SDI Deployment Dress Rehearsal.' "

"Yeah, I saw it. Nice title."

"I need to make a little change."

"There's no such thing as a little change."

"I need to change the title."

Colgate heard a pained sigh at the other end of the phone. Then, he heard some papers shuffle, and finally the editor said, "What's the change?"

"The title should read 'Data Shows SDI Has Been Deployed.' "

"A statement of fact?"

"Yes."

"Pretty cocky. Does Colonel Morris approve?"

"He will," Major Colgate assured the civilian.

"Right. Well, bucko, you defend the content. I just defend word choice, grammar, punctuation, and mechanics. I'll make sure he comes looking for you if he doesn't approve. You know I've got to send a soft copy of the DIN to State, CIA, and NSA before we print—

about two in the morning. You think they'll approve your change as well?"

"Why not?"

"Indeed. If not, they'll think nothing of yanking Morris out of bed."

"I don't think changing the title will make much difference."

"Suit yourself. Anything else?" The editor asked insincerely.

"Not a thing. Good night." Major Colgate stuffed piles of *Yellow Bird*s into his sturdy briefcase. He walked to North Parking, past hundreds of empty spaces to his lonely old Delta 88, the powder-blue pig. He motored down Interstate 95 to his town house—an excellent value in spite of its closeness to Lorton Reformatory. The summer sun went down as he walked through his front door. He found his wife eating a microwave dinner at the kitchen table, apologized for being late, then went to his study to read back issues of the *Yellow Bird*.

Less than nine hours later, a clean-shaven, showered Major Colgate got back into his car and returned to North Parking. Lost in his thoughts, he didn't notice the pigeons and sea gulls that had congregated. He didn't see rising sun. He just mechanically walked into the large granite Pentagon and to his office underneath. He flashed his badge at the NMIC main door, then walked directly to the message center, where he found a stack of that day's DINs. He smiled as he took one from the top of the stack and opened it.

His article wasn't there. He rolled the DIN into a tight cylinder and went to Colonel Morris' office and waited.

Colonel Morris showed up expecting to find Major Colgate waiting for him, and wasn't surprised to hear him say, "No disrespect intended, sir, but just what the hell is going on?"

"CIA Deputy Director Marshall called me last night.

No, not last night—about two-thirty this morning. He told me to pull your article. I asked why. He said he'd discuss that with you. Imagine that? Wouldn't discuss your article with me, only with you. So, Arnold, you have a date with General Marshall next Thursday afternoon, a week from now. Why don't you ask him just what the hell is going on? Eh?"

Major Colgate didn't say a thing.

"Hey, what's the matter? Lighten up. You've got an audience with General Marshall. How many DIA analysts get that kind of recognition from a DIN that never sees print."

Major Colgate managed a smile. "You're right. But why a week from now?"

"I don't know. I didn't ask. One more thing: Marshall asked that you not talk or write about your deployment theory until he's had a chance to speak with you next Thursday. My guess is, you guessed right. Congratulations."

"Thanks, sir." Major Colgate thought, *With a surge deployment, Temple Bay could put the whole system up by Thursday.* He excused himself, picked up his messages from the message center, and returned to his desk where he extracted, then typed in, the ephemeris data—tedious as hell, but the National Security Agency refused to send the telemetry in machine-readable form directly to his computer. More tedious than typing ephemeris data was fighting NSA over data formats, so he typed. Major Colgate's new ephemeris data showed that Felix had landed back at the Temple Bay launch site.

Colgate dug out the cardboard tube and retrieved plots of the Surge Deployment Plan. There could be anywhere from two to five more launches, depending on the payload of each spaceship. What was the payload of the Felix SSTO? Colgate returned to the skunk works where he cajoled his younger friend into letting him see the SDI Surge Deployment Plan. He also retrieved a copy

of the "Felix Single-Stage-To-Orbit Experimental
Spacecraft Design Specifications Executive Summary"
document. He read both at a small desk inside the secure
vault. As he suspected, one problem with setting up a
geodesic dome of Pebbles was that one couldn't reach
all the orbits with one launch. The plan called for a
minimum of three shuttle launches, or eight Delta
launches, deploying between 40 and 120 Pebbles,
depending on options. The surge plan endorsed by NASA
preferred shuttle missions to deploy the Pebbles. A
shuttle crew could deploy the Pebbles with minimum
ground communication. Also, the shuttle enjoyed long
on-station time—fourteen days if necessary, and they
could maneuver to deploy Pebbles in orbits less accessible
to the stodgy Delta rockets.

Colgate read a lengthy paragraph subtitled "Deception
Plan." They planned to deploy the Pebbles under the
guise of other operations. The plan suggested various
medical or biosciences experiments, or possibly deploying
orbiting sensors to monitor Earth's air quality, temperature,
and ozone. A footnote to the "Deception Plan" reminded
the reader that the Strategic Defense Initiative Office
had offered to put sensors on each Brilliant Pebble satellite.
They called the earth science sensors Brilliant Eyes.

Major Colgate chuckled to himself. He remembered
his small piece of the Brilliant Eyes concept during his
tour in the skunk works. The idea required budgetary
cooperation between SDIO, the Air Force, NASA, and
the Department of Energy. The interagency committee
had met three times. First, they drafted their joint set
of requirements. Second, they priced components of
building and deploying Brilliant Eyes piggybacked on the
Brilliant Pebbles System, and each agency left with
instructions to put their piece of Brilliant Eyes into their
budget. In the third meeting, they unanimously killed
Brilliant Eyes, driving a bureaucratic wooden stake through
the heart of the concept, and they heaved a collective

sigh, *Whew! That was close.* Bureaucrats killed Brilliant Eyes before Congress had the chance.

Colgate would have bet big money that Congress would kill SDI's Brilliant Pebbles, too, but they must have come to their senses. Colgate smiled to himself, for he knew that 125 miles above, Pebble satellites were zipping through space at 26,000 miles per hour. The Pebbles served as sentries to end the threat of nuclear missiles, the end of nuclear terror. He wanted to tell everyone the good news. He wanted to call Colonel O'Reilly and tell her, "We've taken the high ground at last."

As a warrior he relished the idea. An antinuclear missile defense gave his country both the strategic and moral high ground—made so much more sense than holding the enemy's cities hostage. He wanted to phone his wife or his mother and tell them, "You're safe, finally safe." He took a brisk walk around the D Ring corridor to burn off some nervous energy. The good news would have to wait. A wave of excitement washed over him like too much caffeine.

Major Colgate hurried back to his office and sent a collections request form to NSA. He asked for enhanced collection of telemetry from the southern hemisphere, especially Temple Bay. He wrote in the comments section that he anticipated three more launches within the week. He wanted more data points, so he could impress CIA Deputy Director General Marshall with his detailed analysis of the deployed Pebbles System. He drew fat red circles around next Thursday on his calendar, grabbed his cap, and left the building.

He bought a small bouquet of flowers from the familiar old vendor who ambushed commuters as they left the North Entrance and passed over the causeway near the Pentagon Officers Athletic Club. He drove home and waited for his wife to come home from her job. Before she could kick the shoes from her tired feet, Colgate sprang the flowers on her, told her he had great news that he couldn't tell her, and invited her out for an early dinner at a Mexican restaurant overlooking the serene Occoquan River. As they waited for dinner, he grinned like a Cheshire cat, plying the wife with margaritas. "My little discovery got me a quick trip up the Potomac River to meet a CIA deputy director."

"That's super, honey."

"Yeah. I could use some friends in high places with all these RIFs coming. Maybe I could get considered below the zone."

"We could get assigned outside D.C."

"No, dear. I'm doomed to the Washington area and Omaha. Maybe a side trip to Colorado Springs."

"I'd love to go back to live on Peterson Air Force Base." Alice Colgate beamed.

The next day, Major Colgate bounced into his Pentagon basement office and rummaged through his messages looking for Temple Bay data. There was none. He picked up the gray phone and called his source at NSA. "Hey, Rick. How could you be late sending my ephemeris data— today of all days?"

The man called Rick replied woodenly, "We're not late."

"What do you mean? DSP confirms another Temple Bay launch."

"You've been cut off."

"Cut off?" Colgate yelled loud enough to attract one of the security guards, who peeked in Colgate's open door.

"Don't yell at me. I don't make those decisions."

Arnold Colgate controlled his voice. He waved the security guard away.

"What about O'Reilly at SPACECOM? You cut her off, too?"

"Yep. All Temple Bay signals have been suppressed for internal NSA analysis."

"Who made that decision?"

"I can't tell you."

"Rick . . ." Colgate sputtered. "Who? You got to tell me."

The hollow voice at the other end of the phone said, "This is not a good time for me to talk. It's busy here. Can I call you back later?"

Colgate suddenly understood and composed himself. *The gray phone might be secure, but who knows who might be standing next to Rick at the other end.* "Oh. I'll be up in the NMIC in two minutes." Major Colgate hung up. He drew a deep breath trying to restore his normal color. Then he walked up two flights of stairs to the National Military Intelligence Center, punched a few keys on the ciphered door, and walked into the dimly lit room filled with shift workers watching computer screens. The chatter of an old teletype clashed with the hi-tech hum of the other machines. A Marine colonel, the shift supervisor, stepped out of his glass booth and raised his voice. "Anyone seen Major Colgate?"

"Over here." Colgate stepped around a cement pillar.

"Pick up the gray phone. Line twenty-two."

Colgate stepped into the booth. A Navy lieutenant handed him the gray phone. "Hello? This is Major Colgate."

Without introductions the other voice said, "I still can't tell you who cut you off. But . . ."

The long pause annoyed Colgate. "But what?" he prodded.

"You'll have to talk to General Harchord to get the Temple Bay ephemeris data switched back on."

"You mean Air Force Chief of Staff Harchord?"

"None other; so save your breath, Arnie."

"Thanks, Rick."

"You can thank me by saying nothing and doing nothing."

"I hear you. Good-bye." He slowly set the receiver back into its cradle.

The Temple Bay ground crew waited anxiously for Felix-C to return. The camp doctor sat with a driver in a van—a makeshift ambulance. He held a portable car phone to his ear, listening to the chatter between the staff in the blockhouse, the pilot, Captain Rogers, and Max Yeager.

The camp doctor transcribed bits of the conversation into his spiral notebook and reviewed his notes. According to Rogers, moments after deploying the last Pebble for this third mission, Mark Holtz had collapsed—wrong word. More accurately, he floated through the cargo bay, tethered by a nylon cord. Mark said he had a pain in his gut. He convulsed like a fish fighting at the end line, apparently nauseous, but there appeared to be nothing in Mark Holtz's stomach, or at least Yeager saw no mess inside Holtz's helmet, just sweat covering the face like a glaze. Yeager described the convulsions as dry heaves. Holtz's face turned ashen, with a blue tinge around the lips.

Orders came from ground control. "Break protocol. Open channel. Send all telemetry."

Moments later, a flood of data, including Holtz's erratic heartbeat, poured through the ground-control computers.

The voice from the ground came back. "Get Mark into the cabin. He may be experiencing an episode of acute angina."

"Speak English!" Max yelled excitedly.

"A heart attack!" Rogers broke in to translate. "Mark's having a heart attack!"

"Angina is not a heart attack," the man on the ground corrected Rogers with a note of contempt. "However, angina can induce a heart attack."

They heard a long groan. Holtz exhaled, "My arms. . . ."

Max Yeager demanded, "Just tell me what to do. Use small words."

Yeager followed instructions. He pulled Holtz back to the pressurized crew compartment. There he unfastened Holtz's pressure suit and removed the helmet. He peeled off his own gloves and pressed his fingers against the stricken man's neck. Yeager reported that he felt no pulse. He asked if you could feel a pulse in zero gravity.

"Of course!" the medic in the blockhouse snapped back.

"Well, I can't find one," Yeager yelled frantically through the comm-link.

"Don't yell. Is he breathing?"

"He's gasping." Max replied.

"Uh-oh."

"What? What are you saying!"

"Telemetry shows cardiac fibrillation. Apply swift pressure directly to the sternum."

"Chest bone. . . ." Rogers added.

"That I knew." Yeager slipped Holtz onto the small sleeping bay and strapped Holtz's limp body onto the cot. He thought, *This must be CPR. I'd give anything if the little prick would speak English.*

Max pushed with all his might against Mark Holtz's chest. Yet all he managed to do was to push himself across the open cabin, where he bounced off the opposite wall, banging his head on a metal strut. "Ow! It's hopeless! I can't help him up here!"

Rogers asked, "What's going on back there, Max?"

Max barked, "I'm a rocket scientist, not a surgeon, damn it!"

The medic in the blockhouse spoke. "Look in the medical expendables and equipment locker."

Rogers translated, "The first-aid kit."

Again the medic. "You'll see an auto-injector with morphine."

Max opened the kit. "I've got it."

"Make sure you've got the one marked morphine—four milligrams. The needle comes out the red end. Hit Mr. Holtz in the thigh with the red end of the auto-injector.

"Okay. I did it. I pulled the needle out. There's some blood."

"Now, take the little oxygen bottle and put the mask over his face. He's still breathing, isn't he?"

Max checked. "A little easier, in fact."

"Put the oxygen mask over his mouth and nose."

Max put the clear plastic mask over Holtz's face and slipped the elastic band behind the ears to hold the mask in place. Max breathed heavily. "He's got oxygen."

The medic prompted Max, "Now look in the locker and take out the small roll of duct tape?"

"Duct tape? What for?"

"Tape the oxygen bottle to Holtz's chest. Then, patch the hole you punched through his space suit."

Those were the first instructions Max understood completely. "Okay. I secured the bottle with tape, and I patched the hole."

"Now figure out some way to apply pressure to the sternum. A strong blow to the sternum can restore the arrhythmic heartbeat to normal."

"I tried that. I just knocked myself across the room." Max argued.

"Well, try something else." The medic prodded.

"How often do I hit him?"

"Three times, one second apart, and pretty hard."

Max climbed across Holtz's chest—weight meant nothing. He managed to wedge himself between Holtz and a storage locker. He used his legs, back, and arms to balance himself and delivered three rhythmic blows to Mark Holtz. Minutes passed. Rogers interrupted to tell Max that they'd reenter in thirty-six minutes; they'd touch down in less than an hour.

"Max," the medic said, "we're looking at the heartbeat from the telemetry. I think you successfully defibrillated him."

"Is that good? He's breathing better. Should I hit him again?" Yeager asked.

"No, no. You've done all you can do up there. Dr. Bocco is already at the landing pad waiting for you to land."

Rogers interrupted. "Max, you've got to buckle him into his seat for reentry."

"You shouldn't move him," called the medic.

Rogers answered. "We have to. When we set down,

he'd be hanging from the wall in his straps. The cot sits on the side wall, not the floor. Bring him up here. I'll help you strap him in."

So Max Yeager unfastened the straps. He slid Holtz's sedated, weightless body from the cot and nudged him toward the flight compartment. Holtz arched slightly as he took shallow breaths. The oxygen bottle lay on Holtz's chest, rolling slightly in spite of the tape. Max steadied Holtz by placing one hand on top of the oxygen bottle and the other hand under his back. Slowly he shuffled his way into the flight compartment, where Rogers helped maneuver Holtz into the seat. They buckled the straps and cinched them tight. They wedged the oxygen bottle into the straps at his side; then they sat Holtz's helmet in his lap: They would keep him on oxygen till the last moment.

On the ground, the camp doctor, Dr. Bocco, prepared a syringe with lidocaine and mentally rehearsed the steps. He'd dealt with one other heart attack in his career, and that one, as they say in the trade, "experienced a negative patient care outcome": The patient died. Most men might have been nervous, but Dr. Bocco saw Holtz's mild heart attack as an opportunity to improve his average to fifty percent.

The ground crew did not cheer this time when the spaceship plunged toward earth, breaking its fall with blasts of fire and clouds of vapor. No, they gathered around and watched the ship settle onto the pad. They watched the van speed to the ship. Two men jumped out. They wore thick, elbow-length, canvas-and-rubber gloves. They held large alligator clips, which they used to grab the legs of the spaceship to discharge the static buildup. Three other men hauled a stretcher from the back of the van. They raised the stretcher through the hatch to extract Holtz—all the while careful not to touch the red-hot skin of the spaceship.

Dr. Bocco jabbed Holtz with the syringe, ordered people

to do things, hurried the stretcher into the van, and sped away to his clinic.

Back at the clinic, Bocco hustled around, barking orders to the medics. "Put him on a nitro drip. What's his pressure?"

"One-forty over ninety-eight."

"Set up for thrombolitic therapy."

"We don't have that kind of stuff here."

"Oh, yeah. I forgot. Well, never mind. He seems to be out of danger." He flashed a light in Holtz's right eye. "Yep. He's going to make it. Arrange a medevac for him. He's going to need angioplasty."

Bocco left to deliver the good news to the people waiting outside the clinic. "Mr. Holtz suffered prinzmetal angina, causing a mild heart attack. It appears that physical distress—something akin to the bends—and severe dehydration, caused the prinzmetal angina. I advised him before the flight that he was dehydrated and shouldn't fly again, but he didn't listen to his doctor, did he?" There is no situation in life so wretched that it cannot be made worse by adding a dose of guilt.

When pressed with questions, Bocco answered, "Of course he'll live. He needs to get to hospital. We'll fly him to Brisbane after we get some fluids in him. His electrolytes are gone."

Max Yeager and Charles Rogers stripped off their flight suits, stinking from three days of nervous perspiration and other excretions. The joy of space travel had worn thin on Yeager, especially during this last trip. Space—that crystal void, that crisp, clear vision of light and dark—was no place for fastidious people. And space—that pure essence of physical science—offers no comfort to those trapped in biological reality. And space—that wondrous leap beyond the heavy, plodding daily routine—was one hell of a place to have a heart attack. Max, knowing he was ten years older than Holtz, shuddered. Max dried himself with a thick towel and sniffed himself. He greatly preferred the scent of new soap to three-day-old Max.

The doctor gave Rogers and Yeager a quick physical exam. As he checked eyes, ears, throat, heart, and lungs, Dr. Bocco explained Holtz's stable condition. "I put your friend on nitro and I'm pumping liquids into him intravenously. His space sickness was worse than he let on. Say 'ah.' " Bocco continued, "You can visit Holtz after dinner."

As Bocco left the room, Rolf Bernard entered. "When I heard the words 'heart attack,' I naturally thought it was you, Max. I guess it was good for Mark that you were there. What a lousy time for the big H."

Emotionally whipped and physically spent, Max merely replied, "I think Mark just had the little H—angina or something."

"How do you know that?"

"I was there."

"Well, thank goodness Mark's work is finished here. We can deploy the last Pebbles without him, can't we? Max, you and Charles can take the Felix prototype up Wednesday, right? You don't need Mark, do you?"

"I think we just saw how useful a third man can be," Charles Rogers interjected. "But we'll manage."

"A third man's not too damned useful when he's having a heart attack, now, is he?" Rolf shot back.

"I think you missed my point."

Max stood between Rolf and Charles. "We're tired; we're hungry; we want to see how Mark's doing. Can we talk to you later?"

Rolf narrowed his eyes, pursed his lips, then answered, "Sure. You guys take a rest. You'll feel like new men after a good night's sleep. Tell Mark I'll be around after dinner." He left.

"What's eating him?" Rogers asked.

"His nerves." Yeager shook his head. "Or maybe he's getting rock fever."

As Rogers and Yeager walked to the dining hall they paused to watch the ground crew roll the Felix prototype to the launch pad. The massive hydraulic arm pushed the huge cone upright. Fuel trucks sat outside the perimeter. Rogers whispered, "I want to go back up."

Max started walking again. "I wouldn't mind having at least one week's rest just to let my bowels sort themselves out."

Rogers glanced over his shoulder at the spaceship. Evening shadows crawled up her sides, but the point of the great cone caught the sun's last fire. Felix stood like a torch against the dim sky. He didn't speak to Max; he spoke to the machine. "God forgive me, I love flying more than life itself."

Chapter 19

Under the cover of the large Temple Bay hangar, the ground crew loaded the last eighty DOOPS pods into the Felix prototype. In what was quickly becoming routine, they dragged her out to the launch pad, set her up, and pumped her full of fuel. Max Yeager recruited Paul to take Holtz's place. Paul beat down his father's objections and joined Max and Charles for the fourth and final flight for Project Green Lid. Paul's presence in Felix-P only heightened Rolf's anxiety: He bounced from euphoria (everything seemed to go so well), to despair (everything else was doomed to fail). Was he pressing his luck or fulfilling his destiny? No man knows until he fails or succeeds.

Felix-P shot into the air, a familiar trajectory. The only heartbeat that truly raced was Paul's. They slipped into space, and in the course of the next day, seeded the heavens with the last eighty Pebbles. They had pushed the last Pebble into the void, and gave the last report, "Last DOOPS out."

Everybody, relaxed—everybody but Rolf. Yeager took a nap. Rogers ate a banana. Paul sat in the back of the cabin trying to will his motion sickness away. The Felix crew settled into the sleep cycle.

The Temple Bay ground control crew relaxed

communications. Knowing how much Rogers despised NASA's hokey wake-up routine, they gathered around a microphone and sang Barry Manilow's, "I Write the Songs." Rogers' groggy voice came back, "Uh, Ground Control, this is Felix-Proto. Easy on the caterwaul, please. We have one nauseous crewman and we're a little low on airsick bags."

Mission Control interrupted, "Captain Rogers, we've got a little school tyke who'd like to ask you a question."

"Oh, brother. . . ."

A woman took the microphone and effected a child's voice. "Mr. Astronaut, sir? I was wondering, what's it like to be—you know—weightless?"

Rogers came back. "I'll tell you what you do, sonny. Just throw your little butt off a tall building. Imagine that the wind isn't whistling past your ears at two hundred miles per hour. You're weightless."

Mission Control whooped it up. Tyler walked in and thought the whole bunch on both sides of the comm-link had suffered a bit of post-mission madness.

That evening, Rolf Bernard worked in the small, private study in his bungalow. He prepared the press release to announce the closure of space. Bobby Tyler knocked on his door.

"Who is it?"

"It's me, Bobby. Are you busy?"

"Yeah, but come in anyway. I just finished our message to the world giving the details of how we closed space. I'd like your opinion."

Bobby opened the door and let himself in.

"Close the door, will you? This air conditioner barely keeps the room civilized."

Tyler shut the door. "When will you arm the Pebble System?"

"I have already armed the system."

"You have!"

"It was very simple. Dr. Abrahamson showed me how.

I must say, it was the most straightforward piece of software I've used in a long time. I just input my special access code, gave the simple enable command. The console read back the list of Pebbles as each responded to the command. All three hundred twenty responded. I'd say we're in business."

"What is the code?"

Rolf's eyes grew wide. "I'm not going to tell you."

Tyler straightened up. He paused to calculate the news. "But I'm your chief of security. If you're not going to tell me, then who in the world are you going to tell?"

"Nobody."

"Nobody!" Tyler turned his back to Rolf to hide the anger and distress that swept over his face. He clenched his fists until his fingernails bit into his palms. In a moment, he had composed himself and turned to face Rolf. "But why? Rolf, you know the risks."

"Of course I do. The risks to my person are tremendous. I figured it very carefully: I put myself in my adversary's shoes. What would I do if I were a spacefaring nation and Mr. Rolf Bernard had armed the Pebbles System, and thereby controlled access to Man's most precious resource—space? I'd kill the bastard as soon as look at him. After all, think of the threat to national security. Spy satellites eventually spiral out of orbit or lose power. Imagine, Bobby, when the comsats give up the ghost, when the Telstars fail, when the weather satellites run down, when the navigation satellites croak. But suppose only Rolf Bernard could disarm the Pebbles, and killing him would seal space for a hundred years—then I wouldn't kill him, would you?"

"But what if you slip in the bathtub?"

"Those poor bastards in the MIR Space Station had better hope I don't. Truth is, any nation kept out of space for twenty years becomes a Third World country. With the Pebbles System, I could ruin a country. So if they kill me, they kill themselves."

Tyler sat down at the foot of bed, stunned.

Rolf continued. "Of course I'd never do such a horrid thing, but the Russians, Chinese, French—maybe even the United States will suspect the worst of me. Heck, they already do, if what I read in the papers is true. Let's face facts. If a spacefaring nation could reopen space by killing me, they would. Wouldn't you?"

"I couldn't say. . . ."

"Oh, be honest. You know very well the danger we're in. I know you do, because you've been wearing your weapon ever since I got here—ever since the Pebbles got here, according to Paul."

"Well, yes."

"And why? Because no nation will tolerate some pip-squeak controlling its destiny. Why, their citizens would throw out the government. So I had to figure out a way to keep the spacefaring nations from putting my head on a stick."

"I don't think they'd rush in. We mustn't get paranoid."

"Paranoid? I'm not paranoid. I've devised a way to ensure that the spacefaring nations will desperately want me alive and well. They'll protect me if necessary. I've made my life at least as valuable as their access to space. To ensure my very life, I have become their access to space, because I alone know the access code."

"Oh, Rolf . . ." Tyler shook his head.

"That's right, Bobby." Rolf stood over Tyler. "I alone know the code to disarm the Pebbles; they stay armed unless I disarm them. I talk directly up the pencil beam to the solar power satellite, which in turn retransmits the code to any one of the Pebbles, which in turn retransmits to each of the others. Nobody—not NSA, not CIA, not the GRU—nobody can even intercept the signal to attempt to decipher it. And if they do, I change the frequency. Four consecutive attempts to transmit the wrong code will shut down the Pebbles communications system, leaving the satellites armed. Even if they could talk to the Pebbles, they couldn't guess right in less than ten thousand attempts. Practically speaking I alone control access to space."

"What if they figure a way to disarm the Pebbles?"

"I'd know soon enough. I'm convinced they'd storm my little spaceport here at Temple Bay and haul me away for a short, show trial."

"What happens if—God forbid—you have an accident, a stroke, a heart attack, or something?"

"I prefer they live with the remote possibility of my accident, than that I live under the certainty of assassination."

"You should give me the code at the very least."

"Not a chance. They could kill me; then put the screws to you. And if you didn't cooperate, they could always point a gun at Mariam's head—or one of your kids. Of course you'd tell them the code: I'd think less of you if you didn't, but by then I'd already be dead and past caring. Trust me on this, Bobby. My way is better. My way, every country out there—as much as they would hate to admit it—will want me alive."

Tyler muttered, "I should have seen this coming."

"What?"

"Nothing." Tyler looked Rolf in the eye. "Do you want me to get you a pistol?"

"No. I've got three hundred and twenty rounds of ammunition overhead. In a way, I feel like the safest man alive."

Arnold Colgate bought a new pair of patent leather shoes and a pair of calf-high socks for his big meeting with General Marshall. The new shoes bit the back of the ankle, and the elastic in the new socks carved circles in the flesh below his knee. He drove his powder-blue car up the George Washington Parkway, turning off to Dolly Madison Boulevard, past the sign announcing CIA NEXT RIGHT.

Colgate pulled up to the remote sentry—an intercom and video camera mounted by the road. The electronic box squawked, "Do you have an appointment?"

"Yes."

"What's your name and social security number?"

Colgate recited both to the box on the post.

"One moment, sir." Colgate knew the drill. The guard would check him against the computer. The voice returned, "Please drive up to the gatehouse, sir."

Colgate approached the guardhouse, posh, metal and glass tollbooths built on islands, with a cement and steel awning overhead. A disfigured pair of signs demanded that he slow to five miles per hour and display the badge he didn't have. At the gatehouse, a man with a Smoky the Bear hat stepped out with a clipboard, asked for a picture ID. The two guards remaining inside the hut stood and watched. Colgate knew well that they each had a machine pistol less than arm's reach away. A German shepherd dog put his nose up to the glass—a dog's idle curiosity. The guard clipped Colgate's military ID to the board and handed both to Colgate. "You'll have to sign the release."

"I know." Colgate signed without reading the form that allowed CIA to search his car and person.

Colgate found the visitor's parking hospitably near the front entrance. His short walk took him past the Bubble, CIA's seven thousand-seat auditorium. Colgate walked past Nathan Hale's life-size statue—Nathan standing, hands tied behind his back, head erect, eyes forward, eternally proud and eternally about to be hung for bungling his mission—seemed to Colgate more a threat to bunglers than a call to espionage. Inside the main lobby, Colgate presented his ID to guards who stood behind polished marble. He took a moment to study William Donovan's bronze statue, the father of the OSS, thereby grandfather of the CIA. Donovan looked like a man set to begin a safari—needing only a pith helmet and a gun.

A bookish man met Colgate at the front desk. Chains and badges dangled from his neck. He quietly led Colgate through the sign-in process, gave him a badge with a clip, and said, "I work for Deputy Director Marshall."

"What do you do?" Colgate made small talk.

"I write his correspondence." The man paused to see if the answer satisfied. It did.

They started down a hall, passing a cold white marble wall embellished with fifty-six bronze stars. Each small, anonymous star memorialized an agent killed. The corridor changed from sea-green to a light blue. The quiet man volunteered, "General Harchord has already arrived. We should hurry."

"General Harchord?"

"Yes, didn't you know?" He answered his own question. "I suppose you didn't."

The civil servant put his badge into one of the turnstiles, keyed in a cipher, and passed through. Colgate dropped his visitor's badge into the slot. The turnstile unlocked and let him through.

"Is there anything else you can tell me?" Arnold Colgate fought a sudden attack of nerves. The Deputy Director and Air Force Chief of Staff would not go to the trouble to personally filet a lowly major—they'd delegate that bit of dirty work. No, Harchord and Marshall wanted something. What did they want so much? Colgate figured he had nothing to lose by asking. "What in the world do Generals Harchord and Marshall want with me?"

"I can tell you that they have your personnel file."

"How do you know that? Aren't there any secrets in the CIA?" Colgate raised an eyebrow. "That's a joke."

"I see." The quiet man picked up the pace as they rounded the corner to a long corridor. "General Marshall sent me to retrieve your personnel file."

"Why are you telling me this?"

"General Marshall asked me to tell you. He's going to offer you a job. And he told me to sell you on CIA."

Arnold Colgate shook his head. "So this is how you sell me on working at the CIA?"

"I don't want to oversell anything to anybody. I do what I'm told, sir. Here we are." He turned a large brass knob and opened the heavy walnut door. He motioned Major Colgate into the dim room. "General Harchord will explain that the Air Force will look favorably on your tenure with the Agency. I think he will recommend that you accept Marshall's offer."

Major Colgate walked through the shadows, past a pair of art deco floor lamps. The two generals stood next to the plateglass windows, looking at the tinted view over the trees. They turned to face young Colgate. Four-star General Harchord spoke. "Come in. Come in. So you're Major Colgate. General Marshall told me about you; I wanted to see for myself. Weren't you in the 149th at Offutt back when I ran the operations center at SAC?"

Major Colgate was nervous, but not addled. He remembered that Harchord had been through his file— but if a general goes to all the trouble to act friendly, the least a major can do is act flattered. "Why, yes, sir. I worked on targeting our missiles."

"Very critical work. . . ." Old pilots like Harchord still had a hard time heaping praise on nonrated men.

General Marshall interrupted. "Let's cut to the chase. You're a clever young man. You figured out what's happening at Temple Bay—almost."

"So it's true! We are deploying the Pebbles System." Colgate stepped forward as they led him to a conversation nook of high-back chairs.

General Marshall corrected him, "I said almost. If you want to learn the whole story, you're going to have to work for me."

General Harchord grinned. "Smells like a promotion to me. Early selection to lieutenant colonel. Take it, Colgate."

Major Colgate looked at Marshall's narrow eyes, then

at Harchord's warm smile. Had he stepped into the wrong cage?

"Is anything the matter? Do you want time to think about it?" Marshall now seemed smooth as oil.

"I'd hate to see my shop at J-Section Current Intelligence go unmanned."

Harchord piped up, "Major Colgate, we need you here at the CIA for now. CIA lacks your analytical specialty and right now, with the Temple Bay situation . . . Let me be direct. If you stay at DIA, you won't get any Temple Bay data. If you come out here and work for my friend, Tom Marshall, you'll get your data back on. And I'll be much obliged. You hear what I'm saying, boy?"

"Yes, sir."

"Good." Marshall put out his hand. "It's settled. You start today. My people will start you through in-processing. CIA has its own drill, you'll find out. Orders have already been cut. Colonel Morris—is that your boss' name? General Harchord's office has already informed him."

Colgate shook the general's hand and asked, "What will I do? What's my job?"

Harchord laughed and shook his head. "My boy—I mean Major—you'll do whatever General Marshall tells you to do. You're in the CIA now." Then he looked at his watch. "Gentlemen, I've got to run. I've got to explain to a bunch of kindy-gartners at the White House why the Air Force shouldn't use F-117s over Macedonia. You got the AP wire? Show it to young Colgate here. See what he thinks."

He walked out to the room, leaving the heavy door ajar. From nowhere a small pale hand reached across the threshold and pushed the door closed. Major Colgate studied General Marshall's face. His mouth kept a steady, uncommitted smile. His voice made smooth, sympathetic sounds. And his soft hands had a manly, trustworthy grip. But his eyes sparked with annoyance.

"Take a look at this." General Marshall reached back

to his desk and plucked a single sheet of paper from a short pile.

Major Colgate took the sheet. It read

GENSER
DT 1200 LOCAL Temple Bay, Queensland, Australia
LEO ACCESS DIVISION, BAP, Inc. (USA)
For Immediate Release
RE: CLOSING ACCESS TO LOW EARTH ORBIT

Effective 2200 hours local Brisbane Australia time, no individual, corporation, nation, or body of nations may launch a space vehicle into low earth orbit, without paying the low earth orbit access fee. LEO Access Division Ltd. (LAD), BAP, Inc. has deployed a geodesic dome of kinetic kill devices, known as the Brilliant Pebbles Antiballistic Missile System.

The Pebbles remain in alert status and will automatically shoot down any launch vehicle that attempts to enter low earth orbit. LAD also cautions against attempts to defeat the Pebbles System by suppressing the Temple Bay ground facility. One person at Temple Bay knows the access codes to disarm the system. If that person could not use the access code, the Pebbles System would remain armed. Each Pebble uses a solar pack and an enhanced battery, giving each Pebble an on-station life of eighty to one hundred years.

LAD will for a fee create a window for a third-party launch. LAD will waive the fee for any LAD-chartered launches. LAD also has a fleet of four Felix-class single-stage-to-orbit spacecraft, capable of putting 8,000- to 15,000-pound payloads into low earth orbit. LAD plans to expand the Felix fleet to meet expected demand. LAD will submit bids to parties who either require a launch window or prefer to buy cargo space on a Felix launch.

Interested parties may contact LAD directly by writing: LEO Access Division, Ltd.; Temple Bay Spaceport; Queensland, Australia; TELEX: 011-65-955-525-02 Answerback LAD; or contact BAP, Inc. Headquarters, McLean, VA: POC Herb Eckert, Sr. VP Finance.

LAD will not be held responsible for loss of property, injury, or death for any unchartered launches that refuse to remit the required space-access fee, which we've initially set at $100,000 U.S.

Released by the authority of Rolf Bernard, President LAD Ltd., CEO and Chairman BAP, Inc.

Major Colgate handed the piece of paper back to General Marshall. "So we didn't deploy the Pebbles System."

"No, we didn't. And we're not convinced that Bernard has deployed it either. The press, so far, seems to be treating the news release as a hoax. As you can imagine, the State Department is up to their eyebrows, and they want us to sort it out. Air Force security has already been to Pueblo, Colorado, where BAP stored the Pebble satellites. They're gone, supposedly hijacked by the Air Force, if you can believe that. The conspiracy theorists will jump all over this news."

Major Colgate interrupted, "I know where they are." Colgate pointed toward the ceiling.

"Don't be too sure. Do you realize the panic this could cause? Do you realize how destabilizing this is? We still have fourteen thousand nuclear missiles aimed at us. The President and Yeltsin have already had one rather acrimonious conversation this morning. The President looks like a liar again. First he promised to kill Star Wars. Then he promised to share operational control with Yeltsin; now, it looks like he deployed the Pebbles System. We'll never get Yeltsin, or anybody else, for that matter, to believe that some American lunatic controls outer space.

No. They'll believe we're behind it. This Temple Bay operation had better be a hoax or all hell could break loose. Needless to say, the CIA will catch unmitigated hell for failing to detect and suppress Rolf Bernard. My career is done for, but to tell you the truth, I don't care anymore. I just want to make sure I've got someplace to retire. Lord only knows who's in control of the old Soviet Strategic Rocket Forces. And who knows what the flower children in the White House will do? I was kind of hoping that you could prove all this is just a hoax."

Colgate shook his head. "They're up there. Whoever flew those four Felix missions from Temple Bay has invested at least—and I mean a bare minimum—a hundred twenty million dollars to do something. I doubt Rolf Bernard or anybody can afford that kind of money for a practical joke."

General Marshall turned to face the outside world through the tinted glass. The rising sun sparkled from the rows of stars on his shoulders. The sunlight shone on his short graying hair and his bald spot, which looked like a monk's tonsure. Marshall looked like a good man standing in the tinted light, looking out to the world through the one-way glass.

Colgate asked, "Sir, why did you and General Harchord cut off my data?"

The older man turned and looked into Major Colgate's eyes. "It doesn't really matter if a nuclear war starts by rumor or by fact, does it? Those three hundred and twenty Pebbles—if they're deployed—can hardly put a dent in a saturation attack. We have a delicate situation. So Major Colgate, we need to control your input—or I should say, your output—regarding these matters. Don't take it personally."

"I understand."

"You're a sensible man." Marshall shook Colgate's hand and led Colgate to the door. He gave instructions to a civilian on how to take care of his new team member.

Then he went back to his desk. The civil servant quietly let himself into the large office and delivered a sealed eyes-only envelope to Marshall's IN box. Then, like a ghost, he left. Marshall tore open the envelope and read the short message from Iago: "RB will not share the access code. Please advise."

"Damnation." Marshall crushed the bad news in the palm of his hand. Please advise, indeed! The whole operation had just turned to crap. Marshall pulled a small lighter from his desk. He lit the small scrap of paper and watched it burn in his ashtray. Then he retrieved a piece of his personal stationery and penned a short letter resigning his commission and requesting retirement no later than—he paused to contemplate a date—August fifteenth, soon enough to divert attention and appease the Administration, and late enough so he could change his mind. He wondered how long General Harchord would last.

General Harchord served on borrowed time. Everybody knew that. The White House had picked their new guy to be Chairman of the Joint Chiefs. But with two dozen hot spots around the globe, the White House delayed sacking Harchord and risking increased anger within the ranks, and criticism from pro-military democrats in Congress.

As the day wore on, Marshall's office grew dim. Periodically, he summoned a fresh thermos of coffee, which he drank as he paced the floor—a most unproductive day. He surveyed a short list of people that General Harchord wanted to see: Dr. Mark Holtz, Dr. Virginia Abrahamson, Dr. Albert Fenster, Mr. Herb Eckert, and Mr. Ted Winston. He dispatched agents to find and persuade them to help their government cope with the rogue Rolf Bernard. General Marshall stressed that he didn't mean normal CIA persuasion, and he apprised the Justice Department of his efforts to solicit voluntary cooperation from certain citizens. He shook his head and muttered, "All I need now is a turf war with the FBI."

General Marshall's phone lit up and a woman's voice intruded. "Sir, the National Security Council has convened an interagency meeting. The director wants you to represent CIA. You'll have to leave within fifteen minutes to get there on time. It's in the briefing vault in the Old Executive Office Building. Can you make it? The director's aide is waiting on the other line for your answer."

"Yes. I've been expecting this meeting. Tell Harry to get the car and pick me up at the front entrance. Find Major Colgate if you can. Tell him to drop whatever he's doing and meet me at the front entrance. Got that?"

"Yes, sir."

With the fifteen minutes left to him, General Marshall dialed General Harchord's number. A colonel answered, and at General Marshall's insistence, interrupted a staff meeting to fetch Harchord.

Harchord picked up the phone. "Tom, have you got confirmation on the Pebbles deployment?"

"In a way, yes. I'm sure it's happened. I'm worried, George." Marshall switched the phone to his other ear.

"So am I." Harchord didn't sound too worried.

"Listen, George. That nut—that erstwhile poker buddy of yours, Rolf Bernard—is the only living being who can turn the Pebble System off. We couldn't get the code."

There was a long pause, then Marshall repeated, "Didn't you hear me? Iago didn't get it. We're in deep trouble, George. I'm supposed to go over to the National Security Council for a three o'clock briefing. What am I supposed to say?"

"Don't tell them anything. Or better yet, tell them almost everything. Tell them you're trying to infiltrate Bernard's organization. Tell them you're rounding up BAP's scientists. Tell them you think Bernard's threat is real. Tell them to shut down operations at Canaveral and Vandenburg."

"But, I just told the State Department to tell the French that we think it's a hoax." General Marshall cleared his throat. "The French plan to launch a communications satellite from French Guiana in about four hours."

"Well, I guess you'd better call them up and warn them not to launch."

Marshall paused. "I don't know, George. It's a surefire way to find out if Bernard's Pebbles System is any good."

"That's pretty damn cold, Tom."

"Oh, what the hell, they're French." Marshall erupted into a belly laugh. Then he collected himself. "Excuse me. This whole business makes me a little crazy. *You* know Rolf Bernard better than I do. How should we go about getting the access code from him?"

"I don't know."

"How about we just stick a gun in his mouth and ask him politely. Do you think he'd be reasonable?" Marshall asked.

"Tom, don't get dramatic on me. It won't work. Rolf knows we wouldn't shoot him. Don't even talk like that. I can see it now—one of your zealots makes a mistake and accidentally kills Rolf Bernard. Good Lord, man! We'd set ourselves back fifty years."

"Have you a better idea?"

"To do nothing is a better idea. Find out what you can from Abrahamson and Holtz. If they can't help us figure a technical way to work around Rolf Bernard, we'll have to hope Bernard can still be bought. In the meantime, I'll try to figure out ways to put a little pressure on him, and you keep your eye on the South Atlantic."

Rolf Bernard's press release didn't play any better at Temple Bay than it did abroad—the only difference was that everyone at Temple Bay believed every word of it. Rolf wisely hid from the flak. Herb Eckert faxed his resignation, adding that the authorities had contacted him. Virginia Abrahamson dissolved into hysteria when she saw Rolf's press release. Rolf watched from the blockhouse as a couple of men threw Dr. Abrahamson and her gear in the Learjet. Rolf thanked God that Mark Holtz had already left Temple Bay. Fifty-six Temple Bay laborers simply quit and awaited bus transport out. Max stayed. Paul stayed. Rolf was grateful for that.

Back in the relative safety of his room, Rolf swallowed his last scotch of the day, and turned the light off. His stomach ached slightly. He dozed off worrying about the hundreds of other things that might soon go wrong.

Weather delayed the Ariane launch for the night, but fair weather returned to French Guiana at 8:43 in the morning. The tall, sleek Ariane IV roared to life and rattled the jungle. The Ariane's onboard computer and ground control exchanged a barrage of data as the rocket made attitude adjustments on its way over the Atlantic Ocean. Then three minutes and eighteen seconds into the flight, the data stopped. Downrange, a French observation ship reported, "The rocket exploded! It just exploded."

Pieces of debris scattered over the ocean, some within sight of the French ship. All but a few pieces of insulation sank to the bottom of the ocean. The staff at the launch site in French Guiana stood with their mouths open as the grim reality set in: contrary to all intelligence reports, Bernard's Pebbles deployment was no hoax.

Tyler beat on the door. "Get up, Rolf. Get dressed and come quick!"

Rolf threw on a robe and followed Tyler into the tropical night, toward the blockhouse. "What's the matter?"

"We got a signal from the system."

"What?"

"The Pebbles System. Pebble 147 just flew. We don't know why. We don't even know where yet."

By the time they reached the blockhouse, a young technician was waiting at the door with a computer printout. He read from the green-striped paper, "Five minutes ago Pebble 147 flew at a target, vicinity 7 degrees, 18 minutes north; 37 degrees, 26 minutes west."

"Where the hell is that?" Rolf snatched the printout from the man's hands and headed for the map.

"East of Kourou, French Guiana. Sensors indicate a hit."

"Those stupid, arrogant bastards! It's their own fault. What did they think would happen?" Rolf crumpled the paper in his hand. "This complicates things."

Tyler raised an eyebrow. "Well, what did you think would happen?"

"Hey. Don't give me that. It's their own fault. They let the cat out of the bag, I didn't."

"Whether you did or not, the cat's out of the bag now. That's for sure."

"I just wish it were the Chinese, the Japanese, or the Americans. The French are so vindictive." Rolf's eyes grew wide. He grabbed Tyler's arm. "Cynthia. Bobby, you've got to get her out of there. I don't care how, just get her out of there. Drag her out by the hair if you have to, but get her out. I don't need that kind of pressure on top of everything else."

Tyler stood half in the light, half in the dark, with his hands on his hips. "Stouffer and the jet won't be back until tomorrow morning. You shipped Ginny Abrahamson down to Brisbane today, remember?"

Rolf stamped his foot. "We have two planes."

"Only Stouffer's can cross the Indian Ocean." Tyler put his hand on Rolf's shoulder. "Here's what I'll do. I know somebody in Paris. I can trust them. They'll make sure the French don't snatch Cindy."

"Make the call."

Rolf walked back to his bungalow. Overcome with worry and unable to sleep, he sipped scotch and flipped through old copies of *The Economist*. Tyler locked himself in his small office in the blockhouse and made one phone call—

to Paris. Then he waited by the phone napping. His phone rang. He caught it on the first ring and sat up, instantly alert. The man in Paris reported that Cynthia Bernard was not in her apartment. Bobby quickly explained the potential danger, told the man in Paris, "Don't call here. I won't be here. In fact, lose this number. I'll find you."

Tyler worried. Had the French already grabbed her? If they had, Tyler could do nothing to save her. He decided that Rolf, who appeared near the end of his rope, was better off not knowing Cindy was missing. Tyler could not fathom Rolf's interest in Cindy. Was it affection? Was it proprietary? Was it worth risking Project Green Lid? Was it worth dying for? Tyler grabbed the night shift supervisor and told him, "Get Stouffer and the jet back here now."

The Learjet 31A landed on the Temple Bay airstrip before the sun came up. Tyler sat in the Land Rover with his briefcase and bag. The plane rolled to a stop, the side door popped open, and out stepped the weary pilot wearing a faded denim jacket with Harley Davidson wings on the back and a Stop-Lorenzo patch on the front. He wore his shoulder-length hair in a neat ponytail with a Cubs baseball cap. He tossed a canvas bag of mail onto the gravel, jumped down, and offered Tyler a copy of *The Truth*. The headline in four-inch, doomsday print read, "SPACE CLOSED!!!" And there was a picture of an Ariane IV rocket on a pad with an inset of a French naval officer holding a small chunk of wreckage in his hand. Tyler handed the paper back to the pilot and asked, "What's the range of this jet?"

"At 400 miles per hour, she'll make about 2,600 miles."

Tyler paused. "How would you like to make some real money?"

"Sure thing, Mr. Tyler. That's the only reason I came to this hole. What's up?"

"How'd you like to fly me to France? We'll pay you double and put you in the hotel of my choice in Marseilles for a couple of nights. All you have to do is be ready to leave on a moment's notice."

"Well, sure. Do you think Mr. Bernard will let you take his jet?"

"We're going to rescue his wife."

The pilot flashed a Midwestern grin. "Come on. Really?"

Tyler opened his jacket exposing the pistol and shoulder holster. "Really. Just do what I tell you, and you won't get into any trouble. Now let's go." Tyler threw his bag into the plane as he asked, "Why does everybody call you Stouffer?"

"I eat a lot of frozen dinners since my divorce."

Stouffer convinced Tyler to join him for a hot breakfast. The plane needed fuel and maintenance to cross the Indian Ocean. Plus Stouffer needed a pot of coffee and a shower.

Tyler did not know how lucky he was to leave Temple Bay behind that day. Rolf threw a fit when he saw the newspapers: "Madman Seizes Outer Space!" The Securities and Exchange Commission halted trading in BAP, Inc. stock, which took a precipitous dive to sixteen dollars. The Senate passed a resolution condemning Rolf Bernard by name, joining his name with Saddam Hussein and Adolf Hitler. Then the fax machine hummed to life with a letter from his board of directors firing Rolf Bernard as CEO and president. Rolf received a warm congratulations from the International Green Party, advice from Lyndon Larouche, and a couple of anonymous death threats from unsigned idiots, whose phone numbers were printed neatly at the top of each fax.

Rolf sat before a large TV screen on which some CNN stand-in reassured the viewers that their anchorman had already left Atlanta for the rainforests of Australia. Rolf gave orders to throw any and all reporters to the sharks.

Then Irwin Kirby arrived. He brought two bodyguards and a lawyer. Irwin did most of the talking. "You lied to me."

Rolf didn't rebut.

"You are a very dangerous man—a renegade. My government asked me to visit you to discuss your future, which I sum up for you thusly. France wants you extradited, but the United States demands a crack at you first. However, most of the folks in Canberra love any bloke, game as Ned Kelly, who can piss off the United States, Great Britain, France, Russia, China, and Japan in one fell swoop. So you've become the rage, a real folk hero. But have tickets on yourself, mate." Kirby paused for emphasis. "The Laborites want to put you on trial. Others think they can co-opt you into serving Australia. To put it bluntly, most of us think you're an asset; others think you're a liability."

"What do you think I am?" Bernard asked.

Kirby sighed. "You're a dangerous asset. Until the government can figure out what to do with you, they've quarantined the Temple Bay area. Nothing flies in or out without Canberra's approval. Australia reserves the right to shoot down anything you launch, so do check with us first. Mind you, we intend to be reasonable at this point. No seacraft will be allowed in or out of Temple Bay. And nothing will come off Bruce Highway to Temple Bay without prior approval."

"I won't stand for that," Rolf blustered.

"Oh, don't get your knickers in a twist. It's for your protection, mostly. Anyway, we're partners, remember?" Kirby motioned with a turn of his head and the lawyer stepped forward.

"What's he for?" Rolf demanded.

Kirby spoke for the lawyer. "This here's my lawyer, Mr. Pibbs, whom I brought up here at my expense to do you a great favor. Tell him, Pibbs."

The lawyer cracked open his leather briefcase and pulled out a manila folder filled with forms. "We think it would be a good idea if you applied for Australian citizenship."

Rolf Bernard looked confused. The lawyer continued with a soothing voice, "Mr. Bernard, you're in a lot of trouble. Fortunately for you, Australia stubbornly refuses to hand over her citizens to foreign powers: We don't extradite our people—probably a holdover from our days as the British gulag."

Kirby chimed in, "Now that you're an outlaw, Rolf, you'll fit right in—a regular ocker. Why you'll be feasting on chip buddies with your fellow dreamers, schemers, and reamers—the spawn of adventurers from the wrong side of the law. Now if you don't mind, I'd like to take a walk about for old times' sake and see our operation. I'll let you and Pibbs sort out the paperwork. Don't worry, nothing final happens until they approve your application and you sign the final documents. In the meantime, these procedures will buy us time while we sort out this little escapade of yours."

Kirby waved and left the small crowd.

Rolf fumed, "I won't sign anything until I see my lawyer."

Mr. Pibbs quipped, "If that were possible . . . He can't get in, and you can't get out."

Dr. Abrahamson waited in the courtyard between the old CIA building and the new glass house. She studied the quarter million-dollar sculpture, a six-foot tall scroll of petrified wood and colored stone, adorned with copper plates, in which thousands of letters were carved in code. She rubbed her fingers over a string of letters.

A lean, gray-haired gentleman wearing a gray pinstriped suit approached. "Dr. Abrahamson?"

"Yes." She turned, slightly startled.

"I'm General Marshall. I'll escort you to the briefing room now." He walked slightly ahead of Dr. Abrahamson through the glass doors. His shoes clicked on the polished, gray and white, Georgia marble. He opened a wooden door and motioned her into the room. "Dr. Virginia Abrahamson, I'd like you to meet General Harchord. You know Dr. Mark Holtz." General Marshall walked Dr. Abrahamson into the small conference room.

She pulled away from Marshall. "Mark! I'm so happy to see you on your feet again. How do you feel? How's your heart?"

Dr. Holtz returned her warm smile. "I'm okay. They gave me a stress test, a little roto-rooter job, and some medicine. If I behave myself, stop drinking, and if I eat nothing but soybeans, they won't crack me open. How are you?"

"I feel like the biggest sucker in the world."

General Harchord reassured her, "We've all been fooled. We trusted Rolf Bernard. Now, you can help us remedy this tragic turn in affairs. We're grateful that you volunteered to help us." He pointed out their seats near the head of the table. "General Marshall will chair this discussion."

Given his cue, General Marshall stood up. "We need to figure out a way to neutralize Rolf Bernard's control of the Pebbles System and return control to a responsible authority, preferably the United States. The question is, how? Our specialists, assembled from government and industry, will, with your input, help us brainstorm a solution."

Mark looked longingly at the silver tray of Danish at his end of the table, but he restricted himself to coffee without cream, without sugar. He absent-mindedly stirred the black coffee and listened to the first proposal. A small man with great, bushy eyebrows recommended that first they must find the Pebbles. He suggested high-powered radar. "SPACECOM can track something not much bigger than my ballpoint pen with their radar."

Dr. Holtz raised his hand.

"Please, Dr. Holtz. What do you think?"

"Radar won't help you. We modified the sheath—that is the outer covering of the Pebble—using stealth materials. You would have a better chance of tracking a

BB flying 26,000 miles per hour more than 150 miles above the earth."

"Can we model their deployment from telemetry?"

Dr. Holtz speculated, "We could find each Pebble's placement within an area about twenty cubic miles, but the Pebbles randomly adjust orbits. I'm afraid we can't find a Pebble unless we can talk to it."

A man from the National Security Agency suggested a plan. "If we can collect even a small piece of the telemetry going to Temple Bay, we should be able to break the code and take over command and control." He turned to face Dr. Abrahamson. "Can you give us some details about Temple Bay's communications with the Pebbles?"

"I'd be happy to." Dr. Abrahamson straightened herself in her seat. "Each Pebble sends lateral signals to its nearest siblings. You can't get in between two Pebbles to intercept their signals, because the Pebbles would shoot you down on your way up. The signal sidelobes are weak, but perhaps you wizards at NSA can collect them if you've already got a bird up there."

"I doubt it."

"The Pebble closest to Temple Bay sends a signal up to the solar power satellite that Bernard deployed in a geosynchronous orbit above Temple Bay. The SPS transmits by means of a laser—technology developed by Loral. The beam has an accuracy of two tenths of a degree of arc. With that accuracy, from here, I could hit a nickel sitting on the top of the Empire State Building. You won't be able to collect the SPS downlink without Rolf Bernard knowing."

The NSA man put up his hand. "Perhaps we don't need to collect current telemetry. Perhaps you could tell me about the encryption protocols you used."

Dr. Abrahamson told him. She told about the randomly generated data pulse rates, the long access number, the trillions of combinations, and the lockout feature for failed attempts. The NSA man blasted her. "You know you're not supposed to develop any encryption exceeding DES standards—especially for commercial use." He turned to General Marshall. "We can't break that code, certainly not without collecting the signal."

Dr. Abrahamson meekly added, "I thought I was developing the code for the government under Project Green Lid. I'll give you my source code if that will help."

"A little," the NSA man snipped.

"And I can disarm the lockout feature."

The man from NSA brightened. "That's much better. We'll just put our computers to work sending codes to the Pebble until they answer. We'll have Rolf Bernard out of business in a matter of weeks."

The air burbled with endorsements. Heads bobbed. Dr. Abrahamson hated to quash this happy room full of owls. "Gentlemen, if the system gets the right code, and if it answers, it will send its answer down the laser to Temple Bay."

"Oh." The man from NSA shook his head.

"Rolf would know that you've broken the code before you know that you've broken it. He'll simply change the access code."

The man from NSA slumped into his chair. He had nothing more to offer. One of General Marshall's men suggested, "I guess we'll have to resort to our first plan: We blackmail Mr. Bernard into releasing the code. Shall I call Paris?"

Marshall flashed an angry look across the room. "Colonel, you're out of line. We'll limit our options to technology for now." An old man with a silver-topped cane stood and tapped the table to get the room's attention. The distinguished doctor from Livermore Labs offered his solution. "So. We can't see the Pebbles. We can't talk to the Pebbles. Nevertheless, we can get rid of them. We shall use electromagnetic pulse, or EMP, to blind their sensors and fry their little computer brains. Then the shoe will be on the other foot, so to speak. After we cook their sensors, the Pebbles won't be able to see us, and they won't be able to talk to each other—or with Rolf Bernard. We believe we can still make a polar launch of an SLBM without activating the Pebbles System. Is that right Dr. Holtz?"

Dr. Holtz agreed, "Rolf deployed the Pebbles coverage to focus on Third World threat. The coverage of the North and South Poles is limited. I can show you exactly where to launch your submarine missiles—you may need to launch about four at the same time to overwhelm Pebbles coverage—for the best chance of getting through."

"Thank you, Dr. Holtz. I recommend we launch to an altitude of two hundred thirty miles and steer the missile toward the equator. Then detonate a one-megaton warhead. The EMP will destroy the Pebbles' onboard electronics, creating a large enough window, so that we can send a shuttle through for more clean up."

A Navy captain asked, "What are we to do with the other nine warheads on the SLBM?"

General Harchord ignored the Navy captain, but challenged the idea. "You'll also knock out another eight hundred billion dollars in electronic gear with the EMP. Are you serious?"

"I see your point. Try this idea. A ground burst. We'll use something very clean—a hydrogen device over the ocean. We can minimize the radioactive fallout since we'll throw relatively little radioactive dust—plus a little steam— into the atmosphere. The EMP pulse will knock a hole in the Pebbles System without a large footprint over the earth's surface. If we simultaneously detonate thermonuclear devices in the Pacific, Atlantic, and Indian Oceans, we could knock out two thirds of the Pebbles."

Harchord spoke. "I don't like that idea at all."

"It's scientifically sound." The man tapped his cane on the table for emphasis.

"But it's political suicide. Why must every solution from Livermore Labs come with a nuclear bang?"

The old man with the cane turned to his fellow scientist for sympathy, "What do you say, Mark?"

"EMP was such an obvious means to disable the Pebbles that we hardened them. You won't knock a very big hole in the system. Plus, at any given time, twenty percent of the Pebbles lie momentarily dormant. You can't blind all their sensors with one blast. I figure you'd need about thirty-four one-megaton detonations at different points around the globe, at different times, to eliminate ninety percent of the Pebbles. You'll never know which ones you've destroyed and which ones remain on station. You'd still run a significant—perhaps forty percent—risk of having a launch shot down."

The only scheme that made sense to Mark Holtz was that the United States and the Soviet Union take the warheads off their missiles, then shoot them, a few at a time, into the Pebbles System, drawing the Pebbles' fire. "Even if Bernard figures out what you're up to, he'll eventually run out of ammunition. Of course, both sides would have to use up all of their missiles to defeat the Pebbles System."

"All of them?"

"Yes, almost ten thousand launches. The Pebbles System adjusts to fill gaps. You create big holes in the system, so each successive attempt to draw down a Pebble has less chance to succeed. You might get the first ten Pebbles with only ten launches; the next ten might require fifteen launches; the last ten could take a thousand launches. But so be it. Can you think of a better way to use up our offensive missiles?"

"That's a great idea. It ties into the Administration's disarmament proposals . . . by God, Secretary Christopher will love it!" The State Department rep beamed.

General Harchord shredded the idea. "That's a very sweet, naive notion. Can anyone in this room make an honest case that the Russian Strategic Rocket Forces would even consider such a proposition?"

The State Department rep squeaked, "Can anyone here make an honest case that the American Strategic Command would even consider such a position?"

The room hushed. All eyes turned to General Harchord, whose face lit up with a generous, if insincere, smile. He turned to his sidekick and asked, "General Marshall. You want to answer that?"

General Marshall walked around the table to the man from State, who squirmed. Marshall stood at a respectful distance, then pronounced, with all the patience he could muster, "My friend, I wish I lived in your world, but unfortunately you live in mine. In your world, people don't need or want nuclear missiles. In my world, we need them; we want them. Everybody wants them. And as long as everybody wants them, we need them. Is this logic too circular for you? Besides, you're talking about wasting trillions of dollars to neutralize three hundred twenty lousy satellites. Does anything I'm saying make sense to you?"

The small man searched the room for any support, and finding none, he cowered. "I'll take it up with my boss."

General Harchord reread Rolf Bernard's press release. He asked rhetorically, "Why do you suppose Rolf Bernard will grant access to space for a hundred thousand-dollar fee? Surely not for the money."

Marshall's eyes widened. "Rolf's smart enough to know that if he simply and arbitrarily denied a country's access to space, we'd all figure we'd have nothing to lose . . ."

"Precisely."

" . . . and so a prudent nation might as well try to grab Bernard and force the code out of him. If he were to die, we'd be no worse off. So he has to provide reasonably painless access to space."

"And there's the fatal flaw in Rolf's strategy." Harchord snapped the press release with his finger. "It might take us a while, but we'll eventually get out of this mess, and we won't spend a trillion dollars to do it. We just need a little luck. And if Rolf will sell us access to space, by golly, we'll take up his offer and see what we can do from up there. We don't have anything down here that can help."

The National Security Council begrudgingly accepted Harchord's recommendation, and the United States joined the Japanese and Russians who had already decided to pay the space-access fee.

Chapter 20

Having parked the Learjet in a small field north of Marseilles, Tyler took Stouffer to the posh Concorde Prado. Tyler brusquely dismissed the disappointed bellhop and took the key. Stouffer slipped the bellhop five Australian dollars and shrugged his shoulders as the bellhop examined the strange bill.

The room faced a voluptuous semitropical garden. Bobby spent just enough time in the room to shower and change clothes. He tossed a small bundle of smelly clothes onto the bed. "All you have to do is hang around for three, maybe four, days. I'll phone if there is a change in plans." Tyler reassembled his modified Glock-17, which he had smuggled through customs. While he snapped the plastic case together, he instructed, "I want you to get my clothes cleaned. I want the jet ready to go on a moment's notice. Enjoy yourself, but I'm warning you, if you get yourself thrown in a French jail, I'll see that you never get out." He slapped the fourteen-round clip into the handle of the sleek pistol with an authoritative click.

Stouffer lay on the bed rubbing his temples. "Why didn't we just fly into Paris?"

Tyler straightened his jacket. "Tougher airports and tougher cops. And we have an old saying in my trade."

Then he chanted a short couplet. "There's more than one way to leave Marseilles."

"Huh?"

"Forget it. Just do what you're told. You won't hear from me until it's time to fly." Tyler left, jumped into his rental car, and sped up Route 7, a great spoke of road leading to the hub of the French world, Paris.

Bobby arrived in Paris in the middle of the night. He drove out to de Gaulle Airport, where he turned in the rental car, bought some francs, and made a couple phone calls. Quickly, he learned that Cynthia and Chip were out of town, and he remembered Cynthia saying that she might take a sailing trip on the Mediterranean. He calculated her return as imminent.

Tyler caught a cab to a new high-rise hotel on the outskirts of Paris, on the way to Versailles. He had always preferred the suburbs of big cities. Suburbs offered the option of hiding in urban chaos or fleeing into the bush. Never knowing which route one might be forced to take, he thought the suburbs offered a compromise. He rang the night bell and a hulk of a man rose from a leather couch, fumbling a great ring of keys. They had a room, and Tyler crawled into bed.

Tyler slept till ten. When he left the room, he nearly tripped over the tray of croissants and coffee set outside his door. He reached down and grabbed one of the croissants. He took a cab to the Eiffel Tower, then walked toward the Hôtel Invalides. A man wearing a dark green beret stepped alongside Tyler and they walked together for a couple blocks without exchanging a glance or a word. Then as they stepped into the shadow of a line of gray buildings, the man gave Tyler an envelope and a set of car keys. Tyler thanked the man and started to walk on, but the man grabbed Tyler's arm. "Monsieur. Moment, if you please."

Tyler turned. The man reached into his jacket and slowly pulled out a pen and a carbonless form. "Do you want to put these charges on your American Express or Visa card?"

"What?" Tyler pulled the man around the corner of the building. "What the hell are you doing? When did we change procedure?"

The man held his chin up and said, "I need the cash flow. Business is slow. Besides, I have given you my sister's car that you will be driving."

Tyler snatched the pen. He dug out his special Visa card, printed the numbers in the form's little boxes, then signed the form. He added, "At two thousand francs a day, I'd better love your sister's car."

"You had better take good care of it." The man tore off the back sheet of the form and gave it Tyler. "Your receipt, monsieur."

Tyler sighed. Then the man saluted and briskly walked away, inspecting the signature on the form. Tyler peered into the envelope and inventoried the false documents and the sundry items. He followed a small hand-drawn map to find the sister's car, a midnight blue, four-door BMW with tan leather interior, sun roof, spoiler on the back, and a parking ticket on the windshield. He stuffed the ticket in his pocket and drove to Cindy's apartment.

He slipped into the building behind a couple of Cindy's fellow tenants. They'd seen him before. Tyler let himself into Cynthia's apartment and quickly assured himself he was alone. From his briefcase, he took a pair of small binoculars and some light equipment to check for bugs. Through drawn blinds, he noticed a black Peugeot parked across the street and two men standing around, reading a newspaper. They waited for Cynthia, too. If they were waiting for Cynthia, they didn't have her—a most hopeful sign.

Tyler waited with them. He didn't use the phone, he didn't turn on lights, he ignored knocks at the door. He expected they might pick the lock, as he had, but they hadn't. He ate various canned soups, cheese, crackers, and the last three eggs. He borrowed her razor and slept in her bed. Her pillow held a sweet, carnal scent.

After two days, the black Peugeot left, and didn't return. Tyler watched the street for an hour, then decided to visit Cindy's other flat. He made his way to rue Saint-Jacques unnoticed. He forced the door and found the room disheveled. He noticed an ashtray filled with cigarette butts—three brands: Dunhill, Marlboro, and another he didn't recognize.

Bobby felt his hands sweat. Whoever sought Cindy knew too much. How many hunters were there? The Americans, the French—but were there others? Had they already taken her? Was she aware of the danger? Had she fled? Or was she coming home and into the snare? He pulled a chair over to the side of the window and watched the street. He saw no loiterers. That didn't mean the street was safe. He looked at his watch. There was nothing to do but wait.

Tyler had just decided to sneak out for bite to eat when he saw Chip's silver Porsche drive up the street and attempt to parallel park. Tyler lunged for the stairwell. He burst through the door and jumped from the stoop to the sidewalk. He sprinted down the walk, sliding to a stop as Cindy casually got out of the driver's side. He grabbed her firmly, and spoke in hushed tones. "Thank God I found you first. We've got to get out of here. Smile and look happy to see me."

"I'm always happy to see you."

He tightened his grip to send her a clue.

"Bobby?"

"No time to explain. I'm sure we've been spotted by now. We're in danger. Come with me." Tyler reached in the door and snatched her purse. He rushed her down the sidewalk. From the corner of his eye he saw a pair of men dressed in overalls toss their gardening tools into the bushes and start jogging after them. Tyler led her toward the Latin Quarter, and with Cynthia's help as a navigator and translator, they ducked into a small restaurant, out the back door to an alley, through a back door into a kitchen.

"Is this that Greek restaurant?"

"Want to stop for some ouzo?"

"You don't get it do you?"

The burly maitre d' stopped them as they came out of the kitchen, whereupon Cynthia rattled off something in French. The maitre d' nodded sympathetically and she planted a kiss on his cheek, saying, "Merci, merci."

"What was that all about?"

"I told him my extremely jealous, homicidal husband sent private investigators after us." She stopped Tyler in the small entrance, where she took a few anise seeds from a bowl, put a few in her mouth, and asked, "Just exactly why are we in danger?"

"Rolf deployed the Brilliant Pebbles System on his own. He's taken control of outerspace. Where have you been? Haven't you heard? Four days ago, the French launched an Ariane IV rocket and one of Rolf's Pebbles shot it down. It's been all over the news."

"I spent the last two weeks on holiday, cruising the Sicilian coast. I don't follow the news when I'm on holiday."

"I'll fill you in." Tyler gave her the details as they backtracked to his BMW. As he put the key in the ignition, he finished, saying, "Rolf, and Rolf alone, controls access to outer space. Nobody can touch him because he's the only person with the access code."

"But the French figure they can get to Rolf through me, right? Well, they overestimate old Smurch." Cynthia boiled.

"He sent me to get you out of harm's way, didn't he?"

Cynthia didn't yield an inch. "Oh, he'd prefer to spare himself the difficult decision—me or his Pebbles. Sacrificing me would look bad in his biography, even a bit ignoble. However, let's not kid each other. I'm expendable. He just cares what the public thinks."

"Or maybe he cares what Paul thinks. Or just maybe—I realize this is a stretch for you, Cindy—he cares what you think. Whatever his reason, Rolf sent me."

"You would have come to save me on your own initiative."

Tyler glanced at her. "You're too smug for your own good." He drove toward Versailles, turning off the road to his hotel, where he parked the car in the underground garage. "I had to put this room on my credit card, so for the sake of our cover, you're Mrs. Tyler tonight."

Cynthia managed a wry smile. "I'm willing to make certain sacrifices to stay undercover with you."

"Cute." Tyler looked into her eyes and saw the spark—dangerous for her, dangerous for him. "We're too smart for that kind of thing, aren't we, Cindy?"

She put her arm in his, and answered, "Smart as a bag of cats. You can call me Mrs. Tyler, dear."

They rode the elevator to their floor, and as Tyler cautiously, quietly turned the lock, Cynthia exclaimed, "I don't have any of my stuff. And my traveling companion, he'll start looking for me. I ought to call."

"We can't go back there. And for heaven's sake, don't use the phone. Chip will have to take care of himself for now."

"You know his name?"

"Yeah, I know a lot." He slipped into the room with his hand inside his jacket, his thumb unfastening the holster strap. He switched on the light and beckoned Cynthia to enter.

She observed, "Twin beds! I'm shocked. I didn't think the French made twin beds. Mrs. Tyler is not amused."

Bobby didn't answer.

"I really must go back to my apartment to get a few things and check my mail. I really need to contact my office. I've been away for two weeks. I've got the Dresden deal—"

"You still don't get it, do you? The French want *you*,

and I don't mean the gendarmes. I mean the deuxième bureau. If they get their hands on you, you'll simply disappear from the face of the earth. There won't be any more deals, because there won't be any more Cynthia Bernard. Geez, for such a smart woman, you can be thick. No one will ever know that the Bureau abducted you, drugged you, interrogated you, imprisoned you. No one will ever know, because you'll never get out to tell. You'll spend the rest of your mortal days heavily sedated, in a straitjacket, praying for death, because death will be your only escape."

Cynthia gasped. "Then this isn't just some stupid ruse to get me back to Rolf?"

"Not on your life."

"Oh, dear. I have to warn him."

"Who?"

"Chip. If they're willing to get to Rolf through me, then they'd be willing to get to me through Chip. I've got to warn him."

"I already have. Anyway, Chip's not worth dying for."

"You're lying, Bobby."

He didn't deny it. He walked over to her and wrapped his arms around her. He pulled her toward him. The scent of her hair recalled the pillow he'd slept on the night before. "I can't protect you out there." He pointed out the window toward the street. "I can protect you here. Chip will have to take care of himself. Besides, they don't want Chip, they want you."

She whispered, "And I want you."

Tyler froze.

Cynthia nuzzled against him. "I know what you're thinking."

Tyler kissed her lightly on the side of her mouth. "Right now is especially not a good time."

She asked him directly, "Do you want me?"

Bobby retreated two steps, stammering, "I. . . ."

Cynthia pressed, "I asked you a simple question."

Tyler took a deep breath and said, "There are so few ways to tell the truth and so many ways to lie."

Cynthia finished his sentiment for him, "And you must choose your answer from so many options."

"Exactly." Tyler clung to her logic the way a drowning man might clutch a serpent. Cynthia sat on the bed, somewhat bemused by Tyler's predicament.

Tyler loosened his collar and changed the subject. He popped open his briefcase and pulled out some papers. "I've gotten us new passports. Tomorrow we become Mr. John Simons and Mrs. Dorothy Dubois-Simons. You finally get a hyphenated name."

"Nice touch. How do John and Dorothy Dubois-Simons feel about each other?"

Tyler threw Cindy's fake passport to her. She spread her legs and caught it in her skirt. She picked it up and asked, "Where'd you get this photograph?"

"A trade secret, Mrs. Dubois-Simons. Remember, we're on vacation. We've only been in France for a week. We flew into de Gaulle Airport. Look at the date stamped for our arrival."

Cynthia stared at the small photo of herself.

"Pay attention, please. What we say has got to match the documents. When they ask you where you live, you can't say 'Paris' and you can't say 'I don't know.' We come from Philadelphia. Your profession is real estate agent, and I'm a lawyer. Can you remember that?"

"Sure. I'll just imagine being in hell. I sell real estate, and I'm married to a Philadelphia lawyer."

Tyler laughed. "Maybe we'd get some sympathy if we got stopped by the police."

Bobby told her his plan to drive south to Marseilles and fly out on a private plane. Cynthia asked no questions and soon Bobby ran out of material. Then Cynthia did ask, "Do you want to push the beds together? That's what newlyweds do."

"No. Cindy . . ."

"Are we in role or out of role?"

"Out. I'm sleeping in the bed by the phone. I get a better look at the door."

"That's so romantic."

Tyler squirmed.

"And where do I sleep?" Cynthia purred.

"Oh, for Pete's sake." He laughed at himself. "You sleep in the other twin bed."

Tyler sweated through another long pause. Cynthia walked across the room and sat on her small bed, bouncing gently to test the springs. "Some beds are built for comfort. Some are built for speed."

Tyler muttered to himself, then spoke directly to Cynthia. "The proper procedure for lying low . . ."

"Yes?"

"Let me put that another way. The proper procedure for hiding out with somebody, as in witness protection programs—"

"You lost me, Bobby. What are you trying to say?"

He took a deep breath. "We're supposed to use room service and stay off the street."

"Could be fun."

"But" —he took another deep breath— "I'd feel much more comfortable if we eat out."

"Okay." She got up from the bed with a little bounce.

Cynthia demanded a half hour to freshen up. She sat in front of a small vanity and nimbly combed her hair and tied it back into a ponytail. She put on a fresh sheen of red lipstick, then lamented that her sleeveless dress limited their choice of restaurants.

Cynthia directed Tyler toward Paris. She insisted that if she were condemned to leave France, then as the condemned woman she ought to get a last meal of her choice. She took Tyler to the Closerie des Lilas, a former haunt of expatriates. They stepped through the door and back seventy years to an era of genteel decadence. Cynthia told how Lenin and Trotsky, Gertrude Stein,

Henry James, and Ernest Hemingway had frequented the Closerie.

Cynthia ordered for Bobby and led him through a leisurely meal. Tyler was in no hurry to get back to the hotel room and face the real perils of becoming John Simons, the imaginary husband. The longer they lingered at the table, the more relaxed Tyler became. By the time the flan and the coffee arrived, Tyler felt serene.

Cynthia said, "I'd go freshen up if I had anything to freshen up with. Do I look that awful?"

"You look very nice."

"Nice? All things considered, I'll settle for nice."

Tyler tried to salvage himself. "I really like your earrings. The windmill on the left ear is upside down."

"Oh, these." She instinctively turned the left earring, turning it a bit too much so that it lay on its side. "Chip bought them for me in a little shop in Delft. How do you know his name?"

"I know lots of things."

"That's not an answer."

"That's the *only* answer. I don't know much about the fellow. What's he like?"

Cynthia demurred. "He's nice enough; we get along. For one thing, he answers my questions. He's actually fairly bright. If I could get him to read. . . ."

"Does Rolf know about Chip?"

"I would assume so. Rolf and I have pursued our own interests over the years. Anyway, I'm surprised you ask. I've always assumed Rolf sent you over to keep tabs on my love interests."

"No, there's no percentage in snitching on the boss' wife. Does Chip know about Rolf?"

"Of course." Cynthia straightened out her silverware around her small dessert plate.

"Well? What does Chip think about the competition?"

Cynthia burst into a girlish laugh and quickly stifled

herself. "Oh, Chip thinks Smurch is an old fool. Chip's more worried about you."

"Really?" Tyler raised an eyebrow. "Why is that?"

"Maybe because you're here and he's not." She wrinkled her nose. She took the earrings off and dropped them into her small purse.

Tyler mulled that over. *What did she mean, "He's not here?" Which "he," Rolf or Chip?* He let it lie. "I'm sorry. I shouldn't pry into your affairs."

Cynthia looked squarely at Bobby. "At least you're curious about me. That's a start. I've always been curious about you."

"Let's take a walk." Tyler needed some fresh air. He paid the waiter, then walked Cynthia up the boulevard. She looked at the old buildings while he watched pedestrians and cars. Most people on the street came in pairs, men and women clinging to each other, making curious, four-legged shadows on the sidewalks. The few loners seemed to be in a hurry to meet someone. Cynthia took Tyler's arm and pressed it against her side, as if to copy the young couple walking ahead of them. Her shoulder pressed against the pistol hidden beneath Tyler's jacket. Tyler turned her around and said, "We've got a long day tomorrow. We'd better call it a night."

Cynthia sighed. "I do hate to leave in summer. I love Paris in the summer." She laid her head against Tyler's chest. "Why don't you quit Rolf and come work for me?"

Tyler patted her on the back. He smelled the soap in her hair, the faded perfume. The crisp smell of fresh lemon came from her hands, and she exhaled a faint aroma of wine, but it was her own sweet, pungent scent rising with the heat from her body that stirred him. He closed his eyes and let his mind wander. Cynthia broke the spell. "Chip must be frantic wondering what's happened to me."

"When we're safe, you can call Chip and put his mind at ease."

Tyler put an arm on her shoulder and led her back to

the car. He drove Cynthia back into the suburbs to their hotel. Tyler checked the front desk for messages, then followed Cynthia to the small elevator. The door slid shut, sealing them from the inquiring gaze of the desk clerk. Tyler exclaimed, "I'm beat. I can't wait to get out of these shoes."

"I can't wait to get out of this bra."

As they approached the door to their room, Tyler gently held Cynthia to the side. He whispered, "I'm suspicious by nature." Then he inspected the tiny piece of tape he'd fastened to the door as a seal. "It's safe. No one paid us a visit.

Once inside, Tyler turned the lock and fastened the bolt. He slid a chair against the door, just in case. And while he fortified the room, Cynthia slipped into the bathroom for a hard, hot shower. In time, the shower stopped and Cynthia stepped out of a warm fog with one towel wrapped around her waist, another held over her breasts as she walked across the room toward her bed. Bobby turned at the sound and his jaw went slack. Cynthia defended herself, saying sarcastically, "I left my flannel nightgown in the Porsche."

She dropped the towel to the floor. Bobby recoiled as if she'd turned a gun on him. "What?" she prompted. "Turn your head or look. I don't care. But I'm not climbing under covers with these damp towels. Hey, you brought me here. I didn't ask to come."

And Bobby faced the wall as she unwrapped the towel from her narrow waist. She tossed it across the room. It hit Tyler across the back. She climbed under the covers. She reached over and turned the lamp off, and from her dark side of the room she said sadly, "Good night, Bobby."

She rolled onto her stomach and buried her face. Tyler turned off the lights, slipped out of his street clothes, tucked his pistol under his pillow and crawled under the covers. White moonlight shone through a part in the curtains, casting a pale glow throughout the room. Tyler glanced across the room and saw Cynthia's form—a sine curve—under the covers. He felt like a young man that night, all knotted inside. Yet he'd behaved like an old man. At least he hadn't behaved like an old goat. He fell asleep with the thought that twenty-five years ago he would have jumped on Cindy in a heartbeat, Mariam or no Mariam, Rolf or no Rolf, job or no job, hell or no hell. Twenty-five years ago, he would have fallen asleep at her side, in a hot sweat, out of breath, crushed under passion's weight, physically exhausted—stupefied into a deep and dreamless sleep. It sounded pretty damn good. *Too damn good.* Yet he felt some sense of relief. The anxiety of contending with Cynthia more than made up for the anxiety of looking for her. Tyler managed to fall asleep.

Tyler woke to the sound of Cynthia's voice. She sat at the small desk, wearing yesterday's clothes. Tyler shook the sleep from his head and focused on her conversation. He understood nothing. She spoke French. He pulled his trousers on and growled, "Cindy, what the hell are you doing?"

She ignored him and continued her phone conversation.

"We're supposed to be hiding. The people we're hiding from tap phones."

She put her hand over the mouthpiece and said, "What are the odds that they'd tap this phone?"

Tyler walked across the room and put his finger down on the button that cut the line. "They use a satellite to listen to all phone calls. They use a big, fast computer to do a keyword search on the conversations—keywords like Cynthia Bernard. Then they listen to your call—trace it, if need be. Given that they probably know exactly who you do business with, I'd say there's a fifty percent chance they made your call. How long were you on?"

"Two minutes."

"That's all they'd need. What did you talk about? Did you use your name?"

"I ordered all my holdings on the Paris CAC and Frankfurt exchange moved to cash. I closed the margin accounts, and I told them to transfer sixty-five million dollars to my Luxembourg holding company—where I pay a bright fellow to play the snake. And of course I used my name."

"The snake?"

"Yes. A snake player trades the spread between various European currencies. My snake player seems to know before the market what the Bundesbank wants to do with German interest rates. He catches nice little moves from time to time. Anyway, it's very liquid. I'm sorry if I messed up your plans, but I can't go into hiding and leave my investments floundering. I've got to make a few more calls. I've got to move everything toward cash."

"Later. You can make your business calls tonight or tomorrow morning. At a minimum, we must assume they know you're still in Paris. But perhaps not." Tyler paced the floor and rubbed his chin. "I've got to make a phone call. I might be able to find out if the deuxième bureau knows we're here."

Cynthia proffered the phone receiver.

"No, Cindy. I've got to assume our phone is dirty now. My source wouldn't want to share a phone line with you— no offense. I must use a pay phone a few blocks away."

"Who's your source?"

Tyler lashed back, "Cindy, you'll get us both killed. Just let me do my job. One more blunder could land us in some French lockup for the rest of our lives—or dead in a ditch. Now, I'm going out for about twenty minutes. I'll check us out of the hotel. Be ready to leave when I return. Don't use the phone. And don't open that door unless you know it's me."

"How will I know?"

"Because I'll sound like me asking you to unbolt the door."

Tyler learned nothing from his phone call. He ran back

to the hotel. He called through the door and his heart sank when he got no answer. The tape on the door frame was split. Tyler used his key. The door swung open. She'd opened the deadbolt, the fool! He ran into the room. He saw no sign of struggle—everything just as he'd left it, except Cynthia was gone. He ran to the window and looked down the street. He saw no loitering men, no black sedans—nothing.

Then a taxi pulled to the curb. Cynthia bolted from the front door into the back seat, and the taxi sped away. "Damn her!" Tyler cursed as he ran down the stairwell to his car.

He drove toward Paris, pursuing a cab that had a four-minute head start toward any number of places. She might go to her apartment. Or she might go to an airport and find her own way out of France. Or she might go to Chip to warn him. Trusting instinct, Tyler drove as fast as traffic would allow toward Boulevard du Montparnasse—ironically, down the street he and Cynthia had walked the night before. He turned left on Boulevard Saint-Michel, where a sixth sense cautioned him to hang back and observe Chip's apartment.

Tyler parked around the corner. He left the motor running and walked to a house on the street, and under the guise of checking the mailbox, he surveyed the street. He spied a black sedan with two men. The man in the passenger seat held a car phone to his ear. The driver held a small pair of binoculars to his eyes. Chip's silver Porsche sat unmolested at the curb, in the same spot Cynthia had parked it.

Suddenly, Chip appeared on the front stoop. He hollered something back into the building, reached in and hauled Cynthia after him, stuffing her into the passenger's side of the Porsche.

Tyler rushed back to the BMW. He rounded the corner in time to see a black sedan pull out to follow Chip's Porsche. Both headed east. Why east? They passed the last turn for the airport. Chip kept to secondary roads. Tyler heard no sirens and saw no sign of gendarmes. The small caravan wound its way through dusty villages. Chip must have figured out the tail, because the Porsche opened up and disappeared over a hill. The black Peugeot lurched forward in pursuit. Tyler's hot BMW had no problem keeping up, but lots of problems looking inconspicuous, so Tyler held back.

The tree-lined, winding roads favored the Porsche. However, Cynthia, frightened and angry, distracted Chip by frantically begging him to stop. "I know what I'm doing," Chip argued. "I've got to get you to Switzerland—out of France."

"Stop this car!" She yelled in his ear.

He shoved her toward her side of the car. "I work for the CIA. I've got friends who can help you."

"You bastard!" She hit him in the face.

He shoved her back. The Porsche lurched across the yellow line to face an oncoming truck. Chip pulled the Porsche back to the right side of the road. Chip yelled, "You stupid, stupid woman!"

"You'll kill us! Please slow down." She began to weep. "Let me out. I'd rather take my chances with them." Her eyes filled with furious, fearful tears.

"Shut up! You'll get us both killed." Yet Chip couldn't dispute her premise. One slip and the Porsche would hit a 200-year-old elm at 130 kilometers per hour.

How could he lose the black Peugeot? He screeched around a corner, barely missing an oncoming farm tractor, and saw the flashing red lights of a railroad crossing. The aluminum road barriers that stuck into the air shuddered. A southbound Très Grande Vitesse, as yet out of sight, barreled down the tracks at two hundred kilometers per hour. Chip figured the train was at least a minute away. He crammed the accelerator to the floor. The Porsche lurched forward to the falling road barriers.

Cynthia screamed. "Stop! Stop!" She tried to grab the

emergency brake. Chip slapped her hand away, then grabbed her by the nape of her neck and angrily shoved her head down and away. The barrier fell faster than he had thought it would. The Porsche barely cleared the first metal pole, but the second pole smashed the car's windshield, shearing off the windshield and roof completely.

The black Peugeot's wheels locked. It fishtailed out of control and came to rest in a shallow drainage ditch just three meters short of the road barrier. The two men jumped out of the Peugeot just as the train blazed by. In less than thirty seconds, the clamor and the train were gone, an ever-shrinking silver rod, going south very fast.

Tyler arrived as the first gate opened. The second gate lay twisted at the side of road. Tyler drove through and immediately saw the silver Porsche, listing in a deep furrow in an asparagus field. He left the BMW on the side of the road and ran through the soft, sandy soil and rows of straw, to the car.

The grisly sight stunned even Tyler, for there strapped into the driver's side of the wreckage sat a headless torso awash with bright wet blood. He ran to the edge of the car and saw a form, a torn and bloody dress, and he feared the worst. Then she moved. She lifted her head, exhaled a groan, then fainted. Tyler quickly checked her pulse. Rivulets of blood ran down her face; her left eye had already swollen shut. She needed stitches to close a scalp wound.

Tyler heard voices behind him. He turned to see the two French agents approach. Quickly Tyler volunteered, "They're dead!"

"*Quoi?* You are American? We will handle these. Go away."

"I said they're dead. I know this woman."

"We will see for ourselves." The agent pressed forward and brushed past Tyler. He saw the remains of the driver. "*Mon Dieu!* But the woman, I think you are wrong about the woman."

In the blink of an eye, Bobby shoved a pistol into the Frenchman's ribs. "I said she's dead. *Comprendez?*"

"Don't shoot, please."

"Tell your friend to lose his gun." Tyler turned the man to use him as a shield.

"My partner understands English. Maybe we should all speak English to avoid a tragedy of a bad translation."

"That's a wonderful idea. My French stinks."

"I could tell."

Tyler spoke to the second agent. "Very easy. Drop your gun on the ground. Thumb and forefinger on the barrel."

The agent with the gun in his ribs echoed, "Do it, Jacques."

Jacques carefully opened his jacket revealing a chrome-plated revolver. With exaggerated precision, he undid the leather strap and plucked the gun out of the holster as if it were a thorn. The frightened man dropped the pistol and stepped away. Tyler rudely frisked his captive and picked a handgun from his body. Then he retrieved Jacques's pistol, which lay on the ground.

"Come here. Help the woman into my car, and be careful. I will lose my composure if she cries out in pain."

The two agents carefully pulled Cynthia from the car. Her shoes were missing. They laid her on the sandy soil to examine her. "She is alive. She needs the sewing up. I think her foot is broken. She may have concussion."

"Put her in my car. Hurry!"

The Frenchmen carried Cynthia to the roadside. Tyler fetched her handbag from the wreckage. They laid Cynthia in the back seat.

"Now walk back to your car. Quickly."

They didn't argue. Tyler walked them to the black Peugeot, then pulled Jacques's pistol from his belt and chambered a round. Jacques fell to his knees, made the sign of the cross, closed his eyes tightly, and begged, "For the love of God, please don't kill me!"

In a businesslike tone, Tyler told the agent who was

still standing, "Tell your friend to get a grip. I don't want him to swallow his tongue when I fire his gun." Then he shot holes in the Peugeot's front tires. Tyler reached through the car window and ripped the handset from their car phone and put it in his pocket. He took the keys from the ignition and tossed them into the field. Finally, he pulled the clips from the French pistols, put the bullets in his pocket and threw the pistols into the Peugeot. "Just a professional courtesy—I know what a nightmare it is when you lose a weapon."

"Thank you, monsieur. You are a true professional."

"Please take your time reporting this incident. If the woman and I get out of France, then I will never be in a position to embarrass you again. As it is, you two can make up any story that suits you, *n'est-ce pas?*"

"I think we can make a special effort just for you. You'd better hurry, monsieur. You can see the Bernard woman needs a doctor. She's no use to any of us dead."

Tyler ran back to the BMW, made a tight U-turn, and doubled back. He sped past the French agents, who crouched behind their black Peugeot. He turned north onto a road that led to a major east-west highway. He might as well leave them guessing his destination: Paris, Strasbourg, Geneva. At the highway, he drove west, then turned south to follow highway signs to Dijon and Lyons.

Tyler heard a doleful sound from the back seat. "I'm a mess."

He looked in the rearview mirror and there she sat, hair matted and encrusted with dried blood. He saw her hold up her hand, streaked with blood, purple and puffy from a sprain. She looked at it, tried to make a fist, but couldn't. "Where am I?" She had no idea where she sat. Her left eye had swollen shut. She had lost the contact lens from her right eye.

"You're back with me. For the moment, you're safe. You are a lot of trouble, Mrs. Bernard; you know that, don't you?"

"I had to warn Chip."

Tyler peeked back through the mirror and saw tears cutting their own path down her cheeks, eroding the dried crud. Were the tears born of pain or sorrow? "So, tell me about Chip. Why did you go off with him?"

"He told me the French had him under surveillance, and that we had to get away."

"He was right about that."

"Chip told me that he worked for the CIA."

"Really?"

"I think my foot's broken."

"You should thank God you can feel your foot. I was afraid you'd broken your neck. How's your head? You've got a cut at the top."

She felt her crown with her good hand. "Ow. It's sticky. There's a huge knot."

"Then the bleeding has stopped. Cynthia we've got a couple of decisions to make. If the French use their civilian police, they'll catch us. I'd bet on it. But we could put ourselves in American hands pretty fast."

"That doesn't sound so bad."

"I'm not so sure I want to get picked up by a bunch of freelance CIA goons like your buddy, Chip."

"Did the men in the black Peugeot get that little bastard, Chip?"

Tyler responded coldly, "Chip died in the wreck."

"Oh, dear—" Cynthia shut her eyes.

"It looks to me like Chip didn't follow his instructions and got himself killed. Just like you didn't follow instructions and nearly got yourself killed. I wish people would just do what they're told. Someday . . ." Tyler caught himself.

Cynthia began to focus through her pain. "What happens if they don't use their civilian police?"

"The Bureau will watch the borders and the airports for a couple of days, so we'll have to lie low. You'll have a miserable time of it, but I think we can get out."

They passed Dijon, and Tyler decided to press forward to Lyons. The sky grew overcast and a light mist rolled up from the south. A police car passed them, but seemed to take no notice. The female cop on the passenger's side read a newspaper, and the male cop, who drove the car, puffed on a cigarette and talked to himself.

They left the highway somewhere south of Dijon. Tyler found a general store. Using his feeble French and bogus John Simons credit card, he purchased some dish towels, a bar of soap, a bottle of shampoo, rubbing alcohol, bottled water, a loaf of bread, a pair of dark sunglasses, and the strongest pain reliever they had for sale. He couldn't find bandages—Band-Aids, yes, bandages, no. But he did find a small roll of cheesecloth. He begged a small bag of chipped ice from the fish case at no charge. And he bought fifty liters of petrol.

He drove to a small grove of trees near a narrow river— a deserted place of tall poplars, high grass, and dragonflies. The rain stopped, but left a gloss on the rocks. Tyler helped Cynthia from her seat. She whimpered as she tested her foot.

"That's all right." Tyler consoled her.

"It's a sign of weakness to show pain." She gritted her teeth.

Tyler laid her down on the wet grass. "Drink this water." He twisted the cap from a water bottle. He looked at the wound on her scalp, dabbing it with a towel wet with alcohol. "It was a lucky thing you ducked back at the rail crossing."

"Chip knocked me down."

Tyler dabbed the wound, pulling strands of sticky hair to either side to get a better look at the cut. "You can thank him for that." He looked at her swollen eye. With thumb and forefinger he spread the swollen flesh of her cheek and brow, and Cynthia made the painful effort to open her eye. "Your eye looks okay. You got a small cut in the eyebrow, but I wouldn't even put a stitch on it."

"I lost a contact lens."

"Open your mouth, please." Cynthia complied and Bobby bent over her face. "I can't see much." He ran his fingers around the inside of her mouth and over her teeth. "You lost a crown on the top right side. I can feel the pin. You've got a couple of loose teeth—top front."

Using her tongue Cynthia found the gap where she'd lost the crown. "I fell off a horse when I was a girl."

Tyler felt the bones in her arms, looked at her swollen hand, poked around her abdomen, then felt her legs and knees. "You've got bruises on your bruises. The sprain on your wrist isn't bad."

He studied her feet. The right foot had swollen to twice the size of the left one. He lifted the injured foot from the ground and pressed the big toe back a centimeter. Cynthia howled, "Oh! Stop, please!" Her chest heaved up and down, and she panted, "Please, don't touch my foot."

"I doubt it's broken, but it might as well be." He wrapped the chipped ice in a towel and draped it over her foot.

Tyler fed her a small handful of pain pills and told her to drink the bottled water. He continued to wipe the dried blood from her face, neck, and arms with towels moistened by rubbing alcohol. "Where would you like to hide out for a couple of days?"

"Avignon is on the way. I know a small pension on the road to Arles. You'll like it: quiet, off the road, in the middle of a peach orchard—I don't even know the name of the place."

"Can we sneak you in?"

She winced. "I'll tell them I fell when climbing rocks at Les Baux. Maybe the proprietor will help me get some medicine."

Tyler slipped his arms under Cynthia to lift her. "Geez, Cindy. You're more solid than I thought." He struggled to his feet with Cynthia in his arms. She fought the pain. Her neck and back ached. Her head pounded. Her foot throbbed.

"Put me in the front with you. I'll show you the way through Avignon to the pension." Tyler propped her up in the passenger's seat and gave her the dark sunglasses to mask her damaged eye.

In Avignon, Tyler swapped cars. He—rather, John Simons—rented a boxy Citroen "for day trips around Provence." He took a tourist map and the keys. Tyler drove the little car off the small lot and around the corner, where he fetched Cynthia. He reached into his pocket, pulled out a crumpled parking ticket, and stuck it back on the BMW windshield where he'd found it.

Cynthia showed Bobby the way out of town to a small road that barely merited a small yellow marker labeled Arles. They turned up a dusty gravel driveway to the Hôtel du Cloître. Cynthia recalled, "I remember now—this place used to be a cloister, a nunnery. It's tiny. Out of season, during the week, we may be their only guests."

The old proprietor and his wife bought Cynthia's story about the fall at Les Baux. The proprietress sympathized, and Cynthia translated bits and pieces for Tyler. "He was an irresponsible husband for making you climb Les Baux— a typical American cowboy stunt. Shame on him. And you should know better too, my poor dear. He was a negligent husband for not getting you immediate medical attention. Look at your poor eye! But not to worry, madame, we French will show your pathetic American husband how to take care of a woman. Maybe he can learn a thing or two!" The old pair seemed very satisfied with Cynthia's translation. The matron actually turned her nose up at Tyler and left the room.

My God! Tyler thought, the old man and woman still run this place like a nunnery. He turned to Cynthia and whispered, "Did you enjoy that?"

Cynthia took a shallow breath and replied, "So far, I'd say that was the high point of my day."

Tyler helped her down a short corridor to their room,

mercifully on the ground floor. A large, old-fashioned tub sat behind a screen. Tyler ran the water and helped Cynthia wash her hair. The soap turned to a pink froth. The clear water rinsed the sticky matter away. Then he filled the tub, helped her undress to her underwear. He saw Cynthia's ribs—black, crimson, purple. She wore a red welt where the seat belt and harness had restrained her. Tyler picked bits of glass from her back and gently touched the large bruise on her hip.

"Ow!"

"Sorry." Tyler helped lower her into the deep tub filled with lukewarm water. He propped her injured foot out of the water on a rolled towel. "We'd better keep ice on your foot until we get the swelling down."

"You're a good nurse, Bobby."

"Now give me your clothes sizes. I'll get you some clothes."

Cynthia also gave Tyler a list of cosmetics to cover her bruises, and list of herbs she said would hasten her recovery: massive doses of vitamin C, zinc, garlic, and gelsemium. Leaving her in the care of the Mother and Father Superior, Tyler drove to the outskirts of Avignon to shop.

When Tyler returned, he found Cynthia sitting on the bed, wearing a pink bathrobe, slowly combing her hair around a bandage. Her purple foot soaked in a large, blue plastic bucket of ice water. Cynthia welcomed him. "At first, the young doctor thought you had beaten me. Then he thought I must have been in a car wreck. The seat belts left distinct marks, and he found some glass stuck in my shoulders."

"What did you say?" Tyler worried.

"I asked him what he intended to do."

"What did he say?"

"He said that if there was a hit-and-run, there will be questions. If nobody asks questions, then he doesn't have to give answers. Except . . ."

"What?"

"He wants to see us both at his clinic tomorrow. He'll X-ray my foot and put a temporary cast on it. He wants to make sure you didn't beat me. That, he would have to report."

"The thought of beating certainly crossed my mind yesterday when you started this wild chase."

"Then I hope he doesn't read minds. Anyway, the doctor put only two stitches in my head. Also . . ." Cynthia rattled a small brown plastic container. "The good doctor gave me these. Better living through chemistry, eh?"

Tyler surmised that Cynthia had already taken a couple.

"And look at the end of the bed—he gave me crutches. And you know something else? The lady who owns the Hôtel du Cloître is his aunt."

"Well, maybe he'll cut us some slack. We can't leave the country yet—the airports won't be safe for a couple of days. We can't change hotels without blowing the John and Dorothy Simons cover. I guess I'll meet your young doctor."

Cynthia could barely move the next morning, she was so stiff with pain. Tyler managed to sit her up and help her dress. He brought her a tray of rolls and café au lait. The matron rapped at the door. Her nephew, the doctor, had called to extract another promise that Mr. and Mrs. Simons would visit the clinic. Cynthia assured the woman they would go.

At the clinic, the doctor came to the door. In English he said, "Mrs. Dubois-Simons, I was afraid I wouldn't see you today." Then he turned to Tyler and said, "Mr. Simons, may I see your hands?"

Tyler held out his hands. The doctor took them with his velvety fingers, turned them once to look at the knuckles and fingernails. He looked Tyler in the eye and said, "So much for that. Would you help Mrs. Simons to my examining room?"

Tyler helped Cynthia to the cold, white room. Then

the doctor asked him to leave. "You may tell my assistant if you desire coffee or tea."

The doctor looked at the Cynthia's bruises again, and checked her eyes. As he worked on her foot, he chatted in French. "Mrs. Dubois-Simons, we doctors are part detective, yes?"

"Yes."

"Your seat belt abrasion—upper right to lower left— shows you were in the passenger's seat. And there's not a mark on your husband, Mr. Simons—not a scratch, not a bruise. He wasn't in the car for the accident; so who was driving the car?"

Cynthia looked startled. "A young friend of mine."

"A man, no doubt."

"Yes."

"Was he hurt."

"I think so."

"How can you be so uncertain?"

"I was unconscious when my husband found me. He'd been following us."

"And your young man-friend? Mr. Simons just left him on the side of the road—just like that?"

"I believe help was called. John took me away to save me from scandal."

"And therefore you made up that pathetic lie about falling at Les Baux?"

Cynthia managed a tear. "I've hurt him enough already. John's a good man—he's taken me back. Please, don't make it worse. Please, let us go in peace. You don't have to make a report of this, do you?"

"Still, you may have broken a French law. True, I know that neither of you were the driver of the car in the accident. But if the authorities call me—"

"You don't have to lie. If the authorities ask, tell them anything you want. Yet I pray that they do not. I only wish to spare John any further humiliation. I promise I'll never cheat on him again."

The doctor looked into her tearful eyes and sighed. "That's so sad." He washed his hands and called Tyler into the room. In English: "Mr. Simons, your wife, she will mend. Give her these pills for pain—a very potent codeine derivative. Don't try to take them into your country. She will mend better if you encourage her to move around. Her muscles are badly bruised. My helper in the front will make for you the bill." As the doctor walked past, he patted Tyler on the shoulder and said, "Mr. Simons, I misjudged you. I'm sorry."

Tyler stepped into the room. "What was he talking about?"

"Later." She smirked.

The cast hardened. Tyler and Cynthia returned to the Hôtel du Cloître. The crusty proprietress greeted Tyler with wreaths of smiles and offered Cynthia nothing but a you-deserve-what-you-get scowl. Cynthia guessed correctly that the young doctor had already given his aunt a complete report. She hoped they could keep the gossip in the family.

A day of rest and the codeine worked wonders for Cynthia. By suppertime she could hobble around on crutches. She took her herbs, drank medicinal tea, and watched the sunlight ripple through the peach trees surrounding the hotel. Meanwhile, Tyler drove back to the commercial section of Avignon. He called Marseilles. Stouffer was more than glad to delay the flight out. "Darned if I'm not even learning some French words!"

He called the little man in Paris and told him where his sister could find the BMW. To pass the time, Tyler wandered through the marketplace—a rough shed with a corrugated steel roof filled with the treasures of southern France: pears and peaches, apricots and kumquats, cheeses and breads, sausages and pâtés made from every kind of innards. He saw pigs, chickens, quail, and rabbits hanging from hooks—all readily distinguishable as he looked into their blank little faces still attached to the skinned and gutted carcasses. He saw oysters, mussels, prawn, octopi, and squid. He saw flounder, perch, grouper, trout, and some primitive sea creatures that man ought not to eat. He saw a blood-covered man sawing steaks from a tuna as big as himself. And he saw flowers.

He bought an armful of flowers to take back to the hotel, giving the bulk of them to the chatelaine, his new buddy, and saving a modest bouquet for Mrs. Dubois-Simons. The old couple took time from their duties to spy on Tyler as he delivered the flowers to his wife—as great an event of charity and forgiveness as ever witnessed in the Hôtel de Cloître. Tyler had no way of knowing, but he had just ensured his safe passage to Marseilles.

Buttressed with codeine, covered with makeup, and wearing her dark sunglasses, Cynthia asked Bobby to take her out for dinner. They found a restaurant with a patio overlooking the Rhone. Cynthia ordered the fixed menu and a bottle of local wine.

"Bobby, be a gentleman and refill my glass, *s'il vous plaît.*"

"You'd better watch the alcohol with these pain pills you're taking."

"How would you know? The prescription is in French." She pulled the small brown plastic container from her purse and raised the small print close to her eyes. "No alcohol, no driving and no heavy machinery. . . . Oh, don't be a jerk. Fill my glass."

Bobby filled the glass, and she thanked him with a nod. They ate in silence until a waiter came to the table and asked Bobby something, to which Cynthia replied, *"Deux glaces, s'il vous plaît."*

She turned to Bobby. "He's bringing the ice cream—it comes with the meal."

Bobby remained silent, but Cynthia prodded, "I'm sorry for running out on you."

"Forget it."

"You hurt my feelings—a woman spurned, you might

call it. I tell you, Bobby, I've loved you for years. I thought perhaps last night, I could make you love me, too."

Bobby looked around to see if anybody had overheard, and Cynthia noticed his discomfort. She reassured and scolded him at the same time. "Few people understand English down here in Provence. If they do, they won't rush over to our table: It's rude." She continued her original thought, "So when you wouldn't go to bed with me, I thought, 'There is no love for me.' I lay awake thinking about you all night while you slept a little more than an arm's reach away. You seemed so indifferent sleeping there. Then I thought, 'No Cindy, you don't need Bobby, you just need a man.' The closest thing I had was Chip. But what I really want—what I really need is you, Bobby."

A solitary tear ran down from behind the dark glasses. Bobby braced himself. The woman was on drugs *and* drinking wine.

Cynthia tried to put him at ease. "You don't have to worry about me for quite a while. I don't feel very" —she raised a napkin to her bruised eye— "attractive at the moment." She lowered her sunglasses. "So you can talk about it. You can't offend me, and if you do, I can't run away. Why won't you make love to me?"

Tyler twirled the melting ice cream with his spoon. He looked at the mush instead of at Cynthia. "We all have a side to life that's conflicted, and if we're lucky, another side that remains constant. You? Your business life has been everyone's dream: success, control, fun; but your marriage—you freely admit—fell apart from the beginning. Rolf? The poor bastard—his business is in chaos—he may yet pull it off. His personal life with you has been chaos. You don't believe it, but he has real affection for you. Me? My career turned to ashes, although thanks to Rolf I make do. Mariam and the kids are the best part of my life. Every now and then you meet the lucky son of a gun who gets it all, but not often."

Tyler looked up at Cindy and saw his smoky reflection

in her sunglasses. "But you know, Cindy, I've been lucky in love; and having watched you and Rolf all these years, I've decided I got the better half of the deal."

"Mariam's lucky. I've always been jealous; she got you. You know why I left Rolf?"

Tyler had often asked, but rhetorically. Now he didn't want to know. "No."

"We never got along too well. You know, of course, that we had to get married for Paul's sake. At first, marriage to Rolf wasn't so bad, but one day I woke up and figured out my relationship—my role—with Rolf."

Bobby looked through the short candle and let her speak.

"To Rolf I was just a good piece of ass." Cynthia smiled and drank her glass to the bottom. "And you know, Bobby, if all you are is a good piece of ass, then you might as well find someone who makes you feel like a great piece of ass. And in spite of his many faults, Chip was, in that regard, a sight better than Rolf."

"Chip was using you."

Cynthia shook her head. "I still can't believe he worked for the CIA. . . ." She slid her sunglasses down her nose, exposing the ghastly bruise and swollen eye. "I ought to cut his balls off."

"That would be a lot of trouble for nothing. Chip would hardly know the difference now."

"Not Chip, I mean Rolf. All this: Chip, the CIA, the deuxième bureau, my eye, my foot—all this is Rolf's fault. I don't know how he manages it. He insulates himself, then sends the rest of us out in the storm with lightning rods strapped to our heads."

"You're bitter and looking for someone to blame."

"Oh, no. I'm looking for someone to get even with. Well, let me tell you something, this time Smurch pays."

Tyler shook his head. "Would your life be so boring if you didn't have Rolf to kick in the shins? I can't think of anything less attractive in this world—to me, anyhow— than a beautiful, bright woman pursuing a vendetta. You are much more interesting when you simply pursue wealth and pleasure."

Cynthia's jaw muscles tightened. She measured Bobby's opinion and dismissed it. "I see. You're interested in pretty, fun, wealthy women—as long as they're shallow. I should be so much more interesting for you if I would just forget this whole mess and get back to spinning straw into gold and working on my figure. It that what you mean?"

"Of course not."

Cynthia laid her small spoon beside the dish and put her napkin on the table. "I used to think that deep down inside, you were your own man, but you're just Rolf's lapdog. I can't think of anything less attractive than being Rolf's lapdog."

Chapter 21

Cynthia spent the next two days shut away from the world. She didn't talk much, just enough to be civil. She soaked her bruised body, only now able to lower herself into the tub. She soaked and read, holding the book at arm's length to compensate for her missing contact lens. She swallowed massive doses of vitamin C and other assorted herbal supplements. When she wasn't in her bathtub hiding behind the screen, she sat in a wicker chair under a shaded colonnade, facing a peach orchard. She watched birds dip and dive among the peach trees, and she drank pitchers of water flavored with fresh lemon slices. A pillar of weatherworn limestone stood amongst the trees. On top of the pillar there was a ball, and on top of the ball, a statue of a woman facing the rising sun.

Tyler kept away. He wondered about Cynthia's preoccupation. Was she brooding about his criticism of her vindictive streak? And how much weight did she put on her Bobby-the-lapdog analysis? Or was she preoccupied with healing? He'd seen wounded animals seclude themselves, focusing their healing power, subordinating all other instincts. Tyler moved into a separate room, a move that the hotel's old matron approved of. After all, the battered Dubois-Simons woman needed long, quiet soaks, and the emotionally bruised Simons man needed time to be apart from his wayward wife—and the Hôtel du Cloître had nine empty rooms.

Tyler took evening meals with Cynthia, peculiar only for the lack of conversation. Cynthia ate soft foods and chewed slowly. Already she'd cut back on the painkillers. Twinges and spasms caught her by surprise, and her face broadcast sudden pains. A piece of ice might settle on her broken tooth like a shard of jagged glass. Cynthia would instantly look tired, worn, and years older.

Tyler looked across the table, pausing from the immediate task of picking small bones from his poached fish with his knife and fork. He carefully set them in a line at the edge of his plate.

Cynthia startled him by speaking, "Bobby or John Simons—I should say John, right? You've been a good nurse."

"You're a good patient." At last, they'd exchanged compliments.

"I've got my faults, but ingratitude is not one of them. I owe you one."

"All I want from you right now, Cindy, is your word that you'll come back to Australia with me."

Cynthia's cheeks turned crimson. "Australia? Rolf's in Australia." She calmed down a bit. "Paul's in Australia."

"I can protect you at Temple Bay. As long as you're Rolf Bernard's wife, you're a target. You don't have to like it, but that's a fact. And I know you have the resources to bolt again. So there's no sense in my smuggling you out of France unless you promise to come to Temple Bay and stay until I say the danger has passed."

"I promise."

The next morning, Bobby packed his and Cynthia's few belongings into a small suitcase he'd bought. They left the Hôtel du Cloître after breakfast, and drove south to the small airstrip outside Marseilles. They abandoned the rental car in the parking lot.

Tyler found Stouffer sitting in front of a TV watching the French version of daytime soaps—a wonderfully coifed woman not wearing much, lying on her back across an antique desk, arguing with someone. Tyler had to tap him on the shoulder twice.

Stouffer grabbed his bag. A supremely bored, mustachioed man stamped their passports and the three took off. The plane climbed through some wisps of clouds, then flew over the Mediterranean Sea.

Tyler and Cynthia sat in the back in the cramped airborne lounge. Tyler poured himself a drink, and Cynthia took one of her painkillers. He said, "You've been angry with me since that dinner at Avignon. I can tell, you've been so quiet."

"No, Bobby. I've been hatching a little scheme."

"What's that?"

"I figured how to turn this whole mess into a profitable transaction. It's what I do: I take sows' ears and make silk purses." She laughed. Bobby had never heard such a chilling laugh before.

Cynthia turned to look out the window at the coast of Italy. A short stack of French newspapers sat in her lap. The sun on her face highlighted the swollen eye, turning yellowish. Cindy talked to herself. "This is going to be a sweet deal."

Cynthia worked on her long list of things to do. She looked up from her pad. "You know I can't go straight to Temple Bay."

She caught Tyler by surprise. "Huh?"

"I've got to spend a couple of weeks in a decent-size city. Brisbane perhaps. I need to see a good internist. I need to see a dentist. I need new contact lenses and reading glasses."

Cynthia moved her pen down her list. "I want an orthopedic specialist to look at my foot. I've got to buy some clothes. No offense, but the two dresses you bought me don't quite make a wardrobe. And I need to find out what's going on in the world. None of those things can I do at Rolf's tropical funny farm."

"But . . ."

"At Temple Bay, or thereabouts, I'll need accommodations for two of my colleagues who'll help me with my next deal. I'll call Andrea Andersen, my mole in Banque National du Paris. She'll help me put the financing together. Also, I must get hold of . . ." Cynthia tapped her forehead. "His name escapes me—the English lawyer who helped me syndicate the Dutch pharmaceutical deal. Oh, Andrea will remember."

Tyler slumped into his seat. Cynthia turned back to her lists. "Should we try Brisbane?"

"I suppose. Mr. Kirby lives there. He could refer you to doctors."

They stopped for fuel at Bombay. Satisfied that the Simons cover had held, Tyler relaxed. He stowed his pistol in the plane. They stayed in Bombay long enough for a hot meal, a hot bath, and eight hours' sleep. Pilot Stouffer refiled his flight plan for Brisbane, and Tyler phoned Temple Bay. He talked to Paul.

"How's my mom?"

"She's fine, but she had a close call. Cindy, I mean your mom, was in a pretty nasty car accident and got banged up: busted her foot, black eye, bruises, a broken tooth—nothing serious."

"That sounds serious."

"It could have been much worse. We've got to put into Brisbane so she can get the right medical assistance. How's your dad?"

"I don't know. One minute he's up; the next minute he's depressed. We get another booking for a launch window, and he walks on air. Then he reads another press article condemning him as a traitor and space pirate, and he skulks around for hours."

"We'll patch things up in time. Calm him down. Tell him he'll go down in history as a real American hero after we sort everything out."

"He'll more likely go down in history as an Australian hero."

"What?"

"My dad's an Australian now. Irwin Kirby arranged it."

"He did what?"

"To avoid extradition, Dad renounced his American citizenship and became an Australian."

"That's plain nuts!"

Paul paused. "I don't think calling Dad nuts is all that helpful at the moment. He wants you back here as soon as possible. The press reported a rumor that the FBI put out a reward for his capture. He suspects some of the hired hands."

"Can you get him to tell you the access code?"

"Nobody can. Anybody who tries, me included, becomes a suspect—as if he'd give me the code, then I'd turn him in. I tell you, it's getting tense up here. I'll try to slip down to meet you in Brisbane. The Aussies put up some kind of hokey quarantine around Temple Bay, so depending on their mood, I may be able to get down to Brisbane, or maybe not."

Tyler hung up the phone. He called Marshall. "Is Rolf Bernard in any imminent danger?"

"Of course he is: Who do you think he's messing with? You just keep that crazy son of a bitch alive until we can think of something."

Cynthia bought a copy of that day's *Financial Times* and the previous day's *Wall Street Journal*—fascinating stuff. BAP, Inc.'s board of directors had elected one of the outside directors, a Mr. Lloyd Swanson, to replace Rolf Bernard. The board fired Rolf as President and CEO, then rehired the former Chief Financial Officer, Herb Eckert, who had resigned his post the previous week.

The Justice Department, in conjunction with the IRS, froze Mr. Bernard's assets. Lawyers for the SEC investigated BAP, Inc. and Rolf Bernard for securities fraud. BAP stock fell to a twenty-two-year low of $14.88. Legal analysts predicted that it might be years before BAP could dig out from the Bernard scandal and the avalanche of stockholder and class action lawsuits. Cynthia pulled out her little spiral notebook, turned to her lists and wrote, "Call Herb."

Back in the air, Cynthia settled into her notebook, and Tyler settled into a light bourbon. He had no idea what waited for him at Temple Bay; therefore, he had no expectations and no plans, and he chose not to speculate. He sat in his seat with the boring expanse of the Indian Ocean beneath him and a small amber drink in his hand.

Stouffer bought fuel in Singapore, then took to the air for the last leg of their journey. The small jet flew over Darwin and kept its southerly heading toward Brisbane. Tyler looked out his window at the flattest continent on earth. The sun set quickly. The land turned black as coal, with a billion twinkling lights above and a rare spot of light below. Cynthia woke from a nap to see Tyler's face pressed against the window.

"What's the matter? You miss old Smurch?" She grinned.

"No."

"Well, I'm sure he misses you, Bobby."

"We'll be landing in Brisbane in another two hours," he said, changing the subject. He excused himself and went forward to sit with Stouffer, who wore little earphones cranking Ry Cooder's music into his head. He tapped his toe, watched the autopilot display with one eye and the night sky with the other. Tyler removed a cup of cold coffee and a bag of rice cookies from the copilot's seat. Stouffer surmised that Tyler had not come forward for conversation.

Tyler sat in the copilot's seat, closed his eyes, and fell asleep. Two hours later, he woke to a gentle poke in the

ribs. The small jet dove out of the sky and landed at
Brisbane's airport just after midnight. Tyler and Cynthia
left Stouffer with the plane. A man pushing an empty
wheelchair met them on the tarmac. Tyler recognized
the man—Irwin Kirby's manservant Archie. "G'day, Mr.
Tyler."

"How'd you know we were coming?"

"Dr. Bernard called Mr. Kirby. Mr. Kirby sent me. Paul
said his mum was bingled, so Mr. Kirby sent me to fetch
you. Paul got permission to fly down tomorrow."

Stouffer stayed to garage the plane. Archie drove Tyler
and Mrs. Bernard to the Hilton near the beach. He told
them Mr. Kirby would check on them before the noon
hour, then he left. The desk clerk handed Cynthia and
Tyler forms to fill out. Tyler asked the clerk, "Give us
two rooms next to each other." Then he nudged Cynthia
and said, "Forget the Simons shtick."

As they filled their registration forms, three policemen
approached. Two wore uniforms, one wore civilian clothes.
They had Stouffer in tow. The plainclothes policeman
cleared his throat to announce his presence. "Mr. Robert
Tyler? Mrs. Cynthia Bernard?"

They turned and replied, "Yes."

Tyler continued, "Who are you?"

"I am Inspector MacAdam. Don't be alarmed. The
Australian government is only concerned for your safety.
May I see your passports?"

Cynthia handed over her real passport. The man flipped
through the pages. "Interesting. I see you were stamped
into France on June 20, but not stamped out. Hmm."

Likewise, Tyler surrendered his real passport. The
inspector mused, "Let's see. You were stamped into
Australia last March. No exit stamp. There's a fairly stiff
fine for evading the departure tax. Yet, you've been out
of the country for more than a week; you managed to
pick up Mrs. Bernard and get out of France without any
record. Very neat work." The inspector casually slipped

both passports into his breast pocket. "We'll just hold on to these for a bit."

"You can't do that," Tyler protested.

"Oh, yes I can. Come down to my office Monday and I'll give your passports back. I'd love to know why you fled France. We got an Interpol bulletin requesting that we hold you. The French want you for tax fraud. However, inasmuch as your husband recently shot down a French rocket, I rather doubt your problem stems from taxes."

"What are you going to do?"

"The French know you're here. We don't exactly know what we want to do. However, I don't want any French mucking about Brisbane looking for Americans who ought not to be any concern of mine. Mr. Tyler, come talk to me on Monday." MacAdam handed Tyler a card.

Tyler looked at Stouffer, who shrugged his shoulders. The three policemen turned and left. Stouffer stayed behind. Cynthia and Tyler watched them get into cars and drive away. Then she said, "What do you think?"

Tyler stared at the empty spot where the policemen had parked their car. He muttered, "I think I know that guy. He's not Australian."

"What?"

"Never mind." Tyler noticed some scrawl on the back of MacAdam's card. He couldn't read it without his glasses, so he tucked the card into his shirt pocket.

The desk clerk emerged from the back office to finish the paperwork and issue the keys to adjacent rooms. Tyler carried the few bags, and Cynthia mounted her crutches and limped to the elevators. Inside his room, Tyler put his reading glasses on and retrieved MacAdam's card. It read: "Marshall sent me."

Tyler slept poorly and got up early. He checked the tape on Cynthia's door, then ducked down to the hotel's little clothes shop, bought a "cozzie" and some "sandshoes," which looked like ordinary beach clothes and sneakers to Tyler. Then he sat by the pool, watching a young mother chase her little urchin around the deck. As morning wore on, he moved into the lobby, where he waited for Mr. Kirby. He recognized Kirby, with Archie in tow, when they stepped through the revolving door.

Tyler intercepted Kirby and said, "I'm Mr. Tyler."

"Oh, yes. Of course."

"Are you here to offer me Australian citizenship?"

"No."

"I'm surprised."

"You needn't be," Kirby assured him, recoiling from Tyler's belligerent attitude. "Don't get sore at me, I'm just the messenger boy. Can we find someplace a bit more private to talk? My car perhaps?"

"No, thank you. Let's just sit by the pool and have a chat." Tyler talked past Kirby. "Archie, why don't you try the Sunday brunch. Put it on my tab. Meanwhile, I promise I won't throw Mr. Kirby in the pool."

Irwin Kirby nodded, and Archie retired to the dining room. While Tyler led the way to the pool, Kirby defended Archie. "You can trust Archie."

"Wrong. *You* can trust Archie. I don't know that I can trust anybody."

"Fair enough." Kirby sat down in a lounge chair in the shade of a palm fern. "Speaking of trust, I hope I can trust you to keep what I'm about to say in strict confidence."

"So, what do you want?"

"I need your help. First, let me give you how things are in Australia. Your lunatic boss has become a bit of a celebrity in Australia, being an international outlaw and all. Because I'm Mr. Bernard's partner, credited with bringing him to Australia, I, too, get some of the dubious credit, and I, too, have become a hot property."

"You should be pleased."

"On the contrary, this kind of publicity always turns sour, and frankly, Rolf Bernard scares me. My government made a monstrous mistake embracing Rolf Bernard, but then, like most democratic governments, Canberra won't contradict popular sentiment. When I tried to warn my people that Bernard's scheme could spell disaster for Australia, they laughed me out of the room. According to the local papers, I'm jealous."

"Why are you telling me all this?"

"As I just told you, popular sentiment never lasts. America and Japan have already started turning the screws on us. Pretty soon the average bloke will feel the pinch. Then I'm going to be the money-grubbing Judas who got Australia into this mess. You are the closest person to Mr. Bernard. We need your help to get out of this pickle."

Tyler sighed.

"You don't look very sympathetic, Mr. Tyler."

"I'm not a very sympathetic guy. What do you want?"

"The problem is that damned Pebbles System. I want that back in the hands of the United States. Our indispensable Mr. Bernard might just cark it in some fool accident, and nobody will get into space for the rest of my lifetime, at least. Next, I want Rolf Bernard's fleet of Felix spacecraft to stay at Temple Bay—just like we planned in our initial partnership."

"And how do I help you get what you want?"

"Actually, you are the key. Rolf trusts you. If anyone can convince Rolf to give up this lunacy, you can. Rolf's got a tiger by the tail and he's afraid to let go. But the truth is, he can't hold on much longer."

"Rolf won't give up the access code—you can forget that approach."

"Then what else is there?"

"Lord only knows."

Kirby gave up the argument. "I hope you're wrong about this. However, all I want you to do is be there when Mr. Bernard realizes the truth. When that happens, you'll have to help him let go of the tiger's tail—so to speak.

Let him know that unofficially, we want to see the Pebbles returned to the United States. Assure him that the Australian government will keep him—he's safe here among friends. Assure him that I will continue to support his Felix operations. Don't let him do something desperate."

"Desperate? Like kill himself? Hardly."

"Desperate people do desperate things. I read about it all the time. You Americans are forever taking a hostage up to your cabin; then, when you're hopelessly surrounded, you kill the hostage and yourself."

Tyler frowned. "I'll see what I can do."

Paul arrived late that afternoon. He found Tyler and Cynthia sitting in the lounge. She struggled to her feet, put her arms around his neck and kissed his cheek. "What have you and your father gotten into now?"

Paul held her hands and stepped back for a complete look at his battered mother. "I should ask the same of you."

Cynthia raised her sunglasses and winked at Paul with her purple, bloodshot eye. "Mischief—naturally. But this time I think we can blame your father's ambition to control outer space."

"I'm really sorry about that."

"Well, give me a hug. Why didn't you meet me at the airport yesterday?"

"The quarantine. The Australian government quarantined Temple Bay for security reasons—partly to protect our operation, and partly to show the rest of the world that they're taking action—whatever that might be."

"What kind of quarantine?" Cynthia asked.

"Oh, it's a joke. It would be like sending a dozen cops to seal off Montana. Anybody can walk in or out anytime, but it's prudent to ask permission. They check the road traffic, air flights, and shipping. Tourists still tramp up

and down the peninsula. They let anybody leave at will.
We just have to make special arrangements to go back."

Tyler asked, "Will we have trouble getting in?"

"No. Kirby made sure our extended party can fly in.
In fact, Kirby wants you back as soon as you can go."

"I know. He told me just this morning."

Paul looked at his mother, then spoke to Tyler. "Bobby,
I don't want you to come up yet. I want you to keep an
eye on Mother."

Cynthia objected. "That's not necessary."

Paul snapped back, "I'll hear no debate." Paul composed
himself. "Besides, there's not much to do at Temple Bay
except swat flies."

"Nothing?" Tyler inquired.

"The Australians have been courting us in an effort to
share our space monopoly—the transportation side of
the operation, of course. We have already scheduled sixty-
three windows for third-party launches, where Dad
disarms the Pebbles and the company collects a $100,000
check, which we deposit into our ANZ account. In two
months we'll be able to operate out of our own cash flow."

"That's commendable."

"Thank you, Mother. Also, we booked 17 Felix flights
at $2,000 per pound—that's $32 million per flight. That's
over half a billion in sales! Not bad for our first month
in business. The Australians want to add to our fleet of
Felix-class spaceships. Max and I have been studying the
Australian industrial base. We could build them here.
Mr. Kirby has certainly turned out to be a decent fellow.
But our next Felix launch doesn't happen until August
twelfth. So Dr. Yeager and about half the crew are waiting
down in Cairns."

"That's a pretty friendly quarantine." Tyler shook his
head. "Frankly, I think the Aussies could be a little more
hard-nosed. Would make my job easier."

"I told you they were easygoing. After you finish in
Brisbane, you ought to consider moving up to Cairns—

a strange place. It's a mecca for scuba divers, but it hasn't got a beach. It's got a rainforest suffering from drought."

"I'll probably stay in Brisbane for as long as I can until Bobby drags me up to Temple Bay."

"It won't be so bad. I'll go back and spruce up your Temple Bay accommodations. I'm going to put you in the marina bungalow."

"A bungalow? Like a shack?"

Paul explained, "Don't worry, Mom. Australian bungalows aren't shacks—not a palace, but very comfortable. And yours is way out of the way, down by the beach."

Before he returned to Temple Bay, Paul found a doctor and a dentist for his mother. In addition to the missing tooth, the dentist found a cracked molar, so Cynthia had to get two crowns—a ten-day process. While she waited for artisans to build her a pair of porcelain teeth, she offered her swollen foot for a little orthoscopic surgery. She persuaded the doctor to give her a more comfortable, removable cast, and the doctor took the stitches from her scalp.

Cynthia leased a furnished office overlooking the Brisbane River. Her two financial technicians arrived: Andrea Andersen, a long-legged Swede with an accent, and Chet Saddler, a little English weasel with a bow tie, but the best securities lawyer in Europe.

While Cynthia worked with Andrea and Chet, Tyler visited Brisbane's cultural hot spots. He watched sheepshearing and wool spinning in Rainbow Valley, where he held his nose and swore he'd never eat mutton again. He sat in the subtropical gardens on Mount Coot-tha until a cloud of midges found him. He tried his luck at Jupiter's Casino and wished he hadn't. He sat on the beach and watched young surfers do things he couldn't. He met Cynthia, Andrea, and Chet for evening meals, where he tried in vain to get them to discuss their work.

In two weeks, Cynthia tossed her crutches away and

took up a cane. Tyler summoned Stouffer. Cynthia left
Andrea and Chet with instructions and flew with Tyler
to Temple Bay. Paul met them at the airstrip in his dusty
Land Rover and took Cynthia to her new home, the marina
bungalow. "It's a bit rustic, but it has a certain charm."

Cynthia peered inside the door and felt a blast of cold,
dry air. She saw a long table with a computer, fax, and
phone. "Paul, I see you got Andrea's package. Is the
software installed?"

"I did it myself."

A ceiling fan augmented the chilled air. She bypassed
the small kitchenette and peered into the bathroom—a
spartan commode, white porcelain pedestal sink, and a
fiberglass shower stall. The small bedroom had one twin
bed, and a simple oak chest of drawers with matching
mirror and night stand. A large window looked from under
the eaves toward the north at the long crescent of sand.

Cynthia squeezed Paul's hand. "I've paid a lot more
for far worse."

"Thank you, Mom."

"If I may, I'd like to rest. Perhaps you could bring some
dinner tonight?" She kissed Paul on the cheek and sent
him away.

Cynthia found the marina bungalow confining—not the
porch, just the interior: the plain white walls, the
omnipresent hum of the ceiling fans, the relentless
chirruping from the gecko lizards. The screened porch
offered a view, the blue bay and sky, wavelets lapping
the sand. She kept her wicker chair facing north to avoid
seeing Fenster's giant rectenna, which marred the bay's
southern vista. Cynthia spent the cool mornings hobbling
up and down the beach, then retreating before the heat
and humidity to her air-conditioned office to talk on the
phone to the Swede. Each day, Paul drove her to Lizard
City for supplies, a hot meal, and a look at the news.
Paul assumed that Cynthia wished to avoid accidental
contact with Rolf.

One morning, Paul took her for a tour of the launch facility. They stood under the inert Felix-C, looking up at the aerospike rocket motors, when Cynthia asked, "How's your father?"

The question startled Paul. "He's fine. He's growing a beard."

"Really? Is his beard still red?"

"Very much. With his hair almost white and red beard he looks like a two-tone Chevy. Dad says he might as well look the part of a pirate, since the whole world calls him a pirate. He's even started drinking rum instead of scotch."

In a mocking tone, Cynthia exclaimed, "That *is* serious."

Then Paul's face fell. "He's acting strange. He's started sleeping locked in his Tempest vault, where he transmits signals to the Pebbles. He's convinced someone's out to kill him. He carries a pistol, now."

"He bit off too much this time, didn't he?"

"He suspects everybody but me, Dr. Yeager, Bobby, and you."

"Not me? How odd." Cynthia shook her head.

Paul walked slowly to keep pace with his mother's limp. They walked over the crushed-coral walkway toward his cryogenics plant. Cynthia leaned on Paul to step over a rut that a recent downpour had cut through the walkway. "I can see how this Temple Bay setup would get on your father's nerves. He's used to having dozens of important people around, soliciting his advice, competing for his favor: White House dinners, embassy parties, power conferences. Although I don't think he deserved it, your father truly enjoyed being admired." Cynthia turned to look Paul straight in the eye. "I suppose it still bothers him that I don't."

"Don't what?" Paul blinked.

"Admire him." She continued, "Now that he's fallen from being universally admired to being universally reviled, I feel sorry for him, I really do."

"But the space transportation business has really picked up."

"That won't make Rolf happy."

During the first week in August, Max Yeager brought the Cairns contingent back to Temple Bay for a launch. A large, covered tractor trailer hauled in a Japanese communications satellite. Buses brought foreign technicians to tweak the satellite, supervise the loading, witness the launch, then adjust the orbits. A veteran astronaut from Japan came to accompany the satellite into space. He immediately sought Charles Rogers.

The increased activity around the launch facility revived Rolf. He shaved his beard, wore khaki shirts and trousers, and dispensed with the shots of Meyer's rum. Max Yeager put his operation back together in a week. The Japanese spent their week scrambling around their big satellite.

The hustle and bustle attracted Cynthia, who spent more time around the blockhouse. As she limped up the path toward the hangar, she spied Rolf walking down the path toward her, alone, muttering to himself, unaware of his impending encounter.

"Rolf!" A flood of indignation swelled inside her, but she checked herself. Her face and tone did not betray her feelings.

Rolf looked up to see his wife. He halted. She leaned against her cane and waited for him to speak. He looked at her cane and followed it to her hand. He noticed Cynthia's white knuckles. Rolf summoned his voice. "How are you feeling?"

"I'm pretty busted up, thanks to you, but I'm on the mend."

"I'm sorry you got hurt."

Cynthia shifted more weight to her good foot. "So am I."

"No, really," Rolf interrupted. He spoke in measured words. "I regret that I was the cause of your accident."

"Accident. . . ."

"I didn't plan it that way, but the French act so irrationally. I've seen you from a distance on your morning walks along the beach. You heal quickly."

Cynthia considered Rolf's half-apology. She'd never heard any such utterance from Rolf, who clung to Benjamin Disraeli's famous dictum, "Never complain, and never explain."

She answered, "I'm getting the strength back to my foot, but the doctor says I'll need six to nine months to get back to normal."

"I see." Rolf looked around. "When things calm down, maybe you, Paul, and I can have dinner together?"

"I don't know. . . ."

"Sure. I understand. I really need to get back to work. We're preparing a launch for tomorrow. I've got to make sure the Japanese letter of credit cleared ANZ Bank. I could use a good finance man now that Herb's gone, but nobody will hire onto our outfit. Care to make any references?"

"No. I couldn't advise someone to sign onto this deathwagon."

Rolf stiffened. "That's not true. We may be outcasts, but only for the moment. We're winning."

"Winning?"

"Oh, yes. In spite of our political problems, we've managed enough business to generate a positive cash flow. Our stock has finally stopped spiraling down. If you still have those puts, you'd better cash them out."

"I have. In fact, I'm a buyer at these prices." Cynthia wondered how Rolf knew about her puts.

Rolf brightened. "Really?"

"Just a bit of speculation. I can't resist a bargain—you know that."

"That much I do know."

"Rolf?" Cynthia's face softened.

"Yes."

"You're trapped up here in the middle of nowhere, imprisoned by your own Pebbles System. I know you—you've got to be bored out of your skull."

Rolf looked around at his small hi-tech camp nestled in his verdant refuge. "I must admit the thrill is gone."

"Then why don't you sell it?"

"Ridiculous. NASA, among others, pays me $100,000 just to type in a simple command and create a launch window for *their* launches. We need the cash flow. We have another sixty-one window openings on the books. Think of it—6.1 million dollars for just opening a door."

"Oh, Rolf—that's chump change. I tell you what I'd do if I were NASA. I'd pay your piddling access fee and launch my full schedule. And while I was up there, I would somehow plant a bug on one of your satellites—or however you rocket scientists do such things. It might take a year to get lucky enough to find a Pebble and plant such a device, but then, at $100,000 a try, who cares?"

"I know that. I'm working on countermeasures."

"You can't beat the whole world."

"Would it upset you if I did?"

"You can't. It's that simple. Four billion minds are better than one. Sell the damned things. You know full well my special knack is knowing when to sell, so you'd do well to take my advice. Sell the Pebbles—they're nothing but grief."

"I can't do that."

"You mean you won't. You could if you wanted to, but you won't, if for no other reason than that I suggested it." Cynthia picked up her cane and started up the hill. "Oh, what's the use, you've never taken my advice before. I should stop taking it personally."

Rolf hollered up the hill after her, "I'd take your advice if you were right."

Cynthia stopped. She tightened her grip on the cane and stood motionless facing the launch area, her back to Rolf. Then without reply, she limped up the hill; she did not look back.

✧   ✧   ✧

The tractor hauled the Felix-C to the launch pad and set her up on her five legs. Although their timing had grown a bit rusty, the fuel trucks ran relays, pumping thousands of pounds of fuel into her belly. When all was ready, she sat and waited for the right hour. Workers gathered on the hill behind the launch pad. Even Cynthia joined the anxious crowd to watch the distant preflight operations. Far down the hillside on the tarmac, Captain Rogers and a Japanese astronaut looked like a pair of ants walking out to a silver stalagmite. Ten men in lime green jumpsuits scurried around checking the stubby feet, the seal on the hatch, the ground for foreign objects, then trotted away.

Throughout the launch area, throughout Lizard City, no person could be seen. Everyone had mounted the hills, taken refuge in the blockhouse, or sat strapped in the spaceship. Cynthia turned and noticed Irwin Kirby standing at her side. As she opened her mouth to speak, the Felix-C spit fire, then boomed and roared. Dust blew up the hillside. The smoke came at them like a wave that didn't break, but dissipated. Felix-C rose into the sky at ever-increasing speed until it disappeared. The crowd on the hill uttered a collective and reverent "Wow" as they shielded their eyes from the sun and scanned the blue sky.

Cynthia felt a tap on her shoulder. Irwin Kirby quickly said, "I thought I should say hello."

Cynthia cupped a hand to her ear. Kirby tried again louder. "I said g'day, Mrs. Bernard! You're looking chipper."

"Good day," she replied. "Did you come up to see the launch?"

"That's part of it. I brought a gentleman to meet your husband." Kirby introduced a small, swarthy, dapper man. "Mr. Eli Adan."

"Pleased to meet you, Mrs. Bernard." The man bowed slightly.

Irwin Kirby added, "Mr. Adan comes from Israel."

"Oh." Cynthia led the way slowly to the path that took them down the hill. "What brings you here?"

The Israeli answered her directly. "I work for the Israeli government. We have a great interest in your husband's work. Some of our more unstable neighbors have acquired medium- and long-range missiles, which causes us tremendous concern. So, my government sent me to see if your husband might entertain a proposal. And I have information for your husband." Mr. Adan smiled warmly.

"Frankly, I hope you've come to buy the Pebbles System, and I hope he sells. But don't get your hopes too high," Cynthia warned.

They reached a fork in the path. Kirby and Adan turned toward the blockhouse. Cynthia took the path toward the beach. On level ground she carried her cane in the crook of her arm. She used it more to poke at things than to walk.

Kirby and Adan could not get into the blockhouse. Rolf, with Tyler's assistance kept the blockhouse staff to a minimum. Rolf suspected all curiosity seekers. The blockhouse guard picked up a red wall phone to announce the visitors. Tyler responded in person, slipping out of the blockhouse and squinting in the bright sunlight.

"Mr. Tyler."

Tyler blinked. "Hello, Mr. Kirby. I heard you'd come up for the flight."

"I brought someone you and Mr. Bernard should meet. Mr. Eli Adan."

The Israeli held out his hand. "How do you do?"

Tyler shook the man's hand. "Let's get out of this dust. Rolf's busy monitoring the launch window. Can I buy you a cup of coffee?"

"Thank you."

They walked toward the dining hall. "What's your interest in Mr. Bernard?"

"I work as a civilian intelligence analyst with the Israeli Ministry of Defense. I study various terrorist groups."

"Oh, you're Mossad."

"I use some of their information, but I'm an analyst."

"You're a long way from your desk, Mr. Adan." Tyler waited for a response and got none. "What do you want to talk about?"

Eli Adan nodded his head. "My government wishes to safeguard the Pebbles System, because it offers us some protection. And my government has uncovered a plot to kill Mr. Bernard."

"Inevitable." Tyler took a deep breath. "I'll set up the meeting with Mr. Bernard. Irwin, bring Mr. Adan to the glass cage in the hangar after dinner." He walked them up the hill to the dining hall.

Tyler told the cook to send some snack food and a chest of cold beer to the glass cage. "Sangers and brew for the Japs?" The cook wrinkled his nose.

Tyler scowled, "First, don't call our Japanese customers Japs. Second, the food is for an Israeli named Adan, me, Mr. Bernard, and Mr. Kirby. Make some of your Australian stuff, but no Vegemite and no chip buddies."

Tyler ate a quiet meal with Max Yeager and Paul. As Tyler pushed his plate away, the cook and another hired hand approached with the chest of beer and a tray of fruit and cheese. Tyler walked with them down the hill to the hangar. Rolf was waiting there with Kirby and Adan. Everyone looked at ease—jovial, in fact.

"Hey, Bobby!" Rolf called out into the hangar. "The mission couldn't be going better. The Japs are delighted. They want to reserve two flights each quarter for the next year!"

"Wonderful." Tyler stopped the man with the beer, reached into the ice, and grabbed a couple cans. With his back to Rolf and company, he handed the cook and his helper a can of beer, then whispered, "I'll take it from here."

Kirby stepped out of the glass cage and helped Tyler haul the chest inside. Tyler turned the Do Not Disturb sign to the outside and locked the glass door.

Rolf Bernard popped the tab on a liter tinny and said, "Let's talk."

Eli Adan said, "I have a business proposition for you, and I have some news from the Middle East that concerns you very much."

"What's your proposition?"

"In Israel, we admire what you've done, and we sympathize with your lonely position in the world. Israel would like to buy your Pebbles System for $300 million dollars."

Tyler couldn't resist. "I'm sure Mr. Adan really does mean three hundred million *American* dollars."

Eli didn't laugh.

Rolf spoke. "If I wanted to sell the Pebbles System, I doubt I'd sell it to Israel—no offense. I'd sell it to my own country."

"And which one is that?" Mr. Adan asked.

Rolf looked at Kirby, then at Tyler. "I'd prefer to sell it to the United States or Australia."

"Have they made you an offer?"

"No, they haven't. You know, you've got some nerve."

Mr. Adan raised his hand. "Do you want them to make you an offer?"

"No."

"All right, then. The Pebbles System is not for sale. We understand each other. I would just feel like such an idiot if I didn't ask, then you sold it to Syria, Iraq, or somebody like that."

"Give me a little credit, will you?"

"If you change your mind . . ."

"I won't."

"Okay." Mr. Adan took a wedge of white cheddar cheese from the tray. "Let me tell you what my people have found out. Certain oil-producing nations that sponsor terrorism—

Iran, Iraq, Syria, Libya and Algeria—have contracted for your death. They've offered almost the same deal as they made for Rushdie, plus some perks. Anyone who kills you before you give up the code—and proves it—gets a cool $5 million. Anyone." Adan pointed around the room.

"That makes no sense. The Arabs don't have space programs."

"That is precisely why it makes perfect sense. The Arab nations cared nothing about space until you put your solar power satellite up. Cheap solar energy will drive oil prices down to two dollars a barrel. Mr. Bernard, you threaten the economic survival of four-hundred million Moslems with your godless machines. Unfortunately, you also showed them the way to save themselves. If they kill you before you divulge your access code, the Pebbles will keep the solar power satellites out of space for at least one-hundred years. Also, with one bullet they neutralize one of the great advantages that the great Satan of the Christian West has over the Moslem world—space technology."

Rolf dropped his can of beer. Tyler snapped the can up and set it aright on the floor.

"We can't keep track of all the freelance assassins out there, but we have learned that Libya gave a contract to a terrorist group called Allah's Mighty Hand. Their success or failure is a two-edged sword."

"Sounds pretty one-edged to me," Tyler exclaimed.

Eli Adan apologized, "From Israel's point of view, of course. I don't mean to be insensitive. If Allah's Mighty Hand succeeds in killing you, then they get back their powerful sponsors. They will rise again, rearmed and remanned, to continue their terrorist campaign. Of course, we don't want that. If they fail, oil prices will collapse in the next decade. Our belligerent neighbors will no longer have the resources, either financial or political, to threaten Israel. We greatly desire that.

"In the meantime, we are delighted that your system

will neutralize the long- and medium-range nuclear missiles recently deployed in Iraq. Hussein plans to go back to Kuwait. He still considers Kuwait a province of Iraq. I hope you won't think me crass, but to sum up our interests—in the short term, we want to keep you safe from terrorist groups; in the midterm, we want your Pebbles System to protect us from a nuclear first strike; in the long run, we want to see the SPS technology bankrupt Israel's adversaries."

Bernard blinked. The color drained from his face. "Do you think this is for real, Bobby?"

"I don't know," Tyler answered, then studied Rolf's face.

"The pity is," Adan continued, "there's not much we can do to keep you alive. They'd think nothing of committing suicide to take you out. Remember your own Marines in Lebanon? The Moslem fundamentalists consider you a far greater prize. Your death would be the greatest triumph their terrorist campaign has ever seen.

"So, Mr. Bernard, you've got a serious problem. If you go into hiding like Rushdie, you can't operate your system, so they win either way. We're still interested in buying the Pebbles System if you change your mind."

Chapter 22

Rolf Bernard stayed in his bungalow. He sat at his desk chain-smoking cigarettes and putting thoughts on paper, doodling around the margins. Rolf needed a plan. He recalled the old wag, Sam Johnson's, flippant bit of eighteenth century wisdom. Johnson commented that knowing one shall be hanged in a fortnight concentrates the mind wonderfully. Not so in Rolf's century. He could hardly string two ideas together, and those ideas that found their way to paper were simple expressions of instinct: fight and flight. The many wadded pages in the trash can attested to Rolf's frustration. He could not devise a plan to suit either instinct.

Max Yeager practically dragged Rolf to the blockhouse to disable the Pebbles System to let Felix-C pass through to land. Supposedly, the Pebbles knew the difference between rising and reentering spacecraft, but Captain Rogers had made Rolf swear many powerful oaths, promising to turn off the Pebbles for his trip out and back. Rolf walked to the bunker, watching everyone along the way. He half expected to see someone produce a pistol and shoot at him. He locked himself in his Tempest vault, and for the first time since he'd armed the Pebbles, Rolf fat-fingered the keyboard and sent the wrong disabling code. He got it right the second time—no harm done. Rolf malingered in the vault, his tiny sanctuary.

On his way back to his bungalow, Rolf ran into Tyler. "Rolf, just a minute of your time."

"Later. I need to lie down. I've got a headache." Rolf started down the path but Tyler stepped in his way.

"Rolf, it can't wait. I've been thinking about Eli Adan and what he said. I'm not too worried about terrorists storming Temple Bay beach. I've been considering the likelihood that someone here at Temple Bay would kill you for the five million-dollar bounty."

"So have I." Rolf glanced from side to side. "So have I."

"A potential assassin must ask himself whether or not he would actually get paid."

"Do you think such a man really thinks that far in the future?"

"I don't know." Tyler put his hand in his pocket and wrapped his hand around a small plastic box, something like a garage door opener. He flipped the metal toggle, took his hand out of his pocket and braced himself.

The air cracked with a blast, knocking both Rolf and Tyler to the dirt. Tyler landed on top of Rolf. A gush of hot air roared by. Chunks and wood splinters rained down. Rolf choked on the dust. "There's your answer, Bobby."

Tyler turned to see Rolf's bungalow, the back quarter blown away, a small fire growing. Rolf helped Tyler to his feet. They brushed the debris from their clothes. Men ran down the hill bringing fire extinguishers. Standing amidst the chaos, looking upon the burning wreckage, Rolf said, "I might have been killed if you hadn't stopped me from going in."

"Let's get to the blockhouse. If the guy can make a bomb, he can buy a rifle." Tyler hustled Rolf back to the blockhouse.

Rolf sealed the Tempest vault door and said, "I need to get out of Temple Bay."

"I agree. We're going to need some help with security."

"You're right, of course."

"I could make a few calls," Tyler offered sympathetically. "Maybe General Harchord could help us."

"Yes, George owes me a couple of favors. Give him a call."

"If you don't mind, I think you'd better plan to room with me until we can get you out of Temple Bay."

"Call Harchord as soon as you can."

"Yes, sir, I'll call Harchord. But what do I tell him? I know what he's going to want. He'll want the code to the Pebbles System. The question is, Rolf, what do you want?" Tyler pulled out a small notepad and a stubby pen.

Rolf thought. Then he checked off a mental list. "I want my assets returned, and that includes my stock, my houses, my cars—everything."

"Got it."

"The government buys the deployed Pebbles System from BAP for 1.3 billion dollars. They budgeted five times that before the cuts, so they should be delighted."

"Okay."

"I want total immunity from criminal prosecution, and indemnity from any civil actions. I want immunity for all the people who helped us put the Pebbles up. I want the government to guarantee any judgments rendered against me or BAP by foreign governments. Also BAP keeps the Felix ships. We want the export licenses to build the Felix craft in Australia."

"Is that all?"

"I'll probably think of something else, and I'm sure the lawyers will think of stuff, but start with that."

Tyler got up and said, "I'll call Harchord as soon as Washington gets back to work. It's two in the morning there."

Rolf opened the vault door, then added "I want my American citizenship restored."

✧   ✧   ✧

After Lizard City settled in for the night, Tyler joined the graveyard shift at the blockhouse and took a quiet desk, made a quick phone call, and waited. He put his head on the desk and closed his eyes. When the phone rang, he bounced his head from the blotter.

"Mr. Tyler?"

"Yes. You got me."

"Is Rolf with you?"

"No. He's trying to get some sleep."

"Did you get the access code?" A different voice chimed in.

"No. Who's on the speaker phone?" Tyler challenged.

"Oh. You just heard General Marshall, whom you know. Also listening is Mr. Jeffrey Brown from legal affairs. I asked him to sit in. Is everything quiet at your end?"

"Yes."

"Well, how is everything?"

"The dynamite blast got Rolf's attention."

There was a short laugh at the other end. Harchord asked, "Nobody got hurt, right?"

"Nobody."

"I would have given anything to have seen the expression on Rolf's face."

"Well, General Harchord, it didn't seem to faze him."

"Ah, grace under fire?"

"You might say that."

"Then good for Rolf. I told Marshall here that a simple dynamite blast wouldn't cause Rolf to give up the access code."

Marshall's voice came over the line. "What will Rolf do now?"

Tyler paused, wondering how best to phrase the next sentence. "The good news is, Rolf wants to sell the Pebbles System, and he wants to sell it to the United States."

"Good. Good." Two voices spoke into the speaker phone.

"Wait till you hear the conditions of sale." Tyler read from his list. The legal affairs guy interrupted from time to time to take notes and ask for details. When Tyler finished, Jeffrey Brown read the list back. Tyler asked, "You see any problems so far?"

"No."

Then Tyler probed. "We got a visit from an Israeli who says Moslem terrorists plan to assassinate Rolf Bernard. Have we got a problem?"

General Marshall spoke. "Could be true. Next to the Israeli Mossad, the French have the best eyes and ears in the Middle East and they confirm it. Algeria pledged a $5 million bounty for Bernard. Mr. Bernard had better cough up that code before it's too late. Sitting around Temple Bay is the wrong answer to his security problem."

"I was afraid of that."

"We'll feed data through MacAdam when we get it."

"Oh, yes. Thanks for the backup."

"Don't mention it."

"Gentlemen, I've gotta go." Tyler broke off the conversation. "Call me any time when you have a decision. Please don't let the boys downtown jerk us around on the small stuff. Make this deal work. Frankly, I'm sick to death of the whole mess." He hung up the phone.

Tyler left the blockhouse and walked down the empty gravel path to his bungalow. Night creatures yelled obscene things at each other and him. Inside his room, the air conditioner in the window droned, and the small refrigerator hummed. A fat moth beat itself against the ceiling light, and a green lizard studied the moth from its perch on a lampshade. No amount of screens, doors, duct tape, or tissue stuffed in cracks, could keep the insects and the geckos out of his room. No amount of men, guns, or electronics could keep terrorists out of Temple Bay.

Tyler did not have to wait long for General Harchord and company to respond. A short message told Tyler to stand by his fax machine, where he waited for the "deal." Twenty-two pages of curled paper fell onto the floor. Tyler collated, then hammered them together with a stapler and sat down for a careful read. The government could guarantee the money. They assured immunity and pardons, but Rolf and his conspirators would have to testify before Congress. The Feds promised to release Rolf's domestic assets, but overseas assets presented problems. The United States would either obtain release, or reimburse Rolf for losses. Jeffrey Brown needed more time to check the process of restoring Rolf's U.S. citizenship. In the meantime, the SEC agreed to drop its investigation into BAP, Inc. if, and only if, Rolf Bernard divested himself of all his common stock. Tyler thought, *Now, there's the bitter pill.*

Tyler called back and asked Jeffrey Brown to explain the SEC's position. Jeffrey Brown said, "We have very little influence with the SEC. Besides—let's face it, Mr. Bernard is through in the defense business. If he keeps his BAP stock, he can control the board of directors. He'd want to run BAP, and he'd need a top secret clearance. No way will that man ever get a security clearance. The Rosenbergs could get a clearance before Mr. Bernard! The bottom line—the Department of Defense needs BAP; it doesn't need Rolf Bernard."

"He won't sell his stock under twenty dollars. It traded over eighty-eight dollars per share just a year ago. He owns twenty percent of the common stock. Who's going to buy that much in this market? He'll drive his own stock down to five bucks."

"I'm no financial guru, but I'd bet BAP stock will go up on the news that Rolf has to sell."

"Would you buy?"

"Sure, why not?"

Tyler sighed. "It's a sad thing to see." Tyler drew a picture of the Felix-P as he took sparse notes.

"Sad has nothing to do with it. Mr. Bernard is lucky to be alive and not rotting in some jail cell. He'll still be one of the wealthiest men in the country. Pardon me if I don't grieve for Mr. Bernard."

"He won't agree to sell his stock," Tyler insisted.

"Then that's a problem." Jeffrey Brown hesitated. "Let me think. Suppose we got him to put his stock in a blind trust. He gets to watch his stock grow back to eighty bucks. He can't vote his stock, which means he can't touch the company."

"Will the SEC agree?"

"I'll see what I can do."

Tyler mulled over his notes. He walked down to Cynthia's bungalow and found her lying on the dock with her face over the edge looking into the water. She wore cutoff jeans, a gauzy blouse tied at the waist, and a floppy hat. She felt a shadow pass. When Bobby stepped onto the boards, she popped up. "You startled me!"

"I'm sorry."

"This business of the bomb in Rolf's bungalow—"

"Nobody got hurt."

"Thank goodness."

"I thought I'd find you inside working." Tyler sat on the dock next to her.

"I'm done. Either Andrea and Chet make the deal work, or they don't. We've raised the capital. We're just standing by waiting for the right time to file the papers."

"What's the deal?" Tyler asked.

Cynthia grinned. "I'd better not say—just yet. There are still a couple of things that could go wrong."

"Maybe I could help."

"I'll let you know." Cynthia stood up. She cast a shadow over Tyler. The sun shone through her loose blouse. She pulled her hat more squarely over her head and said, "Can I get you anything to drink? I made some herbal iced tea—strawberry and lemon grass."

"No, thank you. But I could use some advice." He struggled to his feet and walked with her back to the shaded porch of her rustic home.

"What can I do for you?"

"To make a long story short, Rolf's got to sell the Pebbles System."

"Really? Maybe that dynamite knocked some sense into Old Smurch."

"It would appear."

"So maybe we can get off this rock? My life can get back to normal." Cynthia smiled. "What are you going to do when you get out?" She sounded like an inmate about to see the parole board.

"We're not out of here yet. I'm afraid Rolf won't go for the deal. Rolf gets just about everything he asked for, but the SEC insists Rolf sell his stock or put it in a blind trust. I can't imagine Rolf doing either. What do you think?"

"Rolf will sell." Cynthia stated as a matter of fact.

"I don't think so."

"Oh, yes—he'll sell it all. He'll dump it. He could never be a passive investor." Cynthia shook her head.

"So what happens when he dumps his stock?"

Cynthia smirked. "The institutional investors will grab it up and run the stock back to forty-two dollars."

"Why forty-two dollars?"

"That's the breakup value. BAP's a bargain at these prices." Cynthia poured two glasses of iced tea from a heavy glass pitcher and offered one to Bobby. She winked, and added, "I might even buy a few shares on spec."

Tyler leaned against the rough clapboard walls and sipped the herbal tea.

Rolf admitted Tyler to the Tempest vault, received Tyler's practiced but blunt report, and took the news fairly well at first. Rolf paced the cramped vault to consider the particulars, and slowly percolated to a rage. "Swanson is just running BAP into the ground anyway. I'll just dump the stock, take my cash, and get the hell out. I'm through with the airplane business; I'm in the space transportation business now."

"Yes, sir."

"I'll tell Paul to get out while he can. You ought to tell

Cynthia to dump hers as well. Just watch. BAP will be a penny stock within a week!"

Tyler called BAP's McLean office. The secretary, a new name with an unfamiliar voice, left him on hold for twenty minutes. She came back on the line. "Thank you for holding. Mr. Swanson's not available to take your call at this point in time. Would you give me your name again?"

"Robert Tyler. I told you, I'm calling from Australia."

"Could you spell that please?"

"T-Y-L-E-R."

"And who do you represent?"

"Whom do I represent."

"I said that."

"You said 'who.' You should have said 'whom.' "

"Would you hold please."

The Muzak switched on. Tyler slammed the receiver down. He picked up the phone again and dialed General Harchord's private number. No answer. Harchord languished on Capitol Hill testifying for the Air Force budget, which was already doomed. Tyler punched in another number and reached Harchord's aide, an effervescent and efficient full colonel. Tyler relayed his message. "Tell Generals Harchord and Marshall that Rolf Bernard has agreed to sell the Pebbles System. Tell Jeffrey Brown that Bernard intends to divest, so the blind trust option isn't necessary. And one more thing."

"What's that."

"Tell General Harchord that we can't do the deal without BAP's cooperation, and they aren't cooperating. I can't even place a call to Swanson. Maybe if Harchord explains the deal to Swanson, and Swanson muzzles his harpy in the front office," Tyler said, his voice rising in pitch, "maybe we can close this deal."

Tyler engaged Irwin Kirby's lawyers and they worked with their American counterparts to sew the deal together.

Representatives for the United States wanted to close the deal in Australia, but Rolf refused, and his lawyers concurred. The venue for the transaction had to be in the United States to protect Rolf from future complications. Then both sides haggled over whether the Pebbles System should be disarmed while Rolf traveled. Accidents happen, they argued. Rolf adamantly refused to disarm the Pebbles, saying, "If I turn the Pebbles off, someone will arrange an accident."

General Harchord offered to bring Rolf back on an Air Force jet. Nothing doing. The Justice Department pressured Rolf to divulge his travel plans so that they might provide security. Again, nothing doing. Rolf told them, "I'll just show up when and where I see fit. Make sure you've got the documents ready to sign and I'll give you the code."

Rolf took Max Yeager aside. "I'd like to fly Felix right into Washington. We'll find a nice safe place to land. Speed is security. We could be in Washington in less than five hours. Can you work up the mission?"

"The flight would be a piece of cake. . . ." Yeager shook his head.

"But what?" Rolf demanded.

"The launch has some terrific risks. If someone wants you dead, you can give them no greater opportunity than to strap yourself on top of eighteen thousand pounds of slush hydrogen. You'll never be more vulnerable in your life. As you start to take off, anyone with a high powered rifle could hit you amidships and rupture the fuel tank. Felix would be very easy to hit. No one would hear the shot. You'd never know what hit you."

Rolf looked at Tyler who shrugged his shoulders and said, "We can't sweep a mile of jungle. Even if we could, we can't be sure someone on the Felix ground crew wouldn't sabotage the ship. I agree with Max. We need a jet that can fly nonstop to the States."

"Then we'll need to charter something. Tyler, make it happen."

✧   ✧   ✧

With Yeager's cooperation Rolf plotted a ruse to make
people think that he remained at Temple Bay. Yeager
announced a launch, then ordered the Felix-P rolled into
position for all the surveillance satellites to see. Paul's
small fuel brigade pumped Felix full. Max brought his
Cairns contingent up. Anybody watching would have
expected a Felix launch and would have presumed that
Rolf would have to attend the launch, because he alone
had the key to disarm the Pebbles and open the gateway
to space.

Tyler called Irwin Kirby. "We need non-stop air
transportation to LAX—even better, Dulles."

"I'll charter a Qantas flight."

"I think Rolf would prefer United."

"Qantas has never had a passenger fatality—never.
Besides, a Qantas charter out of Australia wouldn't seem
odd, a United charter would."

"Good point. Shall we fly out of Cairns? Brisbane?"

"I wouldn't. The constabulary in Cairns isn't at all geared
for antiterrorist activities. And as much as you've used
Brisbane, I think your adversaries would watch Brisbane
very closely. I think you'd better hop down to Sydney.
We'll fly you in, hide you if necessary, then spirit you
away on a big jet. I could arrange some security for you."

"No. I'll handle security. You just get me a chartered
plane and give them some fake names for the manifest.
Other than that, not a word."

"Who's flying to the States with Rolf?"

"Me, Paul, and Cynthia. Max Yeager and Charles Rogers
will stay behind to run a dummy launch."

A heavy, fortuitous rain poured down on Temple Bay
like a curtain drawn to hide Rolf's departure. Stouffer
ostensibly prepared for a spare-parts run, supposedly to
Cairns. Under cover of darkness and downpour, Tyler

drove a panel truck out to the Learjet. Draped in ponchos, Cynthia, Paul, and Rolf Bernard slipped out of the van, into the jet. Tyler parked the van next to the fuel shed, then walked the mere fifty feet to the plane holding an umbrella over his head and slogging through ankle-deep water. Stouffer rode out in a separate sedan.

After a turbulent flight, Stouffer landed at Sydney airport's domestic terminal. He taxied all the way to the terminal. From his window, Tyler saw a Mercedes stretch limousine roll onto the tarmac to meet them. Irwin Kirby stepped out. Tyler hopped out of the Learjet and looked around. His face turned crimson. "Kirby, where's the plane?"

"Don't get your knickers in a twist. It's waiting at the international terminal about a mile away. Sydney's got two airfields."

"You should have told me."

"I thought everybody knew that—even Yanks."

"Let's go already." Tyler beckoned the rest of passengers and rushed them into the limousine. After a brief ride to the international terminal, Tyler and Kirby hustled the Bernard family through the automatic glass doors into customs. Each carried a garment bag. Kirby led the small party to a customs official who expedited stamps on visas and collected signed forms and the departure tax. Having satisfied the Australian government, Kirby led the small band toward the public area. "You'll wait in the Qantas VIP suite." Kirby talked to his side while he marched briskly. Rolf and Paul kept pace. Cynthia lagged—her foot ached—and Tyler slowed to help her.

Up ahead, Kirby stopped. "What the devil?"

A news reporter stepped in front of him blocking his progress. The reporter shoved a microphone at Rolf. Tyler saw the intrusion, left Cynthia, and jogged the fifty feet to investigate. He slid to a stop in front of the reporter, grabbed two fistfuls of the man's jacket, pushed him back into a woman holding the camera. Tyler bent him backwards, but held him on his feet, and demanded, "How'd you know we were coming?"

"I won't tell you squat."

Tyler reached into the man's pocket and ripped out his wallet. The woman with the camera came back for a close up. Tyler dropped the reporter onto the polished marble floor. Then he snatched the camera from her shoulder, pulled the cord from the back end, and ripped the tape from the box at her waist. He dropped the heavy camera next to the reporter's head with a loud crash. Tyler read the contents of the reporter's wallet, turned to Rolf and said, "They're from CNN. We've been made. Where's Cynthia?"

Cynthia stood outside the crowd that converged instantly to form a ring around the fracas. The reporter was cursing Tyler and yelling for help.

Tyler grabbed Cynthia by the arm. "Kirby, get us out of here, now. Paul, stay close." Tyler shoved Rolf and Kirby forward, and dragged Cynthia behind. The crowd stayed behind to look after the pitiful pair from CNN.

Kirby pointed toward a corridor. Tyler panted, "We got to get out of here." More people converged on the noise. He shoved one of the gawking travelers, a tourist overburdened with luggage, out of the way. The man fell over on top knocking a small girl to the floor.

The tourist cursed, "Hey, asshole!"

Tyler ignored the indignant traveler and the child, who pointed to her skinned knees and bawled. A woman carrying an infant in a sling rushed over to help the little girl, her elder daughter.

Cynthia wrenched her arm free from Tyler. "Just what do you think you're doing: Are you out of you mind?" She turned to the young mother as she brushed some floor grit from the little girl's knees. "I'm so sorry."

Tyler looked furtively about, checking faces. "Cindy! Come on. We've got to get out of this open space."

Then he saw them. Three men on the open stairwell,

each unzipping a small bag. "Get down!" Tyler yelled. He tackled Rolf and rolled him behind a pillar just as the three men raised their small machine guns and fired bursts.

Cynthia started for cover when she saw the little girl with the skinned knees frozen, her mouth open to scream. The mother dropped a fat gray bag—a baby bottle clattered across the floor. The mother turned her infant from the gunfire. Cynthia dove on top of the little girl.

Rolf felt a sudden pain, like a wasp sting in his hand. His forearm seemed to yank from his elbow. He looked. He saw a dark bleeding hole in the palm of his hand. He turned his hand to see the exit wound.

Then he looked at Bobby. "You're hit, too."

Tyler clenched his teeth. "Don't I know it." Bobby felt a burning wound in his side, but he knew the wound was not mortal. The gunmen aimed at the spot where Rolf and Tyler were hiding behind a cement pillar. Cement chips and lead splinters rained down.

People screamed. The mother clutched her baby and fell to the floor behind a thick planter. Cynthia curled her adult body around the terrified child. She felt a sharp blow to her thigh. Another thud shook her shoulder. Bullets splashed off the stone floor just inches away. Cynthia felt the little girl curled in her arms, pressed against the cold floor, trembling with fear.

The three gunmen ran down the steps, joined by a fourth. They threw their empty clips away, slapping fresh ones into their machine guns. Tyler pulled the Glock-17 from his shoulder holster and returned five shots, dropping one of the men. The three remaining men raised their machine pistols to pour a hail of bullets onto Rolf Bernard and Bobby Tyler.

Then the air was ripped with four or five explosions, blasts from 12-gauge shotguns. The force of the shots jerked the gunmen from their feet and hurled them toward the place where Tyler and Rolf hid from the spray of bullets. Suddenly, the noise of gunfire ended, replaced by the sounds of weeping and groaning. Tyler peeked around the cement pillar and saw the gunmen lying face down, with large ragged wounds in their backs. Two grim men, wearing dark suits and trench coats, trotted forward. Their short-barreled shotguns emitted acrid smoke. They stuffed red shotgun shells into the sides of their weapons while they looked around for more assassins.

Cynthia couldn't get up; she was too dizzy. The small girl crawled out from under her, awash in Cynthia's blood, her hair matted and bawling fearfully. Tyler crawled to Cindy, painfully aware of the hole in his side. He found her bleeding badly from her thigh, where a bullet had torn a gash in her leg. He clamped his hand over the leg wound as hard as he could. He pressed his other hand over her shoulder, where he felt either a piece of metal, a disfigured bullet, or a bone fragment, under her skin.

Cynthia groaned, "How's the girl?" Then she slipped into shock, pale and shuddering. Tyler started to take off his coat to prop up her feet, when, from the corner of his eye, he saw one of the four gunmen—the one he'd shot—pull a hand grenade from his coat pocket. "Rodriguez! Behind you!"

The tall man with the shotgun spun around and fired a blast into the Arab gunman, killing him instantly. The hand grenade rolled across the floor, spinning to a standstill with the pin intact. Both men with shotguns carefully moved among the fallen Arabs and pulled the weapons from their corpses. Plainclothes and uniformed police converged on the area.

Sirens whined outside the airport, then medical teams rushed in. Twenty-eight people had suffered wounds, many from the splash of lead and broken glass. Fortunately, the gunmen had concentrated their fire on Rolf and Tyler, who had had the protection of the cement pillar. Six civilians, including Rolf and Bobby, had taken direct hits from the hail of bullets. Kirby had broken his nose diving behind a kiosk. None but the gunmen from Allah's Mighty Hand perished. The gunfire—first bullet to last—had lasted less than two minutes.

Paramedics took Cynthia before Tyler. One raised her skirt above the wound. The leader spoke into a small radio. "Subject, female, in her late thirties. . . ."

Tyler spoke, "Late forties."

"Check that. Late forties. Severe loss of blood. Gunshot wound to left thigh, severed femoral artery. Gunshot wound to right shoulder, bullet impacted in bone. Subject in shock. I'm putting her on plasma." He put the radio down, put Cynthia on the gurney, and whisked her away.

Tyler sat up and undid his own blood-soaked shirt. He looked at the small hole in his side and momentarily felt queasy. A male and female paramedic team took him. The woman swabbed the blood from his stomach, noticed a web of scars, and said, "This isn't your first, is it?"

"No. And I'm getting a little too old for this."

"We're always too old for this." They hooked him up to a bag of plasma and hauled him to the hospital.

Chapter 23

When they wheeled Tyler into the emergency room, he caught a glimpse of Cynthia. A small crowd of men and women dressed in green hustled her through a double door into a brightly lit room. Tyler tried to sit up, but the pain knocked him flat onto his gurney. Another green-clad doctor came up; he lifted the bandage over Tyler's wound. Tyler muttered, "I need to make a phone call."

The doctor ignored Tyler's muffled voice. He jabbed a syringe into the plasma bag and squirted anesthesia. He tapped the plastic tube with his middle finger to dislodge any bubbles. Tyler's lights went out.

Tyler awoke on a firm bed. The room warped in and out of focus, and he felt as if someone had crammed a broomstick down his throat. A large man sitting next to him seemed to melt, then congeal. Tyler didn't recognize the man in either state. He croaked, "I need to make a phone call."

The man summoned a nurse, who simply noted the time that Tyler came to, then left. Tyler blinked away some of the blur from his eyes. "Do I know you?" he asked, and his head rolled back to the center of the pillow and he fell asleep for another fifteen minutes.

Tyler opened his eyes. "Do I know you?"

"MacAdam, remember? Marshall didn't want you under sodium pentothal without a chaperon."

Tyler blinked. "Oh, yeah." Then he looked under the sheets. They'd painted his shaved stomach with an orange antiseptic. The bandage was much bigger than he imagined it should be. "Will you look at that?"

MacAdam leaned over for a peek. "They tell me the bullet knocked a little chunk off your kidney on its way through."

"Whom did you assign to watch Rolf Bernard's room?"

"Rodriguez and Sam."

Tyler licked his chapped lips. "We've got to get Rolf out of here and close this deal."

"I got the impression, listening to Bernard and his son, that he won't go anywhere without you."

"Then I'll just have to get up and go."

"How do you feel?" MacAdam asked.

"My throat hurts more than my side. What kind of cocktail are they serving?" Tyler pointed at the bag at the end of his IV tube.

"I don't know. General Marshall wants to talk to you as soon as you feel up to it."

"How are Cindy, Rolf, Paul, and Kirby?"

"Rolf Bernard's a tough guy. He had a hole the size of a dime knocked through his right hand. He wouldn't let the doctors knock him out. He let them put a pin in one of his hand bones, sew tendons back together, and close the wound, all with local anesthesia."

"And Cindy?"

"Mrs. Bernard bled herself white, but she's doing fine. They dug a slug from her leg and another from her shoulder, repaired the leg artery, and stitched her up. They pumped three, maybe four, pints of blood in her. She's stuck in bed for a while."

"And Paul?"

"Not a scratch."

"Kirby?"

"He broke his nose—just a typical rugby bump, he called it."

Tyler furled his brow. "Sam and Rodriguez reacted too slowly."

"So they say . . . ." MacAdam looked into Tyler's eyes. "Since you're well enough to critique the operation, I'll wager you are, medically speaking, out of danger. I've got to check on Mr. Bernard."

"You do that."

For two hours, Tyler's mind slipped intermittently between the world of weird dreams and his hospital room. Finally, the world snapped into focus and stayed there, and Tyler found himself staring up at Rolf Bernard. They were alone.

"How are you doing, Bobby?"

Tyler's mind cleared, and a burning pain in his side visited him. "Crank the bed up, will you?"

Rolf found the controls to the mechanical bed and raised the head of the bed so Tyler could sit up. Rolf said, "That was too close. I could have lost Paul, you, and Cynthia." Rolf clasped his good hand on the low bed rail. His other hung in a sling with a cast.

Tyler shifted his weight off of his hurt side. "The Moslems know we're in Sydney. What's on the news?"

"That my wife and I are in hospital with gunshot wounds, pictures of the dead terrorists, pictures of Cynthia and me, interviews with airport security. I'm expected to live."

"They think you are bedridden?"

"I got that impression, yes."

"Good. We can use that to our advantage." Tyler nodded approvingly. Then he added, "We can't stay here, that's for sure. Do you want to try a chartered flight again?"

"I don't think so. They'll watch the international flights. They can plant a bomb on the plane. They could even shoot us down with a surface-to-air missile."

"Maybe you should just give up the code."

"I'm not panicked yet. Bobby, I've got a plan. But you'd have to travel."

"Let's hear it."

"We leave Paul here to look after his mother. We tell the press that I'm much worse off than before—complications—whatever. Anyway, the world thinks I'm under maximum security in the hospital. We leave Stouffer here. I'll fly us back to Temple Bay. Felix-P is fueled and ready to launch. Remember that was going to be our cover."

"That cover's blown now."

"Sort of. Rogers can sneak me aboard Felix. Max can operate the ground controls for the launch. As for our Temple Bay assassin, he's probably halfway to Sydney by now to earn his five million by finishing me in this hospital. And even if he's still at Temple Bay, he's got to figure that I'm in the Tempest vault turning off the Pebbles System for the launch. Logically, I can't be in two places at one time."

"So you want me to switch off the Pebbles System?"

"No, I can preprogram it. But I'll need you to stand by to make sure nothing goes wrong with the equipment. I don't want to find myself in orbit, unable to turn the Pebbles System off. Supposedly, the Pebbles System knows the difference between hot things coming up and hot things going down, but . . ."

"You'd rather be safe than sorry. You want the Pebbles disarmed for your descent."

"Exactly. Also, I'll need you to arrange our landing site in Washington. We won't tell anybody where we're going to land Felix until the last possible minute. Speed and secrecy will be our security."

Tyler smiled and tried to raise himself. "Your plan will work. Get a doctor in here. I've got to take these drainage tubes out so I can out of this bed."

"I'll see to it." Rolf got up to leave. "Oh, I almost forgot. Cynthia told me to give you her best."

"I heard she's doing fine, considering . . . ."

"Oh, she's tough alright. Tough as nails. You don't know the half of it, Bobby. I figured out her little scheme."

"Her what?"

"Her latest deal—what she's been working on for the last month." Rolf sat back down. "She's poised to buy BAP when I sell my stock."

"How do you know?"

"I confronted her. She told me."

"What did you do? What did you say?"

"Nothing. I said nothing. But she's about to find out that running BAP is one hell of a lot tougher than owning it."

"You don't think she's going to run BAP, do you?"

"No." Rolf laughed sardonically. "No, Bobby. She just wants the cheap thrill of taking my company. I know what she'll do."

"What's that?"

"She'll give Paul my job—President and CEO. I know how she thinks." Rolf shrugged his shoulders.

"You seem to take the news well."

"That's because the joke's on her. Paul won't take the job. Paul, Max, and I are going to build spaceships in Australia. Cynthia just bought the geriatric end of the business—yesterday's breadwinner. I get to keep tomorrow's breadwinner."

That evening, the doctor removed Tyler's drainage tube and let him walk around the hospital halls. Walking didn't hurt. Getting in and out of bed did. They wrapped Tyler's torso in a tight elastic bandage to restrict any pressure he might put against his stitches.

Tyler knocked on Cynthia's door. "Cindy? Are you taking visitors?"

"Bobby! Come in. Let me see you."

Tyler walked in stiffly, his bandages acting like a corset, holding him erect. She looked up at Tyler. "You poor dear. Does it hurt?"

"Not too bad. How do you feel?"

"Surprisingly, my bullet wounds don't hurt as badly as my foot. And whenever my shoulder starts to ache, I press this little button and shoot a little joy juice into my supper." She pointed to the tube giving her clear drips from a plastic bag. Cynthia fumbled around for the TV remote and turned the set off.

"Rolf told me you're going to buy BAP."

"That's the plan. Andrea's buying BAP stock under twenty dollars. Breakup value is around forty-two dollars a share. I'm not sure what we'll do. Andrea wants to break it up right away. I'm inclined to keep it a while."

"Is that so? Maybe you could use a good security guy. I'm pretty good at what I do."

"You're good Bobby, but not that good."

Tyler chuckled. "I'm hurt. I really am."

"I've been putting a few pieces together, too. I've got to know. You've been working for the CIA, haven't you?"

"That's crazy, Cindy. That's the craziest thing I've ever heard you say."

"Really? Look me in the eyes and swear you haven't been working for the CIA."

"Cross my heart. I swear."

Cynthia looked into Bobby's eyes. "Then tell me. How does a man steal three hundred twenty satellites, fabricated in a top secret environment, then sneak them out of the U.S. into Australia without help? How can someone show up with forged passports with current pictures at the drop of a hat? How come you knew all about Chip? Maybe Chip worked for you—a disgusting thought, I might add. And you arranged for the SWAT team to protect us at the airport, didn't you?"

"Hey. I don't know where those guys at the airport came from. Kirby perhaps. Anyway, they saved our bacon, so I'm willing to forgive and forget."

The light left Cynthia's eyes. "Who's Rodriguez? The man with the shotgun, whom you called by name. Remember?"

Tyler took his eyes off Cynthia and looked at the ceiling. A minute of pained silence passed, filled with a sense of loss.

"Nevertheless, Bobby, I'm impressed. You had me fooled."

"So, you don't think I'm Rolf's lapdog."

"Not anymore."

"Does that improve my standing?"

"I suppose so. You're a bad man, Bobby Tyler, but you're my kind." Cynthia reached out and took Bobby's hand. "You'd better go now."

Tyler squeezed her hand and left without a word, his next stop Rolf's room. Tyler stood at the heavily draped, sixth floor window. He pulled back a finger's breadth of curtain to look down on the street entrance to the hospital. Rolf sat at a small table with his hospital lunch, focusing his attention on the pineapple wedge and cup of coffee. Tyler closed the curtain. "Here they come. Kirby's man just drove up to the entrance. Let's get ready to go."

Kirby carried a bouquet of flowers and Paul carried a shopping bag with two sets of clothes into the hospital. The guards recognized both and let them pass unchallenged into Rolf Bernard's room. Tyler waited. Paul dumped the contents of the shopping bag—jeans, jerseys, sneakers, and caps—onto the bed. Tyler stripped off his robe and slowly dressed himself in the new clothes. Rolf grimaced as he crammed cast and hand through the jersey sleeve.

Tyler phoned ahead to alert Max and Rogers to launch Felix within ten hours. Tyler would bring the cargo and no one was to know anything about his pending arrival. Then he, Kirby, and Rolf walked out the front door to where Archie waited with the car. They drove straight to the domestic terminal of the Sydney airport, onto the tarmac, and next to Kirby's plane.

Rolf reached over with his good hand, "Thanks for letting us use your plane."

"We're partners, remember? You do remember how to fly an Airstream?"

"Like riding a bicycle."

"One-handed?"

"No hands if I have to."

"Plan on stopping for fuel at MacKay." Kirby unfolded an aviation chart and pointed to the coastline. "Or you could press up to Townsville or Cairns—Cairns is over twelve hundred miles away, and they know you there. In any case, you haven't quite got the range to get to Temple Bay straight from Sydney."

"You need a bigger jet, Irwin."

"Maybe we'll go in halves when you come back."

Rolf flew all day with one stop for fuel at the small airfield in Townsville. Rolf avoided a tall curtain of clouds rising above the Great Dividing Range, clouds that pressed him over the water. The water turned from blue to shimmering black as the sun set.

Stars appeared on the east horizon as they flew into the gray, hazy light called ending evening nautical twilight. Rolf rounded Cape Melville and nudged the plane westerly over Princess Charlotte Bay. Rose-colored fingers reached out through the clouds in the west, the day's last grasp slipping. Rolf poked Tyler with his cast. Tyler's chin bounded off his chest and his eyes opened. "I must have dozed off."

"You need to call ahead to Max. I don't want my voice on the radio."

Tyler rubbed the sleep from his eyes, then keyed the mike. "This is Kilo India Four Niner calling Temple Bay airstrip. Over." He took his thumb off the PUSH-TO-TALK button.

"This is Temple Bay. Yeager speaking. Over."

"How's your launch schedule? Over."

"On time. We're just waiting for cargo. Over."

"Meet me at the airstrip. Tyler, out." Bobby set the

mike in its cradle and turned the power off. He poured a cup of coffee from the thermos and handed it to Rolf.

"Thanks."

Rolf drank the tepid coffee and handed the empty tin cup back to Tyler. "A night launch is a good idea." He looked at Tyler and added, "I feel lucky tonight."

Rolf began the descent. "You see Mount Tozer straight ahead?"

"Mount?"

"A landmark. We'll be on the ground in fifteen minutes."

"Good. Oh, yes. I see the Lizard City lights. They've got the xenon lights on the launch pad. I can just barely see the ship."

"Yeah. I see her. Now I'm going to show you how an Air Force pilot lands a plane—we're talking smooth as ice—finesse and grace. Stouffer lands like a Navy pilot— an ass-smacking, neck-spraining, tailhook-grappling dive at the tarmac." Rolf lowered the landing gear. He let the Airstream slide down to the runway smoothly, as good as his word.

As soon as the plane's engines had been cut, Rolf helped Tyler climb down. Tyler's wound weighed heavily on him now. Max helped Tyler into the sedan and they all sped away to the blockhouse, where unobserved, Tyler and Rolf slipped into the Tempest vault and locked the steel door.

Rolf sat down at the computer terminal. He hummed a tune, stopped, and keyed in a code, typing with one hand. The computer responded with a menu and a prompt. Then Rolf called, "Come here, Bobby."

Tyler walked stiffly to the workstation. Rolf limbered up his fingers and said, "I pick the time to open the Pebble window." Rolf moved the mouse-cursor over a menu prompt titled "Disable." He double-clicked the button and a blinking cursor appeared in a small box shaped like a digital clock.

"We'll launch twenty minutes after midnight, so I type

in zero-zero-two-zero. Skip the date field and it automatically defaults to today. We'll only climb above the Pebbles' field of view for a few minutes as we reach a speed of fifteen thousand miles per hour. I figure we'll start our landing sequence one hour and forty minutes after launch. So now I pick the time to close the system." Rolf moved the mouse to select the menu prompt "Enable."

"We'll give ourselves some slack. I'll fill in the clock with the time: zero-two-four-five. There." Rolf hit the enter key. The computer accepted the sequences but requested the access code again.

Rolf looked at Tyler. "You've got to memorize the code. Never make a hard copy."

"The code?" Tyler tried to keep his best poker face, but his eyes sparked. "Then you changed your mind."

"Of course. Somebody back here has got to have the code. If for some reason Rogers can't land on the first pass, we'll need you to disable the system. This week my code is a line from 'Loch Lomond': 'You take the high road I'll take the low.' And for heaven's sake, don't forget the apostrophe. The first thirty-two characters admit you to the system."

Rolf typed in the code and hit enter. A blinking message appeared on the screen, "Instructions sent." On the next line a message appeared, "Instructions received," then a third line, "New access code sent," followed by a fourth, "Access code recorded." The computer screen slowly inventoried the three hundred nineteen remaining Pebbles on station as the Pebbles zipped around the earth and electronically shook hands. At the end of the inventory routine the screen blanked and the original plain prompt blinked harmlessly, waiting for the access code.

"There you have it, Bobby. You can turn the system off by simply typing in the access code. You select 'Disable,' then enter zeros for all the time and day values. If anything happens to me, I'll trust you to get the code to the National

Command Authority." Then Rolf said, "You look surprised."

' "Actually, yes. I thought you decided . . . uh" —Tyler wondered if it were prudent to proceed— "I thought you would take the code with you to the grave before giving it to anyone."

"That's what you were supposed to think."

"A bluff?"

Rolf changed the subject. "Here's what I want you to do. As we take off, call Harchord and tell them I'm on my way. If for any reason we can't get down within the window, I'll need you to disarm the system. You'd better write this down, Bobby. Tell Harchord to notify NORAD. Tell them I'm going to land somewhere in downtown Washington. Rogers will pick a spot to land on our way down. And I want to see a lot of security. And I want to see Harchord's face when I open the hatch—nobody else's."

"I'll take care of everything at this end."

Rolf rested his hand on Tyler's shoulder. "I'm counting on you. Don't leave me up there with the Pebbles on."

"Don't worry."

Rolf pulled out a cigarette and lit it. He inhaled the smoke. "Another no-frills, no-smoking flight, eh?"

At midnight, Max Yeager drove to the entrance of the blockhouse. Rolf climbed into the passenger side of the pickup truck and they drove down to the Felix-P. Rolf left the truck and hustled to the spaceship, where Rogers waited by the aluminum stairs.

Rogers quietly greeted Rolf, looked at his watch and led the way up into the crew compartment. With little discussion, Rogers showed Rolf how to put on the pressure suit. Rogers handed Rolf a pair of chewable dramamine tablets. Rogers fastened Rolf's helmet seals—then his own. He tested the comm-link, then strapped Rolf into the passenger couch—something like a reclining chair.

Rogers buckled himself into his seat. He looked out the window and saw Yeager speeding away in the truck. The digital clock on the control panel added another minute: 12:18:00.

"Brace yourself, Mr. Bernard. I'm going to fire the motors now. Remember going straight up in a Phantom?"

"Yes."

"Good. You'll like this. . . ." Rogers reached up with a gloved hand and pushed eight small red switches up with a solid click. "The computers will finish their safety checks. . . ."

The ship shuddered as the aerospike motors roared. Sensors measured the thrust. A green light flashed to signal the detonation of the restraining bolts, and Felix lurched skyward. Rolf struggled against the g's and turned his head to look out the port window. The horizon disappeared into the black. Felix rolled over. The dark blue earth lay below. The ship's acceleration kept Rolf squeezed into his seat, yet his vision suggested that he should hang from his shoulder straps. Rogers spoke through his mike, "Are you okay, sir?"

Tyler watched Felix disappear in the night sky. He ducked back into the Tempest vault. He had the code. Tyler thought, *Marshall's been waiting for this code for nine months: won't he be pleased?* Bobby picked up the phone and dialed General Marshall's number. He hung up before it could ring. His eyes narrowed. *What happens to Rolf if General Marshall gets the code before Rolf lands? And what happens to me if they find out I got the code but didn't share it with them? Rolf might let it slip.*

Tyler looked at the clock. I'm late, he thought. He dialed Harchord's office. On the third ring: "Colonel Whitescomb speaking."

"This is Robert Tyler. We've got to act fast. Rolf Bernard is flying into Washington, D.C. aboard a Felix spacecraft. He's coming in and he wants Harchord's protection."

"General Harchord's here." The phone rustled as it changed hands. Harchord's voice came back. "Tyler?"

"Yes, sir. You've got about an hour and ten minutes to prepare to receive Rolf Bernard. He's going to land a Felix spaceship in Washington. You need to assemble some security. You need to alert NORAD to let the flight pass unmolested."

"If Rolf's up there, how's he turning the Pebbles System on and off?"

"He preprogrammed the commands. The Pebbles are off at the moment. He programmed them to arm again soon after he lands."

"How do you know that? Did he give you the code?"

Tyler felt the urge to lecture the general. *Just get the code from Rolf. Finish the deal as we planned. Don't try to get something for nothing.* So Tyler dissembled, "No, sir. He didn't give me the code."

"Very well. Where will he land?"

"I don't know yet. He'll call in and tell me so let's keep this line open."

The Pratt and Whitney rocket motors stopped. Rogers and Rolf felt loose in their straps. Rogers asked, "Well, what do you think?"

"It's gorgeous. Makes me light-headed." Rolf pressed his face close to the window. "Pictures don't do it justice."

"So we've got a couple of minutes to decide where we're going to land. Where to?"

"I've been at enough airports lately. Anyplace but an airport."

"How about the mall in front of the Air and Space Museum?"

Rogers wrinkled his nose. "We're not ready for the museum."

"Okay. How about the mall at the Washington Monument."

"Just like 'The Day the Earth Stood Still.' "

Rolf nodded. "You can be the robot. I'll come out and say *Klaatu Barata Nikto!*"

"Too derivative."

"But a classic. . . ."

"True, but the ground's not level around the monument."

Rolf perked up. "I've got it—the Ellipse. We'll land in the middle of the Ellipse. It's flat. The Secret Service ought to be able to secure the area."

"They've got antiaircraft guns, or something, on the roof of the Old Executive Office Building."

"I think Harchord can handle that. Call Tyler. Tell him we're going to set down on the Ellipse."

Rogers grinned. "You know something odd?"

"What?"

"We're going to land in Washington yesterday. We left Australia on Friday; we're going to land in Washington on Thursday."

"You know, I feel younger." Rolf looked through his window as they crossed the Mississippi. "The world looks younger, too."

Rogers looked at the panel. "We fire breaking rockets in three minutes. Check your shoulder harness."

Rolf tugged at the belts. Rogers consulted the computer's gazetteer, then entered the coordinates for their landing. The computer began the landing sequence. Small jets of forced air slowly turned Felix around. Now Rogers and Rolf could see the western horizon from whence they came. After flipping the ship, Rogers announced, "We're going down."

A moment later, the breaking thrusters fired.

Minutes after getting the word, Secret Service agents swept the Ellipse of people. No explanation—just go. Wooden barricades appeared. Yellow police-line tape cordoned off the area. Fire equipment rushed to positions in front of the Treasury Building. National Airport suspended operations, rerouting air traffic to Baltimore.

District of Columbia police stopped all traffic within five city blocks.

Then, out of the sunny sky came a streak of white light and vapor trail. The fireball fell and grew. The sound finally arrived like a late but boisterous guest. One thousand feet above the monuments, the spaceship hesitated and slipped slowly, more directly over the Ellipse. And with a deafening roar, the ship stood upon an eighty-foot flame. Slowly she set down. She carved herself a scorched platform, blasting chunks of smoldering sod in all directions. Her five legs unfolded and locked into place. Felix effected a half pirouette, then set down.

General Harchord stepped through the police line. A dozen or so security men in civilian clothes walked toward the ship from different angles. In Harchord's mind the scene played like an old fifties movie: Curious civilians approach the red-hot ship, stepping carefully around the charred and smoldering clumps of grass. Then slowly, the hatch opens, and out peers a humanoid—in this case Rolf Bernard. The spaceman looks over the crowd of frightened yet curious people. In the background, the spaceman sees the monuments of American power, large stone buildings and the White House. Everyone waits for the spaceman to speak.

The hatch on the Felix spaceship opened. Heat radiated from the spaceship's skin. Rolf Bernard pulled his helmet off and peered out. He grinned. "George, it's good to see you."

"Welcome home, Rolf."

Rolf squatted down in the hatch. "I can't climb down until the ship's skin cools, or unless you scare up a portable stairway."

"Then we'll just sit here and have a chat."

Rolf mused, "You know, George. I almost pulled it off. I almost turned space into a private enterprise."

Harchord took off his blue cap and wiped his brow. "I'd say you *did* pull it off. You just couldn't keep it up.

But you *did* pull it off—you let the technological genie out of the bottle, nobody can stuff it back in again."

Rolf nodded with a self-satisfied smile. Rogers poked his head from the hatch and looked around at the gathering crowds. He declared the skin cool enough for debarkation. Rolf called down to General Harchord, "Now it's time for you to take me to your leader."

Harchord winced. He looked over his shoulder toward the White House and said with disgust, "I'm sure I can do better than that."

Rolf laughed out loud.

Harchord suppressed his own mirth, "In any case, I'll make sure you don't regret coming back."

"I couldn't stay away, George. I missed the poker games."